LIFE IS BUT
A DREAM

By
Debbie Reis

ISBN: **978-0-557-05397-1**

To my husband, Michael. My best friend, cheerleader, therapist, and soul mate. Day after day you prove to me that love conquers all.

I love you heart and soul, forever and ever.

Chapter 1

Lauren's dream suddenly changed and intensified a few minutes before she awoke. She recognized herself standing on a beach, spying on a man in the far distance, who looked vaguely familiar. He was standing near a towering rock formation, watching the sunset. Her attention fell to the ball of fire changing colors as it slowly descended below the horizon. She couldn't recall ever seeing such brilliant shades of yellows, oranges, and reds before. Lauren could actually feel the gentle breeze fan her long hair, tickling her neck. She felt the soft material of her gown as it wrapped itself tightly around her legs. She turned her attention back to the stranger, and was mesmerized by a glowing white light silhouetting his body. She felt such a tug at her heart that she thought she might lose her concentration and wake up. Even so, she remained focused on the light's aura pulsating around his muscular frame. For a brief moment, she felt their essence had merged to become one and the same. When she tried to center her focus, she awoke with a start.

"Damn!"

Lauren lay still, hoping to recall more, but was confused by the grieving loss she felt. She just wanted to cover her head and cry.

She could still feel his intense loving presence all around her.

How could everything around me be so crystal clear, yet he is so fuzzy? Her mind was whirling the same question over and over. *What does this mean?*

When she felt her confusion turning into dismay, she pulled

herself out of bed, feeling as if she hadn't slept in days.

Please let a hot shower break this irrational spell.

Lauren trudged to the bathroom like a defeated woman, then surprised herself by undressing very slowly and sensually in front of the mirror. When she finally stepped into the shower, it felt like sunshine on her body, waking her senses to the point of complete arousal. She thought of her dream and quickly escaped into the realm of blissful relief.

From the very beginning, Alex felt there was something different about his nightly apparitions, and allowed them to slowly develop. He was having vivid dreams of meeting a part of himself he thought he should already know. He had heard the expression, 'finding one's soul mate,' but thought its meaning was overly simplified. Now he lay in bed fearing the question that kept circling his mind.

Could she be my soul mate? He couldn't believe he was even contemplating such a thing. *And if so, how can I find her?*

He closed his eyes, thinking back to when the strange dreams had first started. They had begun some time ago as shapeless, foggy images. But now to his surprise, they were becoming ever more vivid and real. And Alex wasn't sure whether to be concerned that his nightly visions were now consuming more of his waking hours as well. He could imagine the warmth from the sunset and its brilliant, vivid colors. If he closed his eyes and concentrated, he could create the faint outline of her in the distance. He could see her hair gently sweeping across her face.

Alex could sense the anxiousness creeping into his body as he wrote in his journal, but he refused to stop. Lately, his only dreams had been of her, and his journal was getting full. Not only were the mental pictures increasing in intensity, but he would awaken fully aroused, and sweating, his damp hair pressed against his neck. Each morning, he woke up experiencing such pain that his first instinct was to run to her. In his journal, he described the loss as unbearable.

He wanted to stay in the real world, but prayed this pain was somehow a preparation for some sort of meeting. He wrote about being worried whether it would happen in this lifetime or another. Or worse, had it already taken place, and the dreams were past memories? But if it were real, would he be at the right place at the right time? Would he know her if he saw her? And if so, how would he be able to convince her? The frustration was beginning to weigh heavily on his mind. As bizarre as he knew it sounded, he found her every night, but every morning, he lost her again. During his meditations, Alex had to constantly remind himself to let go, and simply watch the developments.

His encouragement grew when he noticed her becoming slightly more focused in his mind. He thought if he just allowed things to happen, and stayed centered, it wouldn't be long before he would know her face as well as he knew his own. He just had to be patient, and put his trust in everything he had always believed. He knew he must listen with his heart this time, and not his head.

Lauren closed her eyes, silently reminding herself that she was supposed to be a somewhat sensible, down-to-earth woman. With that concept in mind, she tried to smile, if only to reassure herself. It was difficult for her to admit that lately, her thoughts hadn't been on her job, the home, her kids, or her husband. Her frustration mounted as she realized her usual focused and grounded self had somehow been left far behind. It didn't take a genius to figure that out. But she didn't have the slightest idea what to do about it. There were days she didn't think the nights would ever come, that her responsibilities would ever end, or that people would ever stop pulling her in so many directions. Her usual meditations and trusty intuition weren't offering any solutions either. She had even started keeping a dream journal, and was making every effort to interpret them, in the hopes that her subconscious would show mercy, and present her with a healthy-minded answer. Just thinking about it made her emit a loud sigh of frustration.

"I'm beginning to believe that sane and normal no longer exist in my realm of reality. I just want to fall into bed, and sleep until all of this is over." Lauren looked into the mirror and frowned at the dark circles under her eyes. "What am I going to do?" She asked herself.

Lately, her dreams resembled pictures of the aurora borealis, except in brighter, bolder Technicolor. And to further confuse things, each morning she would wake up in a sweat, feeling as if she had just missed an extremely important event. This left her frustrated, and thinking if only she could have slept a little longer, she would have found the solution to all this nonsense. She desperately wanted to believe it wasn't her age playing tricks on her. She needed to believe that she was too young to be getting old. Once a mental note was made to ask her doctor, she tried to refocus on the issue at hand. If only she could remember what that was.

"Damn!"

Another mental request to start writing herself reminder notes. She shook her head, hoping to banish her irritations in the process. Lauren felt almost ashamed to admit she had no right to feel anything but satisfied with her life. She had been a successful business owner for the past seventeen years, having one of the most elite clothing boutiques in Beverly Hills. She and her co-owner, Kevin Costello, had worked long hours to make a success of their shop. The business was doing so well, they were in negotiations with their bank about opening a sister store in Santa Monica.

She glanced over at her bulging briefcase, wanting to blame the growing pressures from the banker for her sudden chaotic behavior. But Lauren knew herself too well to suspect a little outside pressure would cause such a turnaround. She fidgeted in her seat, deep in thought about the situation.

She wasn't worried about her twin daughters. They were away at college, and doing very well. And her husband, Gary, had a successful business that kept him conveniently busy and out of town. She shook her head again. No, she no longer worried needlessly about him either. She glanced at her fingers wrapped tightly around the steering wheel, and caught sight of her wedding band. She and Gary had certainly had their ups and downs throughout their many years of marriage. Admittedly though, most of the years had not been the highlight of her life. Over time, both had grown into very different people. The changes in them used to cause terrible arguments, but now the conflicts had died down. The end result was that he lived his life as he wanted, and she was forced to do the same. The positive side to this arrangement was that it provided her the time to focus on her business and her girls, and less time on the negatives of her marriage.

Lauren quickly transferred her thoughts back on herself.

Perhaps by the time women reach my age, it's normal to re-evaluate their lives. Although today, I feel that I've lived most of it in traffic.

She made another mental note to keep motivational CDs in her car. *Maybe one on memory enhancement too.*

Lauren glanced into the rear-view mirror, and spoke out loud.

"I don't know why I'm worried about my age. A number can't define who I am."

People still complimented her on her appearance. And her daughters would often tell her she looked ten years younger than other mothers her age. But she would be disappointed if they didn't offer such nice compliments.

Isn't that what daughters are supposed to say when their mother has no real personal life of her own?

She eyed the car next to her, and timidly smiled. She still enjoyed watching men looking in her direction, and realized she was far from dead yet. Her attention was drawn back to her rear-view mirror, and the thick dark locks forming an aura around her face.

People were usually caught off-guard by her dark shoulder-length hair and bright almond-shaped blue eyes. She had the habit of blushing and downplaying compliments, then would immediately realize that she should work on being a little less self-critical.

Lauren's beauty showed in a quiet, elegant way. Her posture was like that of a ballerina. Tall, with long legs and a lithe body. Her weight had always been easy to maintain. But lately, she realized she had to work a little harder at keeping her figure in top form. Another cruel reminder of her age.

She would deny it, but one of her most beautiful features was the continuing delicate smile that held her deep dimples permanently in place. And when you looked into her clear blue eyes, it was as if she was seeing deep into your soul. But instead of feeling uncomfortable or violated, their warmth and caring appearance found you gladly inviting them in.

She scrutinized her lips in the mirror, and frowned. Others saw them as pouty and sensual, but she found them large and distracting. She quickly reprimanded herself for being critical, and then focused on her positive attributes.

Instead of her physical qualities, Lauren was more proud of her untarnished reputation. She was respected in the business community, and known as an honest, intelligent, and friendly person to work with. She couldn't deny she had a passion for people, and for life. Although today, she had to remind herself of these qualities, as she saw traffic and people coming at her from all directions.

Lauren took a deep breath, and switched on her music, detaching from the outside world. She was determined to relax and enjoy the ride if it killed her. She was pleasantly surprised to hear 'Street of Dreams' playing, and wondered whether it was a sign.

All right, maybe I'm pushing it, but the lyrics certainly fit.

Lauren quickly shook her head, refusing to allow her fantasies to consume her.

Stop it. It's just a song. Nothing more. What's wrong with me? she told herself.

Lauren took another deep breath, and felt her muscles begin to relax. But not for long, as the car behind her honked, urging her through the green light. She was jumpstarted back into full reality

6

when her cellular phone rang at the same time.

The tension had returned.

"Hello. This is Lauren Wells."

She heard the familiar deep voice of her partner.

"Where are you? You're supposed to return a call to our banker before 2:00. Better do it from the car before he leaves for the day."

Lauren chastised herself for forgetting yet another important appointment.

"Thanks for the reminder, Kev. I'll call you after."

"OK, sweetie. Be careful."

Lauren punched in the number, thinking how grateful she was to have someone like Kevin for a friend and partner.

"At least he's organized, and usually keeps me out of trouble. And until my sanity returns, that's all I can ask for."

The phone rang twice before a young woman with a slow southern drawl answered. "1st Bank of California."

"Mr. Ramsey, please. Lauren Wells calling."

Alex looked up from his computer screen and rubbed his eyes. He realized he had taken too little time for himself, and might need something more interesting to think about. He couldn't recall the last quality time he had spent with friends. And he was glad the eighty-hour workweeks were finally easing up. Recently, the only bright spot in his life had been the few hours each night spent sleeping.

He closed his eyes, and watched the images filtering through from the night before, and chuckled to himself.

"It's as close to a social life as I've seen in a while."

But Alex loved his work too much to slow down for very long. His friends described him as a flowing volcano of knowledge and creativity, never complaining of the dreaded writer's block. He would make light of it, announcing that he couldn't do it without the amazing programming CDs. Right now, he wasn't thinking about his creativity. He had become an overworked hermit, forfeiting enjoyment from the things he had once loved.

Alex looked around and sighed. He lived in a beautiful home on the beach in Malibu. Yet he couldn't remember the last time he had taken a walk, and appreciated its balanced effect. He was pleased that at least he hadn't allowed himself to get too busy to meditate.

Breathing in the crisp ocean air from his balcony eliminated some of the cobwebs from both his mind and his spirit. He knew if he wanted to stay in balance, this was the most important gift he could give himself.

He glanced at a picture of his friends sitting on a nearby table, and smiled, making a quick mental note to start enjoying outside life a little more often.

Alex couldn't have loved his friends more if they were close family members. And he knew he wouldn't be half the man he was without them. They supported his privacy when he worked. Yet when they hadn't seen him in weeks, they would think nothing of knocking on his door with a bottle of wine, forcing him to socialize.

Alex glanced down at his screen, and realized his latest manuscript was finally complete.

"Now I'm in the mood to celebrate."

He stood up with a groan, and walked towards the kitchen, passing a mirror on the way. He caught sight of himself and stopped abruptly. He tousled his hair violently, and then laughed at his disheveled appearance.

"If they could only see me now."

Being a well-known, successful writer, Alex had worked hard, and had accomplished a lot in his life. But everyone agreed he underestimated his good looks and appearance. It never entered his mind that women considered him a very attractive, highly eligible bachelor. The married ones would beg to set him up on blind dates, and the single ones would do everything in their power to be recognized.

But Alex didn't notice his ruggedly handsome qualities. He usually had his long black hair pulled back neatly from his face. His eyes were a deep, dark blue that held a downward dreamy cast. And when he smiled, his dimples penetrated his face, causing deep crevices to appear. He had a permanent dimple in his chin, and a strong sturdy jaw line. It never occurred to Alex that not only was he tall, dark, and handsome, but he exuded warmth and confidence. Everyone highly respected his quiet, calm, and friendly manner. It was difficult to believe he hadn't realized any of his attributes. But, his rare lack of self-worship made him all the more interesting and appealing. It was never an issue for him; not even in the creative, ego-driven world that he had settled his life in. His deep seriousness in meditation, Zen, and other philosophies had always kept his lifestyle and ego firmly intact.

Alex had been married briefly, but his work had taken first priority. He thought of her fondly, knowing he had done the right thing by releasing her. She was now happily remarried, with two beautiful children.

Trying not to make the same mistakes, he now very much believed in his intuition and visionary abilities, taking full advantage of them in his daily living. And they had rarely failed him. It had taken a while, but over the years, he had gradually started listening to his heart, and discovered to his amazement that his life had changed forever.

Alex smiled, satisfied he was making the correct decisions, and that his life was on the right track.

He stood at his kitchen window, watching a sailboat in the distance. He was anxious for sleep tonight. Now that he would be working fewer hours, he was ready for the challenge of bringing the developing visions into focus. Alex closed his eyes, recalling the now hazy details from the previous night.

He remembered having a sense of familiarity, and of watching a woman in the distance. He also recalled waking up in a deep sweat. It was a new experience, and his curiosity was getting the better of him. He was anxious to find out where it was leading; telling himself that if nothing else, a book idea or manuscript may be the prize.

His doorbell rang loudly, waking him from his stupor. His friends were on the other side, banging on the front door, beseeching him to open up. He could hear Donovan's muffled voice shouting through the thick wood.

"Mr. Alex Chandler, open the door and let us in."

Trying to stifle a chuckle, Alex walked slowly to the door.

"Hold on, I'm getting there as fast as I can. My God, you'd think you hadn't seen me in weeks."

Elliot was standing next to Donovan, both wearing wide grins.

"We haven't. And you'd better tell us you've completed the manuscript."

Alex was nonchalant in his reply. "As it happens, I've just finished it, and I'm definitely ready to move on."

Donovan interrupted, walking past him, through the foyer.

"Then our timing was good. See, Elliot, I told you that we're getting as psychic as our friend here. When did you put it to bed?"

Alex closed the door behind them. "Would you believe just a few hours ago? Your timing couldn't have been better."

Lauren's dream journal was increasing in size, with images of fantasy and confusion. And she was beginning to question whether or not it really was all just a coincidence.

She realized the craziness had all started about the same time she had begun questioning the life she was leading. She was consciously beginning to feel there was something terribly absent in her world. Each day, the feeling of urgency was grabbing hold of her soul, and she was desperately searching for ways to control it.

She would try and convince herself that she was beyond the age of being naive. She told herself that she had worked hard to achieve what she had, and she didn't mind working a little harder to keep it. She had actually convinced herself that if she had to give up her personal life to feel secure, then so be it.

Lauren would hear herself praying several times a day, asking for guidance to shake off her schoolgirl fantasies. There was a part of her that wanted to stop dreaming about a person, as well as a passion that she didn't think even existed. To save her sanity, Lauren felt she should get on with life in the real world. And with that thought in mind, she accelerated her speed, heading towards Pacific Coast Highway, hoping to outrun her thoughts and memories. When she saw the Pacific Ocean come into view, her dream automatically floated to the surface. She mumbled sharply under her breath, only hearing every other word.

"Why in heaven's name am I doing this to myself? Surely it's nothing to worry about. I'm just lonely at the moment. It's nothing I can't handle. When the new boutique gets underway, I won't have time to fantasize over these ridiculous dreams."

But her scolding didn't stop her thoughts of him. Lauren let out a sigh of resignation, and allowed the visions to take over. She thought back to him standing near the same rock formation and sandy beach as before. Her concentration was riveted on the water lapping slowly around his feet. She heard the sound of her voice tearing at her own heart.

"He looked so alone."

Suddenly, she felt his loneliness within herself. When she noticed her breathing had accelerated, and her jacket was tightening around her shoulders, she spoke sternly.

"All right, Lauren, you're exaggerating this way out of proportion."

She thought back to her psychology courses in college, and addressed herself with authority.

"This issue will simply go away once I understand what it all means. I'll run over to Moonglows and pick up something on lucid dreaming. I'm sure it's an easy enough process. And maybe once I learn to tap into and control my dreams, it'll just disappear. I've wanted to learn the process anyway. Now I have a reason."

But, even as Lauren was hearing herself speak with such confidence, she saw herself as a big jigsaw puzzle, with one huge missing piece. She fought to ignore the aching in her heart and soul. She didn't know where it was coming from, but she knew it was from someplace deep inside. She didn't think she was ready to locate where that place was just yet, and she wanted to escape.

Lauren felt the frustration trying to creep back in and regain control, so she quickly switched on the radio. Sitting in traffic wasn't one of her favorite pastimes, but today she almost welcomed the time alone. She wasn't in the mood to make intelligent conversation with anyone. She flipped stations, looking for talk radio. She didn't want to hear a song that would bring all the emotions rushing back.

Lauren stopped fidgeting with the buttons and immediately turned her attention to the sound of a man's voice. After a few moments, she increased the volume, trying to decide where she had heard the soothing voice before.

She listened intently as the man was being interviewed about his various accomplishments. He was speaking shyly about the length of time it had taken him to write his current manuscript.

She whispered to herself as she turned her full attention to the radio.

"Who is he? And, why does he sound so familiar?"

Lauren increased the volume again, hoping it would stir a memory.

Instead, she was hit with a strong sensation of déjà vu that was quickly enveloping her. To fight its effects, she raised her voice much louder, and with a pleading tone, she questioned the swirling energy she felt closing in around her.

"Who in the hell is it?"

Lauren's breathing accelerated again, and her heart began pounding through her blouse. She felt the light touch of her fingers as she pushed her skirt slowly up her thighs. She sensed he was talking only to her. But it made no sense because he was telling the interviewer about how he kept himself prisoner within his own house, foregoing a real life to get his work accomplished. He said it had all been worth it now that his current project was complete. The interviewer commented about rumors flying around town about this being his best work to date. He asked Alex in a professional patter what he was doing in his spare time, between writing books and screenplays. Lauren listened closely, wanting to drown in his voice.

"Occasionally, I sing in a little band made up of other misfits like myself. It's a great outlet for the excess energy I seem to accumulate."

Then he added, almost shyly. "The band is great, but I'm not very good. It's more of an amateurish hobby than anything else. And I'm finally getting a lot of much needed rest, too."

The DJ kept to the subject. "Where are you singing?"

Alex laughed, answering mischievously. "Mostly in the shower."

He paused a moment while the DJ understood the humor, then continued.

"Occasionally, we'll play in a few of the local clubs around town."

Still chuckling, the DJ spoke up. "We have a lot of listeners out there who would like to hear your band. Where's your next gig?"

Lauren noticed a poetic charm in his voice.

"Sounds great. My next..."

Lauren's car phone rang loudly, causing her to jump. She answered it out of habit, and then immediately cursed herself for doing so.

"Lauren Wells here."

She realized her tone was irritable, and tried to calm down when she heard the voice on the other end belonged to her banker.

"Hello, Mrs. Wells? I think we have a bad connection. Could you please speak up?"

Lauren forced herself to turn off the radio and hide her anger at being interrupted.

"Yes, I'm here, Mr. Ramsey. What can I do for you?"

The banker paused for a moment, shuffling papers in Lauren's ear.

"I've reviewed your application, and should be meeting with our loan committee this afternoon. I'll give you a call with the outcome by 5:00. Where can I reach you?"

Lauren was fighting to keep her business demeanor temporarily intact. "I'll be at the boutique until 8:00. I'll look forward to hearing from you."

"That will be fine. I'll speak to you soon."

"Thank you, Mr. Ramsey."

Lauren threw the phone down, and quickly switched on the radio. Then she hit the steering wheel in anger when she heard the traffic report now blaring in her ears. She was too late.

She hit the steering wheel again several more times, out of frustration.

"Great, someone else reminding me I'm stuck between a million cars, going no place in a hurry."

Lauren was more than disappointed about missing the writer's name. She felt rage and aggravation, yet she had no idea why. She felt as if she had been close to having an answer to a long sought after truth, only to lose it in a single second.

"Who was he?"

When she felt the hot flashes flaring up again, Lauren impatiently grabbed her phone and called Information, getting the radio station's telephone number. She told herself it was nothing more than curiosity. "I just want to know his name, and where his band will be playing. That's all."

But in her heart, she knew she was being obsessive about something that made absolutely no sense. Her mind couldn't grasp this strange behavior, and she was worried that it was becoming a pattern. More frustration followed when the only answer she received from the radio station was a recording telling her the phone lines were closed.

Alex left the studio humming aloud. He had made it through his radio interview, and was satisfied with its end result. He didn't enjoy public speaking, preferring to put his thoughts on paper. Realizing he couldn't take back a comment once it was heard by a million people scared him half to death. But this interview had been different. He had been dreading it for days, and had trouble controlling his shaky voice in the beginning. Yet toward the end of the program, a feeling of invincible power had suddenly spread over him; a knowledge of being completely confident and in control. He couldn't understand what had put him at peace and helped him get through the interview, but he was grateful for it.

Once on the road, Alex decided to take a detour to a popular bookstore on Melrose. The atmosphere drew him in, and two hours had passed before he glanced at his watch. Now he was enjoying the drive back to Malibu in the comfort of his own solitude. It gave him a chance to clear his thoughts, and listen to a subliminal lucid dreaming CD he had purchased from Moonglows. He was greatly impressed by the store's friendly energy, and he looked forward to returning when his special order came in.

Alex casually tapped his fingers on the steering wheel as he listened to the music. He had visualized himself in dreams before, but this was different. Alex knew he needed assistance to see where this fantasy was leading him. He heard himself talking over the volume of the music.

"I just want to find out why this feels so important to me. And know how much energy I should give to it."

But he knew only too well how much energy he was willing to give; all that he had, and more. He smiled, knowing the day had turned out well, after all.

Chapter 2

Lauren was still deep in thought as she turned a sharp left onto Melrose, searching for a parking space, before finally pulling in front of her best friend's bookstore. She caught sight of the word Moonglows reflecting through her windshield, and smiled. She quickly slid out of her car, anxious to talk with her confidant.

Adriana Dean had been her best friend since college, and had taught Lauren philosophies that had become a way of life for her. When Adriana taught her how to meditate, life began to change drastically. Adriana had come into Lauren's life the first time questions arose about who she was, where she was going, and where she had been. Now, deeper issues regarding the same questions were once again rising to the surface.

It was Lauren's idea to have Adriana open a bookstore, catering to people of like minds. Right from the day Moonglows opened, it had been a huge success. People were ready for a change within themselves, and taking responsibility for their own lives.

Adriana wanted her customers to feel like they were on a retreat when they entered her store. She had designed a large fountain in the center of the main room, with the sound of flowing water being heard throughout the building. Soft, beautiful music filtered through each discovery room, playing intricate melodies from other lands, while intriguing the imagination. The faint smell of incense brought with it pleasant memories of a distant past. To keep the outside noise pollution to a minimum, another large fountain was housed near the tables and chairs on the large wooden patio. Adriana wanted her customers to unwind and learn at the same time. She felt certain that a mixture of both had been achieved.

Lauren opened the door and glanced around the room. She turned when a male voice called her from behind the counter.

"Hi, Lauren. You looking for Adriana?"

"Hi, Mark. Yeah, I told her I'd be dropping by. Is she around?"

Her assistant pointed above him. "She's upstairs. Go on up."

"Thanks, I'll see you before I leave."

Lauren hurried up the stairs and breezed into her friend's office. Adriana was standing next to her desk, looking relaxed and unfazed by the bold entrance.

Her long golden-red hair flowed down past her breasts, and her green eyes sparkled like a beacon of light. The colors stood out prominently against her light complexion and milky smooth skin. Adriana was tall and thin, with a feminine athletic build. She didn't have the classic features that Lauren possessed. Instead, she had a fresh, girl-next-door appeal that made everyone in her presence comfortable, knowing that all must be right with the world.

Lauren was out of breath, but squeaked out a greeting.

"Hi. God, am I glad you were available today."

Adriana approached her friend for a hug.

"That was quite an entrance. What's going on?"

Lauren took a long breath in an attempt to calm her nerves.

"Just girl talk. I'm hoping you can help shed some light on what's going on with me. While you're at it, I'd like you to convince me I'm not going crazy. And before I leave, I want to pick up some motivational and subliminal CDs."

Adriana saw a struggling look in the blue eyes facing her, and smiled knowingly.

"Sit down, and tell me the problem. You know I'll do whatever I can to help."

Lauren didn't want to come off sounding like a lunatic, so she took another deep breath to compose herself. When she was ready, she looked directly into Adriana's equally serious eyes, and then she began.

"Well, I'm not sure myself. I feel like I'm living in a fog most of the time. It's getting to where I can't remember the most common of things. I've been easily distracted, and I'm more sensitive than usual."

Adriana continued shaking her head as Lauren quickly continued.

"I'm having sweats, and I keep getting the feeling that I'm missing something very important, but I can't quite put my finger on what it is."

Adriana's eyes widened and focused on her friend.

"Anything else? Sounds to me like you're falling apart."

Lauren gasped loudly in mock surprise. "Thanks, that's just what I wanted to hear. Gee, some doctor you are."

Adriana smiled in an attempt to keep the mood light. "Oh, Lauren, you know I'm kidding. But seriously, is there anything else?"

Lauren didn't know if she should pursue this, or stop the conversation now. No, she had come here to discuss her symptoms. And she had to admit that her dreams were becoming a real issue and couldn't be ignored any longer. All of her usual tactics weren't helping her stay balanced and in control of her hectic life. She knew something had to be done. She looked down at her shoes and continued.

"This is going to sound very strange. Well, maybe it won't, considering who I'm talking to." Lauren spoke with a grin in her voice.

The corner of Adriana's mouth curled slightly.

"I don't know if I should take that as a compliment or not. I'll wait and see what you have to say."

Lauren's mood turned serious again.

"Adriana, I'm having some weird dreams. It's basically the

same one every night. They started a while ago, but I didn't want to say anything, in case they were temporary."

Lauren bit her lip and spoke slower.

"I'm a little concerned because they're becoming more intense, and I don't feel as if I have much control over them."

Adriana was cautious in her questioning. "Are they uncomfortable or nightmarish?" She waited for her friend's reaction.

Lauren didn't have to think about the answer.

"Oh no, they don't frighten me. But, they're becoming a little uncomfortable."

Adriana was watching her friend very closely now.

"Lauren, why don't you tell me about them?"

Adriana noticed Lauren fidgeting, and allowed her to take her time.

"Well, there's a man in my dream, but his face isn't clear. And the entire dream seems to be played through some sort of sheer curtain. It's odd, because although I can't see him clearly, I can see and smell the ocean as if I were right there. I think I can sense what he's feeling, and he appears very lonely. He's usually standing in the same location, near some tall rocks. And I see the waves breaking around the rocks and at his feet. I can see his hair blowing in the wind. And he's covered in a beautiful light."

Lauren's eyes were bright with the memories. "So far, these dreams always seem to be taking place at sunset." Her eyes widened with enthusiasm. "And, Adriana, I've never seen colors like these. They're dazzling."

Adriana watched as a pained look crossed her friend's face, and heard her voice drop an octave. "And lately, I've been getting a very peculiar sensation. As if I'm observing myself."

Lauren looked down at her hands, not wanting to meet her friend's gaze.

"And, as if it's not crazy enough, I wake up every morning feeling frustrated, and more than a little aroused."

Adriana couldn't choke down the giggle she felt surfacing.

"Lauren, that doesn't sound like such an awful dream."

Lauren looked around the room to cover her embarrassment.

"I suppose it's not, or rather it shouldn't be. Except for an intense feeling I can only describe as absolute loneliness."

Lauren slid her hands through her hair.

"Oh and this terribly frustrating feeling of trying to find what I, or he, or we, have lost. It sounds crazy. I feel as if what was lost was right in front of me, and then it's suddenly ripped away, leaving me to pick up the pieces."

Adriana walked over and sat down next to her friend.

"Since you can't get a clear image of this guy, maybe what you're seeing is just another image of yourself. Perhaps what you're feeling are your own subconscious conflicts."

Lauren stood up and walked to the window, barely noticing her red car parked out in front.

"Normally I would agree with you, except this is something so much different. I just don't know what the hell it is."

Adriana asked the next question with great empathy.

"How are you and Gary?"

Lauren turned away from the window to directly face her friend.

"Me and Gary? That's a good question. We occasionally live in the same house, when he decides to come in town. But we rarely spend any time together. He's always working and traveling. He's got his own life now. Don't misunderstand me, I'm not complaining about the arrangement. I'm busy with my work as well. I'm sure if we wanted, we could find time for each other, but why make waves? It's easier this way."

Adriana continued her gentle questioning, "And the twins?"

Lauren smiled at the thought of her girls.

"Oh, they're doing great in school. In the past week, they've both fallen in love again. No, they're not my problem."

Lauren looked into Adriana's caring green eyes, pleading for an easy answer.

"Maybe it's my age?"

Adriana laughed out loud, breaking the tension.

"Lauren, I can't believe your age would bother you. We're the same age, and I feel twenty-five, so don't give me that crap about it being your age."

Lauren shot her friend a dreary look.

"With that fresh face and perky body of yours, you look twenty-five. Unfortunately, we can't all look like you. So, my dear friend, don't give me any of your crap."

Adriana picked up a pillow, hugging it close to her chest.

"Lauren, you're beautiful and intelligent, you have lots of friends, a successful business, and you have your whole life ahead of you. Count your blessings, sweetie, because you have so very many."

Guilt briefly crossed Lauren's face.

"I know you're right. I'm placing too much meaning in this, aren't I? I need to remember that I'm the one in control, and I am free to think what I want. And if I choose to believe it's a problem, then I also have the power to solve the problem."

"Good girl. Now that's the Lauren I know. And if you can't solve it alone, then by God, we'll solve it together."

Lauren hugged her friend affectionately.

"Thanks for being here. I should be ashamed of myself. Keep reminding me to concentrate on the positives in my life. Oh, and while you're at it, remind me that I'm only as old as I choose to be, too. Now come downstairs with me, while I pick out a few of your most powerful lucid dreaming CDs. I think I'm ready to see what's out there."

Adriana opened her office door, allowing Lauren access to the stairs. "Right this way."

Lauren was in front, and couldn't see the puzzled look on her friend's face. Adriana thought she remembered reading an article resembling Lauren's story, but it was too long ago to remember the details. She also thought there had been a book published decades earlier on the subject. Her mind was drawing a blank, and she knew she would have to do some investigating. In the meantime, Adriana made a decision not to flame Lauren's hopes or fears by mentioning it. If the dreams continued, she knew her friend would confide in her. Lauren was the most rational person she knew, and Adriana was convinced this wasn't a fantasy gone awry. If Lauren was having dreams that seriously concerned her, then it was up to Adriana to support her.

Alex pulled into his driveway, and slowly shifted his car into park. He sat snugly in his seat, allowing his thoughts to drift back to her.

Was she listening today? He shook himself sternly.

Stop being ridiculous. Here I am, thinking about a person that probably doesn't even exist, much less in the same vicinity.

He closed his eyes and listened to what his body was feeling. Alex felt his intuition increasing in frequency, his heart was beginning to ache, and he was tired of feeling that he had misplaced half his soul. Pulling his key out of the ignition, Alex made the decision to trust what was happening. If, by some chance of a miracle, she did exist, he had to find a way of locating her.

By the time Alex had slipped out of his car and walked to the front door, he had decided to confide in his friend, Elliot. Elliot Golden had the kind of focused, open mind that was needed right now.

As he absentmindedly unlocked his door, Alex questioned aloud.

"If there's even the slightest possibility that it's true, what can I do to put power into this dream?"

Then he heard his answering machine, and the lifesaving words of Elliot.

"Hi, it's me. I received your message about dinner tonight. Sounds great. I'll pick you up at 7:00 sharp. I almost forgot,

Donovan might join us. See you soon."

He didn't bother picking up the phone. He had his answer, and he had just enough time for a quick jog. Alex could hear his own voice echoing on the outside steps as he changed into his jogging shoes.

"I've got to come up with an answer. Surely this couldn't be happening for no reason whatsoever. That would be such a waste of energy. The dreams have been going on far too long, and are getting far too intense for them not to have some sort of meaning. No, I'll figure out what I've got to do, and then do it. Either that, or admit I'm completely out of my mind."

There weren't many people on the beach, and Alex hoped he could appreciate breathing the air, and listening to the waves in privacy. Today wasn't going to be one of those days. The moment he began his run, his mind drifted back to his dreams, and to thoughts of her.

Lauren threw the shopping bag full of CDs and books into the back seat of her car. She was feeling a little better now that she had talked over her concerns with Adriana. And she was looking forward to listening to the lucid dreaming CD, and becoming an active participant in her own dreams, rather than a bystander. Lauren had been telling herself that she wanted to control them so the ache would end. Now, she fought another question in the back of her mind.

Do I want the dreams to stop?

She had never dreamed in such detail before. The fact was she rarely remembered her dreams. Lauren had been meditating more than usual, and going deeper each time, too. Adriana had explained it simply. Because she had increased her meditations, she was now getting in touch with, and listening to herself. Therefore, she was remembering her dreams more vividly than before.

Lauren thought back to Adriana's parting words. "Listen and learn from your meditations and your dreams. You'll be surprised what you can find out about yourself."

Lauren knew she had no choice but to take her friend's advice. She eased out of her parking space, and remembered nothing else until Kevin called.

"Lauren, how close are you to the shop?"

Lauren glanced around distractedly.

"Gee, Kev, I have no idea. Wait a sec, while I get my bearings."

She could hear Kevin's laughter in the background. "Where's your head, girl?"

"Obviously not where it should be," Lauren replied heavily. "I've got a few things on my mind. Seems like every time I come down to Earth, something pulls me back into my thoughts."

"Well, come on back to Earth and get to the shop. We should go over a few details before Mr. Ramsey calls."

Lauren looked at her dashboard. "OK, I'll see you by 3:30."

She hung up the phone and tried to remember where her thoughts were before she was forced back to reality. Every time she concentrated on business, her mind would drift back to her dreams, and thoughts of him. It didn't matter that all she had to go on were the vague, unsettling sights, sounds, smells, and sheer essence of his presence. Apparently, that seemed to be enough for now.

She could hear herself responding to her thoughts of frustration.

Him who, damn it?

The only answer came back in the form of her own breath echoing within the car. She pushed her hair away from her face, forcing her mind back to Kevin and the store.

He had been a good friend, and she knew he was worried about her. Hell, she was worried too. She wanted to tell him everything, but didn't know where to possibly begin. He was as dear to her as her own brother, and she felt terrible keeping anything from him. They had grown up together, and now shared a bond that went deeper than childhood memories. They knew every deep and dark secret about each other.

"So, why do I feel uncomfortable telling him about this?"

Lauren thought about all the years they had been partners. Kevin, with his tall, thin frame, wore tailored clothes, and was always fashionable and distinguished in his appearance. He had learned much about the clothing business when he modeled as a young man. Lauren would tease it wasn't fair that he never had to worry about his weight, or his good looks fading. With his thick graying black hair, deep-set brown eyes, and closely shaved beard, he was definitely noticed when he walked into a room. It was his eye for clothing and Lauren's expertise in business that made them such a great team.

Lauren wanted to ask Kevin out to dinner after they closed the shop. She felt she owed him some sort of explanation for her mood, and she didn't want him worrying.

She turned right at the light, and saw the familiar billboard advertising her stylish boutique. The words 'Lauren's Place' appeared ahead. She was temporarily brought back to the real world as she pulled her car next to Kevin's black BMW, and glanced at her watch.

"3:28. At least, I'm not late."

When she opened the door, sounds of New Age music floated soothingly to her ears. Kevin was pouring champagne into a St. Louis flute, obviously for one of his better patrons. Lauren smiled when she overheard a familiar voice from behind the dressing room door, asking Kevin for a smaller size. Lauren knew the spirited voice, and winked at Kevin.

"Mrs. Athens, is that you? You come out here and show off your new figure."

A giggle penetrated through the door.

"Hi, Lauren. Yeah, I've lost another five pounds. Finally at my ideal weight."

Lauren chuckled enthusiastically, "Cindy, that's wonderful."

Kevin handed Cindy the dress, and had a seat on the sofa. While they waited for their model to emerge, Lauren talked excitedly about their new shop.

"I'm not worried about Mr. Ramsey's call. Our accountant says we're in great shape. If you don't have any plans tonight, why don't we go out for a celebration dinner?"

Kevin touched Lauren's hand. "We haven't done that in quite a while. I would love to."

Cindy strolled out, modeling her new figure in mock exaggeration.

Kevin stood up, handing her the champagne flute.

"You deserve the best champagne we have. Congratulations. I know how hard you've worked."

Lauren hugged her friend warmly. "Cindy, it's been too long. You look sensational."

Cindy took one step back, looked at Lauren, and then eyed her own reflection in the mirror.

"Lauren, something about life must be agreeing with you, too. You look great."

"Thanks, I needed that," Lauren said, bending down to hug her again.

Cindy twirled around in front of the mirror.

"The dress really does look great, doesn't it? I don't care how much it cost, I want it. Those last five pounds were hell to shed, and I deserve it."

Kevin took the glass out of Cindy's hand, and kissed her cheek. "Good. I'll wrap it up for you."

Kevin winked, and spoke over the partition.

"Well, Lauren, it looks like our bills are paid for the month."

While Kevin was taking care of the paperwork, the girls sat on the couch to chat for a few minutes. Lauren was eager for light conversation.

"How's Ron?"

Cindy replied in her usual enthusiastic high-pitched voice.

"Oh, he's great. He's been working in the studio, and hopes to have a new CD out before the end of the year."

"That's wonderful. Just make sure my copy is autographed."

Cindy laughed out loud. "I'll make sure of it."

Lauren was beginning to unwind.

"How's your decorating business going? I see your commercials all the time."

Cindy's eyes lit up with pride. "I'm so busy, I've had to hire additional help."

Cindy and Lauren had begun their friendship when the boutique opened. She had been one of Lauren's first patrons. And Lauren was immediately swept up by Cindy's vivacious personality. Lauren then employed Cindy as her decorator, and had greatly admired her creativity. Over the years, they had referred many clients to each other, and in the process, a trusting friendship had developed. Lauren would frequently remark to others that in all the years they had known each other, she had never seen Cindy unhappy, or even having a bad day. Cindy had an infectious smile that promoted happiness all around her.

One of Lauren's goals was trying to keep positive, upbeat people in her life; reliable people who were always there for each other. She would often think of her mother's words when she was a child, and passed them to her own daughters. "You are what you run with." She didn't totally understand the odd expression until she had children of her own. That was when she weeded out those that didn't fit into her curriculum. Lauren was very selective about who she brought into her life, and the lives of her family.

Cindy was one of those valuable people. She was cute, in a pixie sort of way. Petite, with short, curly auburn hair, and twinkling brown eyes that looked as if they were ready to dance. Her little turned up nose added to her perkiness.

Lauren told her friend about waiting for the call from the banker.

"My goodness, Lauren, the proposal was certainly presented

fast. You and I had lunch three weeks ago, and your accountant was just putting the numbers together. When you and Kev want something done, it gets done."

Lauren laughed, "Kevin and I have been discussing it for ages, and now we feel ready to move forward. Why put it off?"

"When are you expecting the call?"

Lauren looked at her watch. "Any minute."

"I wish I could wait with you, but I have an appointment at a gallery in Marina Del Rey at 5:00. If I don't run, I'll never make it on time."

Cindy stood up, pulling down the hem of her short skirt.

"I'll call you if I finish early. Where will you be?"

"I'll have to talk to Kevin, but I suspect we'll go to Pietro's."

"I'll call you on your cell. Good luck."

Hugging both her friends, Cindy picked up her package, sipped her last drop of champagne, and walked out humming a happy tune. After the door closed, Kevin smiled broadly.

"She should package whatever makes her so peppy."

Lauren snickered. "Good, clean living, Kevin. Just good, clean living."

Kevin gave her a doubtful laugh.

"Yeah, that must be it, Lauren."

They were still teasing each other when the phone rang. Lauren casually picked up the receiver.

"Lauren's. May I help you?"

She motioned for Kevin to listen on the other phone.

"Do we have a deal?"

Alex thought he had only been running for a few minutes when he heard his watch alarm go off. He stopped to take a breath and double check the time.

"Where in the hell have I been?"

But, he knew that he had been deep in thought, trying to sort out his near-constant confusion.

"How can something this strange happen to someone like me?"

He had thought about returning to the bookstore.

"Surely, they must know someone who has the answers. If this is real, I can't afford to make any mistakes."

Alex was worried the dreams would stop before he could find out if they were real or just his imagination. He didn't want them to end until he knew who and where she was. He sensed that she held the other half of his soul, or felt sure she at least held the key. But he knew nothing could be accomplished until he let go of the fear that gripped him.

Alex stopped for a moment, speaking to the ocean.

"No, I need to look inside myself, and stay centered and focused. I know an answer will come to me."

Alex continued unconvincingly, "And if not, I'll run by Moonglows, and talk to the owner."

He turned, running faster than usual in the direction of his house. But he couldn't run fast enough to escape the internal whispers.

I feel she's in possession of something I've been looking for all my life.

Alex ran upstairs to his bedroom and out to his balcony. His dark hair was hanging loose, and the wind felt good whipping through it. He looked down at the familiar rock formation that appeared in his dream, and his thoughts were quickly transferred, once again, to his past apparitions. By the time the visions had dimmed from sight, the sun had sunk below the horizon. He realized he had been standing outside in a daze, and knew he was going to be late.

"Damn."

Alex ran downstairs and left a note on the door for Elliot to let himself in. He had just enough time to quickly shower and dress. But first, he had no choice but to release the burning tension that had built up within him.

Alex could hear music playing as he stepped out of the shower, and yelled out his apologies.

"Sorry. Give me ten minutes."

Elliot's voice ascended to the bedroom above.

"No problem. I made reservations for 8:00, thinking we'd have a few drinks in the bar first."

Alex finished dressing and skipped downstairs, taking two steps at a time. He was an impressive sight, dressed in black boots, black jeans, a black tee shirt, and a black leather jacket. His damp hair was pulled neatly back.

Elliot was standing in the kitchen, taking the last drink from a carton of milk.

"Who's the guy on the CD? It's great."

"That's Ron Athens. He's changed his style in this album. It's good, isn't it?"

Elliot walked to the stereo, holding the CD up to the light.

"Yeah. I wouldn't have known it was him. I heard he's coming out with a new one. Two in a year and a half must be wearing him down. Have the two of you thought about joining a twelve-step program for working addicts?"

Alex gave him a side-glance and smiled.

"That may not be such a bad idea. I'll tell him you suggested it."

Elliot threw the carton in the trash, and picked up his keys.

"No problem. Are you ready?"

"Yeah. And, if you don't mind playing the role of therapist, there are a few things I need your advice on."

Elliot opened the door. "Bring the CD, and I'll listen to you both."

Alex looked at his friend and smiled.

Elliot Golden was his age, handsome in a nondescript way, with broad shoulders, short brown hair, rich brown eyes, and long dark lashes. He was just slightly shorter than Alex. But it was his easygoing personality that affected people the most. It was rare to ever see him upset or overwhelmed by a major dilemma. Elliot could always be counted on and trusted. He had been through a divorce at least ten years before, and made a point of letting people know that he wasn't the marrying kind. No one but him seemed to take his comments seriously. He and Alex had met through mutual friends ten years before at an environmental conference in L.A. Alex had just moved to Malibu from Newport Beach. Before relocating, Alex had concentrated his talents towards a national magazine. He was successful, but possessed a nagging desire to write a screenplay. Elliot, being an owner and editor of a magazine, had been his mentor.

The men were driving south into Santa Monica on P.C.H. before the conversation ensued.

"Is Donovan meeting us?"

Elliot talked over the music. "I believe so. When I spoke with him earlier about a client, he said that he was going to try and make it."

Alex sighed in relief. "Good, then I can run something by you both."

Alex and Elliot had met Donovan Barnett through the same group of friends, at the same conference.

Donovan owned a Malibu agency that dealt with many of the writers and musicians on the west coast. He had been a great asset in getting Alex's name established. Donovan was both well known and well liked in the networking circuit, and had made a successful career from it. He knew the right people, and where to find them. He was well liked because you knew where you stood with him. The only issue Donovan seemed to have was with women. He had been engaged several times. It was sometimes difficult keeping track of all the players. His work took first priority, and seemed to tear apart most of his relationships. It was an enigma to everyone how he was able to keep them all as friends. He said that women couldn't stay angry, because he was completely honest and compassionate with them. He took nothing for granted, believing that karma worked both ways. Donovan was very careful not to intentionally hurt the ones that he cared about. He treated everyone with respect and asked for the same in return.

Alex and Elliot thought his current fiancé, Vickie Sanders, might stay permanently. She knew how to handle Donovan. And she had been around and knew how to play the game of life, too. They made such an unlikely couple; everyone felt it had to work.

Donovan didn't look his age because of his endearing little boy qualities. There had been a time when he despised his youthful appearance, and believed that no one would ever take him seriously. Alex helped him to understand how he could use it to his advantage. It actually became his best asset. Donovan was someone that could be trusted, and he was fortunate to look the part, too. It was the best advice he had ever been given. He gave himself permission to be who he truly was.

Donovan no longer worried about his curly tussled blond hair that always looked unkempt. Or his big prankish blue eyes and boyish grin. Once he realized he could do nothing to shed the little boy image, life became easier. A major hurdle was conquered once he accepted himself as he was.

"Is it a business proposal you want to run by us?" Alex heard Elliot ask through his fog.

"No. As a matter of fact, it's something that has me baffled. And it's times like this when I'm glad to have such trusting, unconditional friends. Trusting being the important word here. Because after what I have to say, you both may want to have me committed."

Elliot laughed out loud. "Does it have anything to do with your work? That seems to be the only addiction in your life."

Alex shook his head. "I wish to hell it did. It would be easier to understand. No, this has to do with my personal life."

Elliot laughed. "What personal life? I hate to break this to you, my friend, but you don't have a personal life."

Before he had an opportunity to question his friend any further, they were in the restaurant parking lot, and the valet had opened the car door. The hostess greeted them at the door.

"Welcome to Pietro's. Do you have reservations?"

The two men found a table in the bar and ordered a drink while waiting for their name to be called.

After taking a hearty sip, Elliot looked curiously at Alex.

"Well, what's going on?"

He looked up as Donovan approached.

"Hi guys, how's it going?"

He didn't notice the intense look in Alex' eyes as he sat down at the table. Donovan pushed his blond locks from his eyes gruffly.

"I'm so hungry, I could eat everything on the right side of the menu."

Elliot spoke up before the conversation started in another direction.

"Well, Donovan, it seems that Alex has something he wants to discuss with us. And by the time he finally gets it out, you may have the opportunity to sample the entire menu. I've got a feeling we're going to be here for a while."

Alex motioned for the bartender to bring another round.

"I think we all need a drink before I begin."

He took a much-needed sip from his second glass, and then stared into the liquid.

"Guys, do you ever have vivid dreams?"

Donovan spoke first. "Of course. Well, occasionally... Why?"

Alex blinked hard, trying to decide what words he could use to persuade his friends that he had not been driven insane.

"I've been having some really dramatic dreams for a while now."

Elliot moved a little closer to his friend.

"What kind of dreams?"

Alex looked at the wall straight ahead, ignoring his friends' penetrating stares.

"Concerning a woman."

Elliot thought he understood and smiled.

"Maybe you just need to get out more. You're not exactly

famous in this city for your Casanova style and techniques."

Alex grinned sheepishly at the idea.

"No, Elliot, it's not that type of dream. Although, I do wake up aroused."

Donovan looked curiously at his friend as the hostess called their name. He had known Alex for years, and he had never seen him in this kind of mood before.

After they were seated, Alex looked around the room, and then bent his head down to whisper.

"Have you ever dreamed about someone that you have never met, yet you know them as well as you know yourself?"

He desperately needed a positive response from either of his friends. He knew his question sounded unconventional, even coming from him. But that didn't change what he felt.

Elliot looked casually at Donovan, and shrugged.

"No, I haven't. But it certainly doesn't mean it can't happen. What's it like?"

Alex appreciated Elliot's subtle response.

"It feels great, and it feels awful. It's great knowing I can feel such a fantastic emotion. But it could be a potential tragedy, because I don't know who she is, or even if she exists. So far, I've been unable to get physically close to her. I see her standing in the distance watching me. I'm always standing next to the rocks outside my house. And a brilliant white light surrounds her body. But the strangest thing is the fact that I can feel her, and I can see, hear, and smell the ocean. I can even feel the cool water on my feet. But the acute sense of her presence prevails all else. I get a sense that she's my other self, my soul mate, and it scares the hell out of me. I'm so afraid she's from another time, or from another place. I don't want to believe she's just in my imagination. I know myself better than that. But how in the hell can I find her? I dream of her every night, and each morning I wake up frustrated, aroused, sweating, and depressed. I keep telling myself to just let it happen, and have patience."

Alex was telling them much more than he had planned, and he now wanted to be quiet.

Donovan spoke in an equal whisper. "Have you meditated about this?"

He was taking this seriously because he knew how truly stable his friend was.

Alex responded quietly. "Yes I have, but I'm not really getting anything significant yet."

Elliot interrupted. "The only thing you can do is just wait and listen to your heart. Don't anticipate what you want it to say, but listen to what it's actually trying to tell you. Sometimes, our emotions get in the way of what our intuition is trying to convey."

Donovan joined in. "Yeah, get out of your own way, and see what happens. Try and stay open to whatever comes."

Doubt was creeping into Alex's mind.

"That's fine, but what if nothing happens? What if I never find her, and she just stays in my dreams forever? What if this is just a sick cosmic joke?"

Elliot spoke into the sad eyes staring back at him.

"Alex, what would you tell one of us if we were having these dreams?" Elliot didn't wait for an answer. "I'll tell you what you would say; the very same thing we're telling you now. Get out of your own way and see what happens. Try not to judge the situation."

Donovan had a thought. "Alex, you said that you could sense her feelings and emotions."

Alex looked apprehensive. "Yeah, it certainly seems that way. Hell, maybe they're just my emotions. I don't know anymore. We seem so connected; I can't tell who's thinking what. We're attached, yet separated by something. But by what, I'm not yet sure of."

Donovan continued very carefully. "Have you tried moving closer to her?"

Elliot voiced his thought. "Have you tried to connect with her through mental telepathy?"

Alex had a look of hope in his eyes.

"I've tried to physically move towards her in my dream, but I can't. It's like a magnet pulling me back. Hell, I can't even raise my arms. I haven't tried mental telepathy. I suppose if I can feel her, then maybe, just maybe, I might be able to speak to her. Do you think it's possible?"

Elliot smiled. "Well, if you want my opinion, I think that if it can be done, then you, my friend, can do it."

Donovan spoke in an upbeat tone. "Alex, don't get discouraged. You know as well as I do there's a reason for whatever is happening to you. Just remember that. You'll discover the answer in your own time and place."

Elliot picked up his glass to make a toast.

"If you're looking for someone out there, may she also be searching for you. To new adventures, and may your dreams come true."

Alex took a large gulp, grateful that his friends were so open and unconditional. He continued to tell his friends about the strange tingling sensation that had occurred earlier in the day during his radio interview. He told them about the sudden feeling of being able to do no wrong.

"I know this sounds bizarre, but the sensation came over me so quickly, and felt so profound that I wanted her to be the cause of it."

Donovan added his thoughts. "You said she comes to you when you dream. Do you believe she's also coming through during the day now?"

Alex looked down in frustration, and shook his head.

"I don't know. Today was the first time it happened, and it only lasted a few minutes."

Alex was beginning to see the impossibility of the situation.

"This is crazy. What are the chances of her not only being real, but also living in the area?"

Elliot lightened the mood. "The Los Angeles area is huge. I'm sure in this city, stranger things have happened."

Alex was about to speak when he felt a tingling sensation suddenly overtake him again. His breathing stopped, he stared rigidly into an empty space, and looked as if he were trying to remember something.

Elliot noticed first. "Alex, are you all right?"

But Alex didn't want to answer. He just wanted to bathe himself in this feeling of ecstasy for as long as possible.

Chapter 3

The valet ran towards the car as Lauren and Kevin pulled up in front of Pietro's. Kevin slid out, leaving Lauren alone with her thoughts. "Hold on a minute," Kevin said to the valet, "we don't have reservations."

Lauren sighed loudly. *Why do I suddenly feel so close to him tonight? Am I already anticipating my dreams? Should I be worried about this being just a fantasy, or should I be actively searching for someone that owns the other half of my soul?*

She admitted her thoughts of him were now invading her daily thinking, but had no solution about how to prevent it. She wrung her hands, continuing the private conversation in her head.

As if I don't have enough to think about.

The loan had been approved, and work on the new boutique was to begin immediately.

Maybe this will force me to concentrate on something a little more tangible. There's been nothing to confirm the dreams are anything more than a wonderful fantasy, gone awry.

Lauren stopped arguing when a hot flow of energy quickly ran up and down her spine. She trembled, and instinctively hugged her arms protectively around her body. When she felt wetness in the corner of her eyes and an intense longing in her heart, Lauren could do nothing but voice her question out loud.

"My God, please tell me what's happening here?"

Before she could hear an answer, the door opened and Kevin jumped in.

"There's an hour wait. Do you want to stay, or go elsewhere?"

Lauren was relieved. She just wanted to go home and sleep.

"Kev, would you mind if we postponed our celebration until another evening? It's been a long day, and I'm not as hungry as I thought. I just want to get some rest."

The darkness of the car hid Kevin's look of concern.

"Yeah. That would be fine. I'm a little tired myself."

Kevin chatted on the way back to Lauren's car.

"I thought if Cindy wasn't too busy, we could have her decorate. What do you think?"

Lauren was only half-listening to Kevin's ideas. She was still puzzled over the emotions that had rushed her a few minutes earlier. It was her nature to be analytical about everything she couldn't understand. But tonight, she had more questions than answers.

Where do I begin?

The question was being repeated over and over in her head. *Should I meditate longer? Should I sleep more? Should I be institutionalized?*

She realized it was imperative that she start listening to the lucid dreaming CD immediately.

Maybe it will help. God knows I have to do something. I've never felt so helpless. And if these are fantasies, I must put a stop to them before they take over my life.

But deep inside, Lauren fought the idea of it being just her imagination.

Kevin glanced over and realized she hadn't said a word since they left the restaurant.

"Sorry, Lauren. I've been so busy talking, I haven't given you a chance to say a word. Do you have any ideas about the new store?"

Silence was her response.

"Lauren, are you in there?"

Kevin finally touched Lauren's arm to get her attention.

"Sorry, Kev, I don't think I heard much of your conversation."

Kevin wanted to put her at ease.

"Gee, sweetie, I hadn't noticed. You must have a lot on your mind." He didn't wait for a reply. "Is there anything I can help you sort out?"

Lauren looked over at her friend and touched his hand.

"I wouldn't even know where to start. And even if I did, I would need a lot more time than we have tonight."

Kevin was deeply concerned now. "My God, is it serious?"

Lauren looked out into the night.

"Oh, I don't think so. I don't know. I've just been thinking about life, and where I fit in it."

"Damn. Is that all? I thought it was something important!" Kevin said, with a half-worried tone in his voice. "What can I do?"

As soon as Kevin had parked, Lauren opened her door, and kissed him on the cheek.

"Just be there for me. We'll talk later."

Kevin touched her cheek.

"I'll always be here for you. We're partners, remember?"

She knew he meant it unconditionally.

"Goodnight."

Kevin waited for Lauren to drive off, and sat in the parking lot for a few minutes thinking about what had just happened. He knew her well enough to see that she was sorting out a major issue of some kind. She hadn't been her usual self in several weeks. Without thinking, Kevin picked up his cell phone and called her home.

When her machine came on, he said, "Lauren, it's me. I'm just calling to remind you to have sweet dreams."

Lauren drove home with a subliminal lucid dreaming CD playing softly in the background. As the guitar music relaxed her, she slowly released the death grip she had on her steering wheel. It wasn't long before she was parking her car in the garage. She didn't mind being home alone again tonight. The rooms used to seem empty when the girls had first left for college. Gary was never home anymore, and the silence would sometimes be deafening. More often than not, she now welcomed the quiet.

"Nothing to distract me from my thoughts."

Lauren walked through the kitchen to her office. She immediately noticed the message light blinking on her phone, but preferred to ignore it for a few precious moments. She slipped off her shoes, and when she felt ready, pushed the play button. Her face cast a shadow of doubt when she heard Gary's deep voice.

"Lauren, are you there? I guess not. I'm still in New York, and it looks like I'll be delayed getting back."

Lauren shook her head in defeat, realizing he couldn't even say "getting home" anymore. Now it was just "getting back."

"Hope everything is well with you. I'll call you when I know what my plans are. Take care."

She heard a click as he had hung up. The tone of his voice had been neutral, and Lauren knew he wasn't alone. He rarely was anymore. It had devastated her when she had first discovered his indiscretions. When she confronted him, it was Gary's usual non-committal attitude that made her feelings finally die. He had been honest, and admitted he had been in love with another woman, but stayed in the marriage because of the children. He then let it fall in her lap, saying he would do whatever she wanted.

Lauren thought back to that time. She remembered agonizing over it for months. She had lost count of all the sleepless nights she had had. She remembered how she used to lock herself in the bathroom, and cry until there were no more tears. She finally woke up one day to find it didn't matter anymore. Her life was kept full by the business, her friends, and her daughters.

Lauren realized that neither of them were the enemy. They were just on different paths. It was just 'what is.' They had discussed it and decided that until one of them wanted out of the marriage for any reason; they would live in the same house. Her body often reminded her that she and Gary hadn't shared a bed in over two years. She knew Gary led a discreet life elsewhere, and she had her business.

"Until now, it's been enough." Lauren spoke to a picture of

her daughters.

"And now I'm not sure what I have. I just hope it's nothing beyond my comprehension."

There was another click, and she heard Kevin's voice.

"Sweet dreams." Lauren smiled to herself. "How prophetic. I certainly hope so."

She picked up her Moonglows bag, and ran up the stairs, anxious to begin. Lauren turned on the stereo and began to relax, as the beautiful sounds of Chris Spheeris aroused her senses. She began singing along to, 'Walk With Me.' She turned up the volume and slowly undressed in front of the mirror, allowing her skirt to slip smoothly from her slim hips. Her eyes noticed every part of her body. She slowly touched her breasts, and slid her fingers down to her tight stomach. She watched herself closely in the mirror, murmuring underneath her breath.

"I still feel young, and there's a side of me that aches to be touched."

Lauren shook her head to clean out the sensual response that was heating up her veins.

"I think I need fresh air before I meditate."

She turned off the light, and walked outside to her balcony.

Looking beyond, her eyes adjusted to the black veil in front of her.

Lauren had often marveled at how she could live in one of the largest cities in the world, but from her balcony, it would seem like it didn't exist, with the view of hills and valley during the day, and complete blackness at night.

She walked slowly back into her bedroom, finally ready to meditate. She found the CD she wanted and pushed the button. Her mood instantly changed when the angelic music of Robert Slap began. Lauren sat straight in her chair, and took several deep breaths to relax. After a few minutes, she counted herself down, and completed her affirmations. Her usual mode of meditation ceased at that point.

Lauren immediately began receiving mental pictures. First, she saw herself on a beach. Then she heard a voice, and watched herself turn around in response to the sound. She could vividly see a man she had never met, yet felt as close to as a daughter might feel towards her father. He approached Lauren and hugged her warmly. Then she was asked to remember his advice.

"Become a participant in your dreams, as well as your life. You must find what was lost. Unbury the emotions you've kept hidden for so long. Wake them up and finally be free."

Then he was gone.

Lauren stood on the beach without moving for what seemed like hours. She felt like a child, waiting for the gentle man with such love and devotion in his eyes to return. She was surprised to hear the sound of her own voice rise above the tides.

"But I have questions."

After what seemed like an eternity, Lauren finally counted herself up, and opened her eyes.

"Wow, that was incredible!"

Lauren immediately jumped up to search for her journal, breathless with excitement.

"I've got to get this in writing. I can't wait to call Adriana tomorrow, and tell her what happened."

She stopped her ranting, and thought how odd that she hadn't been frightened.

"On the contrary, I've never felt such peace."

Lauren had decided to keep a diary, when everything in her life began changing.

Who knows, she thought, half-kidding, *if it all comes true, it would make a great book.*

She sat quietly on her bed, staring ahead in the mirror. She knew it was imperative to keep an open mind and not judge what she had seen or heard. She wrote down her experiences and her feelings as she saw them. Then she read the words aloud once more. "Find what was lost."

Lauren yawned, and slipped the lucid dreaming sleep hypnosis CD into her player. She giggled, feeling a little nervous about turning off her bedroom light. That single motion would somehow confirm that she was ready to begin her journey.

She closed her eyes, and worried aloud.

"What if I don't dream of him?"

She wasn't sure how she would handle it.

"Calm down, girl, and just let things happen."

She pressed the button on the player, closed her eyes, and took a deep cleansing breath.

Alex was quiet on the ride back to Malibu. He was still in shock over having such a strong reaction, twice in one day. He was also fighting the weird sensation of being "almost there." Yet at the same time, his mind was screaming out its own question. *Almost where?*

He was beginning to agree with his friends' advice about getting out of his own way, and seeing what would happen. As his thoughts speeded ahead, Alex could feel the frown lines crease his forehead.

"Don't hurry things, but be an active participate. OK, and how in the hell do I do that? I've been able to lucid dream before, but I know this is like nothing I'm capable of achieving alone."

He wanted to get home and try his dreaming CDs. Alex thought that if he could get inside the dream, then perhaps he could do what the guys had recommended, and attempt mental telepathy.

"At this point, I'll try anything."

But he couldn't help but feel a little foolish thinking such a thing could actually take place.

Elliot let the ride pass in peace. He needed time to think about what was happening. He knew that it was difficult for Alex to open up like he did, and he hated to see his friend in such torment. Elliot glanced over to see Alex still very deep in thought.

He cleared his throat, interrupting the quiet.

"Is there anything I can do for you?"

Alex sighed loudly. "Elliot, if anyone had told me I would be going through this, I would have said they were crazy. Hell, maybe I am crazy?" He didn't wait for a response. "In any case, just be there for me. And if I start acting like a lunatic, don't hesitate to confront me."

Elliot replied thoughtfully, "Alex, I don't think you're losing your mind. But I'll be here for whatever you need."

Elliot pulled into the driveway, knowing his friend needed some time to himself. "Alex, I hope you don't mind, but I think I'm going on home, to get some sleep."

"I'm exhausted, too. Thanks a lot. I'll call you tomorrow." Alex pulled himself slowly out of the car, and turned to speak once more.

"Really, man, thanks for your support."

Elliot shrugged. "No problem. Now, go do what you have to do."

Alex unlocked his front door and walked directly into his office. He went to his desk and retrieved the familiar journal that someone had given him several years earlier. He then strolled over to his favorite chair and sank into its welcoming cushions.

Alex slowly flipped to a new page, closed his eyes, and began thinking about how he would write about his new experiences. When his eyes opened, he wrote about how the ache and emptiness refused to go away, and was in fact, growing. Then, he wrote his plan about how he would attempt to contact her in a dream state, and what methods he would use. He ended the page with a promise.

"If she does exist, I'll do everything in my power to find her. Anything and everything!"

After Alex had written all he could, he set the journal aside and gazed at the painting hung on the wall in front of him. It was an original watercolor he had found at Vickie's Art Gallery. Even now, he thought it strange that he would find it so appealing. It was not something most men would appreciate, much less own. He remembered Cindy arguing with him about the colors and portrayal not fitting with his office décor. But somehow, it hadn't mattered. He remembered hearing a convincing voice deep within him, begging him to bring it home. The painting depicted a tropical setting, done mostly in pastels. It revealed a man and woman wearing light clothing, walking on a beach, holding hands.

He smiled, thinking back to Donovan's diplomatic questioning when he walked out of the gallery carrying the piece under his arm.

"Alex, are you sure this is something you want?"

Alex chuckled, remembering the confused look on his friend's face.

Alex squinted, and stared deeper into the canvas. It was several minutes before he finally turned away and shook his head.

"Damn, this is getting too weird."

Alex turned off the light, and took his time trudging upstairs. He didn't want to admit he was almost afraid to proceed on the journey he knew had already begun.

He walked through his bedroom to the balcony, first stopping to turn on his stereo. He began to sing, when the song, 'Walk With Me' filtered through the room. Alex allowed himself time to stand in the warm darkness, and appreciate the light ocean breeze touching his face, and blowing his hair. There was a new moon, and the twinkling stars were out in the billions.

When he felt ready, he deliberately walked back inside, stood in front of the mirror, and slowly removed his clothes. But instead of noticing his dark muscular body, he gazed hard into his own deep blue eyes, hoping to find a trace of her.

When Alex sensed his frustration rising, he switched to a favorite meditation CD, then turned off the lights and stepped back outside.

He got himself comfortable in a chair, and then pulled his thick hair from his face. He looked up at the stars once more, before finally taking a deep breath through his nose, holding it a little longer than usual, then slowly pushing the air out through his mouth.

He wanted to be very deep and relaxed, so he continued this pattern for several minutes. With each breath, he could feel his body progressing to a lighter state. The weight of the day was slowly lifting away as his lids grew heavier. He counted himself down until the feeling of hypnosis overtook him. He felt as if he were in another world, floating on a cloud. He repeated his affirmations, and waited for an answer. It didn't take long.

Alex was instantly transported to a sandy beach. He noticed a familiar woman standing next to him. Her eyes were a soft brown, and her warmth reminded him of his own grandmother. She hugged him closely, and then he looked into the eyes that he had only minutes before stared deeply into. Her voice was delicate and shaky, so he listened carefully.

"My dear Alex, don't give up. It was taken away from you once before. Fight for what belongs to you now. Open your heart, your soul, and your mind. Then trust that everything you need will be there. Find what was lost." She paused for a moment, and added a warning. "But you must be patient and gentle with yourself. You must conserve your energy, and choose your battles well."

He blinked, and she was gone.

Alex opened his eyes with a start. He knew who the woman on the beach was. She came to him often, but this time her words had been startling. He quickly wrote her cryptic message in his journal, ending with "find what was lost."

Alex paced back and forth like a caged animal. He knew he had to calm down, but his mind was spinning by what his guide had said. He finally forced himself to sit on his bed, staring absentmindedly at the dreaming CD for several minutes, waiting for a sign. When Alex finally felt a surge of confidence spread through his body, he took a deep breath, switched on the player, turned off his light, and closed his eyes. He knew if he wanted to find the meaning to the message, then first he had to find her.

Lauren found herself standing on the dark shore. The first

thing she noticed was the full moon and dimly lit stars reflecting off the water. The reflections made the crashing waves a pinkish tint, and the water was a shimmering gray tone.

Lauren blinked hard.

"Where am I?"

She wasn't frightened by her unfamiliar surroundings; instead, calmness prevailed. The sound of the waves had become almost deafening, and she remained in awe of the increased shimmering colors around her. Everything glowed as if the setting had been painted fluorescent colors, and the darkness of the night shone as a black light.

Without warning, she felt her senses heighten. Lauren immediately knew someone was approaching her. Her nerves were suddenly on edge, and waves of heat rolled up and down her body. She was disoriented for a moment, not sure if her emotions were switching to fear, or anticipation.

"What's happening? Who's there?"

Lauren slowly turned around and caught sight of a shadow in the distance. Her dread vanished as the shadow's energy and love immediately encompassed her. She tried desperately to push closer to this personal magnet, but was prevented by a thin shimmering veil she could barely see. It was made almost invisible by the bright golden light surrounding the loving energy in front of her.

She could clearly see the foamy walls creeping around the rock formation beside him. Her eyes were taken off the subject long enough to notice the water ebbing around his feet. Its liquid reflection reminded her of a billion tiny diamonds sparkling in the moonlight.

Lauren's mind was spinning with confusion.

If I can see all of this so clearly, why can't I see his face?

She was screaming the question in her mind over and over again. She felt that she would burst from within if she didn't touch him now. Her whole life depended on it.

Is he my missing piece? Does he possess what I truly need to survive?

She swayed back and forth; allowing her intense emotions to scatter her energy, then fighting to stay centered and focused.

Alex opened his mind's eye, and found himself on the beach. But this time, it was dark, except for the beautiful colors reflecting from the moon. He quickly assessed the location, knowing he was near the same formation of boulders, then he forced himself to stay calm and balanced.

At least I know where I am. Now what?

He was afraid he wouldn't find her.

Is this just a dream? God, please let her be here when I turn around.

He turned, and saw a slight form in the darkness. She was obscure, but the love and warmth emitting from her aura told him she was present. He tried to run in her direction, but was stopped after a few steps.

What in the hell can I do now?

His frustration was overpowering him, and for a moment he lost his focus.

"No, Alex, don't do this. Concentrate on her. Look at her. Center all your energy on her."

He could feel her presence comforting his soul again. Then he remembered the conversation with his friends, and repeated their advice aloud.

"Get out of my own way, and attempt mental telepathy. But how in the hell do I do that?"

He took a few deep breaths and concentrated. He stared directly into where her eyes would be, and mentally spoke to the beautiful source of energy far in front of him.

"Hello, can you hear me? I know this seems crazy, but I'm trying to contact you through mental telepathy. I've never done this before, so if you are getting any of this, try to mentally answer me."

Lauren heard a faint whisper in her head, rising over the ocean sounds. She jerked her head up toward the sky.

"Is this my imagination? Did I hear a voice, or am I losing my mind?"

Alex almost jumped for joy.

"It's me. I'm concentrating on you, so please bear with me. Don't go away."

Lauren looked up as if she were hearing voices emitted from the air.

"Is this really possible?" Lauren asked.

Alex responded shyly, *"God, I hope so."*

Lauren had never felt so much peace. She wanted to ask a million questions, but her energies were being drained very quickly. She felt she couldn't stay much longer.

"Please tell me who you are. Where are you? Do you really exist? I feel as if I may be losing my mind. This has never happened to me before, and it's very frightening."

Lauren waited for an answer. She tried desperately to focus on him, but he was moving further away.

"Oh God, wait! Please help me stay here with you. Tell me, do you really exist?"

Lauren opened her eyes, and lay very still for a moment, not sure where she was. When she heard her CD playing in the background, the grief overwhelmed her.

"No. Dear God, no. Don't do this to me. He was right there. I could feel him so close. Why couldn't I have stayed just a moment longer? Does he exist, or am I going crazy?"

Lauren didn't know what else to do but pick up her journal and calmly write about what had just occurred. After writing the facts, she put her face into her pillow and sobbed, falling asleep in her tears.

When Lauren finally fell into a deep sleep, she watched herself staring at a painting on a wall. She was having trouble with her focus, but she was standing in front of it, as if to make sure it was properly hung. She was grateful when the scene faded. She was exhausted, and didn't want to think anymore.

Lauren had disappeared, but Alex continued screaming for her.

"Wait, please don't leave me! I'll help you."

But her form faded until only the sand dune she had been standing in front of remained.

He heard himself scream to the stars above.

"She's real. I know she's real."

Alex immediately woke up, hearing his CD in the background. Before he analyzed what he had just seen, he picked up his journal and wrote every detail of the event, not missing one second. Then a deep sadness set in when he glanced at the clock. He had only been asleep for a little under two hours.

"How will I find her again? I don't have a clue how I found her this time."

He tossed and turned, thinking about what his dreams had brought him. He thought about how he felt in her presence. He begged to go back to sleep, in the hopes of finding her.

Alex finally pulled himself out of bed and paced. He was angry and frustrated at himself for letting the moment with her slip from his fingers. He felt as if he had misplaced a part of himself.

"There was so much I wanted to say to her."

When Alex finally allowed himself to be quiet, his instincts told him to meditate. He thought he had lost all concentration, but he didn't have the energy to argue. He walked outside into the fresh air and stood for several minutes with his hands wrapped tightly around the balcony rails, before finally taking a few deep breaths. He looked down to see the rock formations that had been in his dream, and sighed loudly.

"It's difficult to believe it was just a few minutes ago. Why can't I look out there and she appear? Why in the hell can't it be that simple?"

Alex felt hot tears stinging his eyes, and sank down in his chair, looking out into the nothingness. He calmed himself before closing his eyes. After counting himself down, he sat still for several minutes. He could feel the scattering of energy, and reminded himself that meditation was more a tool for relaxation than for information.

"Just let it do its job."

He counted himself down again, and took another deep breath. He felt himself being gently lifted from his body. When he opened his eyes, he was on the beach. His maternal guide slowly appeared, and comforted Alex close to her chest.

"Why are you discouraged? You have come further than you think."

Her quivering voice softened. "My boy, don't lose your concentration. Now is the time to train your subconscious mind to stay focused. Find joy that you contacted her. Once you open your heart and soul, only then can true love enter. Patience, my dear boy. Only then will you find what was lost. Remember to look around with new eyes, the reminders are everywhere."

Alex opened his eyes and she was gone. But now, instead of frustration, he felt as if a weight had been lifted.

"So this isn't all in vain?"

He quickly retrieved his journal, and raced downstairs to his desk. He needed to add his latest experience to the ever-growing pages.

His body fell into the comfortable chair with great urgency. As his fingers grasped the book's leather edge, they suddenly became numb. Alex couldn't hold on, and the journal quickly dropped to the floor. As he bent over, his vision was drawn into the painting in front of him. Alex could feel his body heating up as he stared sharply into the canvas. He was amazed to see the well-defined colors and images in much greater detail than he had ever noticed before.

Alex shivered as he looked at his watch.

"My God, where have I been for the last hour?"

He quickly wrote his impressions and the message from his meditation, then closed the book and walked upstairs. He fell into his bed from sheer exhaustion. He was drifting off when the image of the painting came into sharp focus. Then, peacefully, Alex slept.

Chapter 4

Alex awoke the next morning with his telephone ringing near his ear. He turned over and grudgingly answered.

"Chandler here."

It was Elliot on the other end.

"Good morning. Did I wake you?"

Alex looked at his clock. "Yeah, but don't worry about it. What's up?"

Elliot couldn't contain his curiosity. "Well? What happened last night?"

Alex stared at the ceiling, quiet for a moment before responding.

"It was very interesting. I definitely want to discuss this with you, but I need to get up and shower first. Can you drop by later?"

Elliot made a clicking noise as if he were thinking aloud.

"Sure, if it's that important to you. I've got a short meeting in Hollywood this morning. How about after that?"

"Thanks, Elliot, I think you'll enjoy this. I'll see you later."

Alex was about to hang up when he heard Elliot's loud voice on the other end.

"Wait, I just remembered what else I was calling about. After I dropped you off last night, I got to thinking about your dreams. I don't know whether you remembered me mentioning that your story seemed familiar. Well, it was driving me crazy. Then it hit me. I'm almost certain there was a book written several years ago about a couple that had met through their dreams. I don't remember much about it, but I can try to locate the name."

Alex smiled, thinking about how much Elliot meant to him as a friend.

"After last night, I would like to get my hands on that book. Yeah, see what you can find out. Thanks, Elliot. See you later."

Alex stood with his hand firmly attached to the receiver for a long while, deep in thought.

"I need info." It came to him in a burst of excitement. "Moonglows!"

Alex quickly called for the number. Then he picked the receiver up again and punched the buttons in quick succession.

After two rings, a woman answered in a cheerful tone. "Moonglows, how can I help you?"

"Hi, this is Mr. Chandler; I'm calling in reference to information on dreams. I've been having some strange ones lately. Do you have any books on the subject?"

Adriana answered immediately. "Yes, we carry several. What type of dreams are you having?"

Alex was interrupted by the shop's other line ringing. "Sir, can I put you on hold for just a moment?"

Alex continued pacing, but only had to wait a few seconds when Adriana's assistant picked up his line. Adriana mouthed the words, "Mr. Chandler needs information on dreams."

Mark gave her the thumbs up.

"Mr. Chandler, I'm sorry for the delay. Can I help you find the information on dreams?"

Alex spoke quickly. "Yeah, I've been having the same dream for quite a while. There's a woman in it that I think I know, but I've never met her. I know it sounds bizarre, but I can assure you that I'm not crazy, and this is no joke."

Mark smiled into the phone. "Mr. Chandler, I don't doubt you. It sounds interesting. Let me look at our computer, and see what books we have on dreams that might fit your description."

Alex suddenly felt foolish, but he stayed quiet. He knew

explaining any further would just make it sound worse.

Mark finally spoke up. "We have several books on dreams, but I'm not locating anything on your particular subject. Let me do a little research, and I'll give you a call back in a few minutes."

Alex glanced at his watch. "I have an order placed with you. Can you see if it's in? I can just pick it up when I'm there."

He could hear Mark typing on the keyboard.

"Is your first name, Alex?"

"Yes, it is.

"It just came in."

"Good, I'll try to come by today."

Mark responded professionally, "I'll have a list of books included with your order. If you're not happy with the information, just let us know, and we'll find someone to help you."

Alex was feeling relieved to finally have it out, and confronted. "You're very kind. Have you ever heard of anything like this?"

Mark slowed his speech as he thought. "No, but dreams aren't my specialty. However, I'll be glad to find out what I can. Your order will be at the front desk whenever you're ready."

Adriana walked through the room as Mark hung up. "Were you able to help that gentleman?"

Mark looked up briefly from his computer. "He has a special order that he'll be picking up. I'll include a list of books that pertain to his subject, though there certainly aren't many."

Adriana walked over and looked at the screen. "He's having dreams, right?"

"Yeah, but it's the same one every night. He's a little concerned about it."

"Well, do your best to find what you can for him."

"Will do, boss."

Adriana shook her head as she walked upstairs to research Lauren's dreams. "It's not even a full moon."

Alex hung the phone up and walked out onto his balcony. He needed to see the familiar rocks again.

"What I wouldn't give to see her standing there looking up at me." What he saw instead was a couple walking close together, hand in hand. They were laughing and talking in hushed tones.

For a moment, Alex's fingers pressed firmly into the railing. He was envious of such devotion to each other, and was disappointed in himself for having had such a negative response. *Everyone deserves to be happy and to be loved. My time will come when I'm ready.*

Alex knew that he wouldn't have had these thoughts a few weeks ago. He had his work and his friends, and he was equally proud of both. Before now, he could not have conceived there was something missing in his life. Not until he began having dreams of her.

He tried desperately to push his negative thoughts aside, but they continued to intrude.

What if I never find her? Will I have to live with this empty feeling forever?

He turned away from the scene outside.

"Stop thinking like this." He spoke out loud to himself with confidence. "There's a reason for what's happening. Just trust and be patient. Now that I realize something is missing in my life, and I've figured out what it is, I simply have to ask for it, then get out of my own way."

But in the back of his mind, Alex was a little worried that everything he had ever been taught, and everything he had always believed was now being tested. And he had the feeling that it would be the most severe test of his life.

Lauren awoke with a start, as the sound of her alarm intruded her sleep. She rolled over and crudely slapped the clock, turning the noise off. She wanted to do nothing more but lay in place for a while, remembering her dreams from last night.

"He was so close, I could almost touch him. Why am I being tested like this? I thought I had everything I wanted in my life, but

I'm beginning to understand there's much more than this. But what can I do now? I'm at a loss."

The second dream came into focus while she was analyzing her problem.

"Wait! I was hanging a painting," Lauren mumbled louder now.

"It was beautiful, and so real. I wonder what it meant?"

Lauren listened to what she was saying, and caught herself. "Stop it. You're making too much out of it. There are too many other things to think about right now."

But she couldn't control herself as she retrieved her journal and re-read every word.

Her handwriting brought back the memories, and her mind detached from the morning world.

She could hear her voice somewhere in the background. "He has such a radiant spirit. So perfect."

Lauren wrote about the painting and then put the journal aside and slowly undressed. She looked in the mirror, and couldn't stop herself from drifting back to the night before.

When the now-familiar sensation of arousal crept into her being, she stepped into the hot shower, turning her thoughts over to him.

Alex slipped into a pair of jeans, looking forward to the drive to Moonglows. He wanted answers as soon as possible, though he suspected there were no books written about what he was going through.

"If I hurry, I can get there and back before Elliot drops by."

He was almost out the front door when his phone rang.

"Alex Chandler here."

The caller didn't notice his hassled intent.

"Hi, Alex. Ron Athens here. How are you?"

"Hi, Ron. I'm great. How's Cindy?" Alex put his keys aside, and stared at the front door. "Elliot and I were just listening to your CD last night. He thought your new sound was great."

Ron reacted slowly. "That's always good to hear. Cindy's fine. She's been real busy."

Not wanting to seem pressed for time, Alex felt he needed to begin the conversation. "What can I do for you, Ron?"

He noticed Ron's voice had a strained tension to it.

"I'm recording in the studio today, and I've come up against a brick wall." Ron was frustrated. "The sound is not to my liking. I was hoping you could drop by at your convenience to take a listen, and see what you think."

Alex looked at his watch. He wanted desperately to get his hands on the information. But he also didn't want to disappoint a friend.

"Sure, Ron, I'd be happy to. When do you need me?"

There was a grateful tone in Ron's voice. "I'll be in the studio all day."

"OK, let me make a few calls and I'll see you in about an hour."

"I owe you, buddy. Thanks."

Alex immediately punched in Elliot's number; his fingers tapping furiously on the table. "Come on, come on, pick up."

"Hello."

"I'm glad I caught you. I need a favor. Are you still going to be around Melrose this morning?"

"As we speak. Why? What can I do for you?"

"Ron called me and needs a little advice in the recording studio. I told him I'd run by there, but I have a special order at Moonglows that I'd appreciate you picking up for me. They're also getting together some information on dreams. Can you take care of it?"

"Yeah, no problem. Is there anything else you need while I'm over here?"

"No, I don't think so. By the way, have you given any more thought to the name of the book you were telling me about earlier?"

Elliot shook his head, more for his own benefit.

"I still have my thinking cap on. I'll see about getting some information on it at Moonglows."

"Great, then I'll see you later?"

Alex phoned Moonglows, advising Mark of the change of plans.

"No problem, we'll have it ready for Mr. Golden when he arrives."

Adriana turned her attention to the computer screen, and typed 'dreams.' A list of titles immediately flashed on the screen. A new list appeared when she typed 'romance'. Trying to keep her composure, she typed 'love', but the screen stayed blank. Out of frustration, she typed 'non-fiction'. A few generic names appeared.

Adriana spoke harshly to the lit screen.

"Damn. What in the hell is the name of that book?"

Elliot had a difficult time finding a parking place near Moonglows. He finally gave up, and parked around the corner in a rush. He wanted to get Alex's supplies then complete his own errands before the day ended.

When he pulled the door open, he could hear himself breathe an instant sigh of relief. As he looked around, his composure softened. Mark greeted him warmly. "Is there anything I can help you with?"

Elliot turned in his direction, still experiencing the comfortable feeling in the room. "Yeah, I'm here to pick up an order for Alex Chandler."

Mark smiled. "Yes, Mr. Chandler called and said to expect you. I've also included a list of books that might interest him, though I don't think they're exactly what he's looking for."

Elliot looked at the list. "I don't think so either."

Mark thought for a few seconds. "Would you like to speak to Adriana? She's the owner, and may be able to help."

Elliot looked at his watch. "No thanks, I'll give the list to Alex.

He can decide what his next move will be."

Lauren was pouring herself a cup of coffee when the phone rang.

"Hello."

"Hi, Lauren, it's Cindy. How are you?"

Lauren put down her cup, turning her attention to the phone.

"Hi, Cindy. I'm great. How are you? How did your meeting go yesterday in Marina del Rey?"

Cindy had the usual tone of excitement in her voice. "It went terrific. I expect to use a lot of the art from this woman's gallery."

Lauren was curious. "Is she anyone I know? We received approval on our new store. And if you can squeeze us in, Kevin and I want you to personally decorate it."

Cindy's voice raised an octave higher with renewed enthusiasm. "Lauren, I'm honored. I would love to."

"Is there anything in the gallery you think I might like for the store?"

"Oh yes. There are things in this gallery you would love."

Lauren grabbed a pencil and was ready to write.

"What's the name of this place? I'd like to run by there."

"The name is "Del Rey's Arts and Antiques." Vickie Sanders is the owner. She's an intelligent, no-nonsense kind of a gal, with a great sense of humor. And trust me, she knows her art."

Lauren was impressed by the description.

"Do you have the time to drive over there with me today?"

Cindy didn't have to think about her decision. "Yeah, that sounds great, but I need to go over to Ron's studio this morning. Why don't you meet me, and we'll go from there?"

Lauren glanced at the clock on her oven. "What time?"

"How about noon?"

Lauren penciled in her book. "I'll see you then."

She dialed her office, relieved when Kevin picked up on the second ring.

"Hi, it's me."

"Hi, sweetie, how did you sleep?"

Lauren smiled to herself. "Oh, Kevin, my dear friend, we have so much to talk about. But I'm going to need plenty of time for this one. Not to mention, a very open mind."

Kevin chided her. "Gee, Lauren, are you going to tell me that some tall, dark, and handsome man has swept you off your feet?"

Lauren was quiet, not sure how to respond.

"Lauren, are you there?"

Lauren spoke barely above a whisper. "We have to talk."

Kevin raised his eyebrow and returned her whisper. "Lauren, have you met someone?"

"No, not really."

Kevin couldn't hide his concern. "Are you coming to the shop today?"

"That's what I was calling about. I'm meeting Cindy to check out an art gallery in Marina del Rey. She's raving about the place, and we may want to use a few pieces in our new shop. I'll be in later, but I can't tell you when. Is this going to present a problem?"

Kevin shook his head. "No, this is Maria's day to work, so we'll have plenty of help."

Lauren was relieved. "That's great. Then I'll talk to you later."

She hung up and allowed herself a moment to drift back to her memories.

"I wish I could think about anything but this. Please, God, don't let this be just a dream. I really want to find this man."

Gary suddenly entered her mind. "Is this something I need to speak to him about?"

Lauren felt an embarrassing image overcome her. "Yeah, he really would think I was crazy. I wonder if it would be grounds for divorce."

Not that it mattered; Gary was breaking away, and she knew it.

Lauren was beginning to understand that neither one of them were complete. She knew they both needed to get on with their own lives, and their own loves.

"Hanging on is not fair to either one of us. Our past is just that – a past. Neither of us can grow this way."

Lauren knew that Gary was beginning to feel it too. People move in different directions sometimes. It was sad when it happened, but to not realize, or to ignore it and not move on was creating karma within itself.

"Better to let him go with love. If we break clean now, we can still remain friends."

Lauren didn't want a failed marriage. She had never been very good in failing at anything, but she was beginning to realize that one can fail terribly at failing. Her philosophy taught that it was only a failure if you had learned nothing from it. And she had learned many things from Gary. She had learned how to be independent, and she knew that lesson would be used the rest of her life. And he had given her the gift of motherhood. Her girls were everything to her. No matter what problems she had in the past with Gary, she could not deny that without him, she would not have the children she had now.

She believed like most things in life, Gary was brought to her for a reason. She believed it was how a person reacted to these tests in life, both positive and negative, that made them happy or unfulfilled. It was up to each person to determine how he or she would react. She wanted to do this one right. And she wanted no blame from either side. She wanted the karma to be balanced; for her children, for Gary, and for herself. Lauren was deep in thought when the phone rang again. She picked it up absentmindedly.

"Yes."

She heard Gary's voice on the other end.

"Hi, Lauren, just thought I would check in. I didn't expect to find you home. I was going to leave a message."

Lauren wasn't surprised. They rarely spoke anymore, unless it was about their separate itineraries, or about the girls.

"Did you receive my message last night? I'm still in New York, and I can't tell you when I'll be back. Is everything all right there?"

Lauren smiled, no longer comprehending this was the man that used to be her world. It seemed so strange, and so long ago.

"Yeah, everything's great. My loan went through, so Kevin and I are beginning construction immediately."

"That's good news, Lauren. You'll certainly be kept busy."

"I hope so."

Lauren knew she would need to stay busy. She didn't know what surprises were in store for her, and she desperately needed to stay focused.

"You say you don't know when you'll be back in town?" She asked.

Gary's voice changed to a hushed tone.

"No, I can't really say."

Lauren found her tone had lowered too. "I think we need to sit down and talk when you return."

"I agree. We've come too far with each other to ignore the problem. But I promise everything will be fine. Have you made some decisions?"

Lauren felt tears sting her eyes.

"Gary, I think we're both ready to make some decisions. We're trying so hard to be fair to each other, but we're not being fair to ourselves. We both know what needs to be done."

Gary unconsciously dabbed his eyes with the back of his hand.

"Yeah, I think we're both ready to begin new lives. There's a part of our life together that will always be treasured, but I also think that it's time."

Lauren smiled, relieved that she had finally made her move. At least she was going forward. She wasn't sure into what, but at least the feeling of stagnation was beginning to lift.

"OK, we'll talk when you get back. And I'll have our attorney draw up preliminary papers for your review. I want to be fair, and do what's right."

Gary intercepted her thoughts. "You can have the house, and

we'll each keep our own businesses. I'll provide completely for the girls, and anything you may need."

Lauren knew he didn't have to be so generous.

"Gary, I'll agree to most everything except alimony. As long as you participate in our children's lives, then I'm happy. And better, they'll be happy."

"Whatever you want. You work it out, and I'll sign whatever sounds reasonable to you. I know you'll be fair."

Lauren knew she shouldn't say what was about to come out of her mouth next, but she somehow felt compelled to say it.

"Gary, don't worry about how I, or the kids, will react when you remarry. I understand that you have to do what is right for you. The girls will understand too."

Gary sounded relieved.

"I love you, Lauren."

"I love you too. Take care and I'll see you soon."

She hung up before he could say another word. Lauren took a deep breath, allowing the large pressure she had been carrying for so many years to fall away. Now they could both move forward to new beginnings.

Feeling secure that her life was finally going in the right direction, Lauren picked up her keys and headed to her car. She knew there would be tears still to come from her decision. And she still had the girls to contend with, but she now felt strong enough to forge ahead.

Lauren slipped Ron's CD into its slot, and backed out of her driveway. Music entered the vehicle, filling her with energy. She was humming to herself when visions from the night before calmly swept over her.

Will I see him tonight?

Lauren noticed this question was coming up more frequently in her thoughts. "Have I lost a bit of my sanity?" She picked up her phone and quickly punched in Adriana's number.

"Moonglows, how may I help you?"

"Hi, it's me. It happened again last night, but with much greater detail. I'm confused as hell, but it was great."

Adriana couldn't contain her curiosity.

"Oh, for goodness sake, tell me everything."

Lauren spoke eagerly. "He contacted me through mental telepathy this time. We were on the same beach as before, but it was at night. And there was a beautiful full moon shining off the ocean. I couldn't see him well because of that damn veil separating us, but I could see his shadow and form. The energy was incredible."

"Wow, Lauren," Adriana almost shouted, "what did he say?"

Lauren's laughter echoed off the windshield.

"Unfortunately not as much as I would've liked. I couldn't focus for very long, and lost the connection. I didn't have time to find out who he was. Adriana, nothing in my life has ever felt this crazy, yet so normal and right."

Before her friend had an opportunity to respond, Lauren continued.

"I had another strange dream as well. It seems insignificant, but I can't get it out of my mind. All I remember is that I was hanging a painting on a wall. I feel it has something to do with my first dream, but I'm not sure of anything anymore."

Adriana was intrigued. "Lauren, can you remember the details? The colors? Who was in the picture?"

Lauren thought for a moment, tapping her fingertips on the steering wheel, and then glancing down at her speed.

"No, I can't tell you any more about it. You've got to help me here."

Adriana was staring into her computer screen.

"It's driving me crazy too. Your story sounds so familiar, but I can't seem to come up with anything. Maybe now that you've contacted him in your dream state, it'll be easier for you to find him again."

She continued with her advice. "And, Lauren, for God's sake, this is not some cosmic joke. Everything comes to you for a reason. You just need to relax and go with the flow. Don't push for the answers."

Lauren thought for a second, and then spoke in a serious tone. "You're right. Perhaps I won't have it constantly on my mind when we start work full-time on the new shop." Lauren continued without a breath. "I spoke to Gary this morning. We've decided to divorce. We discussed it at length, and decided that neither one of us were doing any good this way. We want to keep it amicable for ourselves, and the kids."

Adriana was surprised by the seemingly natural tone in her voice, but knew this had been a very difficult decision for Lauren to make.

"You know I'm here for you. I don't want you going through this alone."

Lauren felt tears burn her eyes again.

"Thanks. I needed to hear you say that." Lauren intentionally changed the tone of her voice. "Now, I'm off to an art gallery that Cindy found. She's meeting me at Ron's studio. I'll call you later. Oh, and Adriana, I love you. Don't ever forget that."

Adriana smiled. "I know. I love you, too. Talk to you soon."

Lauren turned up the music and daydreamed until she pulled into the studio lot and parked next to an expensive car, making her wonder what a person had to do to afford such an extravagance.

"One day, I'll own one just like that. But for now, I sure don't want to scratch this one," Lauren whispered aloud as she carefully opened her car door. "The last thing I need is for some guy to come looking for me."

The receptionist smiled as Lauren approached. "Hi, may I help you?"

"Yes, my name is Lauren Wells. I'm to meet Cindy Athens here."

"Oh yes, Miss Wells. Cindy's in Ron's office. Should I direct you?"

Lauren was already walking down the hall. "No thank you, I know my way," she called over her shoulder.

She turned right, and continued to the door at the end of the hall, where she knocked softly. Cindy's perky voice was heard from the other side. "Come on in."

Cindy was on the phone, sitting in Ron's chair. Lauren quietly crossed over to give her friend a quick hug, and then sat down. From her vantage point, she could see the marina and began counting the boats in her view. Cindy was in negotiations with a client, and raised two fingers telling her that she would be off the phone shortly.

In a recording studio two flights above, Alex was working on the piano with Ron's music. They had run into a snag, and were working feverishly on correcting the problem. Alex was deep in thought, scoring the music, when he unexpectedly felt an intense rush of energy flow through his veins. All concentration was immediately lost. "Damn."

The intense rush left him feeling too weak and helpless to fight the reaction, and his frustration was beginning to mount. He could barely speak above a whisper.

"Ron, I've got to break for a few minutes."

Ron glanced over and saw Alex staring blankly into space. He followed the direction of his friend's gaze, but saw nothing.

"Alex, what the hell are you looking at?"

The room had become quiet, and a chaotic power seemed to pulsate all around them.

"Alex, are you OK?"

Alex turned robotically in Ron's direction. His voice wasn't his own, and was still barely audible.

"Ron, have you ever experienced a feeling of intense déjà vu?"

Ron fought to keep his voice from sounding confused. "Sure. All the time. It can drive you crazy. Why?"

Alex sat erect, with his head cocked to one side.

He ignored Ron's response and continued.

"I was almost where I wanted to be with the music, when I suddenly had a weird sensation of someone or something being here with me. Someone or something that I'm very familiar with. But damn it, for the life of me, I can't place from where."

Alex narrowed his eyes in fixed frustration, muttering louder.

"There are too many fucking things happening to me lately. I don't know what I should listen to, or what I should ignore. I don't know how much I'm creating, how much I'm obsessing over, or how much of this is destiny. I just don't seem to know anything anymore."

His ravings increased an octave, and Ron felt himself involuntarily flinch.

"What I'm going through feels so right, but I'm getting so damn frustrated, because I simply can't process all of it at once. I don't know what to do next. If I'm not going crazy, and this is all just a sane episode in my life, then I need to know. I'll do anything to make these dreams a reality, but I just don't know how."

Ron stared at Alex in shocked disbelief. He was talking more to himself now, ranting and raving about things that Ron didn't understand. After a few minutes, Ron interjected with a calm voice.

"Alex? Hey man. What are you talking about? Are you all right? Why don't we stop for a while? We can go back to my office and have a drink. Maybe sort things out in there."

Alex blinked hard and gazed into the frightened eyes of his friend. When he saw the concern and confusion looking back at him, he wanted to run away from the humiliation.

Alex closed his eyes, and hung his head. *That's never happened before. Jesus, this poor guy must think that I've lost my mind. If it wasn't so pathetic, it would actually be funny. But Ron's a really nice guy, and doesn't deserve these tantrums from me.*

Anyone would believe that Ron was a musician. He possessed a medium build, with thick, shoulder-length blond hair, and hazel eyes. He and Alex had met through his wife, Cindy, when she decorated Alex's house. Cindy had seen a guitar in a corner of Alex's living room, and had already noticed his beautiful piano. She mentioned that her husband was a professional musician, and the owner of a recording studio in Venice. Before Alex had the opportunity to respond, Cindy had run out to her car and pulled Ron's CD from the player. Alex had initially listened out of politeness, but when he heard Ron's music, he was impressed. By the time Cindy had completed her work, the two men had been introduced and had developed a friendly professional working relationship.

Alex watched as Ron sat down next to him in a chair. His eyes were still filled with fear and concern for his friend.

"Alex, do you want to go to my office?"

Alex tried to lighten the mood. "Ron, is there anything in your office that I need to see? Maybe a few men in white coats?"

Ron looked puzzled. "Just a drink and a couch. Why?"

Alex realized his manner of calming the environment hadn't worked, and interrupted. "Why don't you get me a drink while I compose myself? When you get back, I'll try to explain the reason for my outburst. I promise I'm no lunatic."

Ron's look of concern stayed fixed.

"Ron, don't worry, I'm all right. It's just been a crazy couple of weeks. Now, go get me that drink."

Ron walked to the door, shaking his head in confusion.

When he heard the door shut, Alex put his forehead against the piano, and closed his eyes. He was grateful for the time alone.

"Why does this keep happening? Whose energy continues to merge with mine? It feels so familiar, so warm, so loving, but no one's here. If I'm going to feel someone this close, why can't I have them with me?" He looked up to the ceiling. "Does anyone up there know how frustrating it is to feel what I'm feeling and have nothing to show for it?"

But Alex didn't have an answer, nor did he receive one. In a feeble attempt to center himself, Alex closed his eyes again, taking a deep breath. "I've got to calm down."

He tried to come up with a sane excuse for Ron. He could only imagine how potent the drink would be. "I'm sure he must think that I've either lost my mind or that I'm possessed."

Ron walked into his office, expecting to be alone. His face took on a pleasant smile when he saw his wife on the phone. Ron was as much in love with Cindy now as he was on the day he had married her. When he closed the door, he saw Lauren sitting on the sofa, glancing at a magazine.

"Hi, Lauren, how's it going? Do you and Cindy have plans?"

Lauren put the magazine on the coffee table. "Hi, Ron. Yeah, Cindy and I are driving over to an art gallery. I don't know if she's had time to tell you, but Kevin and I are opening a new store in Santa Monica. We've asked Cindy to decorate it for us."

Ron walked across the room to give Lauren a hug. "Congratulations, that's wonderful news. When's the grand opening?"

A puzzled look crossed Lauren's face. "That's a good question. We begin the design immediately, but when you're working with people that aren't worried about your schedule, who knows how long it'll take. We're praying for a grand opening by the Christmas season."

Ron strolled over to his wife, and put his arm around her.

"And you say you're going to hire my wife to decorate? Well, let's hope you can get her off the phone by Christmas."

They both giggled as Cindy poked her elbow into Ron's ribs. Cindy finally said her goodbyes and hung up.

"Hi, sweetie, I hope you don't mind, I took over your office to conduct some business."

Ron kissed Cindy on the cheek. "Honey, as long as you're bringing in lots of money, I'm happy."

Lauren loved watching her two friends interact. They had their problems like other people, but they had a deep respect for each other, and it always showed.

Cindy turned to her husband. "How long will you be working in the studio?"

A worried look crossed Ron's face. Feeling the couple needed some time alone, Lauren excused herself for tea.

When the door closed, Cindy looked in Ron's eyes. "Jeez, honey, what's wrong?"

Ron turned away, and began mixing a drink. Cindy watched as her husband poured a shot of liquid from a bottle.

"You must be having a rough day."

Ron smiled, "It's not for me. It's for a friend of ours. He's helping me rewrite some music I'm having trouble with."

Cindy looked surprised. "Who is it? You've got the strangest look on your face, and you're obviously in distress."

"No problems with me, but I can't say that for Alex. He's behaving a little weird."

Ron turned to his wife and continued. "I thought we were working fine, when he suddenly went off on a tangent."

Cindy's look mirrored her husband's. "My God. What happened? Is he all right?"

Ron turned and continued mixing the drink.

"I think he's just a little confused. He was working on the score when he suddenly turned pale, and had a very strange look on his face. He was staring blankly at the wall. When I asked him if he was all right, he lost it. He began screeching loudly to himself about what he should or shouldn't believe. He said too many weird things were happening to him. Then he mentioned something about destiny, and a feeling of déjà vu." Ron shook himself. "It was too damn strange for me. He obviously has something on his mind. It's not like him to be out of control.

"In fact, I've rarely met anyone more in control than Alex. Anyway, I told him I'd get him a drink, and give him time to pull himself together."

Cindy spoke slowly, trying to make sense out of what had

happened.

"Not like him? Ron, it's nothing like him. Do you want me to go talk to him? God, I hope he's all right."

Ron headed to the door. "I'm sure he's fine. I think the pressure just got to him. I know how he feels. There are times when I'm so damn close to finding the right connection to finally completing a piece of music, then suddenly I lose it. It was right there, and then it's gone. Let me tell you, I go a little crazy too. I'm sure that's all it is. Don't worry, he'll be fine. He said he'd tell me about it when I got back, so let me get on up there."

Cindy kept the look of concern in her eyes, but she opened the door to let Ron out.

"I'll be here for a few more minutes. If you need me, please call?"

"I promise I will."

Cindy kissed him on the lips, and closed the door behind him.

Lauren was in the kitchen preparing a cup of tea when she felt an intense impression of adoring energy consuming her entire being. It hit her with such force that she had no choice but to collapse in the chair beside her. She tried desperately to focus on reality, but she was shivering uncontrollably as warm tingles ran up and down her spine. She hadn't realized she had been staring at the wall with tears streaming down her face, until she heard her name being called from the hall.

Lauren swiftly brushed at her wet cheeks, glancing at the clock on the wall. "What happened? Where have I been for the past ten minutes?"

She shook herself back to reality, but stood up too erect as Cindy entered. She tried to find a comfortable composure, but wasn't fast enough. Cindy walked around and stood in front of her.

"Lauren, you look like you've seen a ghost. Are you all right?"

Lauren knew she responded too quickly. "Of course, I'm fine." Her composure was fading, and she needed to change the subject. "Is Ron OK?"

Lauren was relieved when Cindy changed her look to one of confusion. "Yeah, he's OK. He's working upstairs with a friend who sort of lost it for a minute. He's sure it's stress."

Lauren was grateful the attention had shifted away from her. It gave her time to analyze what had just happened. She wasn't listening to Cindy's story. She was now deep in her own thoughts. Somewhere in the background, she heard her friend mention someone having a feeling of déjà vu and destiny. She thought to herself, *Join the club.*

She so wanted to understand her own predicament, but she couldn't possibly listen to Cindy and herself too. Cindy won out in the end.

"Lauren, you're not listening to a word I'm saying. What is it with this place today? Everyone's possessed. C'mon, let's go before it begins affecting me too."

Lauren picked up her purse, "Cindy, what are you talking about? Who's possessed?"

Cindy laughed. "Oh, forget it."

Ron exited the elevator and walked quietly into the studio. He found Alex still sitting at the piano, looking pale, but his outlook appeared better. He handed Alex the glass, and sat down next to him.

"Now, would you like to tell me what's going on, or is it none of my business?"

Alex remained quiet, not moving.

Ron continued. "Did you suddenly lose a piece of music? From experience, I know how crazy that can make a person."

Alex laughed nervously, making Ron even more uncomfortable. Noticing Ron's body language, Alex quickly composed himself.

"No, it wasn't anything like that. I just felt possessed for a moment. I've been having some strange dreams lately, and haven't been sleeping as well as I should. Something happened to bring all the emotions to the surface. I can't really explain it now, but I can promise you that I'm fine. I imagine a lot of it is stress related. So don't worry about me."

Alex took a large gulp from the glass, and then completed his thought. "I'm here to help you, not the other way around. So, let's get back to work."

Chapter 5

Lauren and Cindy were driving to the gallery, talking in detail about the ideas they both had on the new store. The tension was finally settling in Lauren's head, when she was taken off guard by Cindy's question. "What was going on back there?"

Lauren hid her look of surprise. "What do you mean?"

Cindy stopped at a red light, and faced her friend.

"I had the feeling I walked in on a very private moment back there in the studio, but you were alone. What's going on?"

Lauren looked out the window. "It's no big deal. You happened to walk in during one of my vivid daydreams. That's all. OK?"

The light changed and Cindy accelerated. "Sure."

Lauren was grateful the ride was finally over, as Cindy pulled into the parking lot. Del Rey's Art and Antiques stood directly in front of them.

"Wow, now that's a classy storefront."

Cindy laughed, getting out of the car. "Just wait until you see what's inside."

Lauren followed Cindy into the gallery, and gasped out loud.

"Oh my God, I've never seen so many beautiful things in one place."

Lauren slowly slid her fingers over a French provincial desk.

"These pieces are unbelievable. I wonder where she gets them."

Cindy walked around to the other side of the table.

"Vickie finds most of the items from estate sales. I haven't seen everything yet. But what I've seen so far has certainly increased my appetite for more."

They turned when someone entered the room.

"Welcome to Del Rey's. My name is Casey. Can I help you?"

Cindy shook Casey's hand. "We're here to see Vickie, is she in?"

"Yes, I'll locate her for you. In the meantime, please feel free to browse."

Lauren was like a child in a candy store, and had already found a few pieces of furniture that would look perfect in her new shop, as well as in her home.

She turned and watched as another woman approached and hugged Cindy. Lauren knew immediately she was the owner. Vickie appeared to be in her forties, with deep red hair, and a tall, slightly stocky build. She looked like a woman confidant with whom she was.

"Hi, Cindy, weren't you just here?"

"Yeah, but I wanted to bring in one of my friends. I told her about your place, and she insisted on seeing it for herself."

Lauren watched as the pair walked over in her direction. She met them halfway with an outstretched hand. "Hi, I'm Lauren Wells. You have a lovely store."

The woman replied with a beautiful smile. "It's very nice to meet you, Lauren. I'm Vickie Sanders."

Lauren immediately felt comfortable with her. "If you don't mind, I would love to have a look around."

Vickie smiled again, obviously pleased with the request. "Please make yourself at home, and take your time."

Lauren strolled to the other side of the room, but could overhear Cindy ask how Donovan was doing. "I didn't have a chance to ask yesterday. Have the two of you made your big wedding plans yet?"

Vickie laughed. "Big wedding plans? No, not yet. I want to be engaged for a while. Donovan is doing fine, as usual. We'll need to have you and Ron over for dinner one night. I'd like to get to know you both better."

Cindy smiled back at her new friend. "Thanks, we would enjoy that."

Lauren turned the corner and their conversation was out of range. She was now in her own world.

Lauren didn't know much about art or antiques, but she knew what she liked, and it seemed the entire store was indeed her fantasy.

When she approached a flight of stairs, Lauren looked around to see if anyone was watching, then questioned whether she should proceed.

"Well, there's no one telling me I can't."

Her curiosity finally got the best of her, as she crept slowly up the stairs. She felt foolish when she reached the top step and saw a sign welcoming her to look around. She was intrigued by all Vickie had hidden away. There was furniture, paintings, clothes, jewelry, books, and accessories. She didn't understand why she would be so fascinated by it all, but she couldn't resist it. She felt like a little girl in her grandmother's attic.

Lauren walked to the rack of clothing hanging in the far corner, and touched the fine silks and satins. "I wish you could tell me your stories of where you've been and what you've seen."

She turned around and noticed jewelry on the other side of the room. "Oh, what wonderful stories they must have."

She quickly strolled in its direction, but stopped abruptly when she was sidetracked by an antique music box. Lauren was immediately drawn to the large wooden box, painted a deep ocean-blue, with a light colored grain bordering the rim of the lid. There were two entwined gold rings painted on the cover. Lauren followed the smooth outline with her fingertips for several moments. The box stood on four delicately carved gold legs. Lauren slowly lifted the cover, and saw that the inside of the box was finished in a royal blue fabric. She was admiring the beautiful piece when something shiny caught her attention. She pulled back a piece of the fabric with her nails, and discovered a ring stuck firmly in the corner of the box. Lauren carefully pushed the fabric aside to get a better look. "Is it a man's wedding ring?"

Once she saw the unusual chiseled pattern on the piece of jewelry, she couldn't resist removing it from its container. Lauren squinted her eyes to almost closing, before she saw the inscription etched on the inside rim of the ring. She moved it towards the light in various positions, attempting to read it. She finally realized it was going to be impossible due to its stained condition. Lauren tried to put it back in the box, but suddenly found it difficult to part with.

"What in the world would I do with a man's wedding ring?"

She tried to part with the ring again, but instead felt the band slide further down her finger. Shaking her head in mock disgust, Lauren tried reasoning with herself. "You don't need this."

She continued to twist the metal around her right index finger, and then held it to the light once again. "It's really quite beautiful."

It was solid gold, with ancient looking symbols embossed over the front in a multilateral design.

She was startled and turned around too quickly when she heard Cindy and Vickie enter the room. Cindy wore the same strange look she had had on her face earlier. "Lauren, are you all right? You've been up here for a very long time."

Lauren glanced at her watch and was astonished. "My goodness, I'm really sorry. I didn't realize I was gone for so long. Uh, where did the time go?"

She was about to make another apology when Cindy interrupted with a giggle. "Lauren, it's all right. I'm glad you're enjoying yourself."

Cindy tilted her head and inquired curiously, "Did you find something that you can't live without?"

Lauren held the ring up to the light once again. "Yeah, I think I have. Though it's certainly not what I came in for."

She held the ring out in the palm of her hand, and pointed to the box. "Vickie, can you tell me what this is selling for, and do you have any history on it?"

Vickie walked over to survey the box before answering.

"Lauren, this box was from an estate sale that I recently attended. It's a relatively young piece, dating back to the 1930s. Unfortunately, I don't have too much information on it. The estate where I purchased it from was not its original owners, so records weren't kept."

Lauren looked at the ring again, and felt compelled to ask. "How much would you take for it?"

Vickie looked hard into Lauren's eyes and saw her eagerness.

"I can sell it to you for $100.00."

Lauren couldn't contain her wide grin of appreciation.

"I'll take it!"

Lauren paid for the ring, and then realized that she hadn't browsed through the remainder of the store.

"Vickie, I apologize for not spending more time looking around. I'll be back in a few days."

Vickie liked Lauren, and smiled warmly at her. "You're welcome here anytime."

When the women pulled out of the parking lot, and Del Rey's was behind them, Cindy couldn't refrain from questioning Lauren on her new purchase.

"Lauren, what is it about the ring that attracted you?"

Lauren looked closely at the metal band and shook her head. "I have absolutely no idea."

When Lauren was finally alone and driving to her shop, she wondered why she was so desperate to have the ring. "It's certainly not something I can use."

She looked at her finger resting on the steering wheel and smiled at the ring's remarkable beauty and character. Lauren picked up the cell phone and punched in Moonglows' number. When Adriana answered, Lauren heard herself speaking in excited confusion. It took Adriana a moment to recognize the voice.

"Adriana, I just bought the most unusual item. And I have no idea why I was so desperate to have it."

Adriana laughed at her friend. "Well, tell me what it is, and maybe I can help you figure it out."

"I bought a wedding band that belonged to a man several decades ago. It's beautiful, but that's not why I had to have it. I actually have no earthly idea why I had to have it, but I knew I wasn't leaving without it."

Adriana's laugh vanished, and she fought to act nonchalant.

"Where did you find it, and what drew you to it?"

In her excitement, Lauren didn't recognize her friend's change of tone. "I went with Cindy to an art gallery in Marina del Rey to look at some items for the new store. Vickie, the owner, also sells antiques. Normally that wouldn't interest me, but when I went upstairs, I found the most fascinating items. She had everything you could think of."

Adriana turned away from her computer and concentrated on the sound of Lauren's voice. She asked her question again.

"What attracted you to the ring?"

"Well, I wasn't at first. I was attracted to a gorgeous musical jewelry box. But out of curiosity, I opened it, and there it was lying off to the side. Adriana, it's the most unusual ring I've ever seen. I argued with myself for the longest time, but obviously to no avail. There was something that told me to buy it."

Adriana was quiet for a moment, but when she spoke, her voice was composed. "Lauren, I would love to see it. Where are you heading now?"

"I'm on my way to the shop."

"OK, I'll see you there in a little while."

Lauren hung up the phone feeling bewildered. "Why did I want this gold piece of metal? Or did it want me?"

Alex left the studio and headed north on the P.C.H. to his home, and back to familiar surroundings. He realized that he had to get his head together and examine what had transpired at the studio.

"What in the hell is going on? Every time I get close to an answer, something happens to make me lose my focus."

His thoughts were still spinning when he realized he had already parked in his driveway. Alex unlocked the front door, and walked slowly into his office. He fell into the recliner in the corner of the room and stared up at the ceiling, silently asking for help.

Please tell me what to do. How can I resolve this problem? I need guidance before I really mess things up.

His eyes immediately sharpened on the pastel painting hanging on the wall in front of him. He blurred his vision until his head ached. The painting that he had never really noticed before suddenly relaxed him. He closed his eyes and slept.

Alex fell into a deep sleep that permitted no participation. He was a bystander, merely watching the activities.

He woke up gradually, softly focusing his attention onto the picture once again. When he suddenly remembered what he had witnessed in his dream, Alex picked up his journal and scribbled as fast as he could.

"I was watching a young and very beautiful woman. She resembled the woman in my painting, but she was distraught and crying. I felt as if someone had died, or that she had lost something or someone very important to her. My heart ached, and I wanted to protect her from her pain. I remember seeing an item in her hand. I watched as she kissed it very gently before placing it in a box. Then the dream faded from my view."

Alex had just returned the journal to its resting place when he heard a knock at the door, then the click from the turning knob. It was Elliot. "Hello… Alex, are you here?"

Alex came out of his study with a dazed look on his face.

"Come on in. I've just been zoning in my study. Were you able to run by Moonglows?"

Elliot handed him a package. "Yeah, it's an interesting place. Very comfortable."

Alex vaguely heard him. He opened the package and searched for the information about dreams.

"Did they say anything about the info I requested?"

Elliot shook his head. "The guy behind the counter said that if you didn't see what interests you, to let them know, and they'll investigate further."

Alex smiled warmly, "Thanks, buddy. Hell, after the emotional roller coaster I've been on in the past few days, they may have to bring in an exorcist."

Elliot glanced at the list, smiling. "Alex, you have to trust me when I say you're not possessed. You're going through something very significant at the moment, even for you. But it's not possession.

"You're frustrated because you usually have everything organized, and so together. Not having the answer is new and foreign to you. But don't get discouraged. I'll bet if you put all the clues together, you'll find that you're moving forward in this quest, not backward."

Alex thought for a moment before replying. "I can't argue with that. I just wish the clues would come a bit slower, or a bit faster. And definitely a bit clearer. I can't assimilate one without another one barging in. It happened today at Ron's. I got so frustrated that I think I went off the deep end and scared the poor guy to death."

Elliot laughed out loud. "I'm sure Ron was fine with it. Granted, you're not particularly famous for your emotional outbursts, but I'm sure he thought it was stress related. You just focus on the issues, and let the rest take care of itself."

Alex knew his friend was right, and couldn't help but tease him.

"How much do they pay you to be a wise old soul?"

Elliot shot him a snide look. "Believe me, not enough! I don't think anyone can afford what I'm really worth."

Alex seated himself in a chair overlooking the blue ocean waters, and stared at the waves crashing below him. He spoke in a whisper.

"So tell me what to do. I felt that same weird sensation again."

Elliot sat across from him on the sofa. "What kind of sensation? You've had so damn many of them lately, it's hard to keep track." Elliot was trying desperately to keep Alex's frame of mind light.

"Dazed feeling. Then chills, followed by the profound power of someone being near me."

Elliot smiled, "Oh, just that, huh?"

Alex heard the lightness, and chuckled to himself.

"I've had these episodes three times in the last twenty-four hours. If I wanted to be an optimist, I suppose I could see it as making progress ."

"Well, thank you, Alex, for allowing the optimism to surface. Has anything else taken place today?" Elliot was curious.

Alex put his hand up in a gesture that demonstrated he would come right back.

In a few moments, he returned with his journal, opened to the page written only a few minutes earlier. Alex began reading his latest entry about the dream. When he had completed his summary, he sat the book on the table between the two men, and then looked over with a question.

"Well, what do you think? And why am I so fascinated by the painting all of a sudden?"

Elliot touched the soft cover of the journal, and closed his eyes for a moment. He spoke slowly.

"Alex, you said that you were looking into the painting when you fell asleep. Do you feel there's a connection between your night dreams, and your dream today? And if so, then what do you think your next step should be?"

Alex picked up the journal and hugged it to his chest. "I don't want it to be just another piece of the puzzle. I've got more than I can deal with now. I want it simplified. Who knows, maybe that's all it was. Just a dream. But you see what I'm doing? I'm obsessing over everything that happens. And I have one question after another. This isn't like me."

Elliot stood up and walked to the window. "But what if it's all supposed to connect?"

Alex didn't have the answer. "I'll think about it later."

Lauren parked her car behind "Lauren's Place", and sat quietly for a few moments, pulling herself together. She glanced in the mirror, looking deep into her eyes. Without warning, her focus blurred and she caught a quick glimpse of someone other than herself. A younger woman. It all took place in a fraction of a second, but Lauren saw the pleading look in the sad eyes that were reflecting back at her. She opened her eyes wide, and the unfamiliar features disappeared.

She tried to shake the confusion out of her head by tightly closing her eyes. When she felt brave enough to open them again, all she saw were her own blue eyes staring back. She leaned her head against the headrest out of frustration, begging for both physical and mental quietness.

Once her heart stopped racing, Lauren forced herself slowly out of the car. "How am I going to describe this in my journal?"

Lauren was talking to herself as she entered the back door.

"Describe who?" Kevin said from the other side.

Lauren lost her train of thought for a moment. "Oh, I was just daydreaming again. What's been going on in my absence?"

She thought about how good she was getting at changing the subject.

Kevin hugged his friend, letting her believe she had got her way, and then walked over to the counter.

"You have several phone messages. Adriana called and said she would be here around six."

Lauren felt certain that she had done the right thing by phoning her friend. Adriana always knew how to help her focus on the issues.

After Lauren had made a few calls, Kevin noticed her gazing

out the window. He slowly approached, wanting to strike up a conversation. Anything to divert her attention away from the glass.

"Lauren, how about you and I go to dinner tonight?"

Lauren gazed into Kevin's brown eyes with a smile.

"I'd love to, but can I take a rain check? There's too much on my mind that needs to be sorted out right away. I wouldn't be very good company."

She felt obligated to confide in Kevin. He had never been anything but a dear friend to her, and she couldn't help but see the worried look on his face. It wasn't fair to keep him in the dark.

"Kevin, Gary and I are getting a divorce." There! She had said it. She waited for a shocked reaction, but instead received a warm, caring hug. Kevin held her close to his chest, and spoke in soothing tones.

"Honey, I'm so sorry. Why didn't you tell me sooner? I feel as if I haven't been there for you."

Lauren pulled away. She turned and sat down on the sofa, staring at her friend in disbelief.

"Kevin, you have always been here for me." She felt her emotions rising, but continued. "It's been your unconditional love and acceptance that has given me the opportunity to explore who I am, and what it is I want."

She began to feel a bit guilty when she thought about it. Kevin had always been her biggest fan. She felt guilty that she hadn't fully realized it before.

"Don't you think I know I haven't been much help around here lately?" Kevin was about to defend her, but she continued. "My mind hasn't been on this job, and you've covered for me."

Without realizing it, tears had formed in the corner of Lauren's eyes. "You haven't questioned me, but instead you've allowed me to just be who I needed to be. Even when I don't know who the hell that person is."

Lauren stood up and walked over to her friend, hugging him with the same appreciation that he had given her.

"Kevin, there's a lot of things happening in my life right now that just doesn't make any sense. I wish I could tell you about them, but I wouldn't even know where to begin. I have a lot of confusion in my head. So much so that there are times when I question what's real and what isn't."

Kevin looked concerned, but Lauren put her finger to his lips and continued, "Don't worry about me. It'll all sort itself out, beginning with Gary. I feel as if a weight has been lifted from my shoulders since we made the decision. It's the best thing for everyone involved, and I don't anticipate any problems. Gary and I remember what we once shared. We won't ruin all those years because of ego and bitterness. We've both learned our lessons."

Lauren poured and handed Kevin a glass a wine before finishing her sentence.

"That part of my life is over, and I'm now ready to move forward. I have to admit that I'm scared to death, but with friends like you in my life, I know I'll survive."

Lauren wanted to confess more. Tell him about the dreams, and about the emotions that were building. But she knew it was best to wait until they had the opportunity to sit down and discuss it without being interrupted. This was something Kevin would have trouble understanding. *And why wouldn't he?* Lauren was questioning her own sanity. *Why wouldn't he?*

Thankfully, they were brought back to reality when the phone rang.

Kevin pulled the phone up to the counter and answered it. She could tell by the conversation that it was private, and quietly excused herself.

Lauren expected Adriana any minute, and she was deep in thought when Kevin walked to the door and cleared his throat. Lauren glanced up and saw him holding his car keys. She cleared her throat back at him jokingly.

"So are you out of here?"

Kevin laughed. "Only if you don't need me."

Lauren shook her head. "No, go have a personal life for a change, and don't worry about me. I'm fine. And, Kevin, thanks for caring."

Kevin winked over his shoulder. "Absolutely no problem, madam."

Lauren waited until she heard the back door close and lock before breathing a heavy sigh. She knew that at least for a few minutes, she would have some peace and quiet. She turned on soft music, and relaxed with a glass of wine until Adriana arrived.

The drive over for Adriana had been thoughtful. She worried about what to say to Lauren. There had been few times over the years when she had to proceed carefully. She knew Lauren was in the midst of a major transformation of some kind, but she wanted to help her stay as near to reality as possible. But Adriana also realized that Lauren should be allowed to fly and follow her dreams. She wanted to try and keep the conversation centered and focused on the issues. She knew that Lauren would have to work this matter out alone, and she could only hope to be a supportive and positive influence. Adriana took a deep breath and stepped out of her car.

Elliot recommended they take a jog on the beach. He knew Alex wanted his opinion, but this afternoon he thought it best they think on their own. It would be enough that he would be there for Alex if his thoughts became scattered.

Alex ran fast and hard, then sat on the beach and watched the sunset in silence.

Elliot glanced over at his friend and saw that he was meditating. It finally gave him a chance to close his eyes and reflect. He knew Alex had to make his own decisions. He also knew there would be no pushing and shoving him into anything. Elliot realized that he could only offer his insight, and let the rest fall into his friend's own lap.

But feeling helpless was not one of Elliot's best assets. He opened his eyes, and quietly walked back to the house.

Elliot decided the best thing for him to do was phone Moonglows again and speak to the owner. Looking back once to make certain Alex wasn't around, he punched in the numbers. Elliot recognized Mark's voice.

"May I help you?"

Elliot stammered. "Yes, hi, this is Elliot Golden. I was there earlier today, and picked up an order for Alex Chandler."

Mark replied cheerfully, "Yes, Mr. Golden, what can I do for you?"

"I have several questions regarding Mr. Chandler's search, and I'm not sure who can help him... help me."

Mark could sense Elliot's unease and tried to make him more comfortable. "Mr. Golden, why don't I have the owner of Moonglows give you a call? She is extremely knowledgeable."

Elliot's mood brightened. "Can I speak to her now?"

"She's not in, and I don't expect to hear from her until tomorrow. But I'll be happy to take your number and have her return the call."

Elliot could hear Alex ascending the steps. "No, that won't be possible, but I'll give her a call tomorrow. Thanks very much for your help."

Elliot hung up just as Alex came striding into the room.

"Did someone call?"

Elliot quickly turned his attention to Alex. "No, I just had some personal business to take care of."

Oblivious to any sign of guilt from his friend, Alex sat down at the bar and asked for a glass of juice.

Relieved that he hadn't been caught, Elliot exhaled in silence. "One glass of juice coming up."

Adriana strolled into the shop with an air of confidence that Lauren immediately felt. She didn't want Lauren seeing concern in her eyes, and it appeared she was a better actress than she gave herself credit for.

"Wow, you're certainly in good spirits tonight. You have a hot date?" Lauren said cheerfully.

"How I wish. Who has time to date? Too busy with everything else."

Lauren knew better. "Sounds like an excuse to me."

"It was the only excuse I could come up with on such short notice. Now, let me see this ring you've become so interested in."

Lauren handed her friend a glass of wine, and motioned for her to move into the office. She sat next to Adriana on the couch, and ceremoniously removed the ring from her middle finger. Adriana moved the lampshade aside for better viewing, and took the ring from Lauren's palm.

Her first impression upon touching it was intense. The vibrations emitting from this small piece of gold surprised her. She knew there was major history associated with the ring, but she didn't want to compromise Lauren's impressions. Adriana composed herself quickly, and tried to get an impression with her eyes open. On visual examination, she could see why Lauren would find it so compelling. It was a beautiful ring.

Adriana had received a few quick psychic glimpses, but didn't say anything aloud. She wanted to think about it before voicing her opinion. But one thing was for sure. She now had no doubts that something was happening here. But her first instinct was the protection of her friend.

Lauren couldn't contain herself any longer. "What do you think?"

Before Adriana had the chance to reply, Lauren continued. "Isn't it the most awesome ring you've ever seen?"

Adriana raised it closer to the light, attempting to read the inscription, while touching the outer symbols.

"I have to admit, it's awe-inspiring all right." Adriana could think of nothing else to say. She tried to examine it closer, when

Lauren spoke up again.

"You can't read the inscription. I've tried every angle and light. I think it's going to need a good cleaning first."

Adriana squinted, and continued her focus on the ring.

Lauren laughed, "I see it has you bewitched too."

Adriana kept the ring between her fingers, and mumbled words that sounded like, "It certainly has."

Rubbing the rough outlines, Adriana was curious. "I would be interested to know what the symbols mean. Are they just designs, or something more?"

Strong currents of heat were pulsating through her hand, causing Adriana to involuntarily grasp the ring tighter. She was getting faint impressions, but couldn't interpret them and hold a light conversation with Lauren at the same time. When she couldn't concentrate any longer, she turned to Lauren and spoke too quickly and too loudly.

"Why don't you leave me alone for a few minutes, while I see what I can get from this thing?"

Lauren understood, and started for the door. "OK, I'll be back in a few minutes."

Relieved, Adriana could finally give this beautiful piece of love her full attention. With the ring firmly clasped in the palm of her hand, she closed her eyes and put it against her forehead. She knew Lauren wouldn't return until she was invited back into the room.

Adriana's first impression was a vivid ball of color. She sensed an emotion attached to the ball, and hoped to get a feel for the person that had previously owned it. The color was a brilliant green, and in a lightning flash, the impression of love and adoration was released into her being. Adriana whispered her findings out loud.

"This ring was worn to represent absolute love. The person had been happy, with many blessings."

Another ball of color emerged, representing different emotions. She felt as if she were a participating bystander watching, but also feeling all the different sensations. Suddenly, without warning, a bolt of black lightning shot through the picture, and Adriana felt as if an unknown intruder had torn her heart out with its bare hands. There was so much sadness associated with this perception that she immediately reacted by pulling in her senses, and bringing a white spiritual light of love and protection around herself. This sadness was the most profound sensation she had ever felt.

When she had finally calmed down, she listened to her heart, and whispered to herself, "No, this ring is not evil. There was intense love, then it very suddenly turned into intense heart-shattering pain. Such a terrible sadness."

Adriana had the impression that the owner of the ring wanted to stop the sadness. Along with the ache came helplessness like Adriana had never experienced. Then it was gone, leaving her very still, and trying to understand her feelings.

"What in the world am I going to say to Lauren? I know there's nothing about this ring to be frightened of. What I felt was the life and energy of its previous owner. The ring probably represented a very happy union, but then something tragic must have happened to cause profound sadness. But overall, the ring held very positive energies." So Adriana decided there was no reason to tell Lauren anymore than that. She believed unless a person was going to be harmed by something that they were unprepared for, there was no reason to inflict her own impressions into their mind.

"Lauren will make up her own mind about the story surrounding this piece of gold. And if it turns out to be significant, then she'll learn of it in her own time."

Adriana opened her eyes, and stared straight ahead for several moments. When she had centered herself and returned to full consciousness, she felt ready to call Lauren back into the room. But first she inhaled very deeply, and brushed the tears from her eyes.

"It's safe to return now," she called out cheerfully.

Lauren tiptoed back into the room, and observed her friend's reaction. Adriana was faster than Lauren at regaining her composure.

"Well, what did you get?" Lauren said suspiciously.

"Don't worry. All went well." Adriana was still integrating her reaction and she answered in a raspy tone. "This ring has some very positive energy, so you won't need to work too hard on cleansing it."

Adriana was curious and asked Lauren about her experience, as she casually handed the ring back. "Have you felt anything from it?"

"No, not really. I just knew I wanted it. Maybe because of its beauty and individuality. The markings are unusual, aren't they?"

Adriana was bewildered why Lauren hadn't perceived any intuitive reaction from the gold band, but thought she probably just had too much on her mind to stop long enough to listen.

"Anything else happen to you since we last spoke?"

Lauren wasn't ready to confide about the vision in her car mirror. Adriana was her best friend, but she didn't want to throw too much on her at one time. So she answered in a non-committal tone. "A little, but I'll tell you about it later. Right now, let's go eat. I'm starving."

Adriana knew Lauren wasn't telling her the whole story, but decided to pull back until she was needed. "Yeah, let's go. I'm hungry too."

Lauren turned off the lights, then stopped at the door in mid-stride. "Adriana, can we go in your car?"

"Sure, if that's what you want. I'll bring you back later."

Lauren sounded relieved. "Thanks, I just don't feel like driving."

Adriana's inner thoughts were whirling. *This is very strange. I knew it! Something happened.* But she kept quiet.

"Do you want me to drive you home tonight? Kevin can pick you up in the morning."

"No thanks, I'll be OK to drive home."

Adriana decided to stay away from her friend's problems during dinner. She chose instead to discuss Lauren's children, their businesses, and the lack of men in her own life. Lauren needed a chance to mentally relax and think about other things. It would all come back to her in bed tonight, and Adriana was hoping for a fresh approach.

She couldn't help but notice how Lauren continuously twirled her new ring around her finger throughout dinner. She knew her friend was subconsciously receiving input, and she was anxious about how she would assimilate it.

Adriana was quiet on the drive back to Lauren's car. She was in her own world until she felt a hug coming from the passenger side of the car. "Thanks for everything. I'll call you tomorrow and let you know how things go." Lauren got out of the car before Adriana had an opportunity to respond.

Lauren knew Adriana was watching, so she quickly forced herself to unlock her car door, and slide behind the wheel before she lost her nerve. However, she was very careful to not look into the mirror. She knew that seeing an unfamiliar face in the darkness of her car would put her completely over the edge. Lauren drove home with the music playing loud, and never once let her curiosity get the better of her.

Alex and Elliot sat at the kitchen bar overlooking the ocean for a long while, talking about music and their work. They spoke of everything but the dreams. Elliot asked about Alex's next manuscript, knowing the conversation would stay in that direction for the remainder of the evening. As the sky was darkening, Alex suggested they go outside and watch the sunset. Sitting on the balcony, the two discussed the shades of colors that were fading as the sun descended, trying to keep the conversation light and relaxed. Without warning, Alex drastically changed the subject.

"Elliot, what am I really doing with my life?"

Elliot put a protective arm around his friend, but wasn't sure what to say. So he spoke from the heart.

"Alex, you should count your blessings. You have most everything a man could want. You have a very successful business, doing what you love. You have your youth, and you have your health."

Elliot avoided the mention of a personal life, but Alex would have none of it.

"Yes, I have those things, but who do I have to share it with?"

Before Elliot had time to argue, Alex continued. "I don't deny that I'm blessed. I am! I've worked very hard to get where I am, and I don't regret the sacrifices I've made. I would do it all over again. But what can I do about the loneliness? It's the one area of my life that is lacking. I never missed it because I had other priorities, but now, I just don't know."

Elliot's mind was a blank. He was in the same situation so could offer little advice. His whole life had been centered on work, and he never thought about what he was missing either. Being in the same situation, Elliot knew that he could offer no words of comfort.

Alex continued. "It took a dream with an unknown entity to make me look at what's really important." His tone turned sarcastic, "And now that I know what I've been missing, I'm afraid of never having it. I can't believe the Gods could be this cruel. I just don't know what to do. In one sense, I say to myself that if I can't find her, then please make the dreams stop." Alex took a deep breath. "Then I turn around and curse myself for thinking such a thing. I'd rather have her in an altered state, than not ever have her again."

Alex was raging more out of frustration than actual anger.

Elliot allowed him the time to vent until his emotions were exhausted. "I'll locate her. I will! It's only a matter of time and then she'll be in my life. One way or the other."

Elliot wasn't going to use this time to bring Alex's confidence down by stating facts. That there could be a possibility of never finding her. That maybe she didn't exist any further than in his own mind. Or that he would never find someone else, because he was basing his needs on someone from a dream world. How could another woman compete with that?

Elliot chose to keep quiet. Alex needed his confidence built up now, not torn down. Elliot had seen first-hand what could be accomplished when one truly believed.

Alex rustled his hair harshly with his open hand.

"God, man, I'm sorry about that. I don't know what's got into me."

Elliot was finally quick with a response. "Since when do we have to apologize to each other?"

Elliot looked at his watch. "Hey, it's getting late, and I have meetings in the morning. You go rest and I'll talk to you tomorrow."

Alex casually hugged Elliot at the door. "You know why you're my best friend? Because you don't say I'm crazy, even when you think I am."

Elliot laughed and opened the door, remarking over his shoulder. "Hell, if they committed you, then they'd have to commit me too. That's why I keep my mouth shut."

Lauren drove home in record time, and parked her car in the garage. Within her own domain, she felt comfortable and safe. When Lauren felt her nervousness about sleep start to subside, she immediately put on her music and snuggled comfortably on her sofa. Listening to the music filter through the house helped her calm down and finally relax as much as she could.

She felt apprehensive and kept glancing at the stairs leading up to her bedroom. Lauren finally picked up a book sitting on the coffee table and sighed loudly, as if to make a point. When she noticed her new ring glittering from the light reflecting from the lamp, she slipped it off for a better look, and rubbed the intricate detailing. She heard herself speaking aloud, but didn't care. "If only you could speak to me."

Lauren suddenly felt she needed to close her eyes, and place the ring in her palm. Then she raised it to her heart. "What do you have to tell me?"

She had barely finished the sentence when she quickly fell into a light sleep, while thinking about the detailed carvings on the object.

Without warning, she was transferred to another time and place.

Lauren was a bystander, watching in awe at what was transpiring in front of her. The view was darkened by a haze, and she couldn't make out the specifics, but she knew enough to let things flow, and try to stay detached. She thought she recognized the jewelry box from the art gallery. "It couldn't be the same one." The haze continued penetrating thickly into her dream state.

Lauren noticed the box was now sitting on a beautifully carved oak table. Nothing else looked familiar.

"Where am I?" No answer came.

Her focus shifted to a photo sitting next to the box. Through the fog, she could vaguely make out what looked like a man and woman. The thick mist lifted just long enough for her to notice the ornately decorated gold frame surrounding the photos. Lauren found herself trying to get a closer look, but the dense fog quickly enveloped her again.

"Do I know these people? Is it my imagination, or do they actually look vaguely familiar to me?"

Before Lauren could concentrate her efforts, the scene quickly faded out of view.

She awoke in a soft, otherworldly state, and allowed her mind to wander. She remembered the box, and thought about the photo sitting on the oak table. But that reality was fading fast, until all she could recall was the box. Still in her dreamy state, Lauren gave in to temptation, and sauntered up the stairs.

Chapter 6

Alex locked the door behind Elliot and walked directly to his piano. Music always put him at peace, and tonight, serenity from his own mind and self-absorbed thoughts was what he desperately needed. He sat at his piano, absentmindedly pressing a few keys. His dark hair fell over his face, but he didn't bother sweeping it away. Instead, he closed his eyes and drew in a deep breath.

He was tired, but knew sleep wouldn't come as long as he was restless. He was nervous about going to sleep. And at times like this, he thanked God for his music. Anything for an escape.

Alex began playing a melody. He completed the song before he realized what he had been playing. He played it again, but this time sang the lyrics. "It seems we stood and talked like this before..."

After he sang the last word, he kept his eyes closed, and began to imagine her just as she stood inside his dream the night before. He knew she was beautiful, and her heart and soul were both pure. He also sensed there was a loneliness inside her that mirrored his. He felt the deep ache, and doubted even the music could extinguish it. His mind drifted back to the melody with a sudden realization.

"I don't remember ever learning that song."

Alex walked methodically into his office, quickly retrieving his journal. He wanted it next to his bed tonight, and hoped it wasn't just wishful thinking.

He was turning to walk out when his eyes glimpsed the painting. He came to an abrupt halt when he noticed a soft light radiating from the area. He squinted, and slowly took one step, scrutinizing it a little closer.

"How strange. It looks like it's illuminating from inside the painting itself."

His curiosity took control as he stepped a few paces back to view it from another angle. The shimmering suddenly vanished, and the painting looked ordinary. Alex timidly walked forward, and gently touched the canvas with his fingertips. He spoke barely above a whisper, "Are you trying to tell me something?"

Then reality set in, and he smirked at himself for being so vulnerable. "OK, I think it's bedtime for me."

Alex walked wearily up the stairs, finding himself humming the tune he had played on his piano a few minutes earlier. He knew the song. He just couldn't remember where he had learned to play it. "I've never even owned the sheet music."

By the time Alex reached the top landing, he was so exhausted that his body was craving the rest it so greatly deserved. He removed his clothes and switched on his meditation music. He took a few deep breaths, letting them out slowly through his mouth, and submerged himself into an unavoidable sleep.

Lauren swallowed her fear and timidly glanced into her bathroom mirror. Her face was close enough to cause a damp fog, as she focused on each eye. This time, she saw something different.

Her eyes appeared younger, and they seemed to sparkle.

She blinked hard, and then looked back into her own blue eyes again. "Please, let me have him tonight in my dreams. Allow me to know this man, and to become a part of him."

She found a bowl, and reluctantly slipped the ring off her finger to cleanse it in a ritual of sea salt and crystals. The last thing was to say a little prayer.

Lauren was anxious and wanted sleep to consume her as soon

as possible. Turning on her CD, she walked out to her balcony and looked up into the clear dark sky, counting the star formations she recognized.

"Can we do this, and still keep our sanity?"

She could wait no longer. She first had to try and locate him, then find out who he was. But she couldn't purge the fear that one night he may never return. There was no way of preparing for that. No matter what words she told herself, he had to be there. He just had to be.

Alex reluctantly opened his eyes. It took him a moment to realize that he wasn't in bed but outside, with dawn approaching. The ever-familiar rock formation was sitting silently in front of him. He immediately noticed the reflection of pinks and oranges from the newborn sun glowing behind the hills, glistening against the wet surfaces. He protested in bewilderment, "Am I sleepwalking, or am I awake? How the hell did I get here?"

Alex felt his anxiety grow when he realized he had missed her. He furiously paced the beach, feeling the sand's coarseness stinging his feet. His eyes kept searching the skies, wanting answers.

"Please, God, tell me what happened?"

He felt shattered, and a sense of loneliness swept over him. Alex sat down, clutching the dry sand between his fingers. He realized he was in a state of confusion, and it angered and frustrated him further when he felt warm tears burning his cheeks.

He closed his eyes, covering his face with his hands. He knew he was overreacting, but didn't know how to stop the downward momentum.

His frustration mounted when he realized his response was completely different from his usual calm, centered demeanor. That behavior seemed to have disappeared; leaving him naked to his raw emotions. He hated not being in control.

"Please, God, let her come to me." He repeated the affirmation aloud, over and over, "Let her come to me. Let her come to me."

Alex opened his eyes and was amazed to see the clear water was no longer in front of him. He jerked his head around and felt comfort at seeing the rocks still standing in their same solid location, and the soft white sand was still underneath his feet. But he was awestruck when he saw an intense deep blue fog swallowing the ocean. The sense of empowering strength washed over him as he watched the fog quickly approaching.

Alex turned his attention to the hills behind him and smiled.

He knew she would be there. He had not awoken on the beach after all. And he realized another lesson had been offered to him. He had overreacted to an episode brought on from his mind.

He centered himself, then focused on her. She was approaching, and he wanted to be calm and prepared. In the corner of his eye, Alex noticed the blue fog had reached the shoreline. He wanted a glimpse of her eyes before it overtook them, but it was too late. The fog rolled in, and she was quickly becoming undefined.

Lauren didn't let the dense haze stop her. She continued her stride toward him until she was near enough to touch him. She stopped only when the fog produced a thin shield between them.

Alex wanted to hurry before she disappeared, and found it easier this time to begin his conversation through mental telepathy. *"I'm so glad you're here."*

Lauren was still unsure of her surroundings, and it took most of her energy to adjust. During waking hours, she would plan exactly what she wanted to say to him, but once his incredible essence was standing in front of her, she forgot everything. She looked in his direction and mentally replied, *"I don't know how long my energy will let me stay. Please, tell me who you are."*

He smiled and was about to answer when his attention shifted to a glowing object radiating from her finger. *"What is that?"*

Even with the dense fog covering them, he couldn't help but

see the gold band.

Alex quickly thought how strange that she would be dim in his view, yet the ring showed bright, each symbol vividly bouncing off each other in various shades of gold.

Lauren looked down. *"How did that get there?"* She was visibly alarmed. *"It's not supposed to be there."* She blinked hard and noticed her hand shaking. *"Oh, God, why is it glowing?"*

Lauren forgot her original question, or what she was attempting to seek from him. Alex had lost interest in her identity too.

"What's on your finger?"

Lauren was in a stupor, but heard herself babbling. *"I bought this ring from a shop. I don't know why, but I had to have it."* She continued stammering in confusion. *"But…but, I…I didn't have it on when I went to bed!"*

Alex wasn't listening. *"How did you get that?"*

The object was glowing in such a way that it now resembled a rainbow, with the colors dancing in an aura around her entire hand.

Lauren slipped the ring off her finger, and tried to pass it to Alex, but the fog wouldn't permit it. He pushed, but the veil refused to be penetrated. In frustration, Alex took a deep breath and concentrated.

"Do you understand its symbols?"

Lauren shook her head. He continued more sternly than before. *"Is there an inscription?"*

She shook her head affirmative. *"But it's so tarnished; I haven't been able to decipher any of it. Maybe once it's cleaned and polished."*

Lauren inspected the inner side of the ring again, and gasped aloud in shock. The tarnish was gone, and the ring now looked brand new. Alex's eyes widened in astonishment. He was now actively fighting to stay focused and centered. Everything had now disappeared from their surroundings except for the glowing ring.

Lauren almost dropped the ring in disbelief when the inscribed words beamed up at her. "This can't be happening."

Alex noticed his own anticipation was beginning to irritate him. His stomach was aching, and he felt as if a hand was gripping his heart. The only thing he cared about now was finding out what the inscription read. He couldn't believe his own voice was speaking out so severe and inpatient to her. *"Can you read the inscription, please? Just tell me what the hell it says."*

Lauren didn't notice his harshness. Her entire being was focused on the ring. With little self-control, and in total amazement, she shouted the words out loud. "Where…When…Remember…My Love."

Lauren heard herself scream the discovery, then she looked up at him in disbelief. *"My God, I swear this couldn't be read before. What's happening?"*

Lauren couldn't see the pained look fall across Alex's face. His anguish and confusion was tremendous, and his energy was spent. But he refused to stop before he had convinced her to interpret the outside symbols too. Nothing had ever meant more to him in his entire life. This glowing circle of gold was his only passion and desire.

Lauren was confused by the current turn of events, and she had no ammunition to deal with the pain she was suddenly feeling. She only knew that she craved to be held, and she wanted everything to stop.

Alex sensed her ache, but wouldn't let her escape. *"Listen to me! Look at the ring and tell me what the symbols read."* As far as he was concerned, it was a life or death obsession. *"Please interpret the symbols!"* Alex saw that dawn was fading into morning, and knew that he was running out of time. *"Please hurry!"*

Lauren put the ring in front of her eyes again in amazement. She couldn't understand what was happening, and was feeling disoriented. The ring was ricocheting colors all around her, and the glow was so strong, it momentarily blinded her. *"I'm sorry, but it's too bright."*

Alex's breathing had become so irregular, he was afraid of

hyperventilating. He was now ignoring her bewildered expression, and was angry that she could remain so calm. *"I beg you, please hurry!"*

She returned her gaze to the shiny object, and noticed its colors dimming. Lauren slowly rotated the ring, and easily read what the circle was trying to tell them. *"Now and Forever."*

His head was aching, and he was heavily perspiring. He realized with a jolt that he hadn't focused on her at all. All of his energy had been spent on the object, now softly glowing from the sun. The fog was quickly burning off, but so was her image. He tried to run to her. *"Please wait. Oh, God, please tell me who you are."*

He could see the sun glistening on her confused tears. She so wanted to be found, but she knew she could no longer manipulate her thoughts. And within a gale of wind, she faded into the breeze.

Alex jerked himself awake. His entire body was shaking and wet, and he was feeling physically ill. He could never remember having such a horrible throbbing headache. He looked at the clock and realized it was morning. But he didn't want the sun. He wanted his dreams back, and he wanted her.

He raised himself painfully out of bed, feeling his hair and body drenched with sweat. Every muscle hurt as he slowly crept into the bathroom. He spent what energy he had left splashing water on his face, then without realizing or caring, he slumped onto the floor, kneeling against the tub. Alex rocked back and forth in a fetal position until grief overwhelmed every cell in his body, and uncontrollable sobs took over.

"She was within my reach. We had enough combined energy to find the missing pieces. But instead, I found nothing."

His fist hit the tub as he continued raging.

"Why in the hell didn't I ask who she was? How could I forget? What could have taken me away from my focus?"

Alex's body became rigid, and his breathing was shallow. His eyes hurt as he felt them grow wide in amazement and fear. His stare was fixated straight ahead into the mirrors surrounding the room. While his mind was whirling and spinning, the dizziness and pain was so overwhelming, he thought he would be sick.

"Oh, God, the ring!"

His hand involuntarily raised up in front of his eyes. "There was a ring on her finger." Alex's mind was in a state of disarray. He knew he was on the edge, but felt too weak to override his mental activity.

"Why in the hell would I use up my energy on a fucking ring?" His agitation was increasing and he was at the mercy of it. The anger was building and he didn't have the strength to control it.

"Why would I do such a stupid thing? All I wanted to do was find her. And what did I do with my chance? I demanded to know about a ring that means nothing!"

Alex was in a wild rage, disappointed and angry with himself. He looked into his eyes in his reflection, eyes that were now burning from the bitter tears pouring down his cheeks. His dark hair was draped over his face, giving him the appearance of a mad man.

"Will I ever have another chance?" His tone was turning into despondency and self-hatred. "Hell no, not after the way I treated her!"

Alex was still sobbing uncontrollably when the phone rang. He heard Elliot's voice on the machine, and grabbed it like a man possessed. "What in the fuck do you want?"

For a brief moment, Elliot thought he had dialed a wrong number. But his gut gripped, and he sensed danger in a way he had never encountered before. "Alex, is that you? I'm around the corner, and thought I'd come by." Elliot's voice was so controlled, it frightened him. He was acting like the calm before the storm.

Alex screamed something unintelligible, emitting sounds that resembled a wounded animal on the run. Elliot heard him violently throw the receiver against a door, the loud thud resounding in his ear.

Elliot screamed into the phone, "Alex, what's wrong? Alex, pick up the damn phone!"

The only sounds Elliot could hear now were of breaking glass and heart-wrenching sobs. He sped down the P.C.H., needing to get to his friend. He knew something had gone very wrong, and Alex urgently needed help.

Lauren awoke to the irritating sound of her alarm clock, and thought it couldn't yet be morning. "Didn't I just fall asleep?"

She had a throbbing headache, and was in an unusually groggy state. She stared hard at the ceiling, recalling the turn of events from the night before. When she realized what had taken place, she was helpless in stopping the reeling and confusion. Every muscle in her body stopped its normal function. All the reminders from the previous night were draining back into her consciousness, and her heart seemed to be in her stomach. She quickly became distraught, and anger overwhelmed her nerves. Lauren shrieked loudly at the walls, which were now closing in on her.

"What in the hell happened? I know less today than I did when I went to sleep last night. I couldn't focus on a damn thing! He's never going to come back!" Her screaming rose in volume. "Never! How could I've been caught up in this stupid illusion anyway? What in the hell is wrong with me?"

Lauren sniffled back a sob, and jerked her hand up in mid-air, crying out in an exasperated gasp. "The ring!"

She violently turned her hand back and forth, slapping the covers around her in a panic. "Oh, God! Where's the ring?"

New fears rushed in until she noticed the crystal bowl sitting on the counter, reflecting through her bathroom mirror. For a moment, she breathed a sigh of relief. She remembered taking the ring off to cleanse it. The feeling didn't last long, as anguish rushed in to take its place. "Dear God! How could I forget to find out who he was? Why was I wearing the ring in my dream?" She wanted to escape her questions.

Lauren's body folded into a fetal position as she lay on her bed facing the bathroom. Her focus was on the glass container that held her memories from the night before. It didn't matter that she was ranting to herself. She wasn't looking for any sort of comfort.

"What does this have to do with me not finding my answers?"

Lauren thought back to the night before and vaguely remembered the ring being on her finger in the dream. She tried to remember more, but nothing came except that it held some kind of significance. She repeated her words in methodical succession. Pent up rage like she had never experienced emerged from the chasm within. "I still know nothing about this man. What in the hell was so fascinating about the stupid ring? Why was I so hypnotized by it?"

She was punching her mattress as she continued her screaming and berating. "Why couldn't I ask the questions? Why did I forget?"

She picked up her pillow and violently threw it in the direction of the bowl. "I still don't know if he really exists!"

Her anger had escalated and she knew the ring was to blame.

Lauren defiantly pulled herself out of bed and marched into the bathroom. She grabbed the gold band from its container and threw the crystal bowl into the sink, smiling as it shattered into a million pieces. Still, her heated adrenalin wasn't satisfied. She stared at the now inanimate object, and felt nothing but hatred for it.

Lauren wanted it far away from her. She ran outside to her balcony, and opened her hand, screeching at the object. "I don't know where you came from, but you're not going to interfere again!"

She wanted to take one last look before she threw it over the balcony to the trees below her. The cool metal was cradled in the palm of her hand when the sun's light captured it, causing it to temporarily shimmer. She stopped her action, and tilted her hand just enough for the rays to bounce off the gold again. Suddenly, everything seemed vaguely familiar. Lauren felt her hair blowing in the wind, and there was a light fog in the morning air. A slight sense of déjà vu prevailed all around her, and she couldn't withdraw her hand from the ring. She stopped breathing, and was now concentrating on the sun's brightness against the shiny object. "The ring? What's going on with this ring?"

She closed her eyes, and watched as faint memories flooded into her mind. Lauren gently placed it back on her finger.

She was admiring the glimmering band when another memory rose to the surface. "Oh my dear God. Wait just a minute!" Remembering the inscription, Lauren tore off the ring, cutting her finger in the process. The stinging and warm blood couldn't distract her thoughts. Lauren turned the gold towards her, attempting to read the unreadable. The tarnish was still attached to every portion of the ring. "I don't get it. I couldn't have read it. It's impossible."

A faint recollection of the symbols appeared in her mind. "What about the symbols?" Then her mind went blank.

Throwing her arms to her side in frustration, Lauren transferred all her mental powers to the most current dream, but her mind still refused to call up the past.

"Did he want to know about the ring? How could I be so stupid? I'll never see him again!"

The mist touched her face and she could smell the woods from the ground below her. Exhausted, she turned to go inside when recognition came to her, and she involuntarily dropped the ring at her feet.

"Wait! I did read the inscription. It looked brand new. I remember reading it to him! Oh my God, the symbols! I read those too!"

When Lauren noticed the ring had slipped from her hand, she fell to her knees searching for it. Her voice rose in pitch as she begged.

"I can't lose you!" In front of her sat the piece of metal, patiently waiting for her to retrieve it. Lauren sat on the floor of her balcony, cradling the ring in her palm. She was humming a tune she made up as she rocked back and forth. Before long, she had gone into a light dreamy state, and didn't care if she found her way back into reality. Lauren put the ring in front of her face, and looked again into its inner core. She could still find nothing coherent.

"How could I have read you in my dream? I distinctly remember reading the words to him. But now I have no idea what you said."

She was speaking in a sad, hushed tone directly into the gold object. The pain overwhelmed her when reality finally surfaced. She realized that it was all just a dream. There probably wasn't a man, and there was no inscription that she had read. It was all just a dream. It was time to start thinking like her rational self again. But first, Lauren put her face in her hands and wept.

Elliot screeched his car to a stop and opened the front door with his key. He wasn't going to wait to be allowed in. He left the door open, and raced up the stairs, not bothering to call out his friend's name. When he reached Alex's bedroom, he stopped in a dead halt. He was startled by his first perception, and it tore at Elliot's heart. He paused briefly, then slowly walked into the dismally eerie gloom that tainted the air all around him.

He found the phone still misplaced, lying against the now broken bathroom door. Elliot scanned the bedroom, and saw nothing out of the ordinary, except for Alex' rumpled bed. He knew there was more than what he had seen so far. There was so much tension, anger, and negativity in the room, he could barely breathe. He stepped in a little further, and could see Alex through the bathroom mirror.

He was crumbled in a fetal position, rocking back and forth. His body was drenched with sweat, his black hair dripping wet, and sticking to his face and neck. Elliot quickly scanned his body, and found Alex's eyes fixed and glazed over. He was emitting quiet whimpering sounds that reminded him of a beaten down little boy.

Elliot grabbed a wet cloth and knelt down beside his best friend.

Alex was extremely hot to touch, and running a very high fever. Elliot allowed his instincts to take over, and spoke calmly, softly, and with confidence in his voice. He gently washed Alex's face, and hugged him for several minutes. He knew Alex needed medical help, and encouraged him to sit up. "Alex, are you hurting anywhere?"

Alex was in a fevered stupor, but turned his attention to the voice speaking in his direction. He looked deeply into the intruder's eyes, and spoke in a hoarse, raspy voice, like all the weight of the world was on his shoulders. "I ache all over. I think I'm burning up, and I blew the only chance I will ever have for happiness. Now, will you just go away and leave me alone?"

Elliot looked into Alex's eyes with a slight smile. "No, I won't go away and leave you alone. We're going to make everything better very soon. The first thing we'll do is get this fever down, and then we'll tackle the other problems. Is that all right with you?"

Alex was too weak to argue.

Elliot carefully dressed his friend and then drove him to the hospital, contacting the doctor on the way. An attendant with a wheelchair was waiting in the parking lot as they approached the emergency room. As calm and efficient as Elliot seemed, his confidence was receding. The only thing going through his mind was a prayer to help his friend get well.

After filling out the forms and making Alex comfortable, Elliot called Donovan, advising him of the problem. He was there within fifteen minutes. Elliot knew that Alex would need their support and care, and he was glad to have Donovan's soothing presence for himself as well. It had unnerved Elliot more than he would let on, and the shock was beginning to settle in.

Donovan waited until he and Elliot were alone before asking. "Tell me what happened?"

Elliot was quite for a moment, trying to formulate his

thoughts. "I don't know much. When I called Alex this morning, he was in a hallucinatory state. I knew something serious was affecting him, so I rushed over. When I arrived, sure enough, I found him on the bathroom floor running a high fever. He had destroyed the bathroom. He was incoherent most of the time, and continued babbling on the ride here about some sort of a dream, and a ring, and his whole life being ruined. He sounded like a defeated man. I stayed calm, but I have to tell you, it scared the hell out of me."

Donovan spoke softly. "So, he's still having the dreams?"

Elliot shook his head, "I know he did the night before last, but I have no idea what happened last night. When I left him, he was going to bed and feeling fine. He told me he'd had a dream about the painting in his office. And he spoke briefly about being lonely, and hoped that he hadn't wasted his life on work. But overall, his spirits were fairly good when I left."

Donovan had a look of concern in his eyes. "Why don't we go check on our buddy?"

They stopped as Alex's physician walked over to their table. "Well, boys, I have good news. Alex came in with a high fever, and to make a long story short, he has a virus, along with a nasty strain of the flu."

The doctor sat down next to Elliot. "Our primary concern is dehydration, so we've got an I.V. in him now. I wanted him to stay overnight, but he refused. He assured me that he could be looked after at home. Is there anyone who can stay with him overnight? I want to see him again tomorrow, too."

Elliot and Donovan looked at each other and smiled. "When can we take him home?"

Lauren was still sobbing quietly on her balcony when the phone rang. She forced herself up and answered as calmly as she could. Adriana was on the other end, and knew the hoarseness in Lauren's voice meant she was upset.

"Lauren, it's me. What's wrong?" Adriana wasn't going to pretend not to notice.

"Oh, this stupid dream I had last night. I hate to continue bothering you with this, but I really need some help. Right now."

Adriana felt Lauren was about to lose control again and wanted to be with her. "You wait for me, Lauren. I'll be there in a few minutes."

When Adriana arrived, Lauren was in her bedroom. She hadn't moved from the space she had been sitting in since answering the phone. Without a word, Adriana sat down next to her friend. Lauren buried her head into Adriana's shoulder and sobbed. She sobbed for herself, she sobbed for her past, and she sobbed for her future.

After several minutes of tears, then a few more minutes of stabilizing her breath, Lauren finally looked up at Adriana. She saw a smile, and a look of encouragement beaming back at her. Adriana didn't speak, but instead, she stood up and walked downstairs to the kitchen. While she was gone, Lauren repaired her body the best she could, though her heart still wasn't in it.

It wasn't long before Adriana appeared with coffee and breakfast on a tray, then she waited for her friend to get comfortable. Adriana pulled a pillow up to her chest and hugged it tightly. She carefully thought about her words before she spoke.

"Lauren, what can I do to help? Together, we will try to fix whatever is causing you such pain. But you've got to be honest with me, and tell me what you're feeling."

Lauren looked at her friend for a moment, then carefully removed the ring from her finger, and passed it to Adriana.

"It's been a crazy time ever since I started having these dreams a while ago. But everything spread completely out of my control with the purchase of this ring."

Adriana examined the ring. She worried that perhaps she had misinterpreted its messages. *No,* she thought, *I know what I felt.*

She had felt both the profound sadness, and the deep love that the ring held in its history. But there was no mistake that both emotions had been extreme. *Maybe she isn't yet strong enough to handle the pendulum effect from her emotions, and those of the ring.*

Adriana looked closely at her friend and saw a profound look of sadness. She took Lauren's hand in hers, squeezing gently, and bringing with it her understanding and encouragement. "Please, Lauren, tell me what happened."

Lauren told Adriana about the obsession that had possessed her when she saw the ring. She admitted to seeing the vision of another person in the car mirror. And about how worried she was that her sanity might be slipping. She told her about the dream she had while dozing on her couch the night before. She told her about specifically taking off the ring, only to be confused when she saw it on her finger in the dream. She ended the story by telling her friend about the man being so insistent about the messages inscribed on the ring.

"I don't know what to believe anymore. One minute, I think it's real, and the next, I feel it's all in my imagination. As you can see, there's no way this inscription can be read. But I swear, in my dream, it became crystal clear. Can you imagine my disbelief when I could suddenly interpret it? We were both so enthralled by that damn ring, neither of us thought about discussing our dilemma. I still don't know who he is, or if I'll ever see him again." Lauren shook her head. "I just don't think I can handle this anymore. Between the dreams, the painting, the ring, my work, and everything else going on in my life, I just can't mentally function the way I need to."

Lauren finished with a doubt. "Of course, I could have already lost my mind. Hell, all of this may not really be happening to me at all. I'm beginning to think that I'm living in a fantasy world, and reality doesn't exist anymore."

Adriana knew Lauren was speaking out of frustration, but felt they needed to find a few answers as soon as possible.

"All right, I want you to tell me what the inscription said. Can you remember?" Adriana asked calmly.

"I don't think so, but hopefully, it'll come back to me."

Adriana continued, painfully slow, "What about the symbols? Would you remember what it read if you were to closely examine it again?"

Lauren was getting agitated again. "No, no, no!"

Adriana was not affected by her friend's frustration. "Next, I want us to drive over to Vickie's store. I want to see if she has any information on the ring."

Lauren completed her line of thought. "Adriana, forget it. I already asked her for information. She didn't have any. There are dead ends everywhere I turn. It's just not worth it anymore. I'm ready to stop!"

Adrian wasn't going to let her friend give up without a fight.

"Lauren, if this is all bullshit, I agree with you. We'll give it up together." Adriana put her hand up to continue. "But if by some chance this is all real, you won't be able to stop until you find out the truth. Your soul will not allow you to stop. So why don't we find out together?"

Lauren looked like she wanted to escape, but Adriana refused to be ignored. "We're going to start at the only place we realistically can. We'll have to start at a place that actually exists in this real world."

Adriana pulled Lauren from her slumped position and walked her toward the bathroom. "You're going to get yourself together while I clean up this glass. After that, you and I are driving to Del Rey's Arts and Antiques. I'm sure Vickie will love to see you."

Lauren was dumbfounded by her response. "All right, you win. I think while I'm there, I may just buy the jewelry box."

Adriana saw it was as much of a surprise to Lauren saying it, as it was for her to hear it. Lauren looked into her friend's eyes and knew Adriana would understand. "In my dream, I just knew the box and ring belonged together. They shouldn't be separated." Lauren spoke barely above an exhausted whisper. "Is that so crazy?"

Adriana smiled genuinely. "Lauren, you've got a heart made of gold." She handed the ring back to Lauren. "Maybe we can do a little hypnosis on you later, and see about that picture you can't seem to get off of your mind."

Seeing Lauren's eyes begin to brighten, she continued. "And about that vision in your car mirror? We'll have to work on that one too. But I hope you're putting all this in your journal. It's going to make a hell of a book someday!"

Lauren finally laughed. "And I suppose I'll find out tonight if this guy is still looking for me, or if he's given me up as completely hopeless."

Adriana put a protective arm around her friend. "We'll certainly have a list of questions waiting for him. And we'll work on teaching you to stay focused, right?" Adriana wasn't finished. "And I have one more suggestion. You may want to think about tearing yourself away from that ring long enough to have it cleaned. How about if we do that first thing? Is that a deal?"

Lauren hugged Adriana close. "Deal!"

Chapter 7

Alex was still drowsy when his friends brought him home. They had taken notes and felt they were prepared to handle any crisis. In Elliot's mind, nothing would compare to what he had witnessed that very morning.

It took a while to get Alex upstairs and into his bed. But once he was comfortable, they began the job of cleaning up the destruction that Alex had created in his heated outburst.

Donovan stepped into the bathroom first and whistled. "My God, did he do all this damage alone? It doesn't seem possible."

Elliot responded in a whisper. "Yeah, can you believe it? I don't know what would've happened if I hadn't called so early this morning. He was totally out of control. By the time I found him, he had no energy left, just a lot of anger. Fortunately, he was too exhausted to do any more harm to himself, or the room."

Donovan picked up glass from the bathroom counter. "I wouldn't have believed this if I hadn't seen it with my own eyes."

The room was destroyed.

Elliot scanned the area and agreed. "Yeah, something drastic must have set him off in a big way. And apparently his fever and illness overrode his usual calm responses. I didn't know he had it in him."

They finished cleaning up, and then checked on Alex. He was sleeping peacefully. It was impossible to believe that someone as gentle as Alex could have been responsible for such destruction.

The two men walked downstairs slowly. They needed time to

relax and get prepared for the unexpected when Alex woke up. They sat on the couch overlooking the Pacific Ocean. The high tides heard in the background helped them to settle down and breathe a little easier. They enjoyed the sounds of nature for a few minutes before Donovan spoke about the condition of their companion. "Do you think one of us should sit with him while he's asleep?"

Elliot smiled. "No, I think Alex would have a fit if he thought we were taking care of him, much less standing guard over his bed."

Donovan chuckled. "Yeah, the sick one won't even admit to having a problem when he wakes up. I think you're right, we're safer guarding him from down here."

A loud noise from upstairs suddenly broke the calm atmosphere, and sent both men running to their friend, fearing the worst.

They found Alex had awakened and had tried to stand up when he fell over into the phone. It had hit the lamp, and fallen helplessly onto the floor. Alex was forced to sit down on the bed, his wet hair hanging over his face. Elliot cautiously approached, and quietly sat down next to him.

"Alex, how are you feeling?"

Alex turned slowly to face his friends. His voice was so weak, the men had to strain to hear him. "Better than I thought. It's been a terrible day. But I'm feeling much better. You don't have to stay here waiting on me."

Donovan stood above Alex. "It's the medication they gave you that's helping."

Alex looked stunned for a moment. "What medications?" Then his memory returned, and he tried to put his arms out in a gesture that meant to say thanks for your help. But he was still too weak. His thoughts were dull, but he was determined to speak coherently. When he saw that he could give only a halfhearted attempt, he lay back down to sleep.

"He won't even remember this conversation," Donovan said, mostly to himself.

After settling Alex back into bed, the guys resumed their talk on the couch.

Donovan watched outside as two seagulls floated in mid-air. "Did he mention anything else going on in his life?"

Elliot shook his head. "No, we just talked about his next manuscript, and about general things. There were really no heavy discussions, except when he spoke about being lonely and hoping that he hadn't wasted his life, or made the wrong decisions. But it was more of an observation than anything else."

Elliot paused, then shook his head again to reaffirm. "No, I keep going over the conversation in my mind, and I come up blank."

Donovan spoke behind him as he walked into the kitchen. "Well, we can only hope that his fever caused this reaction, and not something else."

It gave Elliot a few minutes to think alone. He had been shaken up by the events, and needed to sort out his own emotions. He began to remember pieces of an earlier conversation that he had with Alex. Elliot joined Donovan in the kitchen and sat down on a stool.

"You know, Alex did say a few things earlier when we spoke."

Donovan turned away from the opened refrigerator, and waited for Elliot to continue.

"He talked about getting that rush of emotion again. You remember? Like he had in the restaurant with us?"

Donovan shook his head, remembering the episode.

Elliot didn't wait for a response. "He told me he'd been in Ron's studio when that weird sensation came over him again. Apparently, he lost it in a minimal way while they were working, and was worried that Ron thought he'd lost his mind. I blew it off, thinking it was just writer's frustration, but now, I don't know." Elliot didn't stop for a breath. "Alex also mentioned a dream he had about the picture hanging in his office. He apparently dreamed about the woman in the painting, and hoped it might be the same woman from his dreams."

Donovan closed the refrigerator door and leaned against the sink. "What do you think it means?" Donovan was obviously worried about the change of events. "Do you think he's losing it? Alex is one of the sanest people I know, but some of the things you're telling me sound really bizarre."

Elliot was quiet for a moment, then spoke just above a whisper. "I know Alex better than he knows himself. No, I don't think he's losing it. I think the fever was a contributing factor in today's outburst, and I think the pressure of all this is finally getting to him. He's feeling emotions that are new to him. And what's worse, it's emotions that he can't touch, or smell, or communicate with. He's beginning to question his own sanity on one hand. Yet on the other hand, he knows in his heart what is real. But the poor guy has no solid proof. This is a real world, and we've been taught to deal in realities. If you can't touch it, then it doesn't exist. His right and left sides of the brain are entrenched in a solid battle. We need to help him cope with the flood of sensations that up until several weeks ago had been totally foreign to him. Thoughts and perceptions that we've probably never felt."

Donovan nodded toward the direction of Alex's office. "Let's have a look at that painting."

They strolled into the office, feeling a little guilty for intruding. They both knew the painting wasn't something Alex would have for himself. They distinctly remembered the day he had bought it. He had gone by Vickie's shop to meet with Donovan.

Donovan spoke as if he were miles away. "Yeah, I remember questioning him. It made no sense why he would want it. It's a beautiful piece, but it's not Alex."

Elliot continued the conversation, "He told us that he didn't know why, but he wanted it and bought it right there on the spot."

Both boys turned in the direction of the painting. They agreed it was a beautiful picture, but they still couldn't see the obsessive attraction it held for Alex.

Elliot walked up for a closer look as Donovan switched on the light above the painting. The guys watched as the white glow shone down on the couple. "What do you think? Do you see anything out of the ordinary?"

Elliot shook his head. "No, but obviously Alex does."

Donovan looked closer at the couple holding hands. "They certainly look happy and content, don't they?"

Elliot smiled vaguely. "Yes, I suppose those were the days. Now, have we seen enough?"

Donovan absentmindedly switched off the light above the frame, and the painting immediately darkened.

As Elliot turned around for one last glance, he stopped and blinked his eyes hard. His mouth opened, but he couldn't speak.

Donovan had exited the room and was still talking, when he noticed his friend wasn't behind him. He turned back towards the office and saw Elliot standing at the doorway looking still, and very pale.

Donovan felt an eerie chill, but slowly approached. "What is it?"

Elliot said nothing, but continued his intense glare on the wall across from him.

Donovan spoke up again, "Hey, what's wrong?"

He approached and followed Elliot's eyes in the same direction as the painting, and also fell into a quiet daze.

They had blatantly stared at the painting, but now it was different. Now, it was brighter and alive, bouncing with color. It was as if the light were still dancing on the canvas. Nothing moved within the frame, but the colors had changed into rich, vivid shades.

Elliot tried to compose himself and find the courage to slowly walk over to the wall. As he approached the painting, the colors dimmed dramatically, and the picture looked as it had earlier. It was as if nothing had changed. He quickly turned to question Donovan.

Donovan slid his fingers through his hair, looking confused. Elliot motioned for him to move over to his side of the room. Donovan crept slowly across the floor and stood close to the painting. It seemed an eternity before Donovan blurted out in a tone of confusion, "It's gone. The colors are gone."

Elliot added in a begging tone. "Then we both witnessed the same thing? Right? Is that what you're telling me? You saw it too?"

Donovan put his hand on Elliot's shoulder. "Yeah, I saw it, but for the life of me, I have no idea what the hell it was."

Elliot's speech was slurred. "I don't know. It happened so fast. But what does it mean?"

Donovan walked out the room and sharply turned around with a gleam in his eyes. "That, Elliot, was verification that our friend upstairs is not going crazy. This is the confirmation that all is on track. This happening was the only way to tell us to trust Alex's stories. Now it's time for our aggressive help."

Elliot looked pleased at Donovan's observation. "That's it! Donovan, you're brilliant. We both saw the same thing; it couldn't have been our imaginations. We saw it!"

They took one last look at the painting before going upstairs to advise their friend.

Lauren could overhear Adriana cleaning up the particles of glass while she was in the shower. She felt guilty at having made such a mess. "Adriana, I'm really sorry that you not only have to pick up the pieces of my life, but also the mess I make in the process."

Adriana laughed out loud. "That's OK. If this is as messy as it gets, then I think I can take care of it."

Lauren yelled out a grateful "thanks" and stepped out of the shower to dry off. She was in a hurry today. There was so much to be accomplished, and she knew she had to keep the positive attitude that Adriana had instilled in her. Whenever doubt crept into her mind, she would brush it aside and concentrate on the matter at hand. This was her day off, and she wasn't going to waste it. She knew that doubt would try and creep in when the sun went down. But Adriana had successfully convinced her to keep her options open today.

"Let's concentrate on our priorities just for today," her friend had told her. "We'll worry about tomorrow when it comes."

Lauren was ready to go in record time, and she met Adriana in the kitchen. "I want to thank you again for what you're doing. I feel more confident knowing you're in my corner."

Adriana didn't say a word, but instead she gave Lauren a quick hug. "Let's get out of here and embark on our journey." Adriana made sure she said it with confidence. She had no idea where it would lead them, but she knew the first step had to be taken with her holding Lauren's hand. She didn't want a repeat performance of that morning.

They were almost to the jewelry store when Lauren spoke the words that had consumed her thoughts. "Do you think they'll be able to clean the tarnish off? It's in rather bad condition. I don't want them to ruin it."

Adriana currently had possession of the ring, and took it out of her purse to examine it as Lauren drove. "I see no reason why they can't make it look like new."

Adriana was still studying it when they pulled into the parking lot. She opened her door, but noticed Lauren wasn't moving in the same direction. "Lauren, what's wrong?"

Lauren had a perplexed look of concern on her face. "They'll take good care of it, won't they?"

Adriana looked at Lauren as if she were a child. "Lauren, don't worry. Everything will be fine. Let's get this over with."

Lauren gave an insecure smile and stepped out of her car.

When they walked into the elegant jewelry store, Adriana strolled across the room to a man that looked to be the manager. She put the ring in front of his eyes. "Hello, my name is Adriana Dean." She pointed in Lauren's direction. "My friend has this antique ring. And as you can see, it's quite tarnished. We would like to have it cleaned without destroying its value. Is that possible?"

The manager took the ring from her hand and held it up to the light. "It's quite unusual, isn't it?" He was fingering the symbols as he spoke.

Lauren noticed she had been holding her breath. She didn't feel comfortable having a stranger touch it.

Adriana continued, "As you can see, it has an inscription that we are unable to decipher. Can you clean it to make it look like new?"

The manager was still holding it up to the light, twirling it around. Lauren felt as though she was handing over her own child.

"Please don't drop it."

The manager walked over to the counter and placed it in an envelope. "Yes, this will be no problem to clean. Our person that takes care of this will be in tomorrow. We can have it for you in three days."

Lauren yelled out, "Why so long? I was hoping to have it back today. Please, sir, can't you do something to rush the process?"

Adriana put a comforting hand on Lauren's arm. The manager looked at Lauren and realized this was no ordinary piece of jewelry to her. It obviously meant a great deal more. He assumed it must have belonged to someone very dear to her. "Madam, I wish I could have it for you that quickly, but the process alone takes two days. We use only the gentlest methods to treat such a valuable piece of jewelry. I assure you, it will be taken very good care of."

Lauren didn't know why she was reacting in such a manner. The gentleman was very kind, and she felt he understood its importance. "I'm sorry. Of course you will take care of it. I only worry because it means so much to me, and it's one of a kind."

Adriana spoke up, "Three days will be fine. All we ask is if you see that it can't be cleaned without destroying some of its basic character, you'll stop."

The manager replied, "I'll look after it personally. When you return, the ring will look like new."

The girls walked out feeling assured the ring was safe.

"I hope I didn't put the fear of God into him," Lauren said, chuckling to herself. "I can't believe I reacted the way I did. He must have thought I was crazy."

Adriana looked over at her friend and couldn't contain the giggle emerging from inside her. "You realize he probably thought we were both crazy. But I'll wager a bet he'll be taking damn good care of that ring for fear of what we might do to him if he doesn't." Adriana was excited about the next errand. "Now we're heading to Del Rey's."

"You're going to enjoy this store. It's rather unique. And, I think you'll like Vickie, too. She's rather unique herself," Lauren told her excited friend.

Adriana turned on the CD and they both listened as music penetrated the car and their minds. The remainder of their ride was silent. Ron's music had a hypnotic essence to it. It made each person conjure up their own fantasies.

Before they realized it, Lauren had pulled into a parking space in front of the store. Her excitement was mounting, and she couldn't get Adriana out of the car fast enough.

"I swear, Lauren, you're like a kid in a candy store. I'm moving as fast as I can," Adriana said jokingly.

Lauren opened the storefront door for Adriana and walked in behind her. They stopped in the entrance and Lauren could see her friend's reaction.

Adriana gasped in delight. "Wow, look at this place!"

She was outwardly impressed by Vickie's creativity. She had achieved a sense of warmth and balance. There was a lot of open space for browsing, without the feeling of being smothered by clutter. Yet Adriana was surprised by how much the shop had to offer. An abundance of artwork adorned the walls, with beautiful sculptures placed perfectly throughout on pedestals. The antiques were scattered in various areas, all over the rooms. It added just the right touch of elegance. She heard classical music playing in the background. Adriana turned to Lauren and whispered, "And you're just now finding this place?"

Lauren laughed, seeing her usually calm friend so excited. "Yeah, thanks to Cindy. I knew you'd love it." She took Adriana's hand, and pulled her in another direction. "First, I want to take you upstairs, then we'll look around. You've got to see this music box."

They were heading to the staircase when they heard footsteps approaching from another room. "May I help you?"

Lauren turned around and saw the tall redhead advancing.

"Oh hello, Lauren, how are you? I was just talking about you."

Lauren walked over to her new friend and hugged her. "Who were you talking to?"

"I just had Cindy on the phone. We were making lunch plans."

Adriana walked over to the two girls talking.

"Vickie, this is my friend, Adriana Dean. Adriana, meet Vickie Sanders."

Adriana put her hand out. "Vickie, I'm glad to meet you. Lauren has told me so much about you and your store. Everything she said was true. You have a lovely place."

Vickie returned the shake. "Thanks, I've put all my energy into this little shop, learning quite a bit along the way."

Lauren interjected, "Adriana owns Moonglows. It's a bookstore..."

Vickie interrupted, "That great bookstore over on Melrose?"

Adriana beamed proudly, "You've been there?"

Vickie responded with a smile, "Quite often, as a matter of fact. At least when I can tear myself away from this place. I've been spending more time here than in my own home."

Lauren and Adriana laughed appreciatively. They both understood how demanding owning their own business could be.

Vickie continued, "I've heard so much about Lauren's Place. I plan on coming by one day soon."

Adriana remarked, "You won't be disappointed. I would hang

out there even if Lauren wasn't my best friend."

Vickie noticed Lauren's rush for the stairs. "Why don't we start upstairs and work our way down?"

Lauren winked at her. "You read my mind."

The phone rang and Vickie took it at the counter. "Why don't you go on up and I'll meet you in a few minutes."

The girls were already halfway up the stairs. "Take your time. I'm sure we're going to be here a while," Lauren called back down to her.

They were like two kids racing each other up to the top landing. Lauren took Adriana's arm and pulled her in the direction of the box. Adriana spotted it before they reached their destination and gasped.

"Oh, Lauren, it's beautiful." Adriana placed her fingertips on it gently and stroked the outer texture. She repeated in a whisper to herself, "It's just beautiful."

Lauren slowly opened the empty box. "This is where I found the ring. Do you understand why I felt they belonged together?"

Adriana continued stroking the grain of wood. "Yes. There seems to be so much love here." Adriana was receiving impressions that were unusually strong. "This jewelry box was treasured, and very cherished."

Lauren was proud of her find. "Do you think I'll be able to afford it?"

Adriana looked into a very determined face. "Does it matter?"

Lauren laughed, "Well, actually, no!"

They heard Vickie's heels tapping each step upward. "I thought this was where I'd find you. Are you looking to make a home for the ring you bought?"

Lauren couldn't refrain from smiling. "Yeah, they really do belong together. Isn't that how you purchased them?"

Vickie touched the box. "Yes, they were bought together, along with many other items from the same estate."

Lauren interrupted, "I'm sorry, Vickie, but I really would like to buy this box. How much is it?"

Vickie walked to the counter and pulled a book from the shelf. Her finger browsed down the page until she found the price of the box. She reached for her calculator and started punching in some numbers.

Lauren bit her lip until she tasted blood. Adriana wasn't breathing, and had her arms wrapped protectively around her body.

It seemed to take forever before Vickie finally returned to the anxious women. "Lauren, I've brought the figure down as low as I possibly can. Believe me when I say this is the very best I can do." She handed Lauren a sheet of paper.

Lauren slowly opened the page, knowing the answer could make or break her day. Vickie looked over at Adriana and winked, causing her to instantly relax. Lauren peeked at the numbers and her eyes widened, as a huge grin covered her face, making her dimples jump out. "Is this a joke?"

Vickie looked at the figures on the paper, then at Lauren again. "No, this is the best I can do."

Lauren jumped up and down, hugging first Vickie, then Adriana.

"This beautiful box is mine!"

Lauren enthusiastically handed Vickie her credit card .

Vickie brushed her long red hair out from her eyes, and stared at the box. "It finally has a home again."

Lauren beamed as if all her wishes had come true. "I have to celebrate. Let me take you both out for lunch?"

Vickie turned to the phone. "I'm having lunch with Cindy. I'll call and let her know two more are coming."

Adriana responded, "Great. I haven't seen Cindy in ages."

Vickie made her call and informed them where to meet her. "Let me lock up and I'll meet you there."

Once the box was safely in Lauren's trunk and the ladies were on their way to the restaurant, Adriana innocently asked, "Does the music work in the music box?

Lauren wasn't concerned. "I have no idea. I forgot to wind it up. It doesn't really matter. I would have taken it no matter what."

Donovan and Elliot sped up the stairs. They couldn't wait to tell Alex what had just transpired before their eyes. They walked quietly into his bedroom, and saw their friend still in a deep sleep.

"I don't think we should wake him," Elliot said aloud.

"No, we'd better wait a while. I'm sure he'll be up soon, hungry as hell."

In the hopes that Alex would wake up, they both continued standing in front of his bed. Keeping the strange news to themselves was beginning to frustrate them. But his breathing was slow and even.

"He's not ready to wake up," Donovan said despairingly.

Without warning, Alex opened one eye, scaring the already jumpy guys. "Yes, Alex is going to wake up because Alex doesn't have much choice considering how much racket is going on in here."

Elliot's voice was an octave higher. "Damn, Alex, don't scare us like that. You were in a deep sleep, and we didn't expect you to hear us."

Alex turned over and peered at his friends. "How could I not? Your voices grew louder and louder. Hell, you could wake the dead."

Donovan grinned, knowing his friend was feeling better. "Sorry about that. We just had something to tell you that may be of interest. But since you're a bit grumpy…"

Elliot caught on and continued, "Yeah, we'll just come back later when you're in a better mood."

Alex sat up, propping his pillows behind his head. "OK, guys, I'm awake. Feeling like hell, but I'm awake. What's going on?"

Elliot sat down on the bed. "Alex, the strangest thing just happened downstairs."

Alex interrupted, "No, no, no! I do not want to hear about anything strange. I've had it. No more! If anything strange happened, it was in your little imaginations."

Alex rubbed his eyes, shaking his head in a negative response.

Donovan didn't let his outburst influence him. He took over the conversation. "Let us tell you what happened, and then you can judge what's fantasy and what isn't. OK?" He didn't give Alex time to answer.

Elliot began calmly. "Alex, do you remember what you told me last night about the painting in your office?"

Alex thought for a few seconds, trying to recall everything that had happened in the last few days. "I told you that I had a dream about the painting. I thought the woman in the painting might be the same as the one in my dream. But that was just speculation." Alex was still groggy from his illness.

Elliot's eyes began to sparkle. "Alex, Donovan and I were in your office a few minutes ago. We were looking at the painting, trying to sort out why you would buy it for yourself."

Alex retorted, "Are we going to get into that again? I told you I didn't know why I wanted it. It just appealed to me." Alex was getting frustrated at the conversation. "This is what you guys woke me up for?" He took a pillow and put it over his face, in an attempt to block out his friends.

Donovan stood over him and spoke louder than usual. "Listen to us, Alex. Then you tell us if we're crazy or not, OK?"

Elliot continued calmly, "Alex, we were in your office looking at the painting. We turned to leave, and when I glanced back once more, it looked strange."

Alex's mind instantly sharpened. He slowly took the pillow off his face and sat up a little straighter. "What kind of strange?"

Donovan walked around so that he now stood in front of Alex. "It was sort of glowing. But there wasn't light reflecting on it to make it glow." He put his hands out in front of him, cupping them in the air, as he whispered, "Alex, it just glowed."

Elliot looked straight out onto the balcony, his eyes still dazed from the turn of events. "Man, Alex, if I hadn't seen it with my own eyes."

Donovan's voice was still shaken. "It was so odd. It only lasted for a moment or two, but it was long enough for Elliot and me to realize what we saw. We have no doubts about it."

Alex was wide-eyed and alert now. His body was weak, and he could still feel his head aching, but his mind was awake and excited. "I hadn't had a chance to tell you about that. It also happened to me," Alex said in a surprised tone.

Donovan could barely speak above a whisper. "It happened to you too? When?"

Alex returned the whisper. "Late last night, before going to bed. It seems like so long ago. But yes, it was last night. I remember walking into my office and glancing at the picture. For a brief moment, there was a weird glow coming from inside the painting itself. I just thought I was tired and blew it off."

He looked closely at his friends, making certain this wasn't a joke. No, they were telling the truth. He could tell by the bewilderment written all over their faces. "I'm sorry it frightened you guys, but I can't tell you how glad I am to hear that I'm not as crazy as I thought I was." He continued, "But that doesn't mean that other people won't think us so. Please give me your word that you will not tell anyone about this. Give me time to sort it all out." Alex's eyes were pleading.

Elliot spoke up, "We won't say anything. But you don't have to do this alone. We're all in this thing together now."

Alex looked over at Donovan and found him shaking his head affirmatively. Donovan walked to the bedroom door, with Elliot following behind. "Alex, we're going downstairs to get you some food, and medication. If you need us, just yell."

Alex's weakness returned in full force. He shook his head in gratitude and closed his eyes.

Lauren and Adriana were still discussing the box as they walked into the crowded bistro. They immediately saw Cindy sitting in the bar and crept up on her, giving her a big hug from behind.

Cindy turned and hugged them back. "Hi, I'm so glad you two are joining us." Cindy kissed Adriana on the cheek. "It's been too damn long. What's been going on with you? Besides keeping Lauren here out of trouble."

Adriana looked at Lauren and laughed out loud.

Cindy raised her eyebrows and grinned. "Oh, so it's been Lauren trying to keep you out of trouble?"

Adriana responded, "Yeah, right. All I have in my life is work. I haven't seen trouble for so long, it wouldn't know where to find me."

Lauren winked at Adriana, and slowly changed the subject. "I think work is all we do anymore."

Cindy responded, "That certainly seems to be all that keeps me busy. Now that you're going to have two shops, we'll never get to see you."

Lauren stood behind both her friends, and spoke between them. "That's why it's always nice to have lunches like this. It forces us to get out and socialize, like normal people."

Cindy turned in the direction of the door. "Speaking of lunch, where's Vickie?"

Adriana answered, "She should be right behind us. She had to lock up." The words were no sooner out of her mouth, when Vickie walked in, mouthing apologies.

During lunch, they were all talking at once. Cindy asked Lauren what had taken her back to Del Rey's so soon. Lauren quickly shot a glance in Adriana's direction, then back to Cindy. "I had told Adriana about all the beautiful things I found there. I knew she'd be interested. I also didn't have the opportunity to look around yesterday and..."

Vickie interrupted, "Lauren, I'm afraid you'll have to come

back again because you didn't look around today either."

Cindy glanced questioningly first to Adriana and then to Lauren. "What kept you from browsing this time?"

Adriana was quick to answer nonchalantly for Lauren. "Oh, not much. She just decided to buy the music box that she'd found the ring in. After seeing it, I certainly understand. It's beautiful."

Cindy smiled knowingly. "I knew she'd go back for that box. I just didn't think she'd run back for it."

Vickie spoke up, "I suppose I can expect a return visit. Maybe this time, you'll actually get through the entire store."

Lauren laughed, "Yeah, I need to look at the artwork for the new shop. I can promise you that Adriana and I will both be back, and this time I won't be distracted."

Adriana thought it might be time to change the subject and get the attention off Lauren. "Vickie, is that an engagement ring on your finger? Who's the lucky man?"

Lauren mouthed a thank you to Adriana and let Vickie talk.

She told the women about Donovan. How they had met at an art auction. And about how he owned an entertainment agency in Malibu.

Cindy interrupted, "You'd never put the two of them together if you were to meet them separately. But seeing them together says it all. The perfect couple."

Lauren spoke up, "Like you and Ron. I've always thought the two of you make the perfect pair."

With her infectious smile, Cindy mentioned Ron had been going insane trying to write the music for his new CD.

Vickie mentioned that Donovan had been busy too. "He was supposed to have met me for dinner tonight, but called and said he was spending the night at a friend's house.

Cindy was curious, "Really, who?"

Vickie was solemn for a moment. "He's staying over at Alex's for a day or two. Apparently, Elliot had to rush him to the hospital early this morning. He was suffering from dehydration and the flu.

I think both guys are going to be staying with him. Donovan said that Alex would have had to stay in the hospital overnight, otherwise."

Cindy was shocked. "Alex was working with Ron yesterday. He had quite an outburst from what I understand. That explains it. He was sick, but came over to help Ron anyway. God, I feel awful for him. Is there anything Ron and I can do?"

Vickie shrugged, "Not that I know of. Donovan said he'd explain the best he could later. Whatever that means. Those three guys can be pretty tightlipped about the other when they set their minds to it."

Lauren and Adriana had barely been listening to the other conversation going on at their table. They were both deep in thought. Their thoughts were mutually resting in the trunk of Lauren's car.

They were raised from their stupor when Vickie looked at her watch and shrieked. "Oh, Jesus, I should've reopened twenty minutes ago. I have a million things to do. There's an auction that I must not miss. Cindy, I'll call you later. Adriana, it was very nice meeting you. Now that we're all friends, let's do this more often. I'll say hello the next time I'm in your store, and don't be a stranger to mine." She turned her attention to Lauren, "I want you to enjoy your piece. I know you bought it out of love, and that makes me happy."

Looking at her watch again, she yelled back behind her, "Sorry, I have to literally run. Catch you guys later."

Adriana stood up, "It's time for us to depart as well. We have work to do."

Lauren smiled. "We certainly do."

Alex closed his eyes and fell into a deep relaxing sleep. He had been so worried about his own sanity; now was the first time in weeks that he felt true relief. Now he knew that if he was insane, then his friends were as well. Before drifting off, he had to chuckle at that comforting thought. *I suppose it's time to tell them about the ring. But for now, I need to rest.* He could think of nothing else but peaceful sleep.

Alex knew immediately that he was in a dream state. He was taking deep meditative breaths on his balcony when he heard his name being called. He stopped and calmly responded, "I'm over here."

He heard his name being called again. This time, Alex looked over the railing onto the sand below. He saw a woman he recognized and smiled at her. He ran down the stairs, excited to see his elderly companion.

She returned the smile and gave him a warm, loving hug. It instantly took his body into a much lighter state. Alex remembered that as a child, he used to get the same sensation when his grandmother would wrap her arms protectively around him. She sat down and patted the sand for him to follow. He didn't speak, but rather waited for her to speak first. She was looking out at the ocean and appeared to be waiting for him to tell her his thoughts. He felt such immense comfort being with this older woman, he only wanted to bask in her energy without saying a word. But she would have none of that.

Her quivering voice was soothing. "Tell me how you are feeling, my dear boy."

Alex looked into her eyes and shook his head. "I don't think I've ever felt so sick. My energy is drained, and I worry that I won't ever feel like myself again."

The gentle woman patted Alex's hand and smiled. "Alex, you've built up negative energy, and it had to be released. Your frustrations are tearing you down. Why not let your discoveries build you up instead? Use your optimism to create more waves of positive energy."

Alex frowned, "What discoveries? You say the signs are everywhere and that I should find what was lost. And what do I do? I drive the woman in my dreams away because I'm concentrating on the wrong thing."

His guide chuckled softly. "Alex, you must stay focused, and concentrate on the issue of love. And instead of frustration, focus on the love and renewed faith that your encounters have brought you."

She looked deep into his dark blue eyes. "Alex, I cannot do this for you. I can only remind you of what you are here to find. You started this journey such a very long time ago. You have no memory of it, but it is still your story, not mine. I can only be with you and encourage you." She smiled mischievously, and continued, "And against my better judgment, advise you occasionally by giving little hints. My son, you have done nothing wrong. Your focus was on the element that held the most energy."

The woman put her soft wrinkled hand on Alex's forehead. "Center yourself and think back to your dream. Remember with love, not with disappointment. You were both concentrating on the same situation. It brought with it the same realities. Trust your instincts, son."

Alex was about to protest, but the woman continued. "Hold your focus, and explore your instincts. There is a beautiful woman out there for you. And she misses you as much as you miss her. Keep your heart and mind open. This, dear Alex, you must do."

Alex spoke up, confused, "If this is all meant to be, why can't you tell me where to find her? Why can't you give me the answers I need to make my life complete?"

His guide looked further into Alex's eyes, with much love and patience, but she didn't say a word.

Alex looked down, ashamed. "This is my life, and I have my own agenda, and I have my own answers. This is a karmic tie that I agreed to come back and complete." He looked up with a question. "But what if I make the wrong decision and change my path?"

The woman spoke very calmly, "Then you do. There are no wrong decisions. Any decision you make in life will always set you on a path of some kind. There are many roads to the same destination. You'll eventually reach your goal. But you will be much more successful if you know who you truly are, and why you're taking the path you're on."

She held up her hand before he could speak. "And to erase karma as you travel on your journey, it must always be done with an open heart, with wisdom, and with complete love. That's one of the reasons I'm here with you. To help you remember your paths, and your responses to them. But hopefully with unconditional love and wisdom."

Alex felt like he did as a child when his grandmother had something profound to say. "I appreciate that you're here for me. I suppose I need to be reminded at times. I get so caught up in the drama , I forget there's beauty to be seen as well."

The caring woman hugged Alex. "You're going to feel much better when you wake up, because now you have an open heart. Remember what it feels like so you don't close it again."

Alex hugged her very close to his chest. "Thank you. I love you so much. But I suppose you know that, don't you?"

She smiled proudly at him, "I do."

Alex slowly opened his eyes and looked around the room. Nothing within the room had changed. But he had a quiet new confidence that had failed him before. He didn't know whether it was because he felt better, or because of the discussion he had just had a few moments before that had opened his eyes to new realities. He vowed to do his best to keep his focus, and silently prayed that his wonderful guide would be there to remind him if he should falter.

Alex chuckled to himself and spoke aloud to the walls, "More likely to come back to kick my ass."

Either way, Alex was grateful. He sat up very slowly, and realized that he was starving.

With a weak voice, he made an attempt to call downstairs to his friends.

"Hey, guys, I'm awake and hungry. But I must warn you, do

not enter this room without food."

Elliot and Donovan were below watching television, and looked over at each other, then up at the ceiling.

Donovan laughed out loud. "Well, I think he's gonna make it."

Elliot yelled back to Alex, "We hear your pleas and your wishes will be granted."

Alex had to smile. Elliot didn't know how true he hoped those words would be.

Once in the car, Adriana approached Lauren calmly about the next errand on her mental list. "Lauren, do you think you're up for some work in the altered states?"

Adriana tried to make her voice sound as neutral as possible. She didn't want to intrude if Lauren didn't want company.

Lauren was apprehensive, but excited. "I've been giving this hypnosis thing a lot of thought. As a matter of fact, it's about all I can think about. I think I'm ready to find out if I have anything up there," Lauren said, pointing to her head.

"Then I say let's go for it." Adriana continued before Lauren had time to back out. "Would you prefer that I do the honors, or would you like for me to make a phone call and have someone else do it?"

Lauren looked at her friend in disbelief. "Adriana, of course I want you to talk me through it. I wouldn't feel comfortable discussing this with just anyone. Most people would think I was crazy."

The look of shock on Lauren's face made Adriana burst into laughter. "Lauren, I've heard some mighty strange stories when I've induced hypnosis. Don't worry. I promise this will be our little secret. But you'll allow me to record it, won't you?"

Lauren pulled into her driveway and turned off the engine.

"Won't I know what I'm saying and remember it?"

Adriana had to remind herself that Lauren had never been through a hypnosis session. She wasn't expected to know how to react.

"You'll probably remember everything you say. It may be a little fuzzy, but you should be coherent. Sometimes, you won't think that you're under, until you come out of it. And sometimes, if you're really deep, you may not remember at all, so a recording is always a good idea."

Lauren trusted her completely. "Whatever you say. Let's just get on with it."

Lauren rushed out of the car and opened the trunk very carefully. She picked the box up and carried it into the house as if it were a baby. She didn't bother stopping to put down her purse, but instead marched right into her office and gently placed the music box on top of her desk. She was surprised that it was denser than it looked.

"The music chamber must be made of metal. This thing is really heavy," Lauren said, out of breath.

"Do you need help with it?" Adriana offered, but knew that Lauren would have no one help her. This was her pride and joy. "Let me know when you're ready to begin. I'm going to make a few phone calls in the kitchen."

Lauren was massaging oil into the wood with a soft cloth. "OK, I'll just be a minute."

Adriana spoke over her shoulder. "Since you did buy a music box, why don't you see if the music plays?"

Lauren stopped her circular movements. "Hey, thanks for reminding me. I was so excited to get it home, I totally forgot about the music."

Lauren ceremoniously turned the small knob on the side of the box then opened its cover. The tune surrounded the room. Lauren's eyes first widened, then slowly closed as she swayed to the music. She let the tune flow and play over her body. She was so overcome with emotion, she could just faintly whisper to herself, "My dear God, this is the most beautiful music I've ever heard." She seemed to drift further away on each note.

Only a few minutes had elapsed when Adriana was brought back into the room by the gentle melody. "Lauren, what song is that? It's really nice."

Lauren's eyes flew open, and she closed the lid hurriedly. "I don't know, but it's beautiful. I'll have to listen to it later."

Adriana was a little surprised by her friend's reaction. "Gee, Lauren, I didn't mean to intrude. I just thought you were waiting for me."

Lauren looked over at her friend and felt instant remorse. "I'm sorry. I didn't mean to react that way. I suppose I was in my own little world."

Adriana didn't let it bother her. "I can't blame you. The music would be enough to zone anyone out." She continued with a smile in her voice, "Are you ready to find out what's lurking in that brain of yours, Miss Wells?"

Lauren giggled at how Adriana was swinging her arms about like a mad scientist. "Well, I suppose I am. I think... yes, I am absolutely ready!"

Adriana led Lauren up the stairs. "I promise it won't hurt a bit. I'm very experienced, so you'll be well taken care of."

Lauren lay down on her bed and closed her eyes. Adriana looked over at her and smiled. "First, why don't I explain to you what I'll be doing. I don't want you mentally questioning everything I say. Instead, I want you to listen to me, relax, and allow yourself to follow my instructions." Adriana continued, "I'll turn on some nice background music. Not only will it relax you, but it's also good for noise pollution. Then, I'll verbally take you through your body, while you visualize relaxing all parts. I'll have you bring a light of protection around you. After that is completed, I will count you down. It's basically the same thing you do when you meditate, but I'll count you down from seven to one, two or three times. I want to make sure you're deep. You will go anywhere from mid-alpha to theta, depending on how good a subject you are. And don't expect to perceive an impression any certain way.

Just trust yourself. You may think that you're creating a fantasy in your mind. That's all right; just go with it. Your experience may be visual, or you may receive impressions."

Adriana continued without taking a breath. "You may receive single pictures like the ones you see on slide projectors. Or you may hear voices, or read words. Sometimes, you'll feel like you're actually living the experience, while other times you may be totally detached, just watching as a bystander. And you can perceive through any of these forms at any given time. Just because it's one way one time, it doesn't necessarily mean that it will be that way the next time. It can also change during the same session. So please, Lauren, no preconceived notions. Just let whatever happens, happen. We'll discuss them later. OK?"

Adriana sat down on the bed and placed her hand in Lauren's. "You do trust me, don't you?"

Lauren took the tape recorder from the side drawer and placed it on the nightstand next to her. "I trust you, and I'm as ready as I'll ever be. Don't worry about me. I'll listen to every word you say." And grinning, Lauren added, "And for once, I'll actually follow your instructions."

Adriana laughed and slapped Lauren's arm. "Let me tell you something, girl, the world would be a hell of a lot better off if everyone would listen to me."

Lauren returned the laugh. "M'lady, how right you are. What fools we mere mortals have been."

"OK, I get it. Let's get on with your story, shall we?"

Adriana turned on the background music softly, and pulled out a pencil and paper from the nightstand. She dimmed the lights, and turned to Lauren, who was taking deep breaths. "Get yourself comfortable and let's begin."

Chapter 8

While Alex waited to be served in bed, he thought for a few minutes about what had just transpired. He was weak, but he had to write everything into his journal. He knew that within a few minutes, he would forget most of the inspiring conversation. Alex pulled the book off the nightstand and wrote the words that he knew he would return to again and again. After he completed the last sentence, Alex put the journal aside and propped up his pillows. He stopped when doubt filled his mind. *Did the guys tell me something about the painting?*

Alex tried to think back to their last conversation, but it was a dull memory. *Was I dreaming, or did it really happen?*

He looked around his room and saw nothing out of place. "Did I destroy my rooms, or was that a dream too?"

Guilt overwhelmed him when he realized what had occurred that morning. Then pain developed in his temples, when memories of last night's dream filtered through. *Damn, I can't believe this.*

Alex was ready to deface himself again when he remembered the advice his guide gave him in his dream. "Remember the dream with love, not frustration. Remember it as it was."

Alex opened his eyes and gazed out the window, recalling her soothing words. 'Focus on the love and the renewed faith that your encounters have brought you."

He blinked back tears and felt revived confidence. He mentally thanked her for once again helping him overcome the negativity that had been trying to penetrate his being. He wanted nothing more of that.

Whatever happens, I'll try to be as positive as I can. I know it won't be easy, and I pray that I'll be reminded along the way. But I will do my best.

Alex yelled down to his friends with a smile in his voice. "Hey, guys, I'm really hungry up here. You have me at a disadvantage cause I'm still weak. But you know it won't last forever, and paybacks are hell. Is this punishment for causing you so much trouble?"

He was about to continue when he heard the two men scrambling up the stairs. They immediately noticed Alex had the old sparkle back in his eyes. "Lucky for you that you brought food."

Donovan laughed, "Yeah, that and your meds."

They watched Alex eat heartily. Except for his weakness and being so pale, they would never have known this was the same man who had been incoherent, and had destroyed a room.

Elliot was glad to see his friend coming back to life. "Alex, you seem to be feeling better."

Alex handed him the empty tray. "Much better. I was worried about myself for a while. I still don't think I could go for a walk on the beach, but yes, I'm beginning to feel more like my old self."

Donovan couldn't wait any longer. "Alex, do you remember our earlier conversation?"

Alex looked up at his friends, trying to read their faces, but couldn't. "Yeah, a little. Why? What was said?"

Elliot tried to be cautious, but when he detected a slight twitch in Alex's eye, he sensed his friend had something to say.

Elliot took control of the subject. "We were up here earlier and had a conversation about your painting downstairs. Do you remember what was said?"

Alex couldn't wait another minute. His patience was beginning to run thin. "OK, we spoke about the damn painting. Did you, or did you not see something?"

Elliot and Donovan sat down on the bed and yelled out in

unison. "Yes, we did!"

Alex bolted straight up and yelled equally as loud, "Hallelujah, I'm not hallucinating! You saw it too. This is the only solid confirmation I've had, telling me that I am not going crazy." He laughed and continued, "Not by our standards anyway."

His friends smiled, but kept puzzled looks on their faces.

Donovan spoke up, "Yeah, we saw something, but what in the hell was it? I gotta tell you, it scared the hell out of me."

Alex laughed softly. "You didn't feel threatened by it, did you?"

Donovan thought for a moment and replied, "Well no, I don't think so. In fact, it was sort of pleasant."

Donovan turned to Elliot for validation, and found him nodding his head. "Yeah, it did kind of have a nice glow to it, didn't it?"

Alex was wide awake now. "What do you think it means? I thought I was losing it when it happened to me. At the time, I didn't know if I should mention it or not. How do you go about telling someone your painting glows?"

Donovan put his hand on Alex's shoulder. "It's easy. We would've said you were insane. But we would have supported you. We may not have believed you, but we would have supported you."

Elliot looked out to the ocean in front of him. "Well, thank God we all saw it. Now let's get down to work and see what else we can produce." He spoke directly to Alex. "I'll teach you a few meditations to intensify your dreaming, and we're also going to go through your journal, page by page, to see if we can come up with any clues."

Elliot sat down next to Alex and looked straight into his eyes. His tone was serious. "Alex, you're going to have to tell us what happened last night. Did you dream about her? Can you remember what caused your anger this morning? When you were talking incoherently, the only words I could comprehend were something about a ring, and your life being ruined. Please try and remember."

Alex rubbed his forehead, knowing he had to go over the events leading up to that moment. His weakness was returning, but he was determined to tell his friends what they wanted to know.

"First of all, you must promise me that no one, and I mean no one will hear of this. As of right this minute, anything said to each other will be kept in the strictest confidence."

There was never a doubt in either man's minds. They both nodded their head affirmatively and waited for Alex to continue. Alex propped his pillows up while Donovan took a pad and pen from the dresser. Alex began his recounting of his night.

"Elliot, after you left last night, I was tired but not in the mood to sleep. I sat down at the piano with the intentions of just playing for a few minutes. The next thing I knew, I was playing a tune I'd never played in my life. I knew the song, but I know for a fact that I've never seen the sheet music. I even sang the lyrics."

Donovan's curiosity was getting the best of him. "What song was it?'

"Have you ever heard me play or mention the song, 'Where or When?'"

Both guys looked at each other.

Elliot responded first. "I don't think I know the song."

Donovan shook his head. "No, I can't say that I know it either."

Alex continued, "I've heard the song before, but not since I was a child. You can imagine my surprise when I sat down and played it as if I'd known it all my life." He looked outside and continued, "I was shocked to think that I knew the lyrics as well." He turned to his friends. "Do you think it means something?"

Elliot shrugged, "After everything else that's happened, it seems too odd to just ignore it. Wouldn't you say?"

Donovan glanced at Elliot. "It is a bit strange, isn't it?" He answered Elliot.

Elliot looked back at Alex. "Anything else? What happened

after that?"

Alex hugged his knees to his chest and worked hard at remembering the turn of events. "I was about to go to bed when I remembered the journal was in my office. I wanted it next to me in case I had a dream. As I was leaving the office, I noticed the painting on the wall was sort of illuminating from within. I couldn't believe what I'd seen. It took me a moment to realize what had occurred. I walked around to get another look, but the light was gone. Just like that, it was gone!"

Elliot spoke up, "Yeah, we know what you mean. It certainly got our attention too."

Alex continued, "I'm so glad you guys saw it. I'm relieved to know that I'm not insane. And I couldn't be more grateful about that."

Donovan laughed out loud. "He's grateful to be sane. But it still leaves us questioning our own sanity."

Elliot laughed, "Well put, Donovan, well put."

The mood was lighter now, and Alex was feeling better sharing his experiences with people he knew he could trust.

"I tried to convince myself that I was just tired and therefore seeing things."

Donovan interjected, "Yeah, I feel certain if only one of us had seen it, we'd try to convince ourselves of the same thing."

Alex smiled appreciatively and continued, "Well, by that time, I was so mentally and physically exhausted, I got into bed and immediately fell asleep."

Elliot squinted his eyes narrowly at Alex. "Did you dream?"

Alex took a very deep breath. He was dreading this part of the story. "Yeah, I dreamed all right. I still can't believe what I did in the damn dream."

Elliot and Donovan were shocked by Alex's tone of voice. He didn't sound happy that he had seen her at all. He was almost upset by it.

Elliot continued, looking deeply into Alex's eyes. "Alex, take your time and tell us what happened. Why are you so upset?"

Alex shook his head back and forth. "You're not going to believe what I did to her. I wouldn't blame her if she never returned."

Donovan couldn't stand it another minute. "Alex, what in the hell did you do? For God's sake, tell us!"

Alex sat up straight and hung his legs over the bed.

"I had to wait for her. Actually, I didn't think I was dreaming at all. In fact, I thought I was sleepwalking and woke up outside. But finally, she came to me. Of course, we couldn't touch. But fortunately, we're able to communicate telepathically now. Though only for short periods at a time." Alex stopped for a moment to breathe, and he pushed his dark hair back from his face. "Hell, I say a short time, but twenty-four hours with her would seem like only a few minutes."

Alex shook his head, "No, I don't know how long we were together."

Elliot spoke up to hurry things along. "So, what happened?"

Alex fidgeted with the blankets until the boys wanted to attack him themselves.

Donovan snapped harsher than he had intended. "Damn it, Alex, tell us what happened."

Alex realized he was stalling, and took another deep breath. "When I saw her, I had every intention of finding out who she was. I figured this had been going on too long. For months, we've been trying to get close enough to communicate. Finally, we've found a way. I was all prepared to make this our final dream. I was going to find her in person and stay with her."

Elliot walked over, taking Alex's shoulders and lightly shaking him from his stupor. "Alex, get on with the story!"

Alex looked down as if he were ashamed. "OK. So she shows up. I reach for her, but I can't touch her. I mentally communicate with her, and am about to ask her all the questions that I had prepared, when suddenly, out of nowhere, this ring she has on her finger begins to glow."

Donovan was writing Alex's story on the pad, but looked up in disbelief. "You said it glowed?"

"Yeah, I saw this ring begin to glow, and I forgot about everything else. I became obsessed with finding out where she got it and what the symbols and inscription read."

Elliot interrupted, "What it read? How did you know there was anything on it to read? Didn't you say it was glowing? And if it was on her finger, and you couldn't touch her, then how could you see it?"

Alex ran his hands through his hair. "Hell if I know. This is the most fucked up thing I've ever encountered."

Donovan stopped writing. "OK, continue with the story. Why was it so important that you find out about the ring?"

Alex rubbed his jaw. "I have no idea. It was glowing, it caught my attention, and I knew I wasn't going to be satisfied until the information was in my possession. I can't believe I was rude and totally ignored her feelings."

"How did she react to this treatment?" asked Elliot anxiously.

Alex replied in disbelief. "It was so strange. She was equally as fascinated by the ring as I was. She seemed rather surprised that she was wearing it. I remember asking her what the inscription read on the inside of..."

Donovan interrupted, "You knew there was an inscription on the inside? How the hell did you know that?"

Alex was getting agitated, "That's what I'm trying to tell you. I don't know how I knew any of this. I was obsessed by the ring. She seemed obsessed by it as well. I kept asking her what it read. She said she couldn't read it. I remember getting really pissed off, and I knew she could hear it in my questioning, but for some reason, I didn't care." Alex turned over on his side and faced the balcony. "She did as I asked, and took the ring off. She was shocked to discover that she could indeed read the inscription and the lettering that covered the outside of it."

Elliot asked him very quietly, "Do you recall what she told you?"

Alex shook his head. "Hell no. The only thing I can recollect is whatever she read to me made me sad, and I felt such an ache in my gut. It felt as if it were burning all the way to my soul. The last thing I remember was her standing in front of me, fading away. And she had a tear on her cheek. It tore me up inside."

He closed his eyes as tears stung his own cheeks. Alex was feeling the anger within him begin to emerge again, like a volcano. He immediately imagined light pouring over his body and cleansing him of his anger. All of a sudden, he heard his guide's sweet voice in his head. "Remember, you were both focused on the ring."

Alex instantly calmed down, and continued with his story.

"I woke up this morning feeling terrible. I hurt all over, inside and out. I remember I got angrier than I've ever been, when I realized I had dreamed about her, but then turned around and ignored her. The next thing I know, you both are here taking care of me."

The room was quite for a minute. Everyone was processing the information in their own way. Elliot was finally the first to speak.

"Alex, you were very sick this morning, and running an extremely high temperature. That accounted for why you reacted the way you did. No one can fault you for that."

Donovan interrupted, "Your dream was unbelievable. I'm not really certain how to respond. But we are here to deal with the facts the way they're presented. Right?"

Alex was too tired to answer so Elliot took over. "There was obviously a reason why you both were interested in the ring. I wouldn't feel too guilty, Alex. There was a reason. You need to believe that. Just remember that you both saw the glow." Elliot didn't wait for a response. "The significance here is the fact that you knew there was something written on that ring, and she read it to you."

Alex was waking up from his fog. He was anxious to hear more.

Elliot continued, "We need to find out what she told you. Do you think you could remember?"

Alex thought for a moment. "I doubt it. It's such a blur."

Donovan snapped his fingers. "What about hypnosis? Wouldn't that shake it out of him?"

Elliot never took his eyes off Alex. "I don't know. But in any case, I wouldn't want to consider it until he was healthy again, and off the medications. For now, we can only hope that he remembers. But I see no reason why we can't go to Vickie's to see if she has any information on the painting. At least it's a start."

Alex smiled appreciatively. "Finally, some sort of direction."

Donovan looked over his notes. "We have quite a list here. I'm no detective, but I think we at least have a few leads now."

Elliot turned to Alex and gave him some instructions. "If you're feeling up to it tomorrow, we'll go over to Vickie's and see what we can find. And when you're off the meds, we'll see about getting you hypnotized to discover what was so important about the ring. I don't know what to suggest about the song, except to continue playing it on the piano. See if anything comes through."

Alex smiled apprehensively, "That won't be a problem. I can't get the tune out of my head." A look of concern returned to his face. "Let's hope she comes back."

Elliot winked at his friend. "With any luck, even if she doesn't, maybe we can still get a fix on her."

Alex looked out at the sand where his dreams met, and whispered, "My life would be complete if we could."

His weakness was returning. "If you guys don't mind, I'm exhausted."

The men walked to the door before Alex summoned them again. "Guys, what can I say? You clean up after me, you take care of me, and you help solve my problems. I won't forget this."

They looked over at their buddy lying almost helpless in bed.

Elliot winked and gave him a parting retort. "Just get well so we can all start leading normal lives again. This is exhausting."

Alex smiled, closed his eyes and slept.

Adriana watched Lauren for a few minutes, and waited until she had put herself into a light altered state. The rest of Adriana's work would be relatively easy if Lauren would open herself up and participate.

Adriana directed Lauren to take a few more deep breaths, letting them out slowly through her mouth. She then instructed her friend to focus on the sound of her voice, and the suggestions that she was about to give her. She first relaxed Lauren by having her visualize a bright blue ball of light at her feet, then moving on to one area of the body at a time. Lauren visualized the blue object moving up, cleansing and relaxing her. By the time Adriana had reached the scalp area, Lauren was already well on her way to a deep level altered state.

Adriana then had Lauren visualize a pure bright white light of love and protection to surround her and keep her safe. Adriana began counting backwards, allowing Lauren to visualize her own means of descent.

Lauren saw herself walking down flights of beautiful stairs. She could hear her friend's calm voice directing her down. "Number 7, deeper, deeper, deeper, down, down, down, number 6, deeper, deeper, deeper, down, down, down."

Lauren felt she was floating down the steps. They were vivid, and seemed to come alive with each number she heard. It wasn't long before she heard Adriana say that she had reached number one. Lauren knew she was still attached to her thoughts, but the distance between herself and her physical comprehension was millions of miles.

Adriana told her she was going to take her even deeper. She began counting her down again, beginning at seven. Lauren had never felt so relaxed. She obeyed her friend, and took the stairs downward one at a time. When she had reached the lowest number, Lauren was in a very deep level of altered state consciousness.

Adriana had her take a deep cleansing breath, and then directed her into a room that she could make as comfortable as she liked. "Lauren, this will be your work room. You will remember everything you're asked to remember in this room. And when you're in this room, you will feel no discomfort whatsoever. You will have total control of your emotions. You will be able to stay focused and directed. You will be able to view and describe everything seen as a bystander. Lauren, do you understand what I've told you?"

Lauren nodded her head affirmatively. She had already begun creating, then awaited further instructions from her friend. She couldn't believe her body could be in such a state. There was no pain, no expectation. Just pure bliss and complete rest.

Adriana watched closely and made certain that she had a look of serenity on her face before continuing, "Lauren, you're comfortably seated in your room; I'm going to ask you to first look around and describe the setting." Adriana wanted Lauren to get a feel of what it was like to describe what she was seeing.

"I'm in an open room. It's just the right size for me."

Adriana smiled at her brief portrayal. She knew that she was going to have to be more precise in asking for descriptions. Lauren spoke as if Adriana could see the room, too.

Adriana repeated her words, "Lauren, look around and tell me exactly what you see, and be specific."

"I'm lying on a beautiful dark green recliner. I've never felt anything so soft. There's a beautiful white sofa across from me, with a wooden oriental table in front of me."

Adriana watched her friend's eyes moving under her lids. She knew Lauren was looking around.

"There are large windows on every wall of my room. When I look out on one side, I see beautiful tall snow-capped mountains.

There is a field of blue, red and yellow flowers that lead from my room all the way to the mountains. In the distance, I can see pine trees covering the mountains." Smiling, she commented proudly, "It's magnificent."

Lauren paused for a moment, then continued, "When I look through the other windows, I see a bright blue ocean in front of me. There are no ships on the water. Just blissful miles of blue liquid.

Lauren stopped and sighed. She was induced to the maximum level.

"Lauren, I want you to relax in your recliner and close your eyes." Adriana glanced at the recorder to make sure it was running smoothly. "I want you to remember back to the dream you had last night. I want you to be there and tell me everything you saw, and everything you did. Rewind the memories as if it were a tape. You will feel no emotion while describing the events. You will view it only as a bystander."

Lauren was quiet for a few minutes while the scene was entering her hypnotic consciousness. In her mind's eye, she turned around, and was on a beach being overtaken by a blue fog.

"I'm on the beach. This time there's a blue fog coming towards me. It's blocking the space between him and me."

"Lauren, did you ask him his name?"

"No. Well, yes I did. I told him I couldn't stay long and I asked him who he was. It feels so good being in his presence. I feel whole."

"Lauren, did he give you his name?"

Frustration passed across Lauren's face. "No."

She offered no other explanation, so Adriana continued. "What happened to keep him from telling you?"

Lauren changed her look to one of astonishment. "We looked down at my hand and saw my ring glowing. It was the most remarkable thing I've ever seen. Even with all the fog, we both saw it."

"What happened then?" Adriana was lost in this dream too.

"We forgot about everything else. Looking back, it was almost like a form of hypnosis. I suppose the pulsating light emitting from the ring brought its own form of trance."

Lauren was jumping back and forth as if the story were in the past and present, all in one. She repeated the sentence again, in a whisper, more for verification from her own higher self.

Lauren continued, "He keeps asking me where I got it. And there's a moment of confusion for me, because I knew I had taken it off before going to bed. The confusion just kept intensifying. He's focused on wanting to know about the ring, and I was focused on trying to determine how it got back on my finger."

Adriana watched the lines in Lauren's brow deepen.

"All right, Lauren, let's leave this immediate scene. What's happening now?"

Lauren wasn't finished with her description. Adriana felt Lauren must need to hear herself review the situation, so she let her continue.

"I'm still standing there. The energy is very confusing for us. He's asking me questions that I can't answer."

Lauren had a look of bewilderment on her face. "The craziest thing is happening. The ring is now exploding in rainbow colors. I try to take the damn thing off and give it to him, but something is stopping him from taking it."

Adriana was on the edge of her chair. "Lauren, what is stopping him from taking the ring?"

Lauren shook her head slightly. "I don't know. The wall of fog, I suppose. He's demanding answers that I just don't have."

"What is he asking you?"

Lauren answered in an irritated voice. "He's asking me what the inscription says."

Adriana was confused, "How did he know there was an inscription?"

Lauren was quiet for a moment when a look of disbelief

Debbie Reis

overtook her appearance. "My God, I can't believe it. How did that happen?"

Adriana couldn't contain herself. "What, Lauren? What happened?"

"The tarnish is gone; the inside of the ring can be read. I can't believe it. I watched the words come forward with my own eyes."

Adriana could no longer stand it, and tried very calmly to have Lauren continue with the story.

"Lauren, as a bystander, look into the ring and tell me what the inscription reads."

Lauren said the words loudly, "'Where / when…remember…my love.' What does that mean? I don't understand what it means!"

A tear formed on the outside of Lauren's eyes. She hugged herself and became quiet.

Adriana let her rest for a few moments. She knew Lauren was emotionally spent.

"Lauren, do you want to continue?"

Lauren didn't speak for a while, and then finally spoke up with little energy. "Yes, I want to continue."

Adriana looked at the recorder. She didn't want it running out now.

"OK, let's proceed. Tell me how you're feeling."

Lauren took a deep breath, and continued in a shaky voice, "My soul aches. It burns with a desire that I don't understand. It's as if my body and soul know why it's aching, but my mind doesn't. I wish one or the other would stop."

"What are you physically feeling?"

Lauren squinted, as if she were looking into the sun.

"He wants to know what the outside symbols read. I try to explain that I have no idea, but he refuses to listen to me."

Lauren fell quiet for a moment, trying to compose herself. The look of complete and profound shock was on her face, as well as in her body language. Adriana decided to wait it out and see where

153

Lauren took her.

"The ring is emitting this bright, blinding light. How in the hell does he think I could read anything with such intensity burning into my eyes?"

Adriana could see that it was becoming too much for Lauren to cope with. Her voice was very agitated. She was about to end the session when Lauren gasped loudly. Adriana heard herself gasp in return. She didn't know who wanted the answers more, herself or Lauren.

"Lauren, tell me what you're seeing."

Lauren was immobile for what seemed like hours.

"The bright colors...they dimmed..."

"Lauren, what happened after the colors dimmed?"

Adriana couldn't move a muscle, and her heart was pounding loudly.

"I read the symbols... My God, I read the symbols."

"How were you able to do this?"

"The light dimmed, and suddenly the inscription was as easy to read as a book I've read a hundred times."

With a tone of firm calmness, Adriana had to put this story to rest. "Lauren, tell me what the inscription says."

In a manner of heartfelt pain, Lauren spoke very slowly, as if she were reading the symbols for the first time. "Now and forever."

Adriana echoed her words. "Now and forever? Lauren, is that what it says?"

Lauren repeated it to herself slowly, "Now and forever."

Adriana could hear the anguish and confusion in her friend's voice, and felt tears running down her own face. She calmed herself before speaking again. "Lauren, what are you doing now? Where is he?"

Lauren was openly crying, and her distress and frustration was intense. "He has a look of pain all over his face. The fog is burning off and I'm fading from his view. He hurts so badly right now.

There's nothing I can do but watch until I am back in my bed."

Both women were both caught in the moment and quietness prevailed.

Finally in a small, fragile voice, Adriana heard her friend ask to be brought back to reality. "Please hurry. I can't bear this."

Adriana counted her up with positive affirmations on each count.

"Number five, wide awake Lauren. You're wide awake on number five."

Lauren slowly opened her eyes, and the room was quiet while both women continued sorting out their emotions in their own private ways.

Chapter 9

Alex slept soundly all night for the first time in months. He groggily woke up to the aroma of fresh brewed coffee, and he lay still for a few minutes. He recalled where he was, and wondered who was making such loud noises downstairs. When reality set in, he ran his hands through his dark hair, then touched his face, making sure that he was awake and in his own bed. Alex was afraid of losing balance, so he slowly set one foot on the floor at a time. When he discovered his legs could withstand his weight, he slowly walked downstairs.

He approached quietly behind his friends. "Hi ya, guys. How did you sleep?" Both boys quickly turned around to see Alex unsteady, and holding on to the wall.

Elliot grabbed his chest. "Damn, Alex, with all the weirdness going on in this house, don't go creeping up on us like that."

Donovan was at Alex's side, and helped him to the couch. "What are you doing out of bed?"

Alex forced a weak smile. "I wanted to come down and find out who was making a mess in my kitchen. I couldn't have slept if I'd wanted to with all the noise you guys were making. I'm surprised you didn't wake the dead."

Elliot laughed and handed him a warm cup. "Yeah, I think we have our old Alex back."

Alex gratefully accepted the cup, and blew into the rising steam. "I'm feeling stronger today. I'd like to drive over to Vickie's and see what we can find out about the picture. How does that sound?"

Donovan sat next to Alex. "Are you sure that's such a good idea? You have a doctor's appointment today, and it may be too early to be getting out. Why don't we wait until tomorrow and see how you're doing?"

Alex looked pleadingly into their eyes. "I'll agree to go to my appointment today, but I really must insist on going to Vickie's. Now that we're finally onto something, I don't want to lose the momentum. Surely you must understand that."

It was Elliot's turn to respond, and there was a noticed firmness in his voice. "Alex, why don't we see what the doctor says first? Let's take this one step at a time. You've been very ill. Why can't this quest of yours wait one more day?"

Alex closed his eyes and took a deep breath. "Because I slept soundly last night for the first time in a very long time. Do you know what that means?"

Elliot and Donovan glanced at each other, then shook their heads.

Alex continued, "It means I didn't meet her last night. It means that I may have lost her. And I miss her terribly."

Alex stood up and walked to the glass doors looking out to the Pacific waters. "It means until I have answers, I will not stop today, and I will not stop tomorrow."

Elliot put his hand on Alex's shoulder, admitting defeat. "All right, then let's get some breakfast into you, and get going."

After breakfast and a shower, Elliot noticed Alex was already tiring. He wanted to mention it, but thought better. The decision had been made, and they both knew Alex well enough to know that nothing short of death would stop him now.

The doctor explained to Alex that rest would be required for several days, along with medication.

Alex nodded his head in agreement, and then met his friends in the waiting room, telling them a different story. "Guys, the only advice he gave was to continue the medication and rest when I needed it. That's all. So, let's get going to Vickie's.

Elliot peered into Alex's eyes, giving him a look that said, "We don't believe a word you're saying, but we can't stop you."

Alex looked down mischievously and grinned, exposing his deep dimples.

It was a quiet drive to Vickie's. The music was playing in the background, and the three men were absorbed by their own thoughts.

It seemed like an eternity to Alex before Donovan finally parked in front of Del Rey's.

Alex quickly jumped out of the car, thinking he would go crazy if he had to sit still for another moment. He pulled the door open and burst in, leaving the door to slam shut on his friends.

Vickie was behind the counter on the phone. She looked surprised to see them, especially Alex, who was supposed to be home. She quickly ended her conversation, and walked over to the men, hugging each of them, then planting a firm kiss on Donovan's lips.

"Alex, I'm always happy to see you, but what are you doing out of bed?"

Donovan answered, "We couldn't keep him there, but intend on taking him back when he completes his errands for the day."

A look of confusion crossed Vickie's face.

Elliot continued the conversation, looking past Vickie. "We were commenting on the painting that Alex purchased here, and curious about where it came from."

Vickie stared intently at the trio, then walked over to the counter and pulled out a book. She scanned the pages for what seemed like forever to the men, before finally looking up. "The painting came from an estate sale." She put the book away and walked to Alex, who was now seated in a gold antique chair. "I bought several pieces from that sale. Unfortunately, I have little information about the original owners. I doubt it would be of any help to you. Most of the pieces have been sold, except for a table."

A look of disappointment crossed Alex's face, and he was

quiet for a moment. Then as her words began sinking in, the disappointment was replaced with encouragement. No one else would understand, but she said something he had desperately needed to hear. He smiled and turned to Vickie.

"Show me the table, and please get me all the information you have."

Vickie took the boys upstairs, speaking as she walked.

"Alex, I really don't think I have any information that would help. Sometimes when I buy from an estate sale, the facts on the original owners just aren't available. The pieces are not truly old enough to be considered valuable antiques, and I doubt the remaining family members from the last owners would have much to go on. Based on my experience, I would say it would be a waste of your time."

Donovan gave Vickie a strange look that said, "Don't ask any questions, just give him the information."

Vickie immediately shot Donovan back a look that said, "You'd better get your story straight, because you're going to have a lot of explaining to do."

Vickie pointed Alex in the direction of the table while she searched for the existing records. "It's over in the corner next to a sofa."

Alex didn't need to be told where it was. He was already walking directly to it. He didn't question how he knew. It didn't matter.

Elliot and Donovan watched in awe as he knelt down and lightly touched the beautiful designs carved into the oak.

Vickie walked into the room and couldn't refrain from asking what was happening. "What the hell is he doing?"

Alex was touching the round oak table and humming softly to himself.

Donovan was in total amazement and didn't answer her. Vickie waited a few moments for a response, and then slowly walked over to Alex, and knelt down next to him. "Alex, are you all right?"

Alex was looking sharply and closely at the table, continuing to hum a beautiful tune to himself.

Vickie spoke in a whisper, "Alex, can I help you with..." She stopped when she heard the melody. "Alex, what are you humming?"

Alex stopped and looked at Vickie as if she were a stranger. His voice was hoarse when he finally spoke. "Did you say something?"

Vickie felt as though she were being pulled into a spiraling tunnel. She asked the question again, more adamantly. "What the hell were you humming?"

Alex's trance continued. "Why do you want to know?"

Vickie could feel herself getting anxious. She pushed her red hair from her face and stood up defiantly. She wanted this visit to end.

"Alex, I don't know why the hell I want to know. Why can't you just tell me?"

Donovan saw the situation getting out of control. Both parties were on separate wavelengths. Vickie was not used to being out of control, and unable to explain herself. Alex was in his own dream state, not wanting to be bothered.

Donovan gently took Vickie's arm, moving her away from his friend.

"Honey, are there any other pieces you can show us from the estate?"

Elliot knelt beside Alex and waited. He heard Alex softly humming a tune. He slowly lifted his friend toward him, and walked him over to the nearby sofa.

Alex's eyes were red, and his face was pale. "My God, what happened?"

"You tell me. You were touching the table and humming. Scared the hell out of Vickie."

Alex tried not to smile. "I didn't think anything could scare the hell out of that woman."

The guys were laughing when Vickie and Donovan returned. Alex took Vickie's hand in his. "Are you OK? I didn't mean to frighten you."

Vickie lowered herself to Alex's eye level and looked closely at him. "Yeah, I'm OK. Donovan explained about the illness. I suppose it makes sense why you were acting a little odd."

The boys looked over as Donovan shrugged behind Vickie's back.

Vickie couldn't stop thinking about the tune in her head. "Alex, can you tell me what were you humming? I know the music, but it's driving me crazy. What was it?"

Alex's eyes brightened and focused on Vickie. "The song is called, 'Where or When.'" Alex touched her arm. "Why? Where do you know it from?"

Vickie closed her eyes, trying to remember. "I have no idea." She stood up and walked over to the counter, still shaking her head.

"This has been one very strange week, and I'll be glad when it's over."

Elliot followed her. "Vickie, did you find any information?"

Vickie handed Elliot a piece of paper. "I wrote down the name of the auction company, along with the name of the last owners. But, Elliot, if you want to track down where the painting originated from, then you may have your work cut out for you."

"That's OK, I'm willing to try." Alex hugged Vickie and continued. "I appreciate all your help and understanding with the confusion that I caused today. To make it up to you, I'd like to buy the table."

Vickie looked at Alex in astonishment. "You want to buy the table? Alex, it's an expensive piece, and I have no background on it. Are you sure?"

Alex laughed. "I don't care how much it costs. Can you have it delivered to my house?"

Alex's eyes suddenly fell on a gold frame, detailed in an

intricate lattice design, sitting on top of the oak table. When he felt a warmth flow through his body, he smiled. "I'll take the frame too. However, you don't mind if I take this with me, do you?"

Vickie looked at Donovan and saw him quietly shaking his head.

"OK, just give me a moment to prepare the paperwork. Are you sure you're all right?"

Alex took out his credit card. "I'm going to be just fine."

Alex was glad to be going home. He had a lot to think about, and his body was completely exhausted.

Elliot broke the silence on the drive home. "Poor Vickie. Donovan, you may have to answer a lot of questions when she finally calms down and realizes all the strange things she just witnessed."

Donovan laughed. "I had to come up with a quick story. It wasn't a complete lie. Alex is sick. I just embellished a little, and let her imagination take over." Donovan continued with a smile, "I did find perverse enjoyment in watching the woman I love become a little disoriented and confused. I've never seen her any way but cool, calm, and collected. For the first time since we met, Vickie actually didn't know what to say or do. It was nice to see she's human too."

Alex chuckled under his breath, "You're laughing about it now, but you just wait. Vickie is one of the most intelligent people I know. She's going to track you down for answers, and God pity you, if you don't have damn good ones."

Donovan and Elliot were laughing as Alex continued. "Think about what just happened. We barge into her store out of the blue, demanding information. She finds me hugging a table, while I assume you're both looking on unconcerned. I abruptly decide to make not one, but two purchases. Then, we just as quickly turn around and leave."

The laughter couldn't be contained. Their imaginations were playing the scene over and over in their minds, and it became funnier with each segment.

Donovan mumbled between gasps, "Yes, the look on Vickie's face was priceless. I can't figure out why she had such an obsession about the song though. That was weird."

When they arrived at Alex's home, a dedicated seriousness took hold as Donovan picked up a pen and paper and started the conversation.

"OK, based on what we witnessed in the gallery, it's safe to assume that the table and frame have something to do with the painting."

Alex was holding the frame tightly. "Yes, I would say so."

Elliot continued, "We have very little information about where the pieces came from. I think our next step would be to call the auction house and get whatever info they have on the previous owners, then contact them."

Both men watched as Alex rubbed the frame's ornate latticework.

Donovan spoke in a whisper. "Alex, what do you think?"

Alex continued polishing the frame, while answering, "Yeah, I say we make the call to see what we can find out. I'm ready."

Elliot noticed Alex's body was becoming listless. "Why don't you go take a nap? We'll make the calls."

Alex realized his exhaustion had caught up with him. Physically, he knew he had no business getting out of bed, but his soul felt refreshed, and that was all that mattered.

While Donovan began punching the numbers into the phone, Elliot helped Alex up the stairs. "We'll bring you something to eat as soon as we can. In the meantime, you rest and we'll take care of everything else."

"Elliot, what can I say?"

Elliot smiled, "Thank you will suffice."

Alex looked directly and firmly into his friend's eyes, "Elliot, thank you."

Elliot quietly closed the door behind him.

Alex lay on his side, looking out at the glittering waters in front of him. He pulled his new frame from the table beside him and hugged it. He closed his eyes and said a prayer of thanks as he drifted off to sleep.

After being counted up, Lauren focused on the ceiling for several minutes. Adriana was caught in her own thoughts, and didn't want to bother her. She came back to reality when Lauren reached over and touched her hand. "Thank you. It was difficult, painful, and I ache like hell, but I feel as though a weight has been lifted."

Adriana patted Lauren's hand. "I can't wait to get the ring back from the jewelers. Lauren, you did great. But I can see you're exhausted. I'll let myself out. You get some sleep and I'll call you in the morning."

Suddenly, Lauren was nervous when she found herself alone with her own thoughts. She continued to lie in the same position for a while, trying to establish what had taken place, but now with peace and a detached mind. She would listen to the recording tomorrow. She took a deep breath, feeling like she hadn't been this tired in months. It didn't take her long to remove her clothes and slide under the cool sheets. The moment she closed her eyes, sleep overtook her. There were no dreams tonight. Only peaceful, much needed rest.

Lauren awoke easily when the morning sun crossed her face. She glanced at the clock and immediately remembered what had transpired the evening before. She played it over in her mind before jumping out of bed, heading in a new direction. It was another day and she knew what she needed to do. She picked up the phone and called Adriana, grateful that her friend was home.

"Hi, it's me. Don't say a word until I've finished talking."

Lauren could almost hear Adriana smile as she answered, "Go ahead."

"OK, I would like for us to go back to Vickie's today. I want to insist that she locate any and all information pertaining to the ring and the music box. It's just a hunch, but it's something I'd like for us to do together. Hell, you're as much a part of this now as I am."

Adriana giggled, "And, Miss Lauren, how are you this morning?"

Lauren laughed, relieved that Adriana didn't think that she had lost her mind.

Adriana picked up her purse. "It just so happens that I was on my way out the door. I have a few errands to run first, and then why don't we go have lunch and head over to Marina Del Rey? I'll pick you up. Can you be ready in an hour?"

Lauren walked into her closet, searching for something to wear as they spoke. "Yeah, I'll be ready. See you soon."

She pushed the off button as she pulled a brown pair of pants off the hanger with a tug, then turned and tore a tan blouse off the cushioned rod. Lauren was in a hurry and gave little thought to whether everything matched. After showering and dressing, she finally paid attention to herself in the mirror. She was pleasantly surprised to see an alertness in her eyes that she hadn't seen before. Lauren was turning away from the mirror when she saw a blue flash in the corner of her eye. Then a faint vision of a woman reflected back at her. It took place quickly, but she knew it was the same face she had seen in her car mirror before.

Lauren was momentarily stunned, but quickly found her courage and turned to look directly into the glass. But the image was gone. She was staring into her own almond-shaped blue eyes.

"What happened? I know what I saw," she said half convincingly to no one but herself. Lauren spoke into the mirror in a stronger tone. "Please tell me who you are. Please tell me that you're real. I know I'm not going crazy. I can't be."

The only response that followed was the sound of her breathing. Lauren stared into the mirror for several seconds, then picked up her purse and walked downstairs. She was determined not to let the episode upset her. She walked into her office and straight to her desk without thinking. She needed to validate possession of the music box. To verify to herself that it was solid and able to be touched.

Lauren sat her purse on the table, and pushed herself into the chair. She gently slid the tips of her fingers over the hard rim, and softly hummed the tune that had played from the box the night before. She continued gliding her fingers over the intertwining artistry of the gold rings. Her fingers were methodically roaming from one to the other. The blue color of the box seemed to get deeper and deeper, and the delicately carved golden legs seemed to glow. Lauren was caught in the moment, swaying while she continued to hum the beautiful notes louder and louder. She was suddenly jolted back to reality by the honking of Adriana's horn. Without realizing what had transpired, Lauren picked up her purse and swiftly walked out into the open air.

"Hi, where have you been? I was about to come get you."

Lauren looked at her friend, a bit confused. "What are you talking about? I came out when I heard you honk."

Adriana returned the confused daze. "Lauren, I've been honking for the last five minutes."

Lauren looked over at her house, then back at Adriana, and then down at her fingers, and shrugged.

Adriana spoke up, "I know that shrug, Lauren. What the hell happened in there?" Adriana could see her friend trying to make sense of something.

"I believe that I saw a very faint, very quick glimpse of the woman again in the mirror. It was so fast, I don't even think I could describe her. But I know it was her."

"Are you OK?"

Lauren looked back at her house. "Yes, I suppose I'm all right. Afterwards, I went into my office and looked at my new music box." Lauren shrugged again. "That's all. Nothing else. I didn't even open the lid."

Adriana could sense Lauren getting uptight. "OK, don't worry about it." She quickly changed the subject, "Now tell me, my dear Watson, what's our caper today?"

Lauren released the tension and laughed. "Well, I woke up this morning, after having a complete night's sleep, thinking about where the ring and box came from. Vickie may have bought it from an auction house, but they had to get it from someplace, right?" Lauren turned her body toward Adriana in anticipation. "Do you see what I'm after here?"

Adriana knew, but wanted to hear it from Lauren. "Why don't you tell me?"

Lauren was eager to share her thoughts. "All right, remember when we were at Vickie's store?" Lauren didn't wait for a reply. "We asked her for the price of the box. She pulled out a book and looked at something before adding up the amount."

Adriana continued driving with her eyes fixed straight ahead. "Yeah, I remember. It took her a few minutes to locate the item."

Lauren smiled, "Yes!"

Adriana glanced over and timidly replied. "So?"

Lauren sighed loudly. "Adriana, all we have to do is get our hands on that book. If Vickie can't or won't help us locate the estate, there must be some kind of information from the auction house we can use. Maybe through that info, we can locate him."

Adriana didn't answer, so Lauren continued.

"I've got to do something. I can't stop now. I know without a doubt that he's out there. And he's probably searching for me too. This is the only place to begin."

Adriana sensed Lauren was getting upset. "OK, we'll try it and see what happens. It certainly can't hurt." To ease the tension, Adriana added jokingly, "Just don't get us thrown in jail. Promise me that we'll first ask nicely before we go sneaking around and taking information that doesn't belong to us." There was no response from the other side of the car. Adriana looked over and spoke sternly to her friend. "OK?"

Lauren smiled mischievously and nodded.

Adriana gave in, "OK, let's go to Vickie's first, then lunch."

A wide grin came over Lauren's face. "You're the best!"

Adriana smiled, agreeing, "Yeah, I know."

They pulled up to the storefront, and raced in, with the door slamming behind them. The noise brought Casey out from the back room. "Hi, can I help you?" Then she recognized the women and extended her hand. "What can I do for you both?"

Lauren shook Casey's hand warmly, "I need some information and thought I might have a word with Vickie."

Casey glanced at her watch. "Vickie had an appointment on the other side of town. I'm not sure when to expect her back."

She could see the look of discouragement come over the women's faces. "Is there something I can help you with?"

Adriana thought for a moment and smiled, "I'm sure you can."

She began dramatically detailing a story about how Lauren loved antiques and art. She weaved a web that finally made Lauren have to walk away for fear she would burst out laughing. In the distance, she could hear her friend tell Casey how important it was for Lauren to have as much information as possible for her own peace of mind. She explained how these pieces came alive in Lauren's mind.

She left Casey wide-eyed, looking for any and all information she could find on the pieces Lauren had purchased.

Lauren strolled past the smiling Adriana, and whispered into her ear, "My friend, you're pathetic."

Adriana burst out in laughter and had Lauren take over.

Lauren walked over to where Casey was busy searching through a book behind a counter. She noticed it was the same book Vickie had taken the price from. Lauren tried desperately to push her body over the counter to read upside down.

She was about to lose her balance, when Casey looked up and smiled. "Yes, Miss Wells, I have a little information here."

Lauren quickly regained her composure, and put on her best

performance. "Do you have the name of the seller?" She continued, "I really need that name." Lauren couldn't have sounded more desperate had it been about her own child.

Casey looked at the woman oddly, but realized most of their clients were a little eccentric. She assumed Lauren was no different.

"I have the name of the auction company. They should have the information you're requesting. I'll be happy to give you their number."

Adriana overheard the plea and decided to take control of the downhill situation. She knew it was likely the auction house would not give confidential information to anyone except the dealer.

"Casey, it would be very kind of you to call them for us. You know the information we need." Casey was pleased to help; she had clients that expected much more. Adriana put her hand on her friend's arm. "Why don't we go sit down while Casey makes her call."

Lauren looked at Adriana as if she had lost her mind. She smiled warmly, and squeezed the hand that lay on her arm. "No, I think I'll stay right here."

Adriana saw the determination in Lauren's eyes and knew they would both stand in front of Casey and listen.

Lauren nonchalantly glanced down and memorized the name and phone number of the auction house. She didn't know how far to push Casey. She genuinely liked the girl. Lauren was brought back to reality when she overheard Casey saying thank you and hanging up the phone. She knew Casey had struck gold by the look on her face.

She eagerly handed Lauren a yellow piece of paper that had writing scribbled over the entire sheet. Casey went over the information proudly with Lauren and Adriana. "I spoke to the secretary of the president at the auction house. It took her a while, but she managed to locate a few records." She shrugged and continued, "I apologize that we couldn't find out more for you, but maybe this will be of some help."

Adriana looked over Lauren's shoulder, read the paper, and smiled. "Yes Casey, this will work nicely. You've been a great help."

The girls didn't speak until they were back in Adriana's car.

Then Lauren couldn't contain herself. "God, that was fun. Where did you come up with that crap about me?"

Adriana laughed out loud, "It worked, didn't it? I knew if Casey called the auction house herself, they would ask fewer questions and give a lot more information."

Lauren looked over the paper again. "Is this enough to go on?"

Adriana smiled, "It's a start, and it's more than we had an hour ago. Let's go have lunch and decide what we're going to do next."

Donovan tapped the pads of his fingers on the desk, and felt as if he had been holding the receiver for hours. He had pretended to be an employee at Vickie's gallery, and got through to the auction house with no trouble. He was quickly transferred to the proper station, but he had been waiting ever since. Finally, a young woman with an Italian accent came on the line and quickly gave him the information he had requested.

Donovan hung up and walked toward Elliot, waving a piece of paper. "We've got it."

Elliot snapped the paper from him. "Is this the address where the property came from?"

Donovan was proud of himself, "Yeah, along with the name. I said I worked for Vickie."

Elliot looked at the page again. "It's across the country. Do you think Alex will want to go?"

Donovan picked up the phone and began punching in numbers. "There's no doubt. I'll call my travel agent and arrange it."

Elliot spoke behind him as he started upstairs. "Go ahead and book all three of us."

"Will do."

Elliot tiptoed into Alex's room, just as he opened his eyes. "Hi, I must have fallen asleep. Is everything OK? Have I missed anything?"

Elliot laughed, "Everything's fine. I came up to see if you were awake. How are you feeling?"

Alex fluffed a pillow under his neck. "I'm a little weak, but I feel much better. My appetite is definitely back."

Elliot picked up the frame lying next to Alex. "How would you like to take a trip?"

Alex sat up erect and smiled. "Did you guys actually find something? Did you find out who originally owned the pieces?"

Elliot handed the lattice frame back to Alex and sat down on the bed. "We found where the items came from, but only as far back as the most recent owners. But on the bright side, we do have more to go on now. So, are you ready for a trip?"

There was a new sparkle in Alex's eyes. "You bet I am. How soon can I go?"

"You mean how soon can we go?"

Alex sat up straighter and crossed his legs. "Are you going with me?"

"Donovan and I are both going with you. Donovan is downstairs making the arrangements. Hell, we wouldn't miss this for anything."

Alex chuckled. "I admit I didn't want to go through it alone."

They heard Donovan walking up the stairs and waited until he was in the room to speak. Donovan handed Alex the sheet of paper.

"Is this where we're going?"

"Yep, our adventure begins first thing tomorrow morning. But for today, you need to continue getting rest."

Alex stood up, wobbled, and decided it was easier to sit back down. "What you see in front of you is not a man weak from illness. What you see is a man weak from hunger."

When his door was closed, Alex read the address where his precious items had come from as he hugged the frame. "There is such a place. You did have a home before this one." Alex closed his eyes and prayed a word of thanks, along with a request. "Please have the answers for me. And help me find what I need to make my life complete." He instinctively knew he was going in the right direction. "Next stop, Connecticut."

Alex closed his eyes once more and slept. This time, he was not alone. He found himself in a meadow overlooking a large bay. The cool wind was whipping about him, making him hug his arms tightly around himself. He wasn't sure where he was, but he sensed it was familiar territory. He could see his elderly counselor approaching from over his shoulder. Her gray hair was blowing in the wind. She was wearing an old beige shawl covering her frail looking, yet strong shoulders.

The bottom fringe was dancing in the wind around her.

He turned around and walked toward her, meeting her with a smile. "I'm so glad you're here to join me in my journey. Where am I?"

The old woman looked deeply in his eyes, and spoke with a question, "Tell me, Alex, where are you? Look around. Is this place familiar?"

Alex took a deep breath, letting the air out slowly. He felt this was a test and he was about to fail. He waited as long as he could. "No, I don't know where I am. It feels good here. But no, I don't know this place."

His elderly guide passed him, walking toward the water. Alex followed behind her. He looked slowly around him in a weary attempt to detect anything that might spark a memory. His head was starting to ache, and frustration was beginning to build. He noticed his guide's shawl wrapped tightly around her small body. His mind was temporarily focused on the wind whipping through her hair. *So much love coming from her. So much energy. She reminds me of my grandmother, but she's not. She's the same, yet she's different.* He didn't realize the correlation.

She turned around to face him. "Alex, please don't let frustration work against you. Are you too close to the situation to see with your heart? To see with your soul? Look outwardly with your eyes, but see with your soul. Sometimes you must pretend to be a blind man."

Alex shook his head in total confusion. *Why do I not understand anything being said to me? It all makes sense but...*

She touched his chest with her knobby, right index finger. "You are so well advanced, and know so much. But when frustration takes over your emotions, you refuse to listen to your heart. You lose your essence and immediately turn to what your eyes can only see, and what your mind tells you are so."

Her right hand moved towards Alex's brow as she covered his eyes, revealing only darkness. He didn't know how she could take away all the light by just putting her frail hand over his eyes.

He suddenly heard her crackled voice from above him. "Alex, turn your focus inward." She was quiet for a moment.

Alex was confused, not knowing where to focus his attention. With no light, he could hear the wind howling in his ears, and the blades of grass lashing out at each other in a frenzy. He didn't know what to listen to, or what to block out.

Her voice was now directly in front of him and much stronger. "Alex, you are not trying. Please, son, ground yourself and focus."

Alex turned inward, and suddenly a harmony prevailed. The winds stopped blowing, and he could now perceive a slight hum emitting from within himself. Alex delved further, going deeper. He felt her soft hands lightly massaging his temples. He was sliding further and further within. The humming turned into the music he had played on his piano the night before. It seemed to be coming to him from a distance. He heard his voice aloud. "It's coming through the breeze from within."

He felt her crooked fingers relax around his forehead. "I see a house in the distance. I know this house."

The old woman spoke very softly, "Alex, what else do you see? Remember, don't look with your eyes."

Alex inhaled a deep breath of cleansing air. He knew he could do this. He had done it many times, but had forgotten because of the turmoil within. He knew that he must eliminate the turmoil to be able to see what was real. Not what was made externally with the human eyes.

"I feel the house holds many treasures for me." Alex gasped and tried to describe what he was seeing. "The house! It's shifting like slides on a projector. I saw a large wooden house, then it turned into a small cabin, then a large brick mansion, then it changed into a castle, and back to a shanty house." Alex shook his head in confusion. "I can't keep up. It's the same house, yet different."

His guide was now on the other side of his head, whispering into his ear. "Alex, all these houses belong to you. All these houses are you. You reside within. Which home do you want for your soul?"

She continued, "You seek what was lost to you. What you said you would come back for. But know your home first. Locate your home." She was suddenly speaking from behind him. "Your frustration will only take you further and further away from where you belong. Don't look and see with your eyes. They will deceive you. They will test you."

Alex intuitively knew to open his eyes. He and his guide were surrounded by a bright beautiful aura of white light. Alex blinked several times to get his bearings. The old woman continued speaking as if nothing had happened.

"Alex, your heart is open. Now allow common sense and intuition to come in and prevail. Go beyond the obvious."

She stood face to face with Alex, staring hard into his eyes. When she spoke, he felt her words deep within his own being.

"You will both need to trust the realities of the situation. You're almost across the bridge. Trust yourself and your instincts to put one foot in front of the other. She's walking her path too, and must also trust her instincts. You'll one day meet on the other side of the bridge."

Alex looked into the gentle brown eyes of his guide. "Is that it? Is that all you're going to tell me? Will it be in this lifetime, or another?"

The brown eyes smiled in return. "Alex, sometimes you are very insecure with your own thoughts." Shaking her head in mock amazement, she continued, "My goodness, you have been navigating your life successfully for lifetimes. Why are you so uncertain now?"

He looked towards the ground, ashamed of himself for questioning his own abilities. He knew what he was capable of doing. He had worked hard to learn to trust himself and his instincts. He knew it was the same as always, but somehow it felt so different.

"Maybe it's because I know this is so important. I know I've only been given a glimpse of the person who owns the other half of my soul. I don't want to waste another moment lost from her. But I realize I don't have total control of the situation. I own the other half of her soul as well, and she must find me too." Alex hugged himself tighter. He sensed and knew that he was indeed a much-loved child in his guide's presence. "I am so afraid she'll give up before finding me."

He felt his guide's fingers slide into his long, dark hair and pull him forward to be hugged against her bosom. She was whispering to him. "Sh-h-h-h, there, there." Alex realized he was crying.

"I don't cry from frustration, as much as I cry from fear."

She pushed him to arm's length, and then took a good look at him. He thought of his grandmother again. He remembered she would do this when she wanted his full attention. "Alex, you are well aware of what your capabilities are. No one needs to remind you of that. I am advising you to continue looking inside of yourself, and don't trust your eyes. Do what feels right. Stay inside that place where you were a few minutes ago. Remember what that place feels like. Go there anytime you need an answer. Feel yourself sliding deeper and deeper into where your soul is housed. It will never lie to you. This is where I live as well."

Alex suddenly blinked with new eyes. He finally realized what the old woman had been trying to tell him. He finally understood where his answers would come from. He finally realized the situations would always be different, but the answers were always the same, if you knew where to look in your house. If you were familiar with your home, you could get to any room. Even when it was the darkest, you instinctively knew the way.

She smiled and replied to his thoughts, "Alex, you've always known this. You've used it most every day of your life. You lost your way when you trusted your eyes to 'think' about it."

There was a knock in the distance, and Alex heard a door open. The smell of food entered his nostrils, and he opened his eyes. He slowly scanned the room, surprised when he found himself back in his own bed.

Donovan was standing over him holding a tray. "Alex, where have you been?"

Alex smiled. "Oh, just traveling to familiar territory, that's all. Now, bring on the food. God, I'm starving."

Lauren and Adriana were sitting in a waterfront café overlooking the Pacific coastline on Manhattan Beach, discussing their plans. Lauren was worried. "How soon can we both get away?" They had their calendars sprawled out on the table. "The ring should be ready tomorrow. I'm anxious to have it back in my possession." Lauren tapped the pencil on the table as she continued in a hurried tone. "My curiosity is getting the better of me. What's going to happen if the inscription is different to what I saw?" Lauren took a deep breath and continued, "Or, what if it's actually the same? Either way, I don't know how I'll react."

Adriana smiled from across the table, pulling her light

strawberry-colored hair from her face. Her green eyes were squinting from the bright sunlight flowing through the open-aired window.

"Lauren, I'd be willing to bet what you read in the ring during your dream will be the same as what the inscription reads now. It's just too crazy for it not to be real. You were very certain about this while under hypnosis. In fact, you were amazed at the discovery."

Changing the subject, Adriana pulled her cell phone from her purse and flipped it open. "I'm going to call Mark and find out when I can leave. As it is, he probably thinks I've already deserted him. Let me straighten out my plans, then we'll phone Kevin and convince him you've been kidnapped for a few days." Adriana exaggerated a deep breath and continued. "Then we're going to call the travel agency to book our reservations to Connecticut."

While Adriana made her obligatory calls, Lauren sat back and sipped her tea. Her mind transferred back to a few nights earlier. She could almost see the scene floating in front of her. She could feel the perseverance of the two energies trying to determine what their focus was. And the confusion that took place when they finally discovered what was happening. *Why the ring, of all things?* She could sense the frustration mounting in each of their souls. She could sense his emotions the same as her own, because he also possessed her.

Lauren's eyes were focused on the bottom of the near-empty teacup, her mind swimming among its murky water. She realized her emotions were on the edge, but had no idea how to calm them down. She was grateful for Adriana. *She's the grounding force keeping me afloat.* Lauren knew she had to put everything she had ever learned to the test. She understood that she would need to remember to trust herself, and it frightened her. *If I don't play it just right, I'm afraid that I'll lose whatever this is, for a very, very long time.*

She heard Adriana calling her name, and was suddenly hurled back to the present.

"Lauren, come back to this reality, and let's plan our next

move.

"Mark will cover me until I return. God, I don't know what I would do without him. Thank goodness he loves that store as much as I do." Adriana placed her index fingers to her temples and spoke in an accent. "I see a big bonus coming to him."

Lauren grinned appreciatively, and took the phone from Adriana. "It's my turn. I hope Kevin doesn't want to dissolve our partnership. Maybe I should have a glass of wine first." Then she laughed at her thoughts. "No, maybe he needs the glass of wine first."

Adriana put her hand on top of Lauren's. "Why don't you tell Kevin what's going on? You know he'd understand. And he would be a hell of a lot more willing to assist you."

Lauren was about to protest, but Adriana continued, "You have no idea where this may lead you. Don't you want to be mentally up for it, instead of worrying about your work? Kevin has always been there for you. For God's sake, you're his idol. He would never do anything to keep you from being happy."

Lauren sat the phone down on the table and took a sip of tea. "You're right. It's not fair of me to keep this from him. He and I are as close as siblings. He knows there's something going on, and I know he's very worried about me."

Lauren picked the phone up and punched in the store's number. She smiled when she heard his deep voice on the other end.

"Lauren's Place, how may I help you?"

"Hi, Kev, it's me, you know...Lauren?"

Adriana burst out laughing.

Kevin did the same before answering. "Yes, Lauren, I know it's you. Are you all right? You sound like you've been drinking. Where are you?"

This time it was Lauren's turn to laugh out loud, breaking her tension. "I'm having lunch with Adriana. And no, Kevin, I haven't been drinking, although I've certainly given it some thought."

Before Kevin had the opportunity to respond, Lauren continued, "I need to discuss some important matters with you. There are things happening with me right now, and I'm begging for your complete understanding and support."

Kevin interrupted, "Lauren, you know you have that even before you confide in me. I know you've been going through hell lately. I'm not certain it all has to do with you and Gary. And it doesn't matter. What can I do to help?"

Lauren looked over at Adriana with misty eyes. "Kevin, I don't know how, or what I did to deserve friends like you and Adriana. I promise if you support me right now, I will owe you forever." Lauren took a deep breath as Kevin waited. "Kevin, can you work for me a little while longer? I want to see you tonight and explain everything, but I need to hear you tell me that it's OK for me to be away for a while."

Kevin's voice responded with a sound of concern. "Lauren, I don't know what you're doing, but of course I want to come over tonight." She could hear Kevin's voice soften. "Sweetie, you know you can do whatever you need to do. You don't need my permission."

Kevin reminded Lauren of a time when he had gone through a major lesson in his own life. "You were there for me without questions or demands. I owe you my life. You helped me see who I really was, and how much I was worth. You helped to eliminate the pain. So please, do whatever you need to do. I'll be right beside you, no matter what. We'll get some more help in here. So, don't worry."

Lauren felt relief as she put the thumbs up to Adriana.

"But, Kevin, what about Mr. Ramsey and the bank, and the new store?"

Kevin responded with calmness and confidence. "Don't worry about any of those things. I'll take care of it. And if I run into any snags, you're just a phone call away. This isn't going to be a problem, so don't worry. I'll be at your house tonight at 8:00. We'll talk then."

Lauren kissed the receiver, the smacking sound entering Kevin's ear. "Kevin, that will be perfect. Just come with an open mind. It's going to be tested."

Kevin laughed, "I can't wait for this."

Lauren hung up the phone, and let out a big sigh. "Call the travel agent."

Lauren knew she couldn't control this phase of the journey, and fidgeted until her friend had hung up the phone. She was about to jump out of her skin with anticipation. "OK, tell me when we're going, and what we're going to do when we get there."

Adriana couldn't help but tease her by picking up her sandwich and taking a huge bite from it, aiming her focus directly into Lauren's eyes.

Lauren produced a deviant look, as she took her knife and tapped it lightly on the table. "Adriana, stop that and talk to me!"

Adriana swallowed and took a sip of her tea, before firmly removing the knife from Lauren's hand.

"OK, first you're going to eat lunch, then you're going home to pack. We're on our way to Connecticut tomorrow, early afternoon."

Lauren grinned, causing her blue eyes to glisten, lighting up her entire face. "Oh my God, it's happening. We're going someplace that actually exists. I can't wait to see what we find."

Adriana picked up her sandwich. "Yes, it's going to be quite a journey."

Chapter 10

Alex ate like he had been starving for days. His energy was returning, and his anticipation was mounting.

"Did you guys find a place for us to stay in Connecticut?" He didn't wait for a response. "I've traveled all over the world, but strangely enough, I've never been to Connecticut."

Alex was starting his second helping when Donovan spoke up, "I've been there several times. I used to take side trips from my travels to New York. It's been many years, but I'm sure it's still a terrific place."

Elliot completed the conversation with facts. "We'll arrive tomorrow in the afternoon. I've got us booked at The Willows."

Donovan spoke up, "I've stayed there before. It's a wonderful resort with all the amenities."

Elliot walked into the hall, returning with a suitcase. "Why don't we get you packed? Donovan, why don't you run home, make your calls, pack your things, and meet me back here? When you return, I'll go pick up a few of my things, and take care of my business."

Donovan snapped his finger and pointed it toward Elliot. "Don't you just love this guy, Alex? He's as organized as anyone could be." Donovan picked up his keys, and headed toward the front door. "I'll be back in a few hours. "

Alex laughed. "I feel so damn helpless. Why don't you guys let me do something?"

Donovan stuck his head in the door. "Hey, you are helping.

You're the one who started this crusade. You're the one making all this possible. We haven't done anything this crazy in a long time." Shaking his head, Donovan continued, "No, you just rest. You'll be more help to us healthy."

Elliot was pulling sweaters from the bottom drawer of Alex's dresser. "He's got a point. You just lie there and behave yourself. Trust me, you'll have your hands full soon enough."

While Alex finished his soup, he watched his friend pack. "Elliot, how often do you communicate with your guides, or higher self? Do you communicate only when you meditate?"

Elliot stopped his work and sat in the chair across from Alex.

Alex noticed the sun shining in Elliot's dark eyes.

"No, I don't only communicate when I meditate. Sometimes during sleep, an ongoing communication will occur. I find that when I'm stressed or when I need answers, I tend to be able to reach that state quicker. Meditating and prayer has taught me how to access them at any time. Sometimes, even when I'm reading a book or watching television, I access them. The more you do it, the easier it becomes." He cocked his head to one side and questioned, "Why do you ask? You already know all of this."

Alex heard the wind begin to blow, and the chimes outside began to sing their song to the breeze. "When I slept earlier, my guide came into my dreams. She's come many times before, but this time it was much more profound. I sensed there were lessons I needed to learn."

Elliot stood up and removed the bed tray. "You've had a lot on your mind. Sounds to me like the vibrations are intensifying. What did she have to say? What did she want you to learn?"

Alex looked over to his friend. "We were in a meadow. First there was a house. Then there were many houses. But nothing seemed familiar, or responded to my memory. I was getting frustrated, and my guide was asking me questions that I couldn't answer."

Elliot interrupted his words, "You have questions that have no absolute answers. You have to make up the answers as you go along. There's no outside source to look to, no book to read. You must go within yourself and listen."

Alex glared at Elliot, then softened his gaze. "Damn, Elliot. That's exactly what she was trying to get across to me. Why couldn't I see it? And why am I having such a difficult time accessing and trusting myself? That hasn't been a problem in the past."

Elliot sat down at the end of the bed. "Because you've never had reason not to trust your instincts. That's how you live. That's how Donovan and I live. We trust the process. I can't say I wouldn't hesitate if I were in your shoes. As far as you're concerned, there's a lot at stake. Based on the physical evidence, there have been more questions than answers. You're walking blindly into the unknown. That would frighten even the strongest of us mere mortals. This is the time when you most need to trust the internal process. It's easy to do when there's nothing at stake. The best way to learn that trust is in the beginning, on minor issues. So when the significant ones come around, and they always do, you'll be prepared. But even then, you may have to jump into the void and do nothing more than simply trust. Pretty scary, huh."

Alex closed his eyes and ran his long fingers through his thick dark hair. "I find it especially difficult because I'm not the only one responsible for the outcome of this dream. If I were alone, I may be better able to access the answers. But as it is, I feel as though I must second guess someone I don't know, and have never met."

Elliot walked to the balcony door, then turned and looked back at Alex. The sunlight shown around his body in an aura of pale yellow.

"But that may be where you're losing ground. What if you don't need to worry about what the other heart and soul are doing? Suppose you just trust they know their way. Trust they know their house, just the same as you should already know yours."

Alex's eyes widened in amazement. "Elliot, how do you know

about the house? Do you know about the rooms, too?"

Elliot laughed out loud. "Alex, I only know the rooms in my house. And sometimes the furniture changes and I bump into something I'm not expecting. It's during those times when I try to remember the room is still in the same locality, in the same house. The only thing different is the placement of the furniture. I can walk it in darkness if I need to. But if you don't go to your house and get the feel of your rooms, then when it's the darkest, you won't find your way."

Alex continued staring in disbelief at his friend. "So you're saying I need to know my house and my rooms while the light is shining, so that when it does get dark, I can walk through and know where I am."

Elliot picked up a blanket off the floor. "See, Alex. You're not so dumb."

Alex blinked a few times and ran his hands through his hair again. "I've known you all these years, but I'm still finding out new things about you."

Elliot walked into Alex's bathroom and began taking items out of the cabinet for packing. "I feel the same about you. But you see? That just means we're both still growing. The new is always exciting."

He stopped for a moment and looked at Alex, who was still staring back at him in disbelief. "We're all in this together. There's a reason for it. I feel it. I believe it. So while you're learning, we are too. Do you understand?"

Alex smiled and lay back down. "I believe I couldn't do this without you or Donovan. I believe there are still a few more things to learn. And I pray I have the foresight to see ahead before I run into that real heavy piece of furniture."

Elliot laughed, "Yeah, that's when we receive our ugliest bruises."

But Alex never heard him. He had already drifted back to sleep. He wanted to get his energy back for the upcoming journey.

Lauren and Adriana completed their meal and drove back to Lauren's house in a hurry. Adriana looked straight ahead as she spoke softly, "When I drop you off, do whatever it is that you need to do. I'll meet you at your place tomorrow at noon. By the time we get to Connecticut and settled in to our hotel, the day will be gone."

Lauren turned the music down in the car. "What hotel did the travel agent book us into?"

Adriana pulled into Lauren's driveway and put the gear into park.

"I'm not sure. I'll go by there on the way to my store. She arranged for a car at the airport, too. Hopefully, we'll get there, do what we do best, and then get back before we're even missed."

Lauren opened the car door, then hugged Adriana. "Yeah, if this goes as planned, we can wrap this thing up and be back in no time. Hopefully with a positive outcome." Lauren looked back at Adriana. "Do you think we're doing the right thing? Is this what I'm supposed to be doing? I mean going off to another city looking for my knight in shining armor?"

Adriana stepped out of her car and took Lauren's hand, holding it tight. "Lauren, I think you're doing what you've taught yourself to do. And that is to act instinctively. If you were to pull out your journals and read everything you've written since all of this began, you would see a pattern emerging. You're simply doing what you feel you should do. Don't stop trusting that inner voice now."

Lauren looked down at the pavement below her. "But I'm not as confident as I look. I realize that I'm not the only one navigating these waters. There's someone else out there. I sure hope so anyways. And I sure hope he knows how to steer." She looked up with tears in her worried blue eyes. "What happens if he's steering in another direction? What the hell do I do then?"

Adriana hugged her friend tightly to her chest. "Lauren, I want you to go inside yourself. It's important that you find your center. Then ask for help and guidance. Trust that what you feel and hear will be your truth. You can't make him walk your path. You can only walk your own. If you listen and follow the signs, you will cross paths in time. Just be centered and focused." Lauren looked up at her friend's confident eyes as Adriana continued. "You know how to do it. You've worked hard on this process most of your life. And don't think for a moment that I won't be there cheering you on. If this were not meant to be, you would have stopped long ago. But the signs are pointing you in a direction. Don't doubt yourself, because when you doubt your inner self, then you doubt the whole process."

Lauren touched her friend's light-colored cheek. "Thank you. I love you so much. Don't ever forget that."

Adriana opened her car door. "I won't forget. See you tomorrow. Now you go in and get yourself centered, and do what you have to do before Kevin arrives." With a wave, she drove off.

Lauren stood watching her friend until she was out of sight. She knew that she was stalling, afraid to go inside. She heard her mind speak sternly. *Come on, Lauren, don't just stand here. You have too many plans to make, and too many issues to think about. So, get on with it.* Lauren took a deep breath and opened her front door.

She thought to herself how very quiet it was. She could hear the faint ticking of her grandfather clock. She could hear the chimes dancing in the wind outside on her patio. Yet she felt such stillness. So much stillness it bothered her. She forced herself to walk into her office, and saw the light blinking on her answering machine. She automatically took her shoes off and pressed the play button at the same time. The machine advised her of two new messages. She fell into her leather chair, and waited for the next words to flow from the machine.

The first was from Gary. "Hi, Lauren, just wanted you to know that I have to go to Europe for a week or so. I'll call you when I return. Call my secretary if you need anything. She'll know how to contact me." He paused for a moment, and then continued in a quiet voice, "I hope you're OK. I think we made a lot of progress in our last conversation. And I will abide by my promise to sign whatever papers you want. Just because we're ending our marriage doesn't mean we're ending our friendship, too. Thanks, Lauren. I'll talk to you next week. Bye." And the phone silently clicked off the connection.

Lauren felt a sense of loss and relief at the same time. She could still hear Gary's voice, and she felt responsible to him as a wife.

She shook her head, reminding herself that she was only his wife in name, and even that wouldn't be for much longer. "It's for the best." She knew they would both be happier. She was already feeling a sense of relief, and the pain was lessening each day.

Then the second call started and her focus dramatically changed. "Miss Wells, this is Cohn's Jewelry." Lauren's eyes shot in the direction of the machine. "We'll have your merchandise ready for pick up at 9:00 tomorrow morning. I know you were anxious to get it back. I hope to see you then. Thank you, bye."

Lauren continued staring at the machine, even though it had signaled no other messages.

"My God, tomorrow's going to be a big day." She felt renewed strength enter her veins. She glanced at the music box sitting isolated on the desk, and automatically opened the lid. She sat back in her chair and closed her eyes. The music instantly relaxed her as she melted into the seat and slept.

Lauren was observing herself watching a screen. On the screen was a woman who looked remarkably like herself. It was early afternoon, and she was standing on a beach. The waves were crashing in around her. She looked up to see the full moon blossoming, filling the sky with unusual brightness. She saw herself turn and look behind at the tall hills rising to the height of the sky. She took the time to gaze at the hills and saw they were dotted sparsely with green trees, and a touch of brown from the desert grounds. Turning back around, she looked closely at the blue ocean, watching a small sailboat floating away in the distance. She noticed the light brown shoreline weaving in and out of the water, as the tides continued their continuous forward and retreating journey. The ocean smelled fresh and clean. She couldn't take her eyes away from the scene, or off herself. The rumble from the ocean waves began reaching a high pitch, and she was forced to put her hands over her ears. *It's so loud, I can't hear myself think.*

Suddenly, a large black stone formation stood in front of her, glistening and shiny from the salt-water spray. The stone was flat on one side, with a smooth carved surface resembling a chair facing the ocean. She automatically walked around the boulder and sat down.

Lauren watched the woman on the screen with a sense of awe and confusion. She knew the large rock hadn't been there moments earlier. She watched as the wind savagely whipped her dress all about her, but was surprised to see her hair was laying still on her shoulders. She could hear nothing but the persistently steady sound of the ocean's roar. Lauren watched closely as she saw herself sit down and take a deep breath. How she wished the noise would stop. It was beginning to sound like a train thundering through her head. Lauren watched herself look up at the intensely bright moon, and then back down to the tiny sailboat drifting away from her in the distance. She felt a need to advise the dark-haired woman. She wanted to tell her how to find peace from the awful noise, but she could do nothing but observe.

The pretty woman on the screen closed her eyes and took several deep breaths. Lauren was in awe, and watched as the woman began chanting a familiar sound. Suddenly, the noise around her stopped. There was a beautiful peacefulness she had not experienced before.

Lauren saw the woman smile. She had found a way to conquer the noise pollution from within. She felt a steady vibrational flow coming from somewhere within, much like the purring sound of a cat. Lauren slowly began to realize she was watching herself, but feeling all the sensations the woman on the beach was feeling. Her frame of mind went from curiosity to total astonishment. She noticed the dress had stopped billowing in the wind. The ocean was still bludgeoning the sands, but Lauren no longer let it affect her. She was deep within, and could hear or see nothing except what was inside, far beyond the exterior.

Lauren was so immersed in watching herself on the screen that she jumped when an elderly man suddenly appeared from nowhere. She smiled warmly when she recognized him. Lauren looked closely at the gentleman standing on the beach. He reminded her so much of her wonderful, loving father. Lauren was transfixed on the screen, oblivious to everything around her. She had spoken to him so many times, but had just actually seen him for the first time a few nights ago. Now in front of her, he stood tall and proud, looking so wise and confident. He looked as if he would know the answer to all of the questions in the universe. She watched him touch the dark-haired woman's head. Lauren saw herself open her arms and hug the man. She felt total peace surround her being. These two people were like one. She listened as the conversation began.

"Hello, Lauren. I'm pleased to see you've remembered how to calm the stormy waters and stop the howling from within your mind."

Lauren looked up at the man and smiled. "Yes, although it took me a few attempts. I was getting frustrated and kept losing my focus. I know I should be able to close my eyes and instantly go down to my place, but I get scattered and lose all concentration."

When he smiled, Lauren could actually see the unconditional love emitting from him. It was nothing he had to say that convinced her. It was more of an aura that spread from him, to encompass and shelter her. She knew there was nothing she could do or say to this man that would stop his devotion to her. She could trust him completely.

"Lauren, I know you're learning many lessons right now. And

there is so much frustration entering your heart. This is the time to show your warrior self. Overcome the need to react and pull back. You must charge ahead, knowing in your heart and soul the path you're walking is the correct way to your destiny. We all have our own truths, and we know there are universal truths we must follow as well. Lauren, integrate the two, and make them one and the same. Trust that you know the process. Swim down to your place of light, and learn to live there. As the night gets darker around you, light the candle from within, and continue the journey. If you begin to lose your confidence, pretend it's still strong. And somewhere along the path, you will realize that you are no longer pretending. The signs will guide your way. But the secret is finding that dwelling within. And know that dwelling as well as you know tomorrow is a new day."

Lauren watched herself looking up into his eyes with the same lack of confidence that she had felt earlier. "How do I do that?"

He smiled warmly. "When it rains outside, do you get discouraged?"

She looked at him perplexed. "That's a strange question. No, I don't get discouraged. I happen to enjoy the rain."

He placed his hand on top of her head again. "And why do you not get discouraged?"

She closed her eyes and thought for a moment. "I suppose because I know another day will come, the sun will return, and the birds will sing. I enjoy those days too." She opened her eyes and continued, "I detach from the fact it's raining, or the sun is shining. I find joy in just being able to take pleasure from it. If it rains, I carry an umbrella. If the sun is out, I wear sunshades. I'm always prepared, whether it's dark outside or light. That way, I can enjoy 'what is', and not worry or dread the little things. That's what makes life so much fun. You never know what surprises are in store from day to day."

His eyes gleamed with pride. "Lauren, how do you achieve this?"

Lauren closed her eyes again, still a little confused by the question. "I don't know how I do it. It's just instinctively done every day." She believed every word she was saying, but didn't know where it was coming from.

He hugged her close. "Well, don't you think you should instinctively learn to be as prepared on the inside as you are on the outside?"

She was about to interrupt with a question, but he put his finger to her mouth and continued, "So when your rain falls, or when your sun shines, you aren't unprepared. You know instinctively what to do, where to go, and which path to walk."

Lauren watched herself slowly stand and face the wise man. "You mean like the way I just controlled the noise from the winds and ocean inside my head?"

He took her hand in his. "Precisely. You've always had the knowledge, and you've used it many times. Now, when it's needed the most, don't give up on your abilities. Know it's there, just like the sun and the rain. And be happy for whatever comes your way, because you are prepared."

Lauren was transfixed on the screen, even as she felt tears stinging her eyes.

"It's so simple. Why do we make it difficult? With a little work, any of us can access all the information needed. Why can't we see that?"

The woman was sitting on the dark stone again, facing the ocean waters. She turned to her guide, thanking him for the reminder. "I've just got to work a little harder at trusting myself. Until I no longer have to work at it. One day, it will just be automatic." She smiled at him and continued, "Just please tell me whether I'm going in the right direction to find him."

The old man looked deep into her blue eyes and smiled so warmly, her heart wanted to burst from pure love.

"You know your way, Lauren. Trust that the signs and paths will cross."

She looked at him sharply. "In this lifetime or another?"

He walked behind her and whispered in her ear. "Lauren, place your trust in your own soul. Don't be frightened to do this."

Lauren watched as the woman on the screen turned to ask another question, only to see the man was gone. She couldn't understand how he had vanished. She blinked and he had disappeared from her screen. She focused on the woman, expecting to see a reaction. The woman didn't seem perplexed by it, and instead she continued gazing at the small sailboat in the distance. Her mind was detached. She was training herself to listen.

Lauren blinked again and saw him approaching. She wanted to run to him, but the screen prevented her from doing so. They had not seen each other since that confusing time a few nights earlier. Lauren felt she would burst from all the love possessing her. She desperately needed to be inside the screen. She wanted him to see her. Somewhere in the distance, she heard herself take a deep breath, then serenely watched the story unfold.

He was approaching the woman sitting on the rock. Lauren closed her eyes and took another deep breath. In an instant, the two women merged and became one.

Alex meant to close his eyes for just a moment, but instead, he dozed into a deep sleep. He found himself on the sandy beach, squinting from the bright daylight sun. He looked up and was temporarily confused by the full moon shining back down at him. Then he saw her sitting serenely on a rock. *She's come back. I didn't lose her.* Alex walked quickly in her direction, kicking up sand all around him. *Maybe I'll be able to actually walk up to her, touch her long dark hair, and kiss her sensuous lips.* He was almost within reach when she suddenly stood up and faced him directly.

He stopped abruptly and waited. He couldn't breathe. He could do nothing but stand in awe, staring at her elegant beauty.

They stood gazing at each other for what seemed like forever, neither moving a muscle. The wind started blowing furiously again, causing Lauren's skirt to whip about, the cloth wrapping around her legs. The stiff breeze was pushing her blouse tight across her chest, stretching the fabric fighting to break free. Her hair was raised and blowing outward, framing her lucid face. The ocean waves were pushing and pulling, making a noise of a hundred trains roaring through at once.

The couple continued to be still, feeling the calmness reign. They felt the light-colored aura begin to spread slowly, hugging them both in total warmth. They did nothing but watch each other, neither attempting to speak. They were bathed in a light they both knew represented their love for one another. They instinctively knew this moment would be remembered forever.

Lauren's concentration was focused entirely on him. His long-sleeved shirt was unbuttoned and flowing like scarves in a heavy wind. His long dark hair was pushed back behind him. She could see his muscles straining against the unyielding current.

Alex finally moved first by slowly putting one hand out, his palm pointing toward her. She traced his palm with her eyes, then very slowly raised her palm to touch his. She was afraid the sheer curtain that always intruded would come again to break their bond.

Slowly and tenderly, one fingertip at a time, Lauren touched her palm to his. Tiny sparks from the energy between them flew about, causing Lauren to momentarily pull back. Alex watched as she centered herself, and once again gazed at his open palm. He was patiently waiting for her to make him feel complete. Slowly, she touched her palm with his. As their energy pulsed, a pure white light engulfed their entire being, surrounding them in illuminated brilliance.

Somewhere, he heard the words echoing around him, "Alex, you must remember." He looked up briefly as a dove soared by, gliding through a florescent rainbow, singing its song of freedom. When he looked back, Lauren was gone. His palm remained outstretched, but she had disappeared.

He fell to his knees, crushing the sand below him, putting his face into his now empty palms, and then he cried. He cried from a combination of despair and happiness. He sobbed from his centering place within. He didn't understand how he could be so elated, yet feel such sorrow at the same time. Trying to rationalize what had just happened, he closed his eyes and spoke out loud to himself. "I realize in the past, I probably would have seen the worst of two scenarios. She was here, and then she was gone. This time I know different. I realized instead of sabotaging the moment with self-doubts, I can see it for what it was. I saw the light, and I felt the love. For the first time in my life, I know someone has completely touched my heart."

Alex continued sobbing over the noise of the ocean waves thrashing in about him. "My tears of happiness stem from the simple fact that I have found her again. We were not lost from each other. I remembered the lesson taught to me earlier. We both worked at staying balanced, and we both shared a precious gift. I went into my house within, and found her in one of my many rooms, bathed in light." Alex realized his soul was complete, because she had, and always would dwell there.

He stopped sobbing and looked to where the dove had flown only moments earlier. He cocked his head to one side and listened as he heard a word being whispered once again in his ear, "Remember!"

He closed his eyes and slept.

Lauren opened her eyes and stared at the music box. She picked up her pen and journal, and briefly described what had just transpired within. She didn't have time to stop and analyze. She didn't want to take the chance of forgetting a moment. *I watched myself on the beach, and actually saw myself talking to my guide. I learned a valuable lesson, or rather remembered one. Then he was there in front of me.*

We touched. My God, we actually touched!

Lauren closed her eyes and spoke aloud. "I can still feel the flow of energy pulsating through my body. I can still feel all my senses aroused. Would I know him if I saw him?" The question continued on and on in her mind. Lauren's memory was fading, but she knew the sensation of his touch would always remain.

"I would know his touch with my eyes closed." She repeated the last words again, "With my eyes closed."

It suddenly felt good to be alive.

Lauren turned on her music box and listened, this time with her eyes opened. She sat thinking about what she had learned in the last twenty years of her life, and what she had sometimes forgotten.

"The one thing I know for sure is that my guide was correct. A person must be able to access intuitively and automatically before they can fully trust themselves. Most of us want to give that responsibility to someone else. We'd rather trust the feelings and thoughts of someone else. We must learn to trust ourselves."

She remembered the exercises and made a vow she would continue them, no matter what energy was intruding. "My life can only get better." She refused to add, "Unless I can't locate him in this life." She refused to allow those thoughts to creep in tonight. "I found him on the beach, and those are the memories I prefer to remember."

Her thoughts were unexpectedly halted for a moment. "Remember?"

Lauren was momentarily taken off balance when her phone and doorbell rang at the same time. She laughed, thinking to herself, *Already testing my abilities, huh?*

Alex awoke staring into a darkened room. He had been asleep for a while, and was hungry again. He could hear the television downstairs, and felt comfort knowing he wasn't alone. He quietly turned over and watched the stars twinkling through his balcony door.

"I found her, and she is more beautiful than I could have ever imagined." He looked at the ceiling and smiled. "I touched her."

He turned away from the balcony to touch his newly acquired frame. "I'll always remember, and I'll find her again."

As he closed his eyes, he heard a faint knock at his door.

"Alex, are you awake?" Donovan was whispering over the sounds of the television downstairs.

"Yeah, I'm awake. Come in and turn the light on."

Donovan opened the door, and turned on the lamp in the corner of the room. "How are you feeling?"

Alex sat up and smiled. "Like a million dollars."

Donovan walked closer to observe his friend. "Good, you're not as pale as you have been."

Alex took a sip from his glass of juice, then continued. "How long have you been back? Did you get everything done? When's Elliot due back?"

Donovan laughed. "Whoa, man, you must be feeling better. I've been back for a few hours now. I had several business calls to make, I spoke to Vickie, and..."

Alex gulped down the juice that was held in his mouth. "My God, I had forgotten about Vickie. She's already suspicious as hell. What did you tell her?"

Donovan shook his head. "I'm glad we're such good friends, Alex. I couldn't pull this off for anyone else. Fortunately, I spoke to her over the phone instead of having to look directly into her eyes. I told her there was no time to come by and see her. Then I told her that you have a relative in Connecticut that you insisted on going to see, and since Elliot and I both suddenly had some important business to take care of out that way, we insisted that you not go alone."

Alex looked at Donovan in disbelief. "Donovan, that's the worst lie I've ever heard."

Donovan shrugged. "Yeah. Well, I wasn't very proud of it either. I've never been very good at telling untruths. I'm sure she's convinced all three of us are certifiably crazy."

Alex laughed as he pulled himself out of bed. "I promise when this is all over, you can tell her the truth."

Donovan shirked his shoulders tensely, "If she doesn't have us all committed between now and then."

They heard the front door open downstairs, and footsteps ascending the stairs. Donovan yelled towards the door, "Is that you, Elliot?"

Elliot walked in holding a take out bag from a local restaurant.

"Yeah, I got all my important matters taken care of. Thank God for efficient secretaries. I went home, packed, and here I am with food in hand."

Elliot looked at Alex coming out of the bathroom and smiled.

"Something told me this guy would be awake and growling for his dinner."

Alex took the package from his friend's hand, sat down on the bed, and smelled inside the bag. "I don't know what it is, and I don't care. Let's eat."

They adjourned to the kitchen table to make plans for the next morning. Donovan had the itinerary in his hand, reading it aloud.

"Our flight leaves at 9:00 in the morning. We'll check into the hotel, and go directly to the address given to us by the auction house. That's as good a place to start as any."

Elliot looked at Alex and smiled. "Well, Mr. Chandler, it looks as if you've got your energy and appetite back. I hope you know how lucky you are. Your illness could have turned out much worse."

Alex spoke between bites. "I know, but I've got luck on my side. Good thing too, since I have a lot to fight for right now." Then Alex pulled back his chair and told the men about his most recent dream. He described how centered the couple stayed when everything around them became wild and out of control. He described in detail what he thought she looked like, and what had transpired when they touched.

"Our palms barely touched, but it was confirmation that we belong together. If I wasn't sure before, that one touch confirmed it. I don't know how I'm going to locate her, and I don't know when, but I do know that as long as I stay positive and focused, everything will be all right. I'm going to remember to work like hell to remain in that state. I know there may be several tests, twists and turns in the road, but if I just remember..."

Alex suddenly went quiet, while both men waited for him to complete his sentence, without success.

Elliot finally spoke up, "Remember what, Alex?"

Alex looked over at them with a glazed expression on his face. "I don't know. I just have to remember." His mind kept flashing back and forth from his elderly guide to the beautiful woman in his dream, to his house with its many rooms, and a huge sign in front that read, 'remember.' Before, he had only seen her and she was beautiful. But now, he had touched her. And she possessed such a powerful aura of warmth and love that it penetrated his heart, and soared to his soul. And since that touch, his mind continued playing the same word over and over again. Remember... Remember. Remember?

Lauren invited Kevin in, offering him a glass of wine. He chuckled as he accepted the completely filled glass. "Am I going to need this?"

Lauren returned the laugh. "Kevin, by the time I finish telling you everything, you'll want the whole bottle. Better start drinking up."

Kevin looked suspiciously at her, took the bottle, and sat it on the table next to him. He watched as Lauren poured herself a glass, and then waited for her to get comfortable. She had beside her the journal, the hypnosis recording from the night before, and the music box.

Kevin pored over the paraphernalia that had amassed around his friend before speaking up. "Lauren, what are you doing? You need all this gear to make your point?"

Lauren looked around and giggled out loud. "Kevin, trust me,

I'm not a lunatic. But let me tell you my story, and then you decide."

She told Kevin all about the dreams, and read her journal describing how they had progressed to the point of being able to communicate telepathically. She related how she felt in his presence, and about the painting that she recognized, but didn't know from where. She vividly explained about the ring she had purchased from Vickie's store, along with the dream about the ring and its inscription. Then she played the music box. Lauren ended the story with the meeting that had taken place a few minutes before his arrival.

Kevin stayed quiet throughout her presentation. He listened as she read her diary; he listened to the recording of her hypnosis session, and he watched her cry as she listened to it for the first time. He closely watched her mannerisms and her eyes. He could see she was very nervous about discussing this with anyone. He knew by her body language that she feared he would love her and respect her less. Kevin shook his head silently as he realized Lauren didn't fully understand that his love and friendship for her was unconditional. It had no limits, and no boundaries. They had known each other their entire lives. Kevin knew the deepest part of Lauren, and she did him. He knew she wasn't someone who made up stories for attention. This was very real to her, so in turn, it was very real for him, too.

Kevin smiled when he noticed the bottle was indeed empty after she had completed her story, just as she said it would be.

Lauren finally sat still, looking directly into his eyes.

She noticed him stroking his short beard while she was talking. She saw him working to keep an open mind, and there were times when she caught his eyebrows rising. But he gave her the courtesy of allowing her to continue. She could hear the soft music in the background, and she felt she needed to break the silence, but instead she waited.

Kevin took a sip from his wine, and peered at her. "Is that

what happened when we were going to dinner the other night? Is that when the feeling of, what did you call it, déjà vu took over? Is that why you wanted to go home?"

Lauren felt she was being laughed at. She looked down at her feet, then defiantly back up into Kevin's eyes. "Yes, and that was actually the second time it happened."

Kevin continued rubbing his beard and speaking calmly. "You say you've seen this woman in the mirror how many times?"

Lauren's thoughts were beginning to spiral out of control. *What is this? Is he testing me? Well, I'm certainly not going to break down now.* She took a deep breath and tried to control her anger before speaking.

"I've seen her twice. Once in my car mirror outside the store, and once this morning in my bathroom mirror." She felt she was being interrogated, and had to admit the whole story sounded crazy.

Kevin wanted to try and understand, so he continued warmly. "Let me see if I heard you correctly. You think the ring you purchased from Vickie was waiting for you? And you said you couldn't read the inscription, but in your dream, it flashed colors. Then suddenly, it could be read? And that's what you had me listen to on the recording? Right?"

Lauren was feeling uncomfortable with all the questions, and paranoia was beginning to settle in. She felt she was fighting a losing battle for her own sanity. She stared at her lap and answered softly, "Yes, this is what I felt, and this is what happened." She noticed her voice had grown considerably weaker.

Kevin was asking questions to show he had been listening, and respected everything she said. "So now, you and Adriana are going to Connecticut tomorrow to investigate where the ring and the music box came from, in the hopes of finding this man, or getting some answers?"

Lauren felt violated and ridiculed. She could feel agitation and humiliation begin to flow through her veins, until she could take it no more. "Kevin, I'm sorry you don't believe me. And I'm sorry you think I'm insane. Maybe the story does sound crazy. Maybe I am going off on some middle age tangent. But damn it, it's my dream! And I don't care how crazy they may sound to you, nothing, or no one is going to stop me from pursuing my dreams."

Kevin never took his eyes from her. He slid slowly off the couch, and crawled over to the corner of the room where Lauren had propped herself up. She tried to pull back until he took her in his arms, and hugged her tightly.

"Lauren, what are you talking about? Honey, I believe you. Why the hell wouldn't I? You've never given me any reason to doubt you. You are an intelligent, grounded, and very reasonable woman. I don't doubt you for a moment."

Lauren closed her eyes, wanting to feel his energy, and listen to his words of comfort. She was surprised to see her guide appear inside her mind, smiling and shaking his head. She instantly realized what had just transpired, and was disappointed in herself. She silently told her guide what she now understood.

It wasn't Kevin who reacted negatively to my story. I reacted to my own distrust and lack of confidence. I wasn't strong enough to stand up to him with what I knew were the facts. I started crumbling under what I thought was Kevin's interrogation. I knew I wasn't being true to myself.

Lauren heard her guide speak softly. "You know your truths. Why do you question them just because you feel someone else may? You must be true to your beliefs. Kevin never questioned you. In fact, he believes you. You brought all these unwanted and unneeded emotions on yourself. Your self-doubt can be the downfall of your intuition. Trust in your heart what you know to be true, and don't allow your truth to be swayed, or your judgment to be clouded. Sometimes, we can be our own worst critic. Lauren, remember this lesson. It will serve you well."

And suddenly, she was back in Kevin's arms, feeling safe and secure.

She looked up at her lifelong friend and knew he had done

nothing but listen and support her. She had brought all the negativity on herself. She spoke to Kevin in a whisper. "Self-sabotage can be quite deadly."

Kevin smiled, not understanding what she was talking about, but agreed that yes, it could indeed be very deadly.

They talked and laughed for another hour, then Kevin stood up and walked toward the door, with Lauren following behind. "It's late, and you have a full day tomorrow. Call and let me know how things are progressing. And please, don't worry about anything here. You won't be gone long enough for everything to crumble down around us."

Lauren hugged her friend. "Kevin, I need you and appreciate you more than you could ever know. Thank you."

Kevin returned the hug. "I'll see you in a few days. Have fun, and good luck. If there's anything I can do from this side of the country, call me."

She shut the door behind him and slowly walked up the stairs. She still had a lot to do before her flight tomorrow. "Tomorrow. What a day that's going to be."

Chapter 11

Alex and his friends were up early the next morning. The limo had been arranged, and was waiting in the driveway at the precise time.

It was a quiet drive to the airport. The men were all living deep within their own thoughts, not certain what to expect.

Alex had his hands tightly clasped together, reliving his dream from the evening before. His thoughts remained until he was checked in at the airport and settled into his seat. He closed his eyes, trying to remain calm while waiting for the plane to taxi and finally take off.

When Alex realized the plane was off the ground, he opened his eyes and looked out the window as they circled over the Pacific Ocean, then back over the mountains, heading toward his destination.

He couldn't help but grin. "This adventure is finally taking on real meaning."

Donovan had their itinerary sitting on the tray in front of him. "We should have plenty of time to pick up the car and check into the hotel, before trying to locate the property. Once the auction house gave me the facts, I set out making calls until I had a little information on the house. Because the furnishings were auctioned off, I thought the place might be up for sale. I called a local real estate broker in the area, and sure enough, it is."

Elliot chuckled at the way Donovan was patting himself on the back. "Donovan, I have to hand it to you. Your instincts paid off.

Is the real estate broker going to meet us at the house?"

Donovan smirked mischievously. "I told her that I would call when we hit town. But I want to drive by the place first. I didn't think Alex would want a stranger around when he was getting impressions of the place."

Alex leaned over. He had been listening to the conversation with interest. "Donovan, you're a genius. I still don't know how in the hell you guys have pulled this caper off so far. But I'm a bit worried. I never knew you guys could be so sneaky. We're going to have to work on that when this is all over."

Elliot broke in, "Let's just hope everything goes as planned. We don't know why we're going there, and we don't know if we'll find anything that will be of help." He turned and directly faced Alex. "You do understand that, don't you?"

"Yeah, I understand that. But I feel as though I'm caught between a rock and a hard place. I don't know why I'm going, but I also realize I have no choice."

The conversation was dropped when the flight attendant approached the men, asking for their breakfast order. Short naps and small talk followed until they finally touched down in Connecticut.

They quickly retrieved their luggage and picked up the car. Elliot decided he would drive, while Donovan deciphered the directions.

This allowed Alex the opportunity to let his mind roam free and see where it took him. They were all impressed with the beauty of the location, and how breathtaking the fall leaves were. They quickly checked into the resort, taking little notice of all the amenities it had to offer. They were in a rush to view the house before sunset.

Elliot seated himself behind the steering wheel, then watched as Donovan made a feeble attempt to program the GPS. "Is this going to take all day?"

Donovan squinted firmly in the direction of his friend. "It may if you keep bothering me. I'll have everything organized in a minute."

Alex couldn't hold back a laugh. "Would it be easier if I took a limo?"

Elliot stared at Donovan. "Well, it's too bad that someone didn't think of that before."

The tension was temporarily broken with excitement when the map displayed the house being only fifteen minutes away. Then quietness slowly settled in the car. As they neared the location, Alex began to sweat. He noticed his breathing had accelerated, and his heart felt as though it would pound out of his chest.

Donovan glanced in the back seat, noticing Alex's paleness. "Are you OK? You look terrible."

Elliot interrupted, "Alex, are you sure you're ready for this? Maybe you should have rested awhile. Do you want to go back?"

Alex blurted out much too loudly, "No, I do not want to go back." Then his voice softened. "This is going to sound crazy, but I think I'm worried that I'll find something. Yet I'm also worried that I won't. I know this is a shot in the dark. But damn it, I'm going to keep an open mind if it kills me."

Alex forced his thoughts elsewhere by taking a long deep breath, and concentrating on enjoying the countryside and the smell of the breeze. The air was cool and crisp, and the sky was a clear dark blue. It was a perfect fall day. He noticed the area seemed familiar, but couldn't put his finger on exactly how, or in what way. It wasn't familiar like his home in Malibu, but he felt a sense of déjà vu that he could neither comprehend nor explain.

Everyone had settled into their own quietness and their own thoughts. Donovan was looking back and forth between the GPS map and the address. Elliot was driving slowly, his eyes darting from the road to the countryside, and back. It was a slow pace, but one they were all enjoying.

So it was a screech in the dead silence when Alex suddenly shouted out, without warning, "Turn right! You have got to turn right, here, or you'll miss it."

Elliot looked quickly to Donovan, whose body was rigid. Neither said a word, but Donovan's eyes darted over to Elliot and winked. They didn't want to break the spell. They knew Alex was on to something. Elliot glanced back in his mirror and saw Alex sitting very erect. His eyes were glazed and searching in every direction. He was obviously in a semi-altered state. His paleness was gone, and his eyes were wide with wonder.

Elliot looked straight ahead and continued driving very slowly. They were on a country road, heading east. He could smell the fresh scent of the ocean, and knew it wasn't too far away. Donovan placed a recorder next to him on the seat, and very quietly switched it on. He and Elliot had decided it would be best to record anything that may be of help later on. They hoped that Alex would be as vocal as possible, but felt if he knew about the recorder, he would subconsciously stifle his thoughts.

Alex saw it first, and shouted abruptly, causing the other passengers to jump. "It's here. The house is on our right. There, behind the gate ahead."

There was no street sign, and they had no idea where Alex was taking them. Both men were concerned they were about to trespass on private property.

"Stop the car, Elliot, stop the car!"

Elliot stopped and turned off the engine. The silence had become deafening, when Alex unexpectedly jumped out of the car and stood next to the gate. The wind was gently pushing his hair from his face, and his eyes were wide, taking in all the scenery in front of him.

Elliot and Donovan stayed in the car, watching in anticipation.

Donovan finally whispered, "Wow, can you believe this?"

Elliot continued staring at Alex. "It's unbelievable. I couldn't understand where he was taking us."

Donovan whispered back, "I still don't know where we are. What do you think he's doing?"

Elliot never took his eyes from his friend, who was still standing at the gate, looking straight ahead with great intensity.

"I think he may be going back a long, long time ago. We'll have to wait and see what he does next."

The men gasped as Alex jumped the fence and picked up a sign lying flat on the ground. He read it, then turned it around to his friends.

Donovan looked at the sign, then down at the piece of paper he had unknowingly crumpled in his hand. "Well, I'll be damned."

Elliot smiled in Alex's direction, and spoke under his breath. "Well, what do you know?"

Alex was beaming like a man who had achieved a great goal. In his hand was a for sale sign, with the house address in bold black letters. Donovan looked down at the paper where he had written the address, then back to the map again. He caught his breath and spoke in awe. "Elliot, we've been looking for the wrong address. This place doesn't exist on our GPS.

Alex was holding the sign and swinging it in the air. "I found it. I found it!"

The boys quickly got out of the car and approached him. Elliot couldn't contain his curiosity. "How did you do it? How did you know?"

Alex gently put the sign face down on the ground, then as if to find the answer, he looked up at the sky. "I have no idea. I suppose I just emptied my mind, and without realizing it, boom, there it was. I didn't even realize I had spoken until after you stopped the car." It was obvious Alex was surprised at himself, and very proud of his accomplishment.

Donovan took a step toward Alex. "OK, obviously you're the leader here. What do you want to do now?"

Alex turned away from the men and looked straight ahead, past a large grove of trees, noticing their leaves changing to the fall shades.

"I want to walk up that path and see what we find."

Elliot squinted ahead. "Do you want us to go with you?"

Alex motioned his friends along. "I wouldn't have it any other way."

Donovan let out a sigh of relief. "Good, I would have gone crazy waiting here for you." The other two men quickly jumped the fence and took their places on either side of Alex.

They remained quiet except for the occasional comment about the beauty of the land, as they passed the colorful trees and approached a pond with crystal clear water.

Alex slowed down when they were passing the little pond on the left side of the path. He noticed an old wooden bridge crossing the calm waters. On the other side, his gaze fell on a beautiful gazebo, with a long wooden bench. "My God, look at that." He was having such a difficult time getting the words out, it caused both men to look over in his direction, but neither said a word.

With obvious reluctance, Alex slowly crossed the bridge. The sound of creaking wood with each step seemed to echo all around them. He stood outside the gazebo for a few moments, looking wary, then took a deep breath and stepped inside its center.

The men watched from the other side as Alex slowly turned around several times to view the inner core. He would stop occasionally to gently touch the wood. He was pale again, and seemed to be in a daze. But his friends kept a close eye on him, making sure he was all right. Alex was slowly backing out of the arena when he stopped abruptly, and looked up toward the ceiling. The men continued watching, their curiosity and concern beginning to get the best of them.

Elliot whispered under his breath, "Here we go again."

"Do you think we should go over there?"

Elliot didn't respond, but instead walked slowly in Alex's direction. Donovan followed, pacing himself beside Elliot. They silently crossed the bridge, pausing just on the other side. Neither wanting to intrude on what they were watching in front of them.

Alex was rubbing his finger over the wood on the lower side

of the ceiling. He jerked his head in their direction without warning, and stood frozen in time for a minute. When he finally spoke, his tone was one of shock and confusion. "I knew this was here. I didn't know what was written, but somehow, I just knew there was something to be found inside here. It took me a while to figure out where it was located, and I was about to leave when something sparked a memory of some kind in me. Hell, I don't know."

He pointed toward the ceiling. "You see? The initials of three people, but I have no idea who they are." He brought his arm down to his side, whispering to himself. "But I knew."

Donovan approached first, then motioned for Elliot to follow.

Carved in the wood were the faint writings of someone's initials. Almost childlike, the carvings were written on three lines, underneath each other. N.F., W.W., A.R.

Elliot touched the crude markings. "Where do you suppose it came from?"

But no one was listening. Alex was already crossing the bridge at a fast pace, and Donovan was trying desperately to keep up. He felt in his pocket to make certain the recorder was still running.

Elliot pulled out his camera, taking several quick shots of the location, along with the carved letters, then quickly joined his friends on the other side of the bridge.

Alex continued walking swiftly up the path in the direction of the ocean. Elliot finally caught up and looked at Donovan. He returned the silent glance, shrugging his shoulders.

In a few minutes, Alex stopped short, causing his friends to almost run into him. There was complete silence, and everything was still. Elliot noticed the birds had stopped chirping, and the wind had stopped blowing. There was complete and total silence.

Breaking the surreal setting, Alex took a sharp deep breath, followed by a loud gasp. They looked in his direction, and then followed his eyes.

In front of them sat a beautiful house. It appeared to have a large back yard with another gazebo on the side of the house.

It faced the ocean, with another large yard in the front.

Alex briskly walked around to the front, the men following behind him. Donovan wanted to stay close in case Alex said something worth recording. Elliot lagged behind, taking pictures.

Alex approached the front of the house, finally slowing down his pace. Irritation covered his face when a large screened-in porch kept him from trespassing any further. Without changing pace, he turned to look out on the grounds in front of him, taking in everything he saw.

To his right was a huge oak tree with large, heavy branches. A swing made from an old tire swayed gently on one of the thick outstretched arms. Not far from the tree had been what resembled a flower garden, which had apparently died from lack of attention. Looking in front of him, he viewed a deep-water bay, with the ocean stretching out beyond. There was an old wooden dock at the end of the grounds, half of it fallen into the water in disrepair. He could almost imagine children sitting with their feet dangling over the edge, waiting for the fish to bite their bait. He felt he could easily have been looking at a photograph or a postcard.

Alex could feel his heart aching inside, and could hear his own loud gasp emitting directly from his throat. "Dear God. Where am I?"

Donovan quietly approached, placing his hand on his friend's shoulder to show his support. Alex remained frozen in place.

"Donovan, where are we? This feels so strange, and so surreal. I believe I've actually dreamed of this place, but God help me, I just can't remember."

Alex was about to continue voicing his train of thought, but instead stopped and stared at the house with such intensity that it hurt his head. He moaned to himself in a low, hoarse whisper, "Remember. Come on, Alex, just remember."

Elliot caught up with them, and continued the train of thought in a soft, monotone voice, "Alex, what is it you need to remember?

Can you remember? Remember."

Alex was deep inside himself now, so no one moved. The pain was visible on his face as he attempted to unbury the forgotten memories, or perhaps just merely dreams. But still no one moved.

They were startled when a loud honk of a car brought them back to reality.

Elliot turned to Donovan, mouthing the words, 'shit!' under his breath.

Donovan broke the spell. "Think quick, guys. Looks like we have a visitor. Better come up with a good excuse for trespassing."

No one had time to think. The man and woman got out of their car and approached them quickly. The tall man spoke first.

"Hello, may I help you?"

Elliot took command and answered first. "Hi. Perhaps you can. We're here from California, looking to purchase property. We were actually driving to another place up the road when we saw the sign out front. I hope you don't mind us trespassing. We don't have a lot of time, so we took the liberty of showing ourselves around."

The woman shifted uncomfortably. "You look like nice, respectable people, Mister?"

Elliot approached her slowly, putting out his hand out. "Mr. Golden. And this is Mr. Barnett."

Donovan shook their hands. "That's Mr. Chandler, over there." Alex was walking the length of the porch, peering into the screened area, now oblivious to the others watching him.

The woman completed her sentence, "As I was saying, you all look like nice people, but we're uncomfortable having strangers walking around our property without an appointment."

Alex had a million questions, and quickly turned to join the others. Donovan watched him approach, and looked to Elliot for instruction. An eyebrow was raised, giving the signal. Donovan intercepted Alex, while Elliot slowly walked the couple in another direction. "Oh, so this is your place? It's beautiful. Has it always been in your family?"

In the meantime, Donovan pushed Alex off course in the opposite direction. "Alex, you must let us handle this. The last thing we need right now is for these people to think that we're here for any reason other than to purchase this place." Donovan stepped in front of Alex to look right into his eyes. "Alex, if you want to look around, we'll keep them occupied. Just be very quiet, and make yourself scarce."

Alex shook his head and nonchalantly walked in the opposite direction.

Donovan joined the others without being missed, while Elliot continued the questioning. The woman seemed less apprehensive, which showed itself through a friendlier body language. She was explaining the current history of the property.

"My parents purchased this home many, many years ago. A young couple had originally built it. As far as I know, they were the only other owners of the property."

Donovan felt inside his pocket, making certain the recorder was running. "That's very interesting. Do you know who the original owners were, and why they would sell such a lovely place?" He didn't want to raise suspicion. "I can't imagine someone giving up a place like this, after building it themselves. How old is the structure?"

Elliot looked over at his friend with a slight smile and wink. The woman smiled proudly. "I don't have much information on the couple, except the rumors I heard when I was a child." Her voice dropped an octave, and she spoke as if she were gossiping over the fence to a neighbor. "They were apparently young and very wealthy. Several years after they built this place, the man died in a tragic accident. She died shortly thereafter." Whispering softer for effect, she continued, "It was rumored that she died from a broken heart."

Elliot wanted to know more. "Who did your parents purchase the place from?"

The woman enjoyed telling the story, and was happy for the attention. "My parents told me the house had been put up for auction. They said there were only a few distant cousins left in the family. And they were more than willing to sell the house and its contents, then split the profits. That's how my parents came to own it."

Donovan repeated his question, "When was the house built?"

She thought for a moment and then answered, "In the nineteen thirties."

Elliot wanted to know more. "Do you know the name of the original owners?"

The woman looked at her husband, but he shrugged his shoulders. "I don't remember. I don't think my parents ever told me, and I doubt I ever asked them. I haven't lived here in many years. Both of my parents are recently deceased, so we auctioned off the remaining contents and put the property up for sale."

Elliot was about to ask another question when the woman changed direction, and started walking toward the screen door.

"Why don't I open up the house so you can take a look at it?"

Donovan stayed directly behind her. "That would be very nice of you."

Alex reappeared without anyone noticing he hadn't always been part of the conversation. The woman unlocked the doors, allowing the gentlemen to enter the empty house. All the furnishings were gone, but there was still a slight smell of aliveness to the place.

The couple remained outside, sitting in the two lawn chairs her husband had taken out of the trunk of his car. "We'll stay out here. You don't want people swarming all over you when you're looking around. Go ahead and take your time. We'll wait here."

The three men smiled, then took a few steps into the large foyer. They remained very still, letting the life of the house envelope them. Alex closed his eyes, allowing his energy to come into focus. Elliot pointed toward his camera, motioned to

Donovan that he would catch up with them later, and quietly walked up the stairs.

Donovan kept silent, waiting for some sort of response from his other friend.

Alex took a deep breath, letting it release from his mouth very slowly. He opened his eyes, looking to the right into the dining room. "My God, this place has so many memories. I sense that some were extremely happy, but others were so devastatingly sad."

Donovan spoke to Alex in a low tone, "Do you want some time alone? I could join Elliot."

Alex turned to Donovan and smiled. "Yeah, I think that would be good. I need to be alone to browse around for a few minutes. Thanks."

Once Alex was alone, he took the time to vividly study each room. His eyes started first to the ceiling, and down each wall, to the floor. As he roamed, he began receiving impressions. He felt so many varying emotions stirring inside, he had trouble integrating them all. He found it strange that he could close his eyes, and walk through the first floor of the house, knowing what each room was used for. The residence held such familiar sensations, yet he couldn't figure out what they were.

Alex finally pulled himself away and trudged slowly upstairs. The first room he entered had been a child's bedroom. He assumed it had belonged to the woman waiting outside. He continued his search in each of the rooms, feeling a tug as he approached the end of the hall. Alex didn't know why, but he felt such an ache in his heart, he wanted to stay away from the room beckoning him. As he got closer, his stomach began to flutter, and his heart felt as if someone was crushing it.

He approached little by little, before he had no choice but to open the door. He stood outside the enclosure. He knew he was scared to enter. *Why can't I do this?* Alex was trying desperately to reason with himself. *After all, it's just a room.*

Alex slowly forced himself to take one small step after another, until he was standing in the center of the chamber. At once, he noticed the window shades were raised, with a beautiful view of the bay in front of him. The windows covered the entire wall, taking in the scenery from the front yard, too. He widened his eyes and looked around the room. His fear was vanishing, and embarrassment was taking over as he realized the danger of the room was probably all in his imagination.

The master bedroom was very large, housing a brick fireplace in the corner. Alex sat down on the floor against the wall, and studied the windows, the fireplace, and the complete emptiness of the room. He closed his eyes and took another deep breath. Before he had the opportunity to release it, overwhelming emotions overtook him. He could see in his mind's eye a man and a woman standing before him. They were vague, but he could sense what they were feeling. The room was suddenly engulfed in complete and total uncompromising love. He knew he had never felt this kind of happiness in his entire life. The room came alive with the energy this love invoked. He could hear conversations going on in every corner. Lively conversations with laughter ringing out everywhere. He couldn't help but smile with all the activity going on around him. He desperately wanted to be a part of it.

Then without warning, he heard his own voice crying out in pain, and felt his own hands grabbing at his heart. He felt the agony and distress deep into his soul, and hot tears stung his face. The emotions had changed completely in a matter of a second. He wanted nothing less than death, when a feeling of overwhelming helplessness overtook him. Suddenly, he felt what it must be like to actually die a terrible death. First pain, and then total peacefulness. A sensation of giving up control, and resigning himself to the fact that he was no more.

Alex hesitated for a moment, trying to catch his breath. When he thought he was somewhat composed, he slowly opened his eyes. He gasped when he saw a table sitting in front of him. On the table, he noticed a large box next to a frame with a picture of a man and a woman in each other's arms. The couple was laughing, and seemed very happy. He heard music in the background coming from deep inside the walls. He vaguely recalled the melody, and felt a powerless ache upon hearing its tune. He closed his eyes once again, and saw the table, the box, and the picture disappear.

His guide was kneeling down beside him, hugging him to her chest. "Alex, be strong now, and trust what you feel, trust what you see, and always remember."

He opened his eyes and found himself still sitting on the floor. His shoulders were slumped over, and he had been crying. He put his fingers up to his face, feeling the wetness. He knew he was back in the present, but he longed to go back to that special place in time.

"God, please tell me what to do."

He heard a soft knock, before Elliot slowly opened the door.

"Alex, are you all right? We didn't want to disturb you, but it's getting late. Donovan is outside keeping the people occupied, but I'm afraid they're going to start getting suspicious. I've been waiting here at the door, and felt you were in some kind of distress. But I also knew you wouldn't have wanted any help."

Elliot could feel a fraction of the pain that had been in the room. "Can I help you now?"

Alex saw the concerned, caring look in his friend's eyes. "You're helping me already. You're here with me."

Alex patted the floor, asking Elliot to join him. Elliot set his camera aside, and sat down next to his friend. He could see Alex had been sobbing. His eyes were red, and the tears still stained his face.

"Alex, what happened in here?"

Alex looked around the room, then back to Elliot. He looked as though he would lose his composure again, but instead took a deep breath before speaking. "There is so much history in this room. I felt love and laughter, and just as much pain and agony."

Elliot was quiet. He wanted Alex to continue with his

description.

"I could hear everything that's gone on in this room, but there was no relief between episodes. I heard it all at once. I could hear and feel the whole thing." Alex's voice dropped to a whisper. "Elliot, I closed my eyes and saw the table I bought from Vickie."

Alex pointed in the direction of the window. "It was right there. And on the table was a big box of some kind, along with the frame I bought from her store too."

He turned to face Elliot, and spoke with spent emotion still churning in his voice.

"It was more than I could handle of either emotion. Suddenly, I was filled with heart-wrenching sorrow. I have never known such love and such sorrow at the same time. My body physically hurt. There was such helplessness and distress within, as well as around me. Then there was death."

Elliot looked surprised at the last statement. "Death?"

"Yeah, that's the only way I can describe it. There was a sensation of such love, such pain, and then a nothingness. Almost like a sigh of relief. I had the feeling everything at that moment changed. When I knew I could take it no more, my guide suddenly appeared, advising me to be strong. She also told me to trust, and to remember. That's when I returned to the present."

Elliot was amazed at what Alex had revealed. It was obvious his friend was in the midst of a profound, life-altering experience.

The two men were preparing to stand up when Alex thought of another episode. "Oh, and one more thing. I heard music coming from far away. It was coming from the walls, then flowed all around me. I'm getting the impression that music may have something to do with all of this. But, God, I just don't know how that could be. Maybe I'm too close to the situation. Maybe I'm all wrong." Alex shook his head. "No, I really get that music is the root to this. There's something I need to find from the music."

He stood up, leaving Elliot on the floor, and began pacing back and forth like a caged animal. "Every time I sense an answer may be in front of me, ten more questions rise to the surface."

Elliot stood up to lead Alex out of the room. "Right now, we're going to take you back to the hotel to get some rest."

"OK, go rescue Donovan and I'll be down in two minutes."

When Alex was left alone, he scanned the room, trying to put the picture permanently in his mind. He wanted to remember everything about the energy in the walls. He instinctively put his hand in his pocket and brought out a napkin from the plane. Without giving his gesture a second thought, he took the pen from his jacket, and scribbled words on the paper. He placed it on top of the fireplace mantle, then turned and walked out to meet his friends downstairs.

The couple was putting the chairs in the trunk of their car. "Do you want a ride back to your car?"

Alex spoke up. "No thank you. We'll walk back." He shook their hands and gave them his card. "I'm very interested in the property, and I appreciate your patience in letting us take our time looking around. I'll be in touch."

The woman was taken off guard. She hadn't noticed Alex before. But now there was such a presence about him that she was visibly shaken.

"Th- thank you, Mister?" She looked at his card.

"My name is Alex Chandler."

"Thank you, Mr. Chandler. I would like to see someone nice have this place. It holds a lot of memories."

Alex looked deep into her eyes and smiled. "I have no doubt about that."

Alex and his friends started their walk down the path toward their vehicle, and waved when the couple passed them.

Alex remarked, "Nice people."

Donovan replied, "Yeah, they were. But did you see how she looked at you, Alex? It was almost as if she knew you, but just couldn't place you."

The subject was changed when Alex told Donovan what had

transpired in the bedroom, unaware that his friend was taping his words. The ride back to the hotel was uneventful, and they agreed to meet at the bar after freshening up. Donovan and Elliot were there first.

Elliot waited to speak until the drinks were ordered, and before Alex joined them. "Did you get Alex's experience on tape?"

Donovan smiled, "Yeah, I think between the photographs and recording Alex shouldn't have any trouble reliving his experiences once he gets home. I just hope this comes to a happy ending real soon. It's driving him crazy."

Elliot nodded his head in agreement. "I know. But I've got to admit he seems to be getting closer to some kind of an answer. I was surprised that music may be involved in some way."

Donovan concurred, "I can't figure out what that's all about. He's musically inclined, so perhaps it's just been brought through from the past."

Elliot took a sip of his drink. "You know, Donovan, you just may have something there. It could have to do with the past. But how can he bring the past and the present together to make a future?"

Donovan shrugged, "Certainly, between the three of us, we can come up with a solution of some kind. And we have to remember there may be someone else out there who's trying to do the same."

Elliot downed his drink and ordered another one. "I hope you're right. But in the meantime, we have to devise a way to keep Alex from entirely drowning himself in this undertaking. He needs other things to think about as well. He'll never work it out if he continually obsesses about it. He seems to find more answers when he releases it, then goes with the flow."

"I think you're right. We can find something else to occupy his mind in between the times he's obsessing."

The guys were laughing when Alex approached and sat down. "What's so funny?"

Elliot winked at Donovan. "Not much. I think we're just a little punchy from our excursion. Why don't we have another drink, then eat, and go to bed?"

Donovan interrupted, "Any plans for tomorrow?"

Alex spoke up, "Yeah, why don't we drive around tomorrow and get the feel of the area. Then I think I may put in an offer to buy the property. If all goes well, we can be back in Malibu by the day after tomorrow."

Donovan and Elliot both choked on their drinks, which Alex thought was quite amusing.

"Alex, you're actually going to buy the place?"

Donovan put his glass down. "You can't be serious. What in the hell are you going to do with such a large piece of property so far from home? Who's going to take care of it?"

Alex took a large sip of his drink and laughed. "Guys, don't worry. It'll all fall into place. You've just got to trust me."

Lauren and Adriana were exhausted by the time they had claimed their luggage and were on their way to the hotel.

Lauren had repeated the story to Adriana over and over. Her mind had been consumed by the day's events.

She awoke early, feeling refreshed and ready to start her mission. After packing, Lauren decided she could stand the suspense no longer, and drove to the jewelry store. She wanted to do this alone, fearing she would look foolish if the inscription didn't appear as she had dreamed it. She wouldn't be able to hide her immeasurable disappointment if she discovered it had all been in her imagination.

Driving to Cohn's Jewelry store felt like the ride to hell. Lauren couldn't keep her mind on the road, and was honked at by passing motorists who felt she wasn't keeping up. She didn't care. Her mind was trying to prepare itself on how to rationally deal with the disappointment in case she found out this had all been a horrible nightmare. She was trying to prepare for the worst, scared to death that everything she was beginning to base her life on was a complete and total lie. But in the back of her mind, she couldn't help but be reminded of her guide's advice: "Have complete trust in the process. Trust your intuitive knowledge."

That seemed easy enough to do when your entire life wasn't on the line. She knew if the ring's inscription was not what she dreamed, no one, including herself, would ever believe in her again.

Lauren heard herself speaking aloud, "This is a complete test of faith and competence. God, I hope I'm not insane, or going through a middle age crisis like I'm always reading about."

She was perspiring profusely and turned down the temperature in her car. She noticed her breathing had become rapid and erratic, and she was talking to herself again. "Lauren, get a hold of yourself. You can't change the outcome of what's about to happen, so just try and relax. If you walk into the store like this, they'll surely have you committed."

She broke her own spell by laughing at the scene that could ensue. She imagined the men in white coats coming to take her away. She cringed when she realized she had trusted herself to pursue this in the first place, and now she had come as far as she could without jumping into the void. Everything was on the line, and it was time to take the leap. "I have a damn good reason to be a little nervous." Lauren knew those words would be the only reassurance she would hear herself speak.

She parked the car in a remote area of the parking lot. She needed the brief walk in the fresh air to compose herself. Lauren looked up into the sky after stepping out of the car, and took a very deep breath. She let it out, whispering into the wind, "Please let my dreams be true. Please." Lauren walked slowly across the parking lot, halting briefly before entering the store. She took another quick breath before opening the door.

The manager looked up. "Miss Wells. How nice to see you again."

Before Lauren had the opportunity to respond, the manager

continued, "Your order is in my office. I'll go get it and be back in just a moment."

He was gone before she was able to smile her response. It was probably just as well. Lauren was afraid nothing would have come out of her mouth anyway. She was barely breathing.

She laughed at herself again to break the tension, and thought about what would happen if the rigid manager walked in to find her sprawled out on the floor, gasping for fresh air. And all because of this blasted ring. Lauren laughed for being able to find humor in this awful test of faith, one that she had to endure in public, too.

In a few moments, the manager returned and handed Lauren a small box. He asked her if she wanted to examine it, but Lauren could only smile and shake her head no. She had to get out of the store as quickly as possible. She grabbed the box, and was able to blurt out a quick thank you while scrambling towards the door.

All the while, Lauren tried walking calmly to her car. She didn't want to raise suspicion, knowing that her nervousness was now outwardly showing. "God, I just want this to be over with. One way or the other, I want it to be over."

Lauren found her way to the car, and sat the box in her lap. She couldn't make herself open it. "I can't do it here. No, it would be better in the privacy of my home." She couldn't believe the range of emotions soaring through her body. "C'mon, girl, you've been through tougher times than this." But the insecure child within was threatening to break through and triumph. A quiet, almost frightening calmness overtook her as she drove home. She robotically pulled into her garage, and peacefully walked into her house, directing her steps toward her office.

Lauren gently placed the box on her desk, and sat down in her chair. She looked at the box for several minutes, trying to think of a rational excuse not to open its lid. She had listened to the recording of her hypnosis session with Adriana. She knew and believed what she had seen in her dream. Both Adriana and Kevin knew what she thought she had seen. She couldn't turn back now. She thought back to how she had described it in such vivid detail, and found herself cringing.

Lauren tried reasoning with herself again. "If the inscription isn't the same, that doesn't mean he doesn't exist. It just means what I thought I saw was incorrect."

But her stomach was churning, and she was frightened that she would have to admit her whole life was a total and complete farce. She worried about where that truth would leave her. What part of her life would she have to go back and start over? Which portion of her beliefs would she have to give up, and which would she be able to keep?

She closed her eyes and saw the old man standing beside her.

"Lauren, listen to your heart. Have you forgotten what you have seen? Have you forgotten what you have felt? Follow the path wherever it may lead you. Read the signs, no matter what they may say."

Lauren opened her eyes and found tears streaming down her face. "I believe with all my heart, but I'm also scared to death of being wrong."

Lauren slowly picked up the box and took the jewelry case from its container. She closed her eyes again, and took a deep breath, at the same time she heard the creak from the spring, as she slowly opened the case. With her eyes closed, she removed the ring from its casing and ran her index finger over the now familiar symbols. She realized no matter what it read, she was glad to have it back in her possession. She knew it should belong to her.

With that in mind, Lauren opened her eyes and stared closely into its inner core. "It's the most beautiful thing I've ever seen."

The light forced the color to shine with brilliance. Then shock overtook her when she looked away from the ring, only to be forced back to it again. She repeated this over and over. When she found her voice, she squealed in astonishment. "My God, my God, my God."

Lauren didn't know what to do. She felt as if a boulder had been lifted from her shoulders. She had tried the best she could to prepare herself for a negative outcome, but she had failed to be ready for a positive one. Inside the ring was the most wonderful sight to her eyes, and to her soul. She stopped and read it again, now through solid tears of joy. "Where/when/remember/my love."

Lauren said it out loud through loud sobs. She found herself kneeling on the floor next to her desk, weeping every emotion she had ever felt. She knew the tears were cleansing herself from every doubt she could have had. She was sobbing from the happiness of being able to have her dreams verified so easily. And she sobbed for knowing that while there was still a hard, long path to travel, she knew that at least she was heading in the right direction.

Adriana arrived at Lauren's house early, only to hear intense wailing from inside. Gripping fear took over as she tried to turn the doorknob, but found it locked. She began screaming, kicking, and banging on the door. She rang the doorbell over and over. She was on her way to break a window, when everything in the house suddenly became very quiet.

The outside commotion had brought Lauren back to reality. When she opened the door to let her friend in, Adriana was taken aback by what she saw in front of her. Lauren looked as if she had been whipped. But she was confused by the total look of bliss on her friend's face.

Adriana forced herself through the open door, and grabbed Lauren by the shoulders. "My God, Lauren, are you all right? What in the hell has happened to you?"

Adriana turned her friend toward a mirror as she was questioning her. Lauren looked closely at herself, and began to understand why Adriana was reacting so severely. Lauren's makeup had run all over her face, and her hair was wet, stuck to her face and neck from a combination of tears and sweat. She had a wide grin on her face, and her clothes looked as if she had slept in them.

She resembled a wild woman from the outback.

Adriana turned Lauren back to face her, and then almost carried her into the kitchen. She tried to remain calm, while getting Lauren seated in a chair. While the tea was brewing, she soaked a dishtowel to clean Lauren's face. Lauren couldn't speak, but she also couldn't remove the grin covering her face. Adriana tried desperately to stay composed, but knew she was about to react severely. She could finally hold it in no longer.

"What in the hell is going on, Lauren? What's wrong with you? What were you doing when I walked up? And for God's sake, why in the hell do you have that stupid grin ingrained on your face?"

Lauren had never seen Adriana so out of control, and she burst out laughing in response. Then tried to stifle herself when anger exploded in her friend's eyes.

"You scared the hell out of me, and now you laugh?" Adriana held Lauren's face in the palm of her hand, cleaning it, and speaking to her as if she were a child.

Lauren wiggled away, and looked into Adriana's eyes again.

"I feel free. Totally free for the first time in my life. I believe in myself for the first time in my life, too. And, Adriana, for the first time in my entire life, I know I'm walking the right path. I may not continue on this path, but for now, I have found my direction. And I know that even if he doesn't exist someplace out there, he will always live in my heart. Because, my dear sweet friend, I know that he exists."

Adriana noticed her eyes were shining, and not just from the tears she had obviously been shedding for quite some time. She continued to gently clean Lauren's face, now speaking in a softer tone. "Lauren, please. Tell me what you're talking about. How do you know all of this? What happened?"

But even as Adriana was speaking, she knew in her own heart what Lauren was saying was true. Somehow, she had found her truth. "What happened last night? Did Kevin say or do something?"

Lauren put her hand on Adriana's, forcing her to stop rubbing her face. Adriana felt something slide into her palm. She took her hand away from Lauren, and opened her clenched fist with a gasp. "Oh God, Lauren, it's the ring."

Lauren smiled tenderly. "Look inside."

Adriana walked to the window and turned the ring toward the light. Lauren enjoyed watching her reaction as Adriana's eyes widened in disbelief.

"Oh my God! Everything you said was true, Lauren. Everything!"

Adriana was frozen in place. Lauren peered inside the ring once again, then hugged Adriana. They were both crying tears of joy and disbelief.

"Lauren, this is wonderful. I didn't doubt you, yet I am still shocked."

Lauren laughed, pulling back the hair stuck to her face from the tears. "I know, I felt the same way. I just knew everything that happened was true. It was too crazy for it not to be, but there's that little voice saying, 'what if it's not?' When you actually realize you're not insane, the relief of it all is overwhelming. I don't know how to describe it."

Adriana laughed, hugging her tighter. "I understand. I'm still astonished by all the events that seem unreal."

They sat down at the table, sipping on their tea, hoping to calm down. Adriana looked into the ring again, and then handed it back to Lauren. "I am so happy for you. And I'm glad we planned the trip to coincide with these findings. Would we have gone had the inscription been different?"

Lauren thought for a moment. "Probably not. I would have been so disappointed, I think I would've wanted to stop the entire process at that point. At least temporarily, to gather new strength."

Adriana blew into her cup and continued the questioning. "What if we go to this place, and you don't find what you're looking for?"

Lauren smiled. "Well, then we go and I don't find anything. That wouldn't take away the validity of what has happened here today. This happened, and this is very real. I don't expect every path I take to be the correct one, or the easy one. I may have to travel over mountains and fight my way through jungles. I may occasionally take the wrong turn, but you've taught me to put it in the proper perspective. Aren't they also the right ones as well?"

Adriana smiled. "Yeah, if everything were always perfect, we certainly wouldn't learn much. I've lost count of how many times I thought I would go in one direction, or thought I was going to learn a particular lesson, or thought that I was just going to coast for a while, only to find out later I had indeed learned another type of valuable, life affirming lesson in the process. I am a firm believer in the idea that many close calls are meant to be."

Lauren nodded her head with approval. They had moved on to a conversation on beliefs and theories. And she very much enjoyed this part of their friendship. "Yes, isn't it amazing how you think something was so terrible when it happened, but looking back later, you can see just why it happened the way it did, and all that was learned from it? And more times than not, we're usually much better off because of it. So many better opportunities are brought forth from those encounters."

Adriana sipped her tea, then sat back. "As my grandmother always said, 'When presented with lemons, make lemonade.'"

Lauren glanced at her watch and yelped. "If I don't hurry, we'll be spending our day making lemonade. Look at the time."

Adriana pushed Lauren out of the kitchen. "I hope you can be ready in ten minutes, or we're in trouble."

Lauren raced out of the room, running quickly up the stairs, twirling the ring on her finger. She had to find a gold chain to put the ring on. It was going around her neck, and it wasn't coming off.

On the drive to the airport, Adriana brought up a subject which had been on her mind since the discovery of the inscription.

"Lauren, do you think the other symbols are correct, too? And how do we go about finding the answer to that mystery?"

Lauren continued tapping her fingers to the music playing on the radio. "I don't know. I'm not as concerned about it as I was twenty-four hours ago."

Adriana kept her eyes on the road as they were nearing the entrance to the airport. "Yeah, but you haven't forgotten about it either, have you?"

Lauren looked at her in disbelief. "No, I haven't forgotten for one moment. As if I could?"

The flight was smooth, and both women dozed, chatted, and read magazines to pass the time. Lauren had exhausted herself from all the emotions exerted throughout the morning. Adriana knew there would be plenty to talk about once they had landed. They alternated between discussing the events of the day, and some quiet time to think about what was transpiring. Before they realized they were fully off the ground, they had landed in Connecticut. The day had turned into night, and both girls were tired and hungry.

They found their way to the resort, and walked in exhausted.

"All I want is a nice hot bath, a warm meal, and then a soft bed."

Adriana nodded her head in agreement. "I'll go along with that. We'll get checked in and meet for dinner."

Lauren looked at her watch. "OK, we'll meet in the restaurant at 9:00 sharp.

Adriana was already walking away. "That sounds perfect."

Alex hummed a tune off and on throughout dinner, sometimes a little louder than the volume of their conversation. Donovan and Elliot stopped eating and just stared at him in disbelief, neither saying a word. Alex was obviously in his own world. After several moments of no conversation, Alex looked up to see his friends peering at him.

"What's wrong? Why are you guys looking at me as if I just landed from Mars?"

Donovan chuckled, breaking the tension. "Alex, have you been listening to yourself? I've heard of people humming while they work, but never while they eat."

Alex fell silent, squinting at both men. "What the hell are you talking about?"

Elliot worked at stifling a laugh. "Alex, you have been humming the same tune you played on your piano the other night, over and over. Donovan and I have been trying to carry on an intelligent conversation, in spite of the dinner entertainment. We're glad your meal is worth humming about, but can you cut it out?"

Alex was obviously confused, and continued staring in the direction of his friends. "I have no idea what you're talking about. I've been sitting here eating my dinner, thinking about the house, and the offer I'm going to make tomorrow. That's all. I don't usually make a habit of humming at the dinner table. I think you've both lost your minds."

Donovan tried to speak, but found it virtually impossible. He couldn't see anything but humor in this setting, and the more Alex tried to deny what had happened, the funnier it became.

Elliot looked at his watch. "Alex, what time is it?"

Alex still couldn't find the humor but looked down at his wrist. "It's 9:05, why?"

Elliot looked at his watch again, "Alex, you have been humming, rather loudly I might add, since 8:30. The same tune over and over. What is with you tonight?" He was about to continue, when he saw the now-familiar glazed look fall across his friend's face. Donovan glanced up, catching a glimpse of it as well.

"Alex, what's going on? Don't go trying to spook us again."

Alex didn't hear Donovan's voice. He was far away. The men watched their friend in awe, as Alex crossed his arms, and hugged himself in a comforting manner. When he finally spoke, it was in a whisper. "I feel her again. Rather, I feel something again. It's a sensation of intense energy penetrating every cell in my body. It feels as if each cell is pulsating. I just know there's something I need to be remembering. I never know where this is coming from, and I never know when it'll hit me."

Alex was now sweating and quite pale, and Donovan was getting concerned. "Are you all right? Do you need a doctor?"

Alex surprised them both by smiling. "No, just the opposite. When the pulsating finally stops, a wonderful warm feeling flows over me." Alex looked very cozy. "I feel as if there's nothing I can't accomplish."

Elliot's eyes roamed around the room, scanning each table in his line of vision. There were people everywhere. His eyes were sweeping over the reception area of the restaurant, and continued wandering to the main foyer. He felt his body suddenly tense up, and quickly focused back to the hostess desk, mumbling under his breath. "Wait, I know I just saw a woman standing there. Where the hell did she go?"

Elliot's eyes were quickly darting back and forth among the people in the room. She was nowhere to be seen. "What the hell happened to her?"

Donovan leaned over toward Elliot. "What's going on with you? Am I the only sane one here tonight?"

Elliot looked into Donovan's eyes, and whispered in a serious tone. "I hate to tell you this, but you're not sane either."

Donovan convulsed in laughter, finally breaking the spell at the table. He continued with the conversation that had dominated the day, as Alex and Elliot both remained deep in thought. Alex, thinking about the sensation that had just permeated him yet again, while Elliot's thoughts were with the dark-haired woman he had caught a brief glimpse of before suddenly disappearing into the crowd. He didn't know why it bothered him so.

The men finally finished their meal and relaxed with a cognac. Alex's thoughts went back to the music. "How could I go about finding out, and incorporating music into my dreams? And how do I know if that's what I should be doing? I keep hearing this melody in my head. What does it mean?"

Elliot and Donovan looked at each other, and decided this was the time to make their move. Donovan began first.

"Alex, I think the only way you're going to find the answers is to free up your mind. You need to think about other things right now. Personally, that's how I do my most creative work. I come up with my best ideas when I'm not thinking about an issue. Same with you, right?"

Elliot continued with his opinion. "I have a great idea. When we get back to L.A., why don't you get the guys together, and play a gig or two at the clubs? This was something you planned to do before this took over your life. That way, you'll still be getting the music, and thinking of other things as well."

Alex had a look of concern on his face when Donovan broke in.

"Every breakthrough you've had so far has been when your mind wasn't on it."

Alex's face had a look of defeat, and the guys began to feel guilty, realizing they had been the ones to force him to continue in the first place.

Alex casually slammed his fist on the table. "You're absolutely right. I've done my best detective work when I haven't been thinking so much about it. I get so close, it drowns me, and I stop trusting my instincts. I'll get the guys together as soon as we get back. I know Ron is just waiting for the word to jam."

Donovan folded his napkin, and placed it on the table. "It's been a full day. I'm going to sleep as soon as my head hits the pillow."

The men were waiting for the elevator in silence, when Elliot caught a glimpse of a dark-haired woman. They stepped in as soon as the doors opened, but Elliot suddenly jumped out, yelling back to the others, "You go ahead, there's something I need to check on. I'll call you early for breakfast."

Elliot quickly walked to the other end of the large lobby. He didn't want to think about why he was doing it. She wasn't his type of woman. And he hadn't actually caught a good glimpse of her. There was just something odd about the sequence of events. He remembered Alex was going through this déjà vu thing, when suddenly he looked up and saw this woman. He had received his own impression the moment he saw her. He was walking faster now. *Why am I doing this?* He tried to come up with a quick excuse. *I just want to get close enough to see if any other impressions will come through.*

Elliot felt it had something to do with Alex, or with someone close to him. Frustrated for running around a hotel when he would rather be sleeping, he chastised himself. *What the hell is wrong with me? There's no one here.* The sofas were empty, and no one was waiting for an elevator. He walked into the bar and found it empty as well. He turned away, and walked back to the other end of the lobby. He was agitated with himself and tired. *This is ridiculous. I'm exhausted, but here I am running after a woman I doubt I would even know, much less ever see again. I'm going to bed.*

He approached the elevator doors just as they were closing. "Hold the door please." The doors opened, and Elliot stepped in, punching the button to his floor. There were several people standing around him. He pushed himself further toward the back, knowing his floor would be the last one. It seemed to be taking forever. It felt the doors were opening on every floor, whether someone was getting off or not. He was watching the numbers above him flash at each passing floor, when he glanced over, noticing a tall woman with long straight reddish hair. She had a very comfortable look about her. She glanced over at him, looked briefly into his eyes, and smiled. Elliot smiled back, feeling a huge rush of energy flowing through him. He shivered, and hoped that no one had noticed.

His mind was racing, *This is ridiculous. What the hell is wrong with me? First I'm chasing the halls after a dark-haired woman, then I get a feeling with this one.* He glanced at her again. *She really is a pretty woman. There seems to be something so right about her.* He was talking to himself again, and hoped he was still doing so silently. Elliot tried to rationalize by telling himself he was just tired. He watched in disappointment as she got off on her floor, but didn't look back. *It's just as well. I'm not here trying to pick up women. My hands are full enough with Alex.* The door opened and he gratefully found his room, and was asleep within minutes.

Lauren walked around the lobby several times, waiting for Adriana. A few minutes after nine, she finally decided to call her friend, but found her phone was busy. Lauren was tired and just wanted to eat something light and go to bed. She walked over to the hostess desk of the restaurant, and quickly glanced in. She decided to wait a little longer, before going back to her room. She walked across the lobby towards the shops, but was too tired to find anything that appealed to her.

She was approaching the lobby when a chill suddenly ran up and down her spine. She dropped onto one of the lobby sofas, and wrapped her arms protectively around herself. Lauren frantically glanced around the room, but saw nothing out of the ordinary. *What's happening to me? And why's it happening here of all places?*

Lauren waited until the sensation subsided, then picked up the phone next to her and called Adriana's room. Hearing the same busy signal, she yawned. "That's it. I'm tired, and I have no idea when she'll be off."

She picked the receiver up again, and phoned room service, ordering a snack for both her and Adriana, then took the elevator back to her room.

Adriana tried to phone Lauren's room, but found her already gone. She had been tied up with business, and couldn't get away to tell her to go ahead without her. Finally, at 9:30, she took the elevator down to search the lobby for her friend. There was no sign of her. Finding the house phones, she dialed her friend's room. When Lauren picked up, instead of a hello, she simply said, "Where were you?"

Adriana giggled, "Sorry Lauren, there were shipping problems at the store. I had to work that out, and make a few other calls. Everything is all right now, but I lost complete track of the time. Are you still hungry? I'm downstairs."

Lauren laughed, "Sorry, I'm tired. I ordered room service for both of us. I assumed you were busy, and wouldn't have time to eat. You'd better get back to your room before it arrives."

Adriana blew a mock kiss into the phone. "You're the greatest. What did you order me?"

Lauren responded in a mysterious voice, "Sweetie, you're the psychic. You tell me. Good night, I'll see you early in the morning."

Adriana said her good nights and headed back to the elevators. She was getting frustrated on the flight up. "What the hell is happening here?" The doors were opening on each floor. She looked up as each number lit up, and then down at her watch. She caught a glimpse of a handsome man standing in the corner. She had noticed his glance too, but she was too tired to pursue it, and instead gave him a half-hearted smile. The door opened to her floor, and she strolled out. As expected, her food was waiting at her door.

Chapter 12

Lauren awoke early the next morning, feeling refreshed. She phoned Adriana, and then met her in the coffee shop for a quick breakfast.

As soon as they walked outside, Lauren took a deep breath, and buttoned her jacket. "Now this is what air is supposed to smell like. What a beautiful day. Just look at the leaves, and the bright blue sky. Isn't it gorgeous?"

Adriana looked around her, buttoning her own jacket. "Yeah, I could get used to a place like this. I had no idea the sky could still be this clear, and the air this cool."

They made their way to the car, and then took a few minutes to program the GPS. Adriana slid behind the wheel, and adjusted the mirrors. "Lauren, let's get our bearings before we leave. How long did the real estate agent say it would take to drive to this place?"

Lauren was sliding her finger over the GPS map, reading the street names. "She said it would only take a few minutes. I didn't bother to ask if her few minutes were in L.A. time, or Connecticut time. You know there's a big difference between the two."

She heard no response from her driver, and glanced over. She found Adriana staring blankly at her. Lauren tried to sound intelligent about the point just made. "Well, there is. This is the country. Things are much slower here." She saw she wasn't making headway with her friend. "OK, I forgot to ask her how long it would take. I know it's not far. Does that help?"

Adriana smiled warmly; her point had been well made without uttering a word. "Let's see the directions."

After a few moments, the women seemed to have their bearings, and drove off the hotel property. Except for the occasional comment about the beautiful countryside, their drive was quiet. They were both spellbound by the place. Once they realized the property wasn't as far as they first thought, Adriana slowed down so they could enjoy the scenery.

Lauren opened the windows to take advantage of the clean crisp fall air. Every so often, when they would pass an old house, an old fence, or an old tree, Lauren would turn her head, and watch it intently. Finally, she voiced her thoughts, "Do you feel as if you've been here before?"

Adriana looked over and smiled warmly. "Well, I don't know if I've been here before, but I know it's a place I wouldn't mind coming back to."

Lauren returned her smile, "Yeah, perhaps that's what I'm feeling. It seems like such a wonderful place. But I keep getting this sensation of déjà vu. It's like so many little things remind me of something, but I just can't put my finger on it."

Adriana didn't want to taint Lauren's impressions, so she just nodded, keeping her attention on the road.

By the time they neared the old road that the house was on, they had both returned to their own thoughts.

Without realizing her words, Lauren calmly stated, "This is a little tricky here. You have to make an immediate right."

Adriana knew Lauren hadn't looked at the map or her notes for several minutes. They were both too involved with the sights and sounds of the countryside. She casually glanced over at her friend and found Lauren had a fixed look on her face, appearing completely relaxed, and at ease. Adriana responded by turning the wheel to the right.

Lauren was quiet as they continued driving up the old country road. When she spoke again, Adriana couldn't put a face with the voice that she heard. "You can stop at the gate ahead. The house is on the right, further up the drive."

Adriana slowly drove the car to the metal gate and stopped. The fence was closed and locked, and they would have to wait for the agent to arrive. Adriana couldn't see a house, but suspected it was ahead on the right. Quietness prevailed in the car for a few minutes, until Adriana couldn't wait any longer. She saw no signs saying the property was for sale.

"Are you certain we're at the right place?"

Instead of responding, Lauren opened her car door, and stepped out. Adriana quietly unfastened her seatbelt. She didn't know what was going to happen next, but she wanted to be prepared for anything. Lauren gently closed the car door and stepped to the gate. She looked all around the immediate area, her eyes scanning each treetop, then down to each blade of grass. Adriana continued to watch from the car. She thought it was harmless sightseeing until Lauren began climbing over the gate. Adriana quickly scrambled out of her car, running to her friend.

"Lauren, what are you doing? You're going to hurt yourself. We don't even know if this is the right property. And if it is, then we need to wait until the agent arrives."

Lauren wasn't listening, as she brought her other leg over to the opposite side of the fence.

Adriana tried again. "Lauren, listen to me. You can't be doing this."

Lauren didn't hear her. She walked over to an object lying flat on the ground. Adriana waited. It was obvious that her words weren't getting through. Lauren bent down and picked up a sign. She turned it toward Adriana, pointing to the phone number and address painted on the piece of metal. "Is this the agent's phone number?"

Adriana dug into her pocket, pulling out a card. She looked up at the sign being held high in the air, then back down at the paper. "Yeah, it's the same. Congratulations."

But Lauren had already thrown the sign back to the ground in a tangled heap and was strolling down the dirt driveway.

Adriana didn't know what to do. She looked over at her car, not knowing whether to leave it behind, jump the fence and follow Lauren, or wait until the agent arrived and drive through the gates like a sane person. She didn't think for long. She jumped the fence, yelling, "Wait for me."

By the time Adriana caught up with Lauren, neither wanted to interrupt the sounds of birds singing, the crunching of the fallen leaves as they were trampled on, and the scraping sound of a large stick that Lauren had retrieved, and was now grating on the dirt behind her. Though they were quiet, Adriana watched Lauren closely. With a look of absolute confidence, she seemed to know exactly where she was going. She looked so confident that Adriana was leery of speaking for fear Lauren wouldn't know who she was. She knew that was nonsense, but there was still a faint doubt in her mind. She followed alongside, just watching and listening.

Lauren followed the trees until she came to a pond. She crossed over to Adriana's left, and followed the path leading to an old wooden bridge. Adriana could hear her humming a melody as she crossed, walking in the direction of the gazebo standing nearby. Adriana chose to sit down on the bench and observe. Lauren was humming loudly to herself, oblivious to anyone around her. Adriana watched as Lauren stood in the middle of the open gazebo, gazing out onto the fields. She had a hint of a smile on her lips, and her eyes were alert and crystal clear.

Adriana involuntarily jumped when Lauren quickly turned around and started frantically looking for something inside the gazebo itself. Her eyes covered every square inch of the building. Just when she looked as if she was going to walk away filled with disappointment, she turned swiftly around again, and pointed to something on the peaked ceiling.

Adriana couldn't make out what it was. Her friend motioned impatiently to her. "Come see."

She walked quickly in her friend's direction. "What is it?" Lauren kept her finger pointing toward the area that had caught her interest. Adriana approached, her head tilted up. She was momentarily confused. "This is what you came for?"

She looked into Lauren's eyes and saw a faint glow of remembrance. In a barely audible voice, Lauren choked out, "I knew it was here. I don't know what it means, but I just knew it was here."

Adriana looked up again and saw the letters. Slowly, she read aloud what had caught her eye, "N.F., W.W., A.R.

She ran her finger over the rough markings. "What does it mean?"

Lauren stood beside her, eyes wide. "I don't know. I feel as if I should know, but it's just not coming to me."

"Have you dreamed about this place, or these initials?"

"No. Not that I'm aware of." Lauren was flushed, and sounded as if she were in the distance somewhere. She was thinking, trying to remember something, anything that may help. "I should know this. I mean, I knew it was here. Right?"

Adriana nodded her head.

"Then why don't I know what the hell this means, or how I knew it was here in the first place? I've never been psychic. Certainly not like this anyway."

Adriana was about to speak when she heard a honk in the distance.

"Damn, the agent's here. You stay put. I'll run meet her, then drive in to get you." Adriana was already crossing the bridge and talking behind her. "I don't know how far the house is from here."

Lauren interrupted, "It's just up the driveway and around the corner. I'll meet you there."

Adriana watched as Lauren crossed the bridge and began her walk.

Adriana mumbled to herself, not sure what to say to the agent about Lauren's disposition or whereabouts. "I suppose I could always say that Lauren was in awe of the place. And being the free spirit that she is, I decided to let her roam the area alone." Shaking her head back and forth, she mumbled again, "God, that's a terrible excuse. It all sounds too strange. She'll believe everything she's ever heard about California. Better come up with something else, quick."

As Adriana approached the gate, she saw the older woman innocently standing next to her car, and knew she couldn't come up with anything better.

The agent met Adriana on the other side of the fence. "Hi, you must be Cathy Owens. I'm Adriana Dean." Adriana extended her hand and continued. "We appreciate you taking the time to meet us here first thing this morning." Adriana was trying to stay calm, and maintain control of the conversation. "Lauren found this place to be so beautiful, she didn't want to wait. She decided to walk, and said that she'd meet us at the house. I hope that's all right." Adriana knew she was speaking too fast, but she wasn't used to having to make up stories. At least not on demand.

The older woman smiled. "That's quite all right. I was concerned when I didn't see anyone in the car."

Adriana worked at continuing the conversation, "I couldn't hold Lauren down for very long." Adriana was still mumbling to herself as she slipped behind the wheel of her car, following the agent's car in front. "Lauren, I hope you're not up there doing something we're both going to regret."

Jerking her head from one side to the other, she didn't see Lauren anywhere in sight. They had already driven slowly past the pond, and the gazebo. "Where are you?"

She was attempting to drive safely on the dirt road, and search for her friend at the same time. By the time she had put the car in park, she had almost run into the agent's car several times. As she slowly stood up, she looked ahead and momentarily forgot about her friend. "Wow, what a house."

She continued staring, and talking to herself in amazement.

"There's another gazebo. My God, these people must have had the bucks."

Cathy approached with a smile on her face. "You're impressed, I see."

Adriana was visibly affected. "Yes, it's quite a home."

Cathy continued her sales pitch. "It would be a wonderful retreat for the right person."

Adriana was searching the grounds for Lauren, again. "It certainly would."

"Miss Dean? Miss Dean?" Adriana was fantasizing about what she was going to do when she found her friend. She vaguely heard an irritating high-pitched voice calling her name. "Miss Dean?" It was the agent's voice.

Adriana was back in the present. "Yes?"

"If we could locate Miss Wells, perhaps we could go into the house. Would that be satisfactory?"

This woman was much too stiff for Adriana, and she found it difficult to relax around her. She just wanted to do what had to be done, and be gone. Unfortunately, she knew she would have to entertain her while Lauren roamed the grounds unsupervised.

Adriana took a breath, turning slowly to the woman. "Why don't we look for her?"

Cathy leisurely walked around one side of the house, while Adriana ran around the other. She found Lauren gently swaying in a tire swing attached to an old oak tree.

Adriana quickly and carefully assessed the situation, then moved slowly and calmly in her direction. "This place is sure beautiful, isn't it?"

Lauren was humming softly to herself. She looked around, and then turned her attention to Adriana. "The flower garden is dead. Can you believe it? At one time, it was beautiful."

Adriana looked around, noticing the brown withered twigs. "Yes, I'm sure at one time it was very lovely." She squatted down in front of her friend, now trying desperately to hide her worry.

"Lauren, are you all right? The agent's waiting for us. And I'm sure she's already questioning our sanity. Can you help me out here?"

Lauren looked out over the bay. "The water's calm today. It's been a long time since I've seen water like this."

Adriana glanced at the water, noticing the dock was in need of repair. She was fighting to stay focused and keep her voice calm. "Lauren, have you seen the house yet?"

The swing momentarily stopped, and Lauren looked in the direction of the massive screened-in porch. "Yeah, I want to go inside, but it's locked. I can't imagine why." Her voice was delicate, far different from the one she normally possessed.

Adriana was now visibly shaken. She firmly grabbed her friend's shoulders. "Lauren, look at me."

Noticeably disappointed, Lauren's attention was focused on the dead garden again. Adriana looked to her right, and spotted Cathy coming around the house. She only had a few moments to bring Lauren back to reality.

She lowered her voice and spoke more sharply now. "Lauren, if you don't focus for a few minutes, this woman will never allow us in this house. Do you understand what I'm saying? We would have come all this way for nothing."

Lauren was still humming the same tune as before. Her attention had switched and was now focused on the front porch. She didn't seem upset in the least. "Adriana, don't worry. I'm OK." Lauren was speaking in a dreamy, faraway voice. "She'll let us in."

The agent was quickly approaching. Adriana braced herself by standing up straight, introducing her friend, and hoping for the best.

Lauren stood up when the older woman came closer, and firmly shook Cathy's hand. Adriana noticed the wispy tone of her voice was still present, but the agent had never met Lauren before, and wouldn't know any different.

Adriana smiled, "Let her think Lauren's a little odd. It's too late to cover it up."

Adriana took Lauren's arm as they walked in the direction of the big house. "Lauren, why don't we go inside and see what we find?"

She announced it more as a hint for Cathy to walk ahead of them, and unlock the doors. Adriana continued talking to keep suspicion down. "This place is gorgeous. Tell me, Cathy, do you know its history?"

The woman looked down at her paperwork. "You'll have to excuse me. This is not my listing. It belongs to a friend of mine. She's out of town, and asked me if I'd help out. I'll try and answer the best I can." She looked down again, and paraphrased the information.

"This property has had two owners. The last one had it for many years."

She was about to continue when Lauren stopped her in mid-sentence. "Who were the original owners?"

Adriana interrupted before Lauren got herself into trouble. She knew where the question was leading. She spoke up with a smile in her voice. "What she means is, who originally built the house, and how old is it?"

The woman unlocked the door, stepping aside while the two young women walked into the foyer. The woman was scanning for the information when a gust of wind blew the papers out of her hands. Adriana saw the woman scramble to retrieve them, and stooped down to help. Lauren never noticed, and immediately left their side.

Adriana scooped the papers up from the ground, and then gently took the agent's arm, leading her to the front porch. "Cathy, why don't you tell me what you do know about the house?"

Cathy's forehead wrinkled. "As I said before, I don't know too much. Don't you think your friend may want to be shown around?" In a friendly and professional manner, the agent tried to release herself from Adriana, but she would have none of it.

Adriana continued to smile with great interest. "Cathy, Miss Wells is a bit of a loner. Why don't we let her walk around the house by herself for a few minutes? If she needs us, I feel certain she'll call. She couldn't possibly get herself into any trouble. Right?"

Realizing she had been defeated, the confused woman sat down on the steps of the front porch, and began putting her papers in order. She was visibly resigned to the fact that she was no longer in charge of the situation. "If you think that is best, Miss Dean."

Adriana felt guilty for treating this nice lady the way she had, but knew Lauren needed her privacy for as long as possible. "Thank you, Cathy. That's very nice of you." Adriana sat down next to the woman and continued the conversation. "Now, why don't you tell me all you know about the house?"

The agent read to Adriana what little information she had in her possession. It was obvious she hadn't done her homework, and she was doing this strictly as a favor to a friend.

Adriana smiled, and pretended Cathy was quite a sales lady. She listened to every word, and asked questions when necessary.

Lauren never heard the line of questioning going on, on her behalf. She closed the door and found herself in a different era. She didn't realize she was humming a tune one minute, then talking softly to herself the next.

Her self-guided tour began in the large foyer area, when she gasped in pleasure, and spoke aloud, "My God, the energy here is incredible." She felt safe, and knew her guide was with her. Lauren continued forward, then to the right, walking into the spacious dining room. Her fingers reached up to lightly stroke the walls. She continued her conversation, "Such parties and wonderful dinners in this room."

She crossed to the other side, and walked into the formal living area. She stood in the middle of its vastness, and faced the large stone fireplace. She could almost see the flames leaping over the wood, being consumed. "That fireplace was always too hot to sit near."

She was going with whatever thoughts occurred to her. She walked toward the back of the house, strolling through the living room. "This must be the library." The room was beautifully paneled, with bookshelves on two walls. She inhaled and noticed the room had the scent of musky wood. "I like this room."

She could almost visualize the books of all shapes and sizes lining the wall. Lauren was exiting through the rear of the room, when she momentarily caught sight of another fireplace against the wall. Above the fireplace was a picture of two people on a beach. She quickly turned her head in that direction, but the wall was blank. She squinted harder, and barely breathed. "I know a painting was on that wall. I just know it. I'm not crazy. I know what I saw." She was desperately trying to convince herself. "Damn it, I know what the hell I saw."

When she could come up with no logical answer, Lauren held her head high and defiantly marched into the kitchen. The walls were painted a cheery yellow and white. She walked over to the counter, and looked out the window. Her eyes immediately roamed past the back yard and deep into the trees beyond. She sensed something was out there, but couldn't remember what it was. She was growing more impatient, and could hear her fingers tapping hard against the counter top. "I'll go look in a few minutes."

Lauren heard the sound of her own voice, and stopped. Shock registered as she began realizing what thoughts had transpired verbally in the last few minutes. "My God. This is all so familiar to me. No, it was all once familiar to me." She shook her head violently, looking down to the floor. "I don't know what I'm saying."

Lauren took a deep breath to center herself, and smelled freshly baked pastries. She began humming again, while instinctively walking to the stove. "Everything looks different, yet it's all the same." She realized what she had mumbled, and cradled her forehead in her palm. "What am I saying? Where is this coming from?"

Lauren stood with her eyes closed for a few minutes, and saw her guide standing next to her. "Don't be frightened. Just light your candle, and trust the process."

Lauren opened her eyes. "My candle."

She trudged very slowly away from the kitchen, making her way up the stairs. She realized the house was making her feel happy and carefree, yet so very tired and sad too. "What is happening to me?"

She could hear voices outside, and knew Adriana was keeping the agent busy. "Thank God for Adriana."

Lauren stopped when she reached the top of the stairs. Her mind was running in a hundred directions, but her body refused to budge.

"OK, Lauren, you can do this. For God's sakes, let me move my feet."

She was talking louder now. "You will never forgive yourself if you don't finish what you've started here. Now move it!"

Lauren picked up one foot and placed it in front of the other. "That's right. Don't stop. Everything is all right. There's nothing here that can hurt you." Lauren was giving herself a pep talk, and it was working. She was beginning to see the beauty of the house. "There's such a wonderful feel about this place."

She walked into each room, glancing out the windows to view the back yard and the trees beyond. She looked in the closets, up at the ceilings, and down the walls. She smiled, realizing there was nothing in these rooms to frighten her. "This house makes me feel just fantastic. Almost like a child again. There are some wonderful memories here."

Lauren began humming the familiar tune, oblivious to the energy pulling her straight ahead. She walked out of the smaller bedroom, continuing down the hall, when she caught a glimpse of a door in front of her.

She suddenly felt an eerie, unsettling sensation, and froze dead in her tracks. Her intuition was appealing to her heart. She thought it was telling her she was about to enter an area she said she would never return to again. "That's ridiculous." But she couldn't move, and the only sound she heard was her own heart beating out of her body.

She took a deep cleansing breath, forcing herself to remain calm. But knew she was losing the battle. "Lauren, you will do this. It's just a room." She refused to give in to the fear, and forced herself to the door. Lauren put her head down as if in prayer, and visualized a glowing white light of protection around herself. She slowly raised her hand, placing her long fingers on the knob. It fit perfectly in her hand as if she had used it a million times. Lauren stood in place for what seemed like hours, until finally, her curiosity prevailed. "Damn it, there's something about the room that I must investigate." She was no longer afraid of what she would find. Her only fear was of how she would react.

Lauren centered herself, and gently opened the door. The room was well lit, and appeared cheerful and friendly. She opened the door wider and entered, feeling silly for reacting so harshly. "It's a beautiful master suite. Nothing more than that."

She stood just inside the door, first proving to herself she had courage before stepping further into the room. She approached the large bay windows and stopped. "What a lovely view. This room is just wonderful."

Lauren walked to the door, and slowly turned to scan the entire room before leaving. "I can't imagine anyone wanting to sell this place." She knew she was making casual conversation with herself, trying to ignore the chill running up her spine. She instinctively hugged herself, still not sure what was happening. Lauren closed her eyes and shivered, as if to shake the sense of sudden dread from her soul.

When she opened them, she was in her previous dreamy state. She felt light, and very different from the woman she had been a few moments before. Lauren was only vaguely aware of what was happening, and fighting to stay in her real world. "Where is this coming from?" She leaned her body against the door for support. An illuminating image overtook her, and she slumped to the floor.

The entire room had changed. Furniture had replaced the empty spaces, and a roaring fire was burning in the fireplace. She could unmistakably feel a sense of love penetrating every cell of her body, coming from someplace she couldn't identify. There was music in the distance, and she wanted to calm the pounding of her own heart, so she could listen to the tune beckoning her.

"Where have I heard that before?" She was humming the melody to herself. Lauren sensed a presence and glanced around, but saw no one. Even so, she knew there was another energy sharing her space. The temperature was rising in the room, and she felt beads of sweat forming on her forehead. She squirmed, as if to get out of her own skin. "There's so much intense passion in here." She found herself near the center of the chamber, and felt the heat from the burning logs in the fireplace. "Where's it coming from?" She smiled when her gaze fell on a beautiful oak table placed in front of the bay windows. A light fog had enveloped the room, and Lauren was having trouble making out the detailed markings on it. But she was now totally immersed by the happenings around her.

"I know this table. I've seen it before. I know I have." She didn't approach it, but stood staring at it through the multi-layers of fog. Suddenly, her blue eyes seemed to penetrate the ethereal mass around her, and she spied a large box sitting atop the oak furniture. Next to it was a beautiful frame that held a picture of a smiling, and obviously happy couple.

Her eyes returned to the familiar box sitting on the table. She studied its handiwork. It was deep blue, with a light colored rim. "I know there's something on top of the box." She didn't try to approach the table, preferring instead to stay on the floor. She looked through the fog, and saw four beautifully carved wooden legs. Her eyes widened in disbelief when she suddenly heard music penetrating the entire room. "Oh my God, that's my music box. I own that. It's mine!" She tried to have a closer look, when her eyes once again caught sight of the framed picture.

"I've got to see who these people are." She crawled on the floor, trying desperately to fight her way through the heavy mist. The music began to slow down and soften. At the same time, Lauren could feel the panic building within the walls and herself. Something wasn't right anymore. Something in and around her was beginning to ache and hurt. She began to hear the soothing words of her guide echoing within the walls. "Open your mind, and your heart will follow. Find what was lost to you."

She was pushing the fog away, but stopped when a wave of anguish and pain soared through her soul. The ache was so severe, Lauren grabbed at her chest, trying to rip it out of her body. She could feel hot scalding tears burning her eyes. She could hear herself gasping, and fighting for every breath. She had never experienced such pain in her entire life. She had no idea this kind of agony even existed. She hardly recognized the tortured sound of her voice, "Please, let me die too. Please, please, let me die, too."

The muscles in her body froze, and she became still and quiet.

Then she heard herself whimpering in a childlike voice, and it frightened her. "Did I just say that? Did I just say I wanted to die?"

Her dark hair was wet and had fallen in her face, and her eyes were wide and crazed. She felt dizzy and sick to her stomach.

"God, please tell me what happened. I don't understand."

Lauren looked around and saw she was still on the floor, but was now crouched in a corner like a frightened animal. The ring she wore around her neck had found its way to being cradled in the palm of her hand.

She looked slowly around the room, and heard her voice become dry and flat. "It's empty. There's no furniture here. No music. No fire in the fireplace."

She closed her eyes, and hugged her legs tightly to her chest. "What happened to me? What happened to the people who had loved so fiercely, and lost so much? How could there be such a drastic contrast in emotion? How could anyone stand it without going crazy?"

Her body was feeling the aftermath from the assault to her senses. She became very quiet, realizing it had become imperative that she listen to what her heart had to say. Otherwise, she knew she would go crazy, herself.

Lauren could hear the old man somewhere around her, very faintly. "Open your mind, and your heart will follow."

Lauren looked closely at her ring. "Your heart will follow? I don't understand."

She closed her eyes to get her bearings before having to face the women downstairs. She knew she had been gone for a very long time. But she couldn't shake the faint voice that had barricaded itself in her mind. Somewhere in the distance, she could hear words being repeated over and over. "Find what was lost to you."

Lauren sniffled, took a deep breath, and spoke aloud, "I'm trying to remain very calm. But I think I know what I saw." She sniffled again. "And I definitely know what I felt. It was wonderful, and then it was tragic. I wanted to die." The words came from her lips, but she couldn't comprehend them. "I wanted to die?" She shook her head, "No, I didn't want to die. But someone did."

Lauren was too confused to comprehend, and her head ached to be given a rest. She sat in the corner, staring at the room for a few minutes, then slowly stood up, and held on to the mantle until the dizziness subsided. Once she stabilized herself, she took her time trudging to the door, then turned to look back into the room once more. She felt tears stinging her eyes. "Such history." She could think of nothing else to say. She pushed her hair out of her face, and took a deep breath. "I need some fresh air. I have to see that life exists outside of this room."

Lauren was closing the bedroom door, when she heard a voice inside of her head. "Stop!" Every muscle in her body turned rigid, and she was stuck to the floor. She instinctively closed her eyes.

"Open your mind and your heart will follow."

Lauren kept her eyes closed. "Please tell me. What is so important that I'm not paying attention to? I don't understand. How can I open my mind any more than it already is?"

Her mind was questioning one thing, but her body was telling her something else. Her instincts were strong now. Every nerve in her body was ablaze. She kept her eyes closed and listened to the rhythm of the house. She listened to her body and she listened to the energy pulsating around her. Not a muscle twitched.

When Lauren opened her eyes, she was standing near the mantle in the bedroom. She didn't think to question how she got there. She listened carefully, and then raised her hand to the mantle, lightly touching the wooden shelf. Her first instinct was to pull back when she felt something soft brushing against her hand. But instead, she grabbed the object between two fingers, and swiftly brought it down to eye level. Turning it over in her hand, she saw it was a white napkin with writing on it. Lauren was in disbelief. "Oh my God. Where did this come from? How did I know where to look? How did I do it?" Her fear had been replaced with excitement. She noticed the napkin was folded over in the center. She put the paper next to her skin and smelled it, then gently rubbed it against her cheek. A chill ran over her entire body, as she ceremoniously opened the napkin.

"I wonder who wrote it?" She looked on the other side, but found no signature. "Looks like a man's handwriting."

She closely examined the writing once more, then read it aloud.

"Time will hold the answers to the questions in our hearts.
Memories of you keep my love strong.
Every second that we're apart."

Lauren wiped fresh tears from her eyes.

"That's the most beautiful thing I've ever read."

She walked to the door, then stopped and looked down at the note. No longer having the strength to question her actions,

Lauren placed it very carefully in an empty envelope, then took out a blank sheet of paper and a pen from her purse. She didn't have to think about what she wanted to write. It came easily for her. She placed her note on the mantle, and calmly walked from the room.

She had just closed the door when she heard Adriana approaching, out of breath. "Are you all right? You've been gone for a while. I've been trying to keep the agent talking." Adriana giggled at herself. "I know all about her family, her friends, and her entire life."

Lauren smiled, but Adriana wasn't finished. "You look as if you've seen a ghost. What happened in there?" She opened the bedroom door and gasped.

Lauren looked at her closely. "What do you see?"

Adriana walked into the room. "Only one of the most fabulous rooms I've ever seen."

Lauren looked around. "You don't see or feel anything unusual?"

Adriana looked at her strangely. "No, why? Should I? It just feels really nice in here. And the room looks out over the yard, and the water? Wow, what a gorgeous view."

Lauren looked around again. "I agree with you on that count, but I've had the strangest things happen to me in this house, particularly in this room. I can't wait to tell you about it." Lauren was digging in her purse. "But first, I want to show you what I found on the mantle."

She pulled out the napkin, and placed it carefully in Adriana's open palm. Adriana read it several times, then handed it back to her friend, visibly moved by its content. "Where did it come from?"

They were walking down the long hall toward the stairs. "I don't know. I was leaving the room when I felt a tremendous urge to approach the mantle. This is what I found."

When the women reached the head of the stairs, Adriana stopped at the window overlooking the back area of the property. "Isn't it beautiful out there?"

Lauren stopped talking and looked where Adriana was pointing.

She felt the chill return, running down her spine, causing her to shiver uncontrollably. She heard herself speak in an unfamiliar voice. "There's something out there, and I must find it. I know it's there."

Lauren could hear the trees summoning, and she wanted desperately to run outside, and frolic among them. She felt Adriana's stern pull to her shoulders, and was thrown back into reality.

"Lauren, what's going on? What are you sensing? What happened in this house?"

Lauren felt slightly dazed. "That's what I was trying to tell you. The room changed its appearance. I think I saw it the way it must have looked in another time. It drew me in, and there was music all around. I felt a loving, happy energy. I saw an oak table, with a picture frame sitting on top of it. There was a man and a woman in the picture."

Adriana interrupted, "Could you see who the people were?"

"No, just like in my dreams, there was a fog preventing me from crossing over. But the most exciting moment was seeing my music box on top of the table."

Adriana looked surprised. She wasn't sure if her friend was hallucinating, or had fallen asleep and dreamed. "How do you know for sure that it was your box?"

"I just knew. The damn mist was covering it, but I know without question the music box I own not only came from this house, but it sat on an oak table in the master bedroom."

Adriana looked puzzled. "If you saw all this flow of energy around you, why do you look as if you have just been through hell and back?"

Lauren's face fell, and her eyes filled up with tears as she remembered. "Adriana, I don't know if you believe me or not. I see the doubt in your eyes, but you have got to trust me. I didn't believe it either. But when I found the note, I had to stop questioning what I saw." Lauren took her friend's hand. "I had no choice but to trust."

Adriana looked deeply into the woman's moist eyes and saw the bittersweet pain. "All right, Lauren, why don't you tell me what happened."

Lauren took a grateful breath. "It was beautiful, and then it was awful. And I don't begin to understand any of it. One moment, there was so much joy and laughter in the room. Then everything changed, and there was such tremendous pain. What brought me out of it was the sound of my own voice begging to let me die." Lauren looked into her friend's eyes. "I said, 'please let me die too.'"

Adriana had a look of disbelief cross her face.

Lauren was suddenly concerned, "What's wrong?"

Adriana sat her down on the top stair, and warmly took her hand. "Lauren, the agent told me a story. Actually, she said the story had been a rumor around here for years. But as far as she knew, there's no proof of it being true."

Lauren's curiosity was getting the best of her. She squeezed her friend's hand. "What? Tell me what you heard."

Adriana swallowed hard. "The story goes that this house was built by a young couple in the nineteen thirties. She wasn't very clear on the year. Poor thing, I didn't want to push her."

Lauren squeezed her hand again. "Keep going. Don't get off the subject."

"OK, OK. Anyway, they were a wealthy couple, and both were writers. Apparently, they were very much in love, and inseparable. But one day something tragic happened to the husband. He died in an accident, and she never got over it. Soon after, she also died. Isn't that just horrible?"

Lauren pursued the story. "So, how did he die? How did she die? How did the next family come to own this place?"

Adriana shrugged her shoulders, "I don't know. Neither does the agent."

Lauren was agitated. "What kind of agent is she? She doesn't even know the history of this place? I need answers."

Adriana stood up, "Well, you have the only answers she can give you. She's not the listing agent, so I'm glad we got as much as we did."

They were halfway down the stairs when Lauren paused. "Adriana, would the agent know if this place had been shown before? Wouldn't they keep a list at the office?"

Adriana stopped behind her friend. "I would suppose so. Why?"

"Couldn't we have her check with the office? This way, we may get a lead on where the note came from. What do you think? I know it's a long shot, but it wouldn't hurt to ask. Right?"

Adriana looked at her watch. "OK, I'll go down and have her call the office. I seem to have made a friend. Why don't you go out back, and look around."

Adriana was startled to hear herself make the suggestion. She wondered if Lauren had noticed the difference in her voice.

"OK, I'm going to see what I can find out there. It's definitely calling me."

Adriana opened the front door and walked out, still perplexed. She could see the agent still on the phone, so she sat on the steps, grateful for a few minutes of quiet.

Lauren unlocked the back door and stepped out into the cool, crisp autumn breeze. The sunshine warmed her body, making her feel alive. She took a deep cleansing breath, and then laughed at herself. "If I keep doing this, I'm going to hyperventilate." But the air was clean and stimulating to her lungs.

She walked out toward the grove of trees about a hundred yards from the porch, noticing the leaves had started turning various shades of orange and red. "I wish I could take this back home with me." She thought about the snow falling in the winters, and how the beauty must be breathtaking. "I wish I could be here to see it."

Lauren continued walking slowly through the trees, touching several along the way. "How odd this is. I feel as if I'm saying hello again." She repeated herself again in a whisper, "How odd this is." She felt an urge to sit down among them, and have a picnic.

Lauren stopped abruptly when she came across a beautiful area of open land, with large trees surrounding it. She looked down and noticed several colorful rocks of all sizes in front of her on the ground. She bent over and touched one. "These rocks don't belong here. They were put here by someone. I wonder why?" Lauren picked one up, turning it over several times, feeling the familiar smoothness of the jewel in her hand.

When she heard Adriana calling her name in the distance, she carefully placed the rock back on the ground. Lauren would stop every few yards to glance behind to the tiny clearing of land. "What am I forgetting?"

But her friend's incessant calling forced her toward the house.

Adriana was standing on the back porch. "Did you get any impressions out there?"

Lauren looked through the trees behind her. "I feel a pull, but I don't know why. Maybe I'm just taken in by the beauty of it all. Did you find out if they've shown the house lately?"

Adriana shook her head, "Sorry, they haven't shown it."

"That's odd. I don't feel the note has been here very long."

Adriana looked at her closely, "Why do you say that?"

Lauren looked up at the sky, "I don't know. I just don't think we've been the only people here lately."

The girls thanked the agent for her time, and slipped into their car.

Lauren looked back once more at the property as they drove away.

"I hope someone special buys this place. I wish it could be me, but I couldn't afford it."

She turned away and became quiet before her voice registered the tears already in her eyes.

Chapter 13

Alex was anxious to go over his ideas with Elliot and Donovan. He waited until 8:00 to call and make arrangements for breakfast. By the time they arrived, he had ordered for his friends, and was sipping coffee at the table. "Good morning. I trust you both slept well last night."

Elliot and Donovan looked at each other as they took a seat.

Alex didn't notice and continued, "I was up most of the night thinking about how I would purchase the property and..."

Elliot interrupted, "Alex, you're serious about this? Why would you do that?"

Alex felt confident, "Because I love the place. Because it would give me someplace to live when Malibu starts driving me crazy. And because I couldn't bear to see it sold to someone that wouldn't appreciate it."

He could see the look of worry cross the faces in front of him. "Look, guys, the moment I saw the place, I knew it was in my blood. That property should belong to me."

Donovan studied Alex's dark blue eyes. "Have you made an offer yet?"

Alex smiled, assured of the outcome. "No, not yet. If you don't mind, I'd like to take another drive out there after breakfast. I'd like to see it once more."

They quickly finished their meal and had their car brought to the entrance. Elliot got behind the wheel again, with Donovan on the passenger side. Alex slid into the back seat.

Alex immediately started humming, and didn't stop throughout the duration of the drive. It didn't take long before Elliot and Donovan found themselves humming the same catchy tune. Elliot drove to the locked gate and parked the car. With Alex taking the lead, the boys jumped the fence and began their walk down the driveway.

Donovan reminded them they were trespassing again, but Alex laughed, "It's just a technicality. In a few days, this place is going to be mine."

Elliot looked back at their car as they passed the pond on the left. "Yeah, but today we could get arrested."

Alex wasn't worried. His head was clear and he knew what he had to do. The property would soon belong to him.

As they approached the house, Elliot nudged Donovan. "Alex, we're going down to the dock. It looks like it's going to need a lot of work. If you need us, just yell."

Alex didn't answer, and continued walking around to the back of the house. Before he was out of sight, Donovan felt driven to ask the question he didn't really want the answer to. "Alex, are you planning on going inside?"

Alex continued his pace, "That's my intention."

"How the hell are you getting in? Are you going to add breaking and entering to your deeds today?"

Alex laughed and waved to the men as he turned the corner. He jumped onto the back porch, and pushed open a window he had noticed unlocked the day before. The window opened with ease. Feeling no guilt, Alex pulled his other leg over the sill, stepping onto the parquet floor in the library. He smiled to himself. "That was easy enough. Almost too easy. I'm going to have to take care of that window."

Alex turned around and noticed the living room straight ahead.

He gazed at the large fireplace for a few minutes, enjoying the calmness that swept over him. He heard himself mumble, "A lot of good times around that fireplace."

He walked up the back stairs towards the master suite. All the other rooms held no interest for him today. He knew he was there for one purpose. He didn't want to question why something deep inside himself was compelling him, almost daring him to come back and walk into the large room at the end of the hall. But he could feel its tug. He hoped the overwhelming positive energy of two people very much in love would still be present. He wanted proof that he wasn't deceiving himself, and needed to believe that he wasn't overreacting. He hoped that most everything appearing to him the day before would reappear today. And prayed the disturbing moments would stay far away. He wasn't sure he had the energy for it.

Alex approached the door and turned the knob very slowly. As he reluctantly stepped in, he saw nothing had changed, and he felt less apprehensive about the revisit. He crossed the room to the bay windows and watched his friends talking near the dock. He was beginning to feel more confident, and focused his attention back into the room, immediately noticing the fireplace in the corner.

"It's a beautiful room, and it has wonderful energy. But it's just a room."

He wanted to love the room for different reasons. Alex pushed down the question of his own sanity, as he stood for what seemed like hours, not sure what he was waiting for. He finally grew tired, and sat on the floor, gazing at the fireplace. He meant to close his eyes for just a moment, but a dream state overtook him almost immediately.

Alex saw the room had been transformed. He stared in awe at the oak table that now belonged to him. He saw the frame, with its mysterious photo of a happy couple. His ears started ringing, and he suddenly heard voices and laughter swirling in the air all around him. The room's energy was pulsating, and his body felt as if he were being pushed against the wall. His emotions intensified within his mind's eye, and he fought desperately to keep the panic he was feeling from overwhelming him. "Stay calm, stay calm." The sound of his own voice gave him temporary reassurance.

Alex forced his focus on the oak table again. He was startled to see a beautiful music box. The lid was open, and a magnificent melody was circling the chamber. He was peacefully humming along in a trancelike state, when reality touched him for a moment. His ears almost exploded with the truth of what they heard. "It's the song. It's the song!" He tried to stand up several times, but the pulsating energy kept him tied firmly to the floor. "Stay calm, stay calm," he repeated the words over and over until it resembled a chant.

The memories of the day before rushed by, and he fought panic and dread. He didn't think he could bear feeling the anguish and pain that had completely overwhelmed him.

Alex watched what was happening as if he were viewing slides, one after another. He heard his voice register deeper than usual. "Why is this so familiar? Why? Why? Why?"

He forced his attention to the wooden table once again, but what he saw next made him lose his breath, and gasp painfully loud. He was fixated on a faint vision of a woman in desperate pain. His heart was pounding as he watched her bending over the box. She was taking something from her hand. He watched her tenderly kiss the object, and then place it in the container. The music stopped abruptly, and the only sounds penetrating his being were her deep sobs of distress. He felt as if he had been hit in the stomach. He felt her pain as if it were his own. He could hear his whispering pleas between gasps for air. "Oh God, please help her." Then, as suddenly as it had all started, it stopped, and he was once again alone in the room.

Alex waited several moments before finding the courage to blink. He sat in a daze, his eyes never leaving the area where the action had just taken place. He found it impossible to sort out how just a few moments before, there could have been a music box playing an all too familiar tune, along with a terribly sad woman in the same room with him.

He heard himself whispering his chant again. "Stay calm, just stay calm."

He wanted desperately to be back in his real world again.

When the dizziness had subsided, Alex slowly pulled himself up from the floor, feeling relieved when the unseen energy didn't push him back down again. He physically tried to shake off what he had just witnessed by forcing himself to the window. "Please be there."

He was relieved to see the past had vanished, as he watched his friends throwing rocks into the bay. Never had a sight looked so good.

Alex was still in a state of shock, but convinced what he had seen was real. And he knew what he had to do next.

"I know this house is mine. It needs me as much as I need it."

Alex was closing the door behind him when he remembered the note he had left on his last visit. Feeling certain that it was still lying on the mantle, he smiled as he walked out of the room to join his friends. As he was approaching the stairs, he heard wind whistling from behind him. "How can that be?" Puzzled, he walked back to the end of the hall, and opened the door. He shook his head when he saw no evidence of blowing wind, and noticed instead an eerie silence. He tried shutting the door behind him again, but instead felt himself walking to the mantle. His hand reached up, feeling for the napkin, at the same time as his eyes widened in disbelief when he realized it wasn't his note he could feel.

"What's happening here? This is crazy." He looked on the mantle, and found it now empty. He frantically searched around the empty room, hoping his note had fallen on the floor. "What the hell is this?" His mind was in such a state of turmoil, he couldn't get his thoughts in order. "No one else has been here. This cannot be." He was talking loudly, trying to drown out his confusion. His sturdy jaw line was clenched, and his dark hair had fallen into his eyes. He realized he was in a state of internal chaos, and had to somehow calm himself before he could proceed any further.

Between gasps, he noticed his voice taking on a softer tone. "One thing after another is happening here. I have got to center myself before I lose my mind. C'mon, Alex, center and focus. Center and focus."

He looked down at the note and found the writing wasn't his own.

He knew it was from a woman. "For God's sakes, Alex, open the damn thing up and read it." He cursed himself when he felt fear gripping his throat again.

His eyes slowly read the first word, then following it to the end. He read the words silently several times, and felt the long awaited tears flow freely down his face.

"Where did this come from?" He looked at his watch, trying to reason with himself. "I was just here yesterday. It's still early today. No one could have been here. I don't know what to think."

Alex neatly folded the note and put it in his pocket. "I've got to find the guys. They're not going to believe this."

He got as far as the top step when his eyes were drawn out the window, leading to the back yard. "What was that?" His breathing was heavy, and he felt as if he had run for miles. "I know I saw something down there."

He stared hard, but saw nothing out of the ordinary. His chest was aching but he hurried down the stairs, crossing through the dining room, running through the kitchen, and across to the library. He was about to climb through the window when he noticed something out of the corner of his eye, pulling his attention above the library fireplace. When he looked again, there was nothing but a blank wall. "Wait a second. I know I just saw something up there." Alex was beginning to feel uncomfortable again, but continued his steady gaze at the empty wall above the mantle. "This is getting too creepy for me."

He shook his head and quickly climbed over the sill, pulling the window down into place. His excitement was building again as he thought about showing the guys what he had found. "They'll help me make sense of all this."

He was walking to the side of the house when he felt an invisible pull from another direction. "Damn it, I know there's something out there." He looked in the direction of the trees several yards out. The wind was beginning to blow, and he could smell pine and cedar in the air. Alex suddenly felt dizzy, and took a deep breath, trying to steady himself.

He heard a voice coming from the wind. "Find what was lost to her."

He jerked his head, quickly scanning the area. Without warning, another stiff breeze blew through, but he was deaf to all outside noises. "What did you say?" But he heard nothing.

Alex looked around once again, trying to maintain some sort of balance and control. He fought hard, but when he felt his soul being pulled toward the trees, he knew he had lost the battle. By the time reality temporarily took command again, Alex was in the middle of a small grassy area. He was gazing down at several colorful rocks on the ground. He sat down among them, picking up one after another. He noticed a nearby tree, and crawled over to sit against it. Among his find, he noticed one rock away from the others. The sparkle was so intense, the light was reflecting back in his face.

Alex was mumbling to himself under his breath, "It looks as if it's been played with, then tossed aside." He picked the stone up and gently rubbed. "The stories you could tell. Where did you come from? How did you get here?" He was so drawn into the moment, he wouldn't have been surprised if the stone had answered him.

Alex was drained, and let himself drift off as he rolled the cool, smooth stone slowly around in his palm. While he lightly dozed, he began receiving impressions. He took a slow deep breath and kept his mind empty. He watched as a beautiful young lady suddenly appeared in his mind's eye. He couldn't help but spy as she walked through the trees, obviously with one goal in mind. He watched with eyes wide open as she dug a hole, and then placed something in the ground. She was sobbing as she looked around, before quickly covering it up. He could feel her inconsolable sorrow, and instinctively knew she wasn't going to live much longer. He kneaded the stone in a frenzy, trying to remain detached. His instincts also told him that he wasn't ready to feel that kind of pain.

Suddenly, the scene changed and he saw the woman he had touched only a few nights before on the beach. She was there, in his dreams. He smiled and tried to get her attention, but to no avail. "Why can't she see me?" He noticed she wasn't on a beach this time. "Where is she? Focus on her, Alex, where is she?" He watched her walk into a grove of trees and vanish.

Alex blinked back frustration when he found himself sitting against the tree alone, stroking the shimmering rock.

Without warning, a deafening quietness came over him while he silently contemplated all the secrets around him. He concentrated on what the trees and the house were trying to tell him. His head was cocked to one side, as if he were listening to advice from the wind. After a long while, Alex shook his head, acknowledging what had been whispered.

He took a breath so deep it hurt his lungs. Then he looked down at the ground again and smiled. With an empty mind, and using the stone as a shovel, Alex began digging the dirt in front of him. He was painfully aware of what he was doing, yet he deliberately kept himself detached from the labor.

Elliot and Donovan was beginning to worry that Alex had been gone too long without being heard from. They had grown bored with their conversation, and were tired of skipping stones into the bay. When they rounded the house, they both caught a glimpse of their friend sitting on a small patch of open ground, surrounded by trees. Donovan stopped short, with Elliot running into him from behind. They watched for several minutes, before Donovan whispered quietly to his friend, "Surely he hasn't been out there all this time."

Elliot responded in a curious tone, "I'm more concerned about what he's doing out there, rather than where he's been."

Both men watched Alex digging furiously, as they stood there without moving a muscle. Alex was perspiring, and speaking aloud between each breath. "You know it's here. You saw her bury it. Just keep digging. You've got to find it for her."

The hole had become very deep when the rock would go no further. Alex slapped the ground once more and felt something solid. He methodically placed the rock next to him, and then began scraping the ground away from the object with his hands.

The guys sensed they would soon be needed, and slowly walked around the grove of trees, coming up quietly behind Alex. They stopped and watched what was transpiring in disbelief, listening to every word he was muttering to himself. "You've got to find it for her."

Alex finally pushed the remainder of the dirt away from the object and brought out a small wooden box. He blew the dirt away, and slowly opened the container. They heard him gasp a sob and scream into the vastness, "I found it! I'm not crazy. It's here. I really found it."

Elliot was the first one to him. "Alex, are you OK? What did you find?"

Alex was gasping for breath, crying and laughing at the same time. He felt as much pain as he did relief. "I'm not crazy."

With the little energy he had left, Alex ceremoniously opened his hand. This time, it was his friends who gasped in disbelief when they saw a tiny box with a woman's wedding band inside. Before anything else could be said, Alex closed the lid, placed it in his jacket, and zipped it up. Then they silently started their walk back to the house.

As they passed the trees, Alex stopped. "Wait, I'll be right back." He quickly returned to the clearing, and picked up the colored stone, stuffing it in his pocket. "This is coming home with me."

Elliot waited several minutes before he felt it safe to question what he and Donovan had seen. "Alex, what happened?"

Alex shook his head and laughed. "You're not going to believe me. It'll take the entire trip home to explain. And let me tell you, it's quite a story."

Donovan spoke up, "Does that mean we're heading home?"

Alex shook his head. "Yep, right after I put in the offer and sign the papers. If we're lucky, we'll be on the last flight home."

Elliot and Donovan wanted to try and reason with him, but he seemed far too content with his decision for them to bother. As they reached the gate, Alex picked up the For Sale sign and put it in the trunk. "Let's get this done and go home."

Donovan shook his head. "You're the boss."

Lauren and Adriana drove back to the hotel and quickly packed their bags. Lauren confessed there was nothing more she could do, and wanted to catch the next flight home. "I feel as though I came for confirmation, and that's what I got."

Once they were settled on the plane, Lauren pulled the note from her purse, and read it over and over.

Adriana glanced over Lauren's shoulder and saw the masculine writing on the napkin. "I look forward to seeing what impressions I get from this. It's too bad the guy didn't scribble his name and phone number on it. That would certainly have made it easier for you to locate him. At least you would have known if this was the same guy."

Lauren opened her mouth to comment, when suddenly her eyes widened. She looked over at Adriana and back down at the paper. "Damn!"

Adriana jumped. "Jeez, Lauren, what's wrong?"

Lauren looked back down at the paper. "Damn, damn, damn!"

"OK, Lauren, what the hell is wrong?"

Lauren slapped her palm up side her head. "You're not going to believe what I did, or rather what I didn't do."

Adriana took Lauren's hand off her temple and held it in her own. "What am I not going to believe?"

Lauren was angry at herself, and it was reflected in her tone of voice. "I left behind my own personal note." Adriana was about to speak but Lauren continued. "I fantasized about the writer of this note returning to find mine."

Adriana broke into a grin. "Yeah, I think that was a wonderful idea. So, what's the problem?"

Lauren's usually composed face suddenly darkened. "The problem is, I forgot to sign the damn thing. I can't believe I forgot. How does someone forget something so important?"

Adriana took the napkin from Lauren's possession. "I suppose the same way he forgot to sign his. Anybody could make the same mistake."

"Great, and I suppose a potentially lethal mistake as well. Where has it got either of us? I'll tell you where." She answered her own question, "Not far."

Adriana patiently shook her head. "Lauren, you've got to trust the process. How many times have you told me this in the last several days? You found his note, didn't you?"

Lauren still looked frustrated, "I found a note. I hope it's his note, but how will I know, now?"

Adriana smiled. "Ye of little faith. The same way you were led down this path. Why don't you trust the process and find a little humor along the way."

Lauren looked at her friend as if she had lost her mind. "Humor? You want me to find humor in this fiasco?"

Adriana was still smiling. "Lauren, one of your most endearing traits is that you tend to find humor in the littlest things. You've always found good in the worst possible scenarios. Don't let me down now. You've got to trust that everything will work out."

Lauren placed the note back in her purse and sighed loudly. "You're right. Actually, I have no choice but to trust the process. But, is it natural to question my own sanity?"

Adriana laughed and patted her friend's hand. "Of course it is. Now try and rest. And by the way, you're not crazy."

Lauren turned her face toward the window and closed her eyes. She hummed herself to sleep, napping until the plane touched down in L.A.

By the time the girls had stored their luggage in the car, it was late and Lauren wanted to get home. She was hoping to dream, and tell him what she had found. But she doubted her dreams would be significant tonight.

After Adriana dropped her off with promises of lunch the next day, Lauren walked into her empty house. She walked past her office and straight up her stairs to her bedroom. "I'll check my messages tomorrow."

She quickly took off her clothes and stepped into the warm shower. "If I don't relax, I'll never get to sleep." She was having trouble releasing the day's events from her mind. After reliving it again, she toweled herself off and slipped under the soft sheets. Lauren refused to admit her anticipation as she quickly closed her eyes, said her nightly prayers, called in the protection of the white light, and immediately dreamed.

Excitement overwhelmed her senses when she saw him standing among a grove of trees. Lauren automatically pushed further into the ethereal vision, and noticed he was holding an object in his hand. She squinted, but still couldn't make out what it was. She was surprised when the incident didn't upset her, and how easily she could remain detached and observant. "I must be even more exhausted than I thought." The scene slowly disappeared from her view, and Lauren dreamed of walking through a grove of trees, humming a beautiful melody. Finally, she felt peace.

The men barely made it to the airport in time to catch the last flight back to L.A. It had taken most of the day to put in the offer and sign the necessary papers before leaving the remaining business to the agent. Alex wanted to make certain the bid was in, and the house would be his. He didn't want to leave anything incomplete.

When they had finally relaxed in their seats, and had been served a drink before takeoff, Alex told his anxious friends what had transpired on their second visit to the house. He told them about the life changing events that he would never forget. "I'll try to remember to always trust my instincts first. I've never had such soul-affirming events take place."

His friends were in awe of the story, and of the proof he submitted.

Elliot took the note written in feminine script, and read it out loud.

"Words of hope, and words of love. I will keep these things in my heart and soul. And I promise that I will remember. Words to remind us of our past, and to remember that I have loved you. Words in the present, I love you still. And words for our future, I will love you always and forever. No matter where, no matter when. I will love you."

Alex brushed a tear from his eye. "Those are the most cherished words I've ever read. I don't know where they came from, but I suspect they could come from only one person. I'm just not sure whether this person is from my past, my present, or my future."

Donovan spoke barely above an emotional whisper. "Couldn't she be from them all? Read her words again, Alex. Couldn't she be?"

Alex didn't answer, but instead pulled out the tiny wooden box. He looked at the dirt imbedded in the grain from so many years of interment beneath the ground. "Who do you suppose this belonged to? Would I be crazy to wonder if this is the ring I've seen in my dreams? I admit I can't remember what it looked like. And rationally, I know I should just say that it's all a coincidence. But every cell in my being is telling me that we both now possess what the other is missing. I've known that since the first time I laid eyes on her. I thought it was just my soul that she owned." He raised the ring up to eye level. "But it's more than that. I may just have proof now. However, I fully realize most people would say that I was crazy, but they weren't there. I know I was sent to those trees for a purpose. I knew that I was the one who had to locate this object. It had to be me." His voice trailed off.

Elliot took the ring from his friend and turned it towards the light. "Very elaborate symbols. Wonder what it means? I have a friend in town that deciphers this kind of stuff. Perhaps he can make sense of it." He looked inside the gold circle's core. "Did you read what it says in here?"

Alex didn't look over. "I made out some of it, but not all. I'll have it polished tomorrow. All I can make out is w-h, and the slash and then e-n, and further around, v-e. Can you make out any more than that?"

Donovan took the ring from Elliot and looked at it closely. "That's all I can make out, too. But I'm sure it will all make sense after it's polished up. This is amazing. How did you do it, Alex?"

"I don't know. I just remember working at calming myself down, and then letting my mind go blank. I dreamed of a woman burying something. God, she was so unhappy. Then it changed, and I watched the woman from my dreams walking through the trees. The next thing I knew, I was digging the ground in front of me. The last few days have been the most enlightening of my life."

Donovan was casual in his remark, "It's too bad she didn't sign her name."

Elliot closed his eyes, knowing the disappointment his friend felt.

Alex took a deep frustrated breath. "Yeah, I've thought about that a thousand times already. I'm angry with myself for not adding my name, but I didn't think anyone would see the note. I don't even know why the hell I wrote it. It's certainly not something I would have normally done. I'm trying desperately not to get too upset, and just hope that it all works out. For my own sanity, I have got to believe that. Because if I thought I had come this close, and the only thing standing between this woman and myself is a signature, I don't think I would ever get over it. So, as difficult as it is to do, I just have to trust."

Elliot spoke up, changing the subject. "And when you get back, you're going to call Ron and set up a gig at Tom's place. Right? What's it called?"

Donovan answered, "Jupiter's."

Alex interrupted, "I need my music right now. I know that'll keep me sane until I come to the next bend in the road."

Elliot remarked, "Appropriate. Sounds like a song."

Alex turned his overhead light off, and closed his eyes. All he could hear and see was music. That was what he dreamed about until the plane landed in Los Angeles.

Arriving back in L.A. was a relief. He felt desperate to get home. He needed some time alone to sort out his feelings.

Elliot and Donovan said their swift goodnights in the driveway and left Alex to himself. He walked into his house, taking his shoes off at the door. He could see the light from the full moon peeking through the back window shade, and he was glad to be home. He could feel the carpet's softness against his feet, and he pressed them deeper into the floor as he walked over to his piano.

Alex closed his eyes and allowed his fingers to move to the melody in his mind. He played for a few moments, and then began singing the lyrics to the song he would never be able to forget.

"It seems we stood like this before. We looked at each other in the same way then, but I can't remember where or when."

He sang the words louder and louder for what seemed like just a few minutes. But glancing at the clock proved him wrong. Alex blinked hard, and forced himself to stop playing. He opened the window shades to see a light morning mist coming off the ocean. "There's no way I could have played the piano all night long." He pulled himself from the seat and walked up the stairs to his bed. "I'll just nap for an hour or so." Alex fell into a deep sleep before even getting his clothes off.

Chapter 14

Lauren awoke early the next morning and stayed in her sleeping position for a long while. She couldn't get the events from the day before out of her mind. *It seems as though it was all a dream.* The same words ran over and over in her mind. *I know it wasn't a dream.* She had a ring to prove it. She had a beautiful message from someone as well. With a start, Lauren suddenly jumped out of bed. "I must take care of that right now. Right now."

She retrieved the note and read it several more times before putting it in a plastic container, and placing it in a metal security box in her closet. "I can't let anything happen to this. It's all I have of him."

She sat down on the bed and stared at her closet door, fighting doubt. "But, how do I know it's from him?" Shaking her head vigorously, she responded to her own question. "I just know." She giggled as she stood up and walked into her bathroom. "Stop arguing with yourself, Lauren. You'll lose every time."

Before jumping in the shower, she made a point of reminding herself that it was going to be a productive day. Lauren realized stability was what she needed, so she dressed quickly, skipped breakfast, and drove straight to her store. She needed a balance between the real world and the one of her dreams. She knew getting her mind off her adventures might just bring the needed solutions she was after.

Lauren listened to motivational music while she drove on the hectic L.A. freeways. She was so happily caught up in the music and lyrics, she temporarily forgot there was a hostile existence outside of her car. She stopped at a traffic light a few blocks from her store and noticed herself busily tapping her fingers on the steering wheel to the music. But her smile disintegrated when she saw her fingers weren't moving with the tune coming from her speakers. They were instead moving with the tune humming from her lips. She listened to herself for a moment and temporarily lost focus with her surroundings. The music in her car was loud and clear. The tune she was humming sounded like the same one she had been humming for days. "Why am I so attracted to the song from my music box?" She was listening to the music on her CD, but only heard the melody from the past few days. "As if this can't get any stranger than it already is? Damn!"

Lauren turned up the music to the point where it hurt her ears. But all she heard was the now familiar tune. "How can I listen to one song and sing another at the same time?" She shook her head vigorously again. "This is crazy. Would someone up there please tell me what it is I'm supposed to be hearing?"

It finally struck her that someone or some thing may be trying to tell her something. She quickly guided herself internally, hoping to connect with her higher self, her guide, or at this point, just about anything positive who might drop by with some answers.

"What is it?" She spoke to her guide, instantly locating the older gentleman within her own higher self. "What am I supposed to do with this tune? Come on, I need some help over here."

The only response she received was one from the car behind her. The honking brought her back to reality. She lifted her hand up as if to say sorry to the driver behind her.

She tried reasoning with herself. "Lauren, you know it could just be that you're just fond of the melody. Why are you making such a big deal out of everything? You're usually reasonable. And now's the time to be reasonable here."

Lauren reached her destination and quickly stepped out of her car. She unlocked the back door and strolled into the store, turning on the lights. Her mind temporarily forgot about the 'why' for now. Fortunately, Kevin walked in right behind her, giving her a big hug. "Welcome back. That was a quick trip. Did you find anything?"

Lauren talked while she prepared coffee. "Yeah, I found that my life is drastically changing. And if it isn't, then I would propose that someone commit me."

She brought Kevin up to date on the events that had taken place in Connecticut. When she was finished, Kevin sat on the edge of her desk looking deeply into her eyes. It made Lauren feel self-conscious.

"I wish you wouldn't look at me like that. I can't tell whether you believe me or not."

Kevin took her hand and smiled. "Of course I believe you. I'm just amazed at the events taking place in your life. I can't wait to read your note. Do you remember the words?"

Lauren smiled. "What do you think? I can recite it backwards, if that's what you want. I didn't make it up, Kevin. Adriana was with me. She saw it. And how do you explain the inscription inside the ring?"

Kevin cupped Lauren's face in his palms. "Lauren, why are you doing this? You don't have to convince me of anything. Have you ever thought I may be envious of you? I can be a romantic too, you know."

Lauren looked at him in shock. "Me? Why in the hell would you be envious of me? My husband and I are divorcing, and with it goes the life that I've always known. It's literally falling away as we speak. The only stability I can count on are you, Adriana, and my children. I don't know half the time if I'm sane, or if I'm going out of my mind. I've never enjoyed riddles, rhymes, or puzzles. And I don't read mystery books. And as you know, I've never felt comfortable not knowing what's around the corner. Any corner. So the way I see it, I'm therefore not prepared to know what steps I'm supposed to take. I'm questioning everything that I was brought up to believe in. I'm in love with a man I don't even know exists in our everyday reality. I have clues all around me, but that doesn't help much when I don't know what to do with them. And I don't know if I should jump in the void, attempting freefall or flight, or opt for the parachute. And you envy me?"

Kevin listened to her with love and compassion in his eyes. "Lauren, don't you see what I see? I'm envious because your life is virtually changing right in front of us. And you're luckier than you think. You are being given clues. And you're fortunate to be able to pursue them. You've already been forced to jump into the void, and you're currently in flight without the parachute. You have to believe you'll have the ability and forthrightness to know where to land. Just listen to the clues."

Lauren looked confused and was about to protest, but Kevin continued, "You have been given a wonderful gift of renewed life. And you have been given the opportunity of looking in that window and seeing true, unconditional love for what it is. Whether you ever find this man or not, you've seen what it's like to know that feeling, and that passion. And because of that, you will never be the same again. Your life had to change. You couldn't go back. So, enjoy the flight and look forward to seeing where you land. Then think about all of us here, supporting you and loving you. You have so many wonderful reasons to be grateful."

Lauren had never heard Kevin speak this way before, and was quiet for several moments. She was enjoying the trip inside his heart.

After a few moments, he broke the silence again. "Now, would you please recite the note for me?" Then he teased her, adding, "That is, if there is such a note."

Lauren pushed him off her desk and watched as he tumbled onto the sofa cushions, laughing. She turned serious, and took a moment to compose herself. Kevin noticed her voice had changed to a husky whisper when she finally spoke.

"Time will hold the answers to the questions in our hearts.

Memories of you keep my love strong. Every second that we're apart."

Kevin was quiet for a moment, then spoke in a whisper, "Gee, Lauren, I don't know what to say. It's as if this person was confirming your thoughts, and trying to make you feel better about the situation."

Lauren smiled. "Yeah, I know. That's what I thought too."

Kevin continued, "Do you mind if I ask you what you wrote in your reply?"

Lauren looked down, embarrassed. "No, I don't mind. Why should I keep it from you? You already know everything else. Just promise me you won't think it's silly."

Kevin gave her the same look she had seen from him a few times in the past week. She knew he wouldn't judge her.

"Words of hope, and words of love. I will keep these things in my heart and soul. And I promise that I will remember. Words to remind us of our past, and to remember that I have loved you. Words in the present, I love you still. And words for our future, I will love you always and forever. No matter where, no matter when. I will love you."

Kevin swallowed hard, and took Lauren in his arms, hugging her very tight. "God, you are high in flight, lady. Very high in flight. All you can do now is have hope, and trust in yourself."

Lauren smiled, hugging Kevin back. "Yeah, I've been advised to do that already. Trust myself. Easy to say, very difficult to do."

The phone rang and Kevin reached to answer it. After a few moments of small talk, he handed the phone to Lauren. "It's Adriana."

"Good morning, Adriana, how did you sleep?"

Her friend smiled into the phone. "Fine, as usual. I can't get this stuff out of my mind though. How about dinner tonight?"

Lauren looked at her calendar. "It'll have to be a late one. I've got a million things to do today. I'll call you later."

She hung up the phone remembering that Adriana and Kevin

always put her in a good mood. She smiled to herself, realizing that she was indeed a woman blessed. Lauren turned on the stereo to the new age music that seemed to bring customers into the store, and then walked out to the front with Kevin.

"I feel it's going to be a busy day." And indeed it was.

Alex slept soundly until late morning. He awoke and looked at the clock beside his bed.

"I must have been more tired than I thought. There are a million things I need to get done today."

Alex showered and quickly dressed. He ran downstairs, grabbing a piece of toast as he flew out the door to his car. His first stop was to Malibu Jewelry. Elliot and Donovan had mentioned they were the best in town. "If you want to read what the inscription says without destroying the finish, then Jeff is the guy to see."

Alex entered the store in a noisy rush. A man approached him, asking if he could be of service. "Are you Jeff?"

The older man excused himself, mumbling something about getting his son. A few minutes later, a man who looked much younger than his years entered the room. "Hi, I'm Jeff. May I help you?"

Alex was apprehensive about handing over his most prized possession, but didn't see how he had much choice. Alex shook his head and spoke up.

"Hi, Jeff, my name is Alex Chandler." He was about to continue when the young man interrupted.

"Oh, Mr. Chandler. Of course. I know who you are. You're a fine writer. It's a real pleasure to meet you."

Alex was always forgetting that strangers would occasionally recognize his name. "Thank you very much. I was given your name by friends. They said you were able to clean tarnish from gold? I'm very protective of this particular piece of jewelry. I need your assurance that you can clean it up without damaging it. I don't want to take any chances."

Jeff had a look of concern cross his face. "Let's take a look at it, shall we?"

Alex pulled the small ring from his pocket and reluctantly passed it to the man. "Please be careful."

Jeff took it, and walked to a nearby magnifying glass. "It's quite unusual and beautiful, isn't it?"

Alex answered numbly. "Uh huh."

Jeff could see the apprehension on Alex's face. "Mr. Chandler, I can clean this up for you just fine, with no damage. We'll have it looking brand new."

Alex exhaled and smiled. "Great. What time can I pick it up?"

The young man grinned openly. "I'll need to keep it for a few days. But I give you my word it will be taken very good care of."

It was obvious Alex was upset about having to leave it overnight.

Jeff repeated himself, "I give you my word I'll take care of it personally, and I'll call you as soon as it's ready."

Alex gave the required information, and grudgingly walked out, still not feeling confident of his decision. He was talking to himself as he stepped into his car. "It's not like I had a choice. It's imperative that I know what the inscription reads." He kept reassuring himself that it was only going to be out of his possession for a few days.

He pulled out of the parking lot and headed south to Ron's studio. Alex knew Elliot was right. "Until I can find a way to meet this woman, I need to work on other projects. It'll come to me. I just know it." Alex turned on the radio, hoping to drown out his thoughts. By the time he pulled into the studio parking lot, he found himself humming the tune he had been playing on the piano a few hours earlier. "Why can't I get it out of my head? Why?"

Ron was standing in the reception area when Alex walked in.

"Alex, I hear you were quite ill. How are you feeling?" Ron didn't want to mention the outburst in his office a few days earlier.

He assumed his illness was the cause. "What are you doing over in this area?"

Ron motioned for Alex to follow him. Once they reached his office, Ron offered him a chair. Alex smiled excitedly.

"I know we've talked about playing a few gigs around the area. I've been sidetracked lately, and haven't felt up to it. But I think if you're ready, and if the others aren't busy, then we go for it."

Ron laughed through his reply. "I say let's do it. This has become a tradition with us. I was afraid you'd lost interest."

Alex could feel the old tensions melting away. "On the contrary, I think it's exactly what I need. Do you think we'll have trouble getting the other members together?"

Ron picked up the phone. "Well, why don't we find out?"

Alex continued excitedly, "If we practice all week, do you think next week is too soon to play? There's some new stuff I want to try out, but if we work hard, I think we can get a solid sound by next week."

After the last call was made, Ron put the receiver down. "Well, it looks as though our merry little band is in session. At least for the next few weeks." Ron couldn't refrain from showing his excitement as he rubbed his hands together in anticipation. "We start practicing tomorrow, and we'll play Jupiter's a week from Saturday."

Alex walked to the door. "Splendid! Are we going to practice here, or at my house?"

Ron thought a moment. "Since all the equipment is set up, why don't we do it here? How's 7:00 tomorrow night?"

Alex continued the conversation while he walked out of the office, "Nothing will keep me away from this. Give my love to Cindy. And tell her to invite everyone she knows. We need as many supporters as possible."

Ron laughed out loud. "You're telling me. But fortunately for us, our public has always been forgiving in the past. All they expect is a bunch of over-the-hill businessmen to entertain them. Right?"

Alex grinned. "Better have Cindy bring relatives too."

When Alex returned to his car, he phoned the real estate agent in Connecticut. "Have we got a deal?"

"Yes, Mr. Chandler, we do indeed. The owners approved your bid just a few minutes ago. The paperwork will be faxed to you, and the property should be yours within a few days."

Alex was on top of the world. "Excellent. Keep me posted. And thank you for speeding up the paperwork."

Alex drove home in great spirits, tapping his hand on the steering wheel, developing new music in his head. "I've got to get this on paper before I forget. This is good."

Lauren completed her workday after 8:00, and was exhausted by the time she called Adriana. "Adriana, I apologize for getting back with you so late. You'd have thought we were giving things away. It's just a good thing I had extra help. I had Kevin take some much-needed time off. But if business keeps up like this, maybe I should leave town more often."

Adriana laughed. "I'm starving, and since I'm only a few minutes from your house, why don't we meet there? You have anything in your fridge?"

Lauren was already locking up. "Sure, I can be there in thirty minutes. If you get there before I do, use your key."

"OK, I'll see you then."

Lauren hurried to her car. She was looking forward to going home and relaxing with Adriana, and a nice glass of wine. She absentmindedly started the engine, and glanced into the rearview mirror, flinching in shock when the familiar yet strange face suddenly loomed in front of her. She heard her voice turn to fear.

"Dear God. Who are you? What do you want?"

There was no answer; just an eerie, icy silence prevailed.

Lauren looked away, but curiosity finally overpowered her. She slowly raised her eyes, trying not to flinch again.

She saw a dim bluish glow around the glass, and a faint shadow around the eyes. She found they were soft, beautiful and vaguely familiar. Not the kind of eyes that she should be frightened of.

Lauren pushed aside her fear, and focused all of her energy into the mirror. She heard her voice soften. "Please tell me who you are?"

The eyes were so hazily faint now, she could barely see them. But they were clear enough for Lauren to make out the love, as well as the pain. She watched as the bluish aura suddenly became more pronounced.

"Please, let me help you."

But the eyes closed at the same time as her inside light dimmed, then went out. Lauren was left in the darkness and silence of her car.

"My dear God, please tell me what that was? The pain in those eyes, mixed with such love. Where are they coming from? Who do they belong to? What do they want from me?"

She automatically drove home, pulled into her driveway, and walked into her house without fully realizing how she did it. Luckily, Adriana was already sitting at the bar, with another full glass sitting beside her.

Adriana watched as Lauren walked in, absentmindedly tossing aside her purse and briefcase on the table. She watched her remove her shoes, flipping them one at a time in the corner of the room. She noticed the intensity on her friend's face, but her body was going through zombie-like motions. Adriana slipped off the stool and quickly walked in Lauren's direction. She stood directly in front of her.

"Lauren? Lauren?" Lauren looked right through her friend. Adriana touched her shoulder, making her look directly into her eyes. "Lauren, where are you? Time to wake up."

Lauren blinked twice, then looked at Adriana as if for the first time. Her eyes widened, as she looked around the room. When Lauren spoke, it was in a quizzical tone, louder than usual.

"Hey, what are you doing here?" She looked around at her

surroundings. "Wait. How did I get here?"

A worried look crossed Adriana's face again. "Lauren, you don't remember driving home? You don't remember walking through the door and looking right at me?"

Lauren walked over to the bar, and took a large sip from the full glass sitting on the counter. Her forehead was creased and she was noticeably pale.

"Adriana, I don't remember anything since I spoke to you on the phone." She turned to her friend. "I did speak to you on the phone, didn't I?"

Adriana's concern carried over in her voice. "Yes, Lauren, you spoke to me. You told me you'd be home in thirty minutes. You made it in twenty."

Lauren fell into her couch before she fell on the floor. She sipped her wine, trying to remember what had happened in the twenty minutes prior to her arrival home. Adriana sat on the floor and stared up at her.

"Are you all right? Your eyes look as though you're in pain."

Lauren blinked hard, her eyes lighting up with recognition.

"Of course! Now I remember. Oh, Adriana, this is so weird. Maybe you can tell me how or why this would affect me in such a way."

Adriana was confused and stopped her friend's babbling.

"What is so weird? What are you talking about? What happened to you?"

Lauren slipped down onto the floor with Adriana. "I saw the face again." She stopped and corrected herself. "Rather, I saw the eyes."

Adriana squeezed Lauren's hand. "You mean the one in the mirror?"

Lauren's eyes were sparkling now. "Yes. But I just saw the eyes, and there was a blue light surrounding them. They looked familiar in an odd sort of way, but I can't place them. I was frightened at first, but then something changed."

Adriana couldn't control her anticipation. "What changed? What?"

Lauren stood up and paced around the room. "The eyes were lovely, and they had a warm loving aura to them. I asked what they wanted with me, but I never received an answer. Then I saw the pain living inside those beautiful eyes." Lauren turned to face her friend. "Adriana, I could actually feel the pain. I asked what I could do to help."

"And? What happened next?"

Lauren sat back down next to Adriana. "Nothing. They disappeared, along with the light around them. Next thing I knew, you were calling my name, here."

Adriana stared at the wall in front of her for several moments while sipping her wine. Lauren finally couldn't stand it another minute.

"Tell me what you're thinking. What do you think it was? Was I abducted or something? You're beginning to scare me."

Adriana smiled at her friend. "Of course you weren't abducted. I see no strange probing marks on you. You were only gone for twenty minutes. My God, it would take them that long just to shut you up."

Lauren immediately noticed the smirk on her friend's face, and realized she was desperately trying to add some humor into the room. All the tension disappeared as they both burst out laughing. Adriana walked into the kitchen, keeping the conversation going.

"Lauren, it obviously has something to do with your dreams, your ring, your music box, and your note. And anything else you might have accumulated on this journey of yours. It doesn't take a genius to figure that out, but that's as far as I can understand it. You're obviously on the right path."

She was going to continue, but Lauren stopped her.

"I was going to ask you about that. I also want to give you one more thing to think about."

Lauren walked into her office and opened her large music box.

The melody floated into the room. Lauren swayed to the music for a second, bordering on getting carried away.

Adriana loved the tune as well, then realized they had come into the room for a reason. "What were you going to ask me?"

Lauren left the lid up, allowing the music to flow.

"I'm beginning to think this song, this tune, whatever it is, is a clue. A message of some sort. I don't want to sound as though I'm losing my mind. But I cannot get this tune out of my head. It never goes away. I don't even know the name of it." Lauren looked down at the box, wishing it could give her the answer. "There's a way of finding out? Right?"

Adriana closed the lid, and quietness prevailed. "Yeah, we can record it, then take it to the music store. Surely someone must know what it is." But Adriana cautioned her friend. "It may be nothing more than you simply liking the tune."

Lauren wasn't going to be put off. "Perhaps so, but I feel it's a clue. It's not something I'd been thinking about. It's something that came to me while I was driving to work. Either way, I have to check it out."

Adriana agreed. "Yeah, after everything else that's happened, you'd be crazy if you didn't. You can take care of that tomorrow. Now, back to the eyes."

"I'll tell you what. Let's find something to eat, have some wine and watch some TV. I'm mentally exhausted, and don't want to think about anything serious at the moment."

Adriana gave her friend a surprised look, but agreed. "I think that's an excellent idea. We both worked our butts off today. Who says we can't completely relax for one evening?"

Lauren brought a variety of cheeses and bread into the living room while Adriana poured them fresh glasses of wine. Within five minutes, they were curled up on opposite ends of the couch, sleeping peacefully through the night.

Lauren awoke first, glancing at the grandfather clock on the opposite wall. She noticed Adriana was fast asleep at the other end of the couch, and she tried to get up without waking her. But her body was stiff and sore. She mumbled to herself as she trudged slowly into the kitchen to make coffee, "I've got to get back to my dance class."

She looked at Adriana, fully spread out on the couch, sleeping peacefully. "Oh, is she ever going to be sore and stiff when she wakes up. She's going to blame me for sure."

Lauren looked outside towards her back yard and beyond, while the coffee was brewing. Her mind went back to the events from the night before. "I can't get those eyes out of my mind. As if I need one more thing to think about."

She walked into her office, still remembering Adriana's suggestion. Lauren took the recorder from her top desk drawer, opened the music box, and switched on the recorder. After she filled the tape with music, she slowly and silently closed the lid, and sat still. She felt exhausted.

"I'll just sit here for two minutes, then wake Adriana up." Lauren was admiring the music box, when her attention suddenly focused on the exterior of the bulky, wooden container.

"It has such an odd shape to it." She stood up and walked around the wooden object. She knocked lightly on the sides and top of the box. Then she slid her fingertips over the legs and slowly slipped her hand underneath. "Something just isn't right."

She sat down at her desk, her attention never wavering from the box. Adriana slowly plowed into the room, clenching her own back.

"God, you look like hell."

Adriana yawned. "I could say the same about you. Don't you offer your houseguests a bed to sleep in? I thought I rated better than a couch."

Lauren grinned. "Don't complain, I was on that couch too."

Adriana noticed Lauren's full attention was on the box.

"What's wrong? Is the damn thing floating in mid-air now?"

Lauren let out a giggle. "No, I recorded the music a few

minutes ago. Then something about it caught my eye. I can't figure out why it's so oddly shaped. It seems to be hollow on the bottom. Yet it seems bottom heavy. Why would they build it that way? There's just something about it."

Her voice trailed off silently into the air.

"I don't know. I found it odd, too. It's a beautiful box, but there's something about it that makes it look different than most. I can't place it either. Beats me."

Lauren thumped its side.

"I wonder why it sounds hollow in this area?"

Adriana yawned again, thinking more about coffee. "Perhaps the builder was going to add a drawer to the lower section, and just never got around to it."

Lauren ran her fingers over the top again. "That doesn't make any sense. But who knows? I wish I could figure it out. It seems awfully heavy to only be housing the music chamber and a jewelry section."

Adriana shrugged, walking toward the kitchen. "I don't know. Maybe it was built with heavy wood."

Lauren followed her friend in the kitchen for coffee. "Thanks for your input. Remind me never to have you build me a house."

Alex still had the melody of a new song playing in his head when he opened his front door. "I've got to get this on paper."

He rushed into his office and opened the bottom drawer of his desk, pushing aside future manuscript ideas and old musical compositions, until he found the blank composition sheets he was looking for. He was on his way back to the piano when he heard something fall from the pages and hit the floor. In his rush to start work, he hadn't noticed a small book amongst the stack of papers he had gathered up from his desk. He bent over to pick up the opened book.

He noticed the page number before absent-mindedly closing it. Alex turned it over and read aloud. "Think On These Things.

Selections from the Edgar Cayce readings."

He rubbed the face of the book a few times, trying to recall where it could have come from. "Hmmm. Maybe it was a gift."

By the time he reached his piano, Alex's mind had returned to center stage. He tossed the book on top of the piano, placed a pencil behind his ear, and sat down. He proceeded to direct his attention to the music in his head. He played a few notes, then feverishly wrote as fast as he could. He was so engrossed in his music that he only vaguely heard his phone ring. He didn't want to be disturbed, but grumbled an excuse to get up. "I need a break anyway." He reached the phone as the message machine was about to switch on. It was Elliot. "Hi, buddy, how's it going today?"

Alex smiled into the phone. "Great. I've already had a full day. I ran out to Ron's and organized a jam session with the guys, starting tomorrow. We're going to be playing at Jupiter's a week from Saturday. You think you can make it?"

"I look forward to it. Did you take the ring to the jewelry store? What about the property? Have you heard anything?"

Alex replied slowly as if his thoughts were somewhere else.

"Yeah, Jeff was very helpful. He said it would be ready in a few days. And I spoke to the agent for the property. The paperwork should be completed in just a few days, and then it'll be all mine."

Elliot sensed Alex's distance, and knew his mind was on either another manuscript or a song.

"I know that tone of voice. What are you working on?"

Alex laughed, now fully back in the present. "You've been around me too long. Actually, I was sitting here composing a new tune that's been eating at me all morning."

As he spoke, Alex turned in the direction of the piano, immediately noticing the book. "Elliot, while I've got you on the phone, let me ask you a question."

"Go ahead."

"Did you ever give me a book published by the A.R.E.? It's called 'Think on These Things.' It's selections from the readings of

Edgar Cayce?"

Elliot thought for a moment. "No, it wasn't me. The last one I gave you was the new one from Sutphen. Speaking of which, have you seen him around lately? The last I heard, he was touring Europe. I know his seminars have become very popular."

Alex smiled, "I never did thank you. It was great book."

Alex's eyes shot across the room again. "I wish I could figure out where I got this one on Edgar Cayce. I don't recall ever seeing it before, and suddenly here it is. Are you sure you didn't give it to me?"

Elliot thought again. "Sorry, buddy, it wasn't me. What's so noteworthy about it?"

Alex shook his head. "Nothing in particular. I just don't know where it came from. I'm probably just being paranoid. I seem to be questioning everything nowadays. It's probably been right under my nose the whole time."

Alex lost his train of thought when a new chord came to him. "I hate to run, but I really need to get some of this stuff on paper before I lose it. If you're in the area later, drop on by?"

Elliot shook his head. "I'll try. Go back to work."

With the tune roaring in his head, Alex quickly hung up, and headed back to his piano. He glanced as he approached the bench, noticing the book wasn't in sight. He blinked hard and looked again.

"I know I put it up here." Alex was touching and exploring the area where he knew he had put it.

"This is ridiculous. I know I'm not going crazy. Where is it?"

Alex glanced on the floor again, and saw the book lying next to the piano, opened, face down.

He picked it up and turned it over. Alex was surprised to see the book had fallen on the same page as before. He wanted to close it, and place it elsewhere, but instead casually turned it over again. His eyes focused on the page, and time stopped for a brief moment.

He read silently to himself several times before finally reading it aloud, as if to grasp its meaning.

"Only music may span that space between the finite and the infinite… Music may be the means of arousing and awakening the best of hope, the best of desire, the best in the heart and soul of those who will and do listen. Is not music the universal language, both for those who would give praise and those who are sorry in their hearts and souls? Is it not a means, a manner of universal expression? Thus, may the greater hope come."

Alex read it once more silently. Then he flipped the page back when his eyes caught another verse.

"Love goes far beyond what you call the grave."

He closed the book and silently held it to his chest. Alex felt the room spinning, and shut his eyes. Appearing before him was his guide. Alex waited, but she didn't speak. She was looking into his eyes with intent, inquiring what he had discovered, and smiling outwardly. Then she was gone.

With eyes still closed, Alex sat down on the bench and put his head down. He tried to stifle the sobs of relief, but found he couldn't do so. The weights were being lifted, one at a time. After several minutes, he quietly stood up and walked into his office, first stopping in front of the painting he knew in his heart was alive with spirit, where he asked aloud, "Is this what I think it is? Music? Can it be something so simple? Will she understand the music? Will it bring her to me? What music, and how?"

The painting didn't change. No answers came, and there was no glow or penetrating colors emitting from it.

He wiped the tears from his cheek. "It doesn't matter. I know the answer is inside me."

Alex stood in silence and felt what was happening to him. He felt the energy inside of his soul grow more confident, and he felt a new surge of hope emerging. There was no way to verify it, but he knew he was still being led on the right path.

Alex sat in front of his piano and played with a passion he

hadn't felt in years. He felt one step closer to her, and because of this, his energy was ageless. He had found another way of reaching her. The energy of music. And the remembrance that love is never-ending. He remembered the music in his dreams of her.

He recalled something his friend Dick Sutphen had said to him many times. He heard his own voice repeating his friend's words of wisdom. "There are times in life when you must have enough faith to let go and stop trying to manipulate your circumstances. Surrender, know that there are reasons for what you are experiencing, and they are beyond your understanding."

Alex looked out to the ocean, and smiled. "Yes, Richard, I believe you are correct. Every time I surrender and get out of my own way, answers come to me. I don't always have to go searching for them. I'm still learning to trust the process, and that's not an easy lesson for me to learn. You always said that I feel more comfortable being in total control at all times. But I think I'm beginning to understand. And I'm trying not to get upset when I don't have that control, or when I don't understand what is happening. I trust she will be brought to me. And in time, I know she will be mine. I just need to trust the process."

With fingers poised on the keys, Alex continued to compose his song, this time with a smile on his face. He had a lot of work to do before tomorrow's jam session.

Lauren and Adriana talked over coffee, before Adriana excused herself, with promises to be in touch later in the day.

"If I don't get out of here now, I'm going to be late for my meeting. I'll call you later."

That meant Lauren had to force herself upstairs to her bedroom. She turned on her music, and the tune 'Walk With Me' permeated the room, instantly relaxing her. Lauren stepped into the shower, humming to herself to drown out the other tune that was breaking into her thoughts. As the water softly pelted her body, she couldn't force the sight from the previous night out of her mind.

"Such pain-filled, loving eyes. I feel she was trying desperately to tell me something. Surely, after everything that's happened, this can't be my imagination."

Lauren dried herself, rubbing so hard her skin burned, and then she pulled her hair in discomfort, as she brushed it up in a ponytail. But still, she couldn't escape the presence in her mind's eye.

"What could all of this have in common? I don't see a connection, but common sense tells me there must be one."

Lauren dressed quickly, put the pocket recorder into her purse and stepped into her car. She kept sounds to a minimum on the drive to the music store. She wanted to hear her thoughts. But the rhythm of the now familiar tune would not let up, and she had no choice but to release, and hum along. What seemed like hours were only a few minutes before Lauren finally reached the music store. She swung the door open much too hard, and approached the first person she saw. He looked to be a young man about twenty years old. Lauren immediately began to have doubts as to whether this boy could help her.

"Excuse me, I've recently purchased an old music box."

Lauren took a deep breath and retrieved the recorder from her purse.

"I don't know the tune, and hoped someone could help me figure it out."

She didn't want to appear irrational, and worked hard to keep her rambling down to a minimum. But she wished she could somehow get across to this guy just how much was riding on his answer.

She noticed his confident smile, and relaxed a little.

"Let me listen. We'll see if I can help you."

Lauren handed him the recorder, and watched as he walked to the corner of the room and switched it on. For a short time, the tune softly played in the background. He listened again and again.

Lauren knew the kid was just doing his job, but she was losing patience.

"Any ideas what it could be? I'm sure it was before your time. Is there anyone older that may be of some help?"

The young man smiled again with confidence. "Yes, I know the tune. It was originally from a musical done long before I was born. My grandmother used to play it. She was…"

Lauren interrupted him. "Can you tell me what the song is?"

"I'm sorry." His friendly smile stayed. "It's called 'Where or When'."

Lauren turned pale and leaned against the wall for support.

"Miss, are you all right? Can I get you a chair?"

Lauren tried to compose herself before she frightened the boy.

"That would be nice, thank you."

She needed time to reason with herself while he was gone. Her mind and stomach were both spinning and churning.

Oh my dear God, oh my God, oh my God! What is happening here? What is happening?

She felt for the chain that held the ring around her neck. Her fingers grabbed the circle of gold and held on for dear life.

How can this be? What do I do? Oh God, please tell me what to do.

Lauren was desperately trying to calm herself before the young man came back. She took a slow deep breath.

OK, Lauren, stay calm. Just get out of here quickly and use my phone.

The young man came back with a chair and a glass of water. Lauren sat down, and gratefully accepted the water. It gave her time to think while she drank it slowly.

"Thank you. I didn't have breakfast this morning. I suppose I got a little dizzy." Lauren shook her head while she was speaking to him. *God, Lauren, that's a pitiful excuse. Think of something coherent, and then get out of here.*

"Would you like to purchase the song in its entirety with the lyrics?"

Lauren looked up in surprise. "You mean there are words?"

The boy's smile returned. "Sure. They're beautiful. They just don't make songs like that anymore."

Lauren stifled a giggle. "Your grandmother must be very proud of you. Yes, I would like to buy it."

The boy left, and Lauren breathed a sigh of relief.

God, there's lyrics too? I knew it, I just knew it. It had to be a clue of some kind. Just get me out of here so I can figure out what to do next. If he's not back in two minutes, I know I'm going to scream.

Lauren finished the water and rubbed the edge of the glass furiously, oblivious to the loud squeaking sound being emitted.

Please hurry. I can't keep this mock composure up forever.

The young assistant returned, and Lauren quickly paid for her item and thanked him profusely. Then she calmly exited the store, and quickly walked to her car. She flipped up her phone and immediately called Adriana. "Please answer. Please answer."

Adriana picked up on the fifth ring. Lauren heard her cheerful voice. "Good morning."

Lauren was out of breath. "Adriana, oh God, Adriana. You have got to tell me what to do. I am in a state of shock. I don't know what to think."

Adriana grabbed the receiver with both hands. "Lauren, what's happened?"

Lauren was speaking too fast. "I took the recorder to the music store and found what I needed to know. You'll never guess what the name of the song is."

Adriana made a noise of frustration. "Damn it, Lauren, tell me!"

"Where or when."

Adriana didn't understand. "Where or when, what? What are you talking about?"

Lauren caught herself giggling. "No, Adriana, the name of the song is 'Where or When'. 'Where or When'! Just like the inscription on my ring. Where or When."

Adriana was caught off guard, and the phone almost slipped

out of her hand. "Jesus! Are you sure about this?"

"I can't believe it either. I just bought the CD. It has lyrics too, but I haven't had the courage to listen just yet. I would prefer to be someplace other than my car. God only knows what they say, but either way, I want to be prepared."

Adriana was having trouble catching her breath. "Are you sure? Where or When? Lauren, there must to be something to this. It's just too incredible."

Lauren noticed she was still sitting in the parking lot, not sure what her next move should be. "What should I do now?"

Adriana thought for a moment. "Go to your office and get your work done. Don't listen to the song. Tonight after work, I want you to go home and listen to the song over and over. Then I want you to meditate. Hopefully, you'll get an idea about what to do next."

Lauren was apprehensive. "Please, Adriana, come over tonight. I want you there with me."

Adriana smiled over the phone. "No, Lauren. You need some quiet time alone to listen and sort this out. If you hit a brick wall after that, then I'll be there to help you. But first, you must try and do this alone."

Adriana was about to continue, when a thought struck her.

"I just had an idea about the book I've been trying to remember the name of. It had to do with a couple that met through dreams. Remember?"

Lauren tapped her fingers on the steering wheel. "You're still trying to come up with a name?"

"Yeah, but I just had an idea. There's something about the words 'Where or When' that's reminding me of the book, but I don't know why. I have my own investigating to do tonight. If you get into a bind, call me, otherwise I'll talk to you first thing in the morning."

Lauren was nervous about the evening. "Are you sure I should do this alone?"

"Lauren, you'll be fine. Call if you need me. But do not listen to the song until you go home and get relaxed. You'll want your full attention focused on this."

Lauren knew she had lost the argument. "OK, I'll go straight home this evening, and do what I have to do. Thanks for being there. I was losing my cool, and didn't know what to do to get it back."

Adriana laughed. "So what's new? Just remember to have fun with it. And don't go into it with expectations. Easy to say, right? Just remember it's leading you in a direction. You just need to listen and follow. I'll be right behind you, so don't worry. I love you."

"I love you too." Lauren turned the phone off and drove to work in silence.

Chapter 15

Alex refused to pull himself away from the piano for lunch. The music and lyrics were flowing like water.

He had the note he had found on the mantle in Connecticut, along with a copy of his own note in front of him. The music energized him, making him feel alive. Lunch would just have to wait. It was after nine before he finally felt his energy depleted. Though tired, Alex was excited about his new venture.

"This music will do the trick. I just know it."

His friends weren't surprised when he phoned, advising them he was too busy for a visit. Donovan and Elliot both gave him the same piece of advice before hanging up. "Don't overdo it, Alex. I know how consumed you get when that creative urge slaps you upside the head. Get your rest, eat, and call me tomorrow."

Alex had to smile. "Don't worry. I'll either see you tomorrow before I go to practice, or for dinner after."

That seemed to satisfy them, and he felt reasonably certain he would be left alone for the remainder of the evening. Alex documented his new song into the recorder, and pushed the piano bench in. "I don't know if I'm feeling more hungry or tired." He was reminded of how much he enjoyed feeling this way. "It's my way of knowing I've made good use with the day. A very creative day."

Alex spent the remainder of the evening making copies of his arrangement for the other band members. By the time he was finished, he was too tired to eat.

"The only thing I want is a hot shower and my bed."

He couldn't help but wonder whether he would see her. "I want to try and infuse my new song into the dream."

But he couldn't keep the doubts from intruding.

"What if she doesn't grasp it? We never have much time, and the energy is depleted so quickly. I wish I knew what to do about that."

Alex removed his clothes and stepped into the shower. He immediately noticed the feel of hot liquid running down his chest, dripping onto his flat stomach, then flowing between his legs.

He began singing his new arrangement to the point of arousal.

"Great. Is it because I haven't had a woman in a very long time, or is the music doing it to me?" He was amused by the notion.

Once satisfied, he stepped out of the water and walked onto his balcony. Alex was now consumed with his plan to reach her, to touch her soul. He wanted everything to be right. His thought was interrupted by another, causing him to race downstairs to retrieve his recorder, grabbing a sandwich along the way.

He returned to his balcony, still naked, where he relaxed in a chair. The waves were crashing in a beautiful symphony around him. But he refused to let their beauty and sounds take precedence over coming up with a plan to reach her.

"I'll meditate while listening to the song. I'll ask my guide and higher self to intervene. They must know how much I need her. She's become my life. Everything I do now, I do for her, and because of her. I know in the deepest part of myself that she's not a fantasy. And, I know she's looking for me too. I'll find a way to reach her. This I know with every fiber of my being."

Alex refused to let negativity intrude on his prayer to the universe. He looked up at the stars and took a deep breath.

He instantly went down to his place of comfort and found he was very deep in trance. He saw himself and the pages from the Edgar Cayce book floating in front of his inner eyes. The words suspended in florescent colors.

"Music may be the means of arousing and awakening the best of hope, the best of desire, the best in the heart and soul of those who will and do listen."

Alex felt the music fusing itself to his soul. He knew there was a way to her heart. In his inner mind, he looked up to the sky and saw the words that gave him confirmation.

"Love goes far beyond what you call the grave."

His guide suddenly appeared before him. It still surprised him how much light and love she brought forth with each visit. She was looking at him, but not speaking. He wanted her nearer. He wanted her to comfort him and reaffirm his dedication in what he believed.

She slowly approached, and took his hand. When she spoke, it was barely above a whisper. "Alex, your music is beautiful. Perhaps the best you've written in this lifetime. It truly comes from the heart. It is time to bring it to her as your gift. She will determine whether or not to accept it. Do your best, Alex. She knows of your attempts, but she must be a willing participant as well. Fear and confusion must be cast from her soul before you can go any further. The love for you has always been in her place. She's never lost the love. But false fear has destroyed many loves. Do your best, and she will come to you."

Alex was taken aback by the speech. "You tell me of things that are fear based. Why do you say these things to me? You know I'm doing my best. I would be the last one to wish fear into her heart. I love her with everything I am, and with everything I have ever been. I feel I will be nothing more without her."

The old lady touched his forehead. "Do not say these things, Alex. You will be you, with her, or without her. I caution you not to add your fears to her story. Do not add your burdens to this. You will be everything you are meant to be, whether she chooses to join you or not. Do not play the role of martyr. She loves you. Until any further developments take place, be happy with this. Don't give up your efforts either. Do what must be done, and do your very best. But you must not pour your expectations over this issue, regarding what should be, or shouldn't be handed to her. She has her own decisions to make. You are more learned in your powers than she is. She's catching up with you very quickly, so don't worry about her energies not matching yours. They're coming along nicely. But you will need more patience."

He looked down and shook his head in frustration. "Will I know her in this lifetime? You've already as much as said that she's been with me before. I assumed as much, considering how intense this feeling is, but am I doing all of this for nothing? Will this lifetime be a waste? Am I destined to continue this game throughout this lifetime?"

The woman gently cupped his face in her hands. "Either way, this is not a game. Anything that brings you closer to your loved ones, no matter in which lifetime it may be, is an affirmative action, and not a game. I will try and answer your question the best I can."

The old woman took Alex's hand again, and squeezed. "This is yet to be decided. You both have the capabilities to make a reunion. But she must conquer her fears, not to mention your passion to want to control and influence the situation. Let her come to you with the level of comfort you already know in your heart. You wouldn't want it any other way."

He shook away from her, knowing her words hit very close to his own thoughts. "I will continue to do my very best. I will do everything I can with only the best of intentions. I don't want to lose her again. I feel in my soul there has been far too much tragedy already. It's time to start again. But this time, with her. If she lets me assist her freely, I will help her conquer her fears. I will not insist that she hand over her fears to me so I can heal them myself. But I think it's all right to assist her if she is willing. I can help her if asked, but I cannot influence? Am I right?"

She smiled at him. He could see the energy of light flowing through her. "You are correct. You can assist her if she truly wants the help. She's not as far from you as you may think. Her love for you is strong and very real. She acknowledges that freely. That is a very large step in the right direction." The old woman patted Alex's heart, and continued, "You may not want to be reminded again, but you both acknowledged and accepted these needed lessons on the other side. You both must learn to accept freely, and then cast away the fears of living without the other. You are correct in your assumption. She was very much consumed by anger and frustration with the tragedies that were involved. She could never possess herself, without also possessing you. And, you, my son, were no different. The love should be unconditional and freely expressed with no expectations whatsoever. A difficult task, but not impossible. You've both grown in this life. You both have acknowledged your enlightened souls, and have worked hard to build them stronger. She hugged Alex close to her. "Alex, the love has always been there. There was a promise made between the two of you long ago. Do your best, my son. And in doing that, so will she."

Alex opened his eyes and was alone, fighting for self-composure.

"My God, I've never been given so much information before. This must mean that I'm closer to her spirit."

Alex looked up at the sky and spoke softly into the breeze. "I won't desert you again. This time, I will be there for you when you need me."

He quickly wrote down the volume of words that were spoken, then felt exhaustion set in. He put his new music on repeat, and fell into his bed.

With Kevin gone most of the day, Lauren was able to keep herself busy. It was bad enough that he had noticed something was amiss in just the few minutes that he was with her.

"Lauren, you keep glancing at your watch. You have a hot date tonight, or something?"

Lauren hadn't realized she had been acting as if she would bolt from the store at any moment.

"No, it's going to be a quiet evening for me."

She wanted to change the subject. "What are your plans for the evening?"

Kevin purposely took the bait. "Terry and I have plans with some friends. Probably drinks and dinner. You want to join us?"

Lauren smiled. "No, thanks. I'm looking forward to an evening alone."

She didn't bother going into an explanation, and Kevin didn't push the subject.

At precisely 7:00, Lauren put the closed sign out and quickly locked up the store. She was in her car and gone in a matter of a few short minutes. The drive home was quiet and relaxing. Lauren opened her sunroof and welcomed the breeze now blowing softly through her hair. She tried to ignore the CD lying next to her, but her anticipation was growing. When she finally reached home, she pulled into her garage and jumped out of the car, rushing into her house in record time.

Lauren threw her purse and briefcase on the table and slipped her shoes off before finally taking a deep breath.

"God, it's great to be home."

Lauren hurried into her office and opened the music box. When the music started playing, she realized it was time to do what she had been dreaming about all day. She stared at the CD cover for several minutes. "What am I afraid of? My goodness, it's just a song. After everything else that's happened, this should be simple."

But her hand never moved to take the CD from its wrapper.

"I'm being ridiculous. There's nothing to be frightened of. I've waited all day for this. What could I possibly find that would upset me?"

She realized how silly she was being, and closed the box.

Lauren picked up her shoes and CD case, and defiantly walked upstairs. She intentionally undressed very slowly, allowing herself plenty of time. After what seemed like hours, she stepped into the shower, letting the warm drops touch every part of her body. She wanted to rid herself of all the day's tensions, and start anew. Then she slipped into her most comfortable pajamas, and turned off the telephone. She wanted no disruptions tonight. She was going to follow Adriana's advice to the letter.

Lauren pulled the note out from the metal box, and picked up her journal. She touched the ring that fell to her chest, giving her comfort and strength. Slowly, she put the CD into the player, pressing the repeat button.

"I'd better like the song, otherwise this is going to be a very long night."

She opened her journal to a blank page, then waited for some kind of reaction. Lauren instantly heard the now familiar tune that she had come to love so much. Her heart was pounding out of her chest as she waited for the lyrics to follow.

"It seems we stood and talked like this before... we looked at each other in the same way then, but I can't remember where or when... the clothes you are wearing, are the clothes you wore... the smile you were smiling, you were smiling then, but I can't remember where or when."

Lauren seemed frozen in time. Her mind was spinning, but she forced herself to write her first impressions. After the song played in full, she looked down at her page and was shocked at the words she had written.

"It's as if I wrote the lyrics myself. But I know that's impossible. There's something about it that's bringing back a faint memory. It's almost as if I'm supposed to remember something of importance. Something I promised I would never forget. Almost as if I gave my word to always remember."

Lauren looked up to the ceiling and pleaded aloud, "But what is it?"

She played it again, this time singing along to the music. "So it seems that we have met before, and laughed and loved before, but who knows where or when."

She softly rubbed the ring for comfort and strength, listening to the song over and over. When Lauren finally looked down at her journal, she was surprised to see how much had been written. She didn't recall writing anything more in the book, but the blank pages were now full. She had written the inscription of the ring over and over. 'Where / when… remember, my love.'

"My God, I must have written it a hundred times. Why would I do that?" Lauren shook her head violently. "I've got to get a grip on reality." But her thoughts immediately returned to the question that she couldn't answer. "What must I remember? I gave my promise to always remember something, now and forever. But what?"

She read her journal over again. 'Where / when… remember, my love.'

To prove she wasn't losing her mind, Lauren made a list of what she visibly had in her possession, then read it back aloud, "I have a ring, a handwritten note, a music box, this song, and my hypnosis tape."

Lauren closed her eyes in frustration. "I made a promise. To whom? About what? Why am I afraid to remember?"

Lauren shivered as a chill spread up her spine. But she took a deep breath and spoke the words again.

"Where or when… remember… my love."

Tears of frustration came to her eyes as she began putting all the pieces of the puzzle together. Lauren whispered to him as if he were in the room.

"I know this has to do with you. I know there must have been a promise made. The song was supposed to be a reminder, wasn't it? Please help me put it all together. I think I'm beginning to remember bits and pieces. But most of the time it makes no sense to me. Am I supposed to remember that I love you?"

Lauren rubbed her eyes to clear the tears, and then turned off her light. She slid under her covers and prepared for her meditation. But she fell asleep instead.

Lauren looked around in shock when she found herself standing inside the gazebo, staring at the old wooden bridge crossing the pond. *I'm in Connecticut? What am I doing here?*

She stared at the pond for a moment, and then remembered the initials carved in the open building. She immediately looked up to verify her surroundings, and found the jagged edges of the letters scrawled into the wood.

Lauren read aloud, "N.F., W.W., A.R."

She was back in the gazebo she so dearly loved, and smiled. Then she patiently sat down and waited. She wasn't sure what would happen next, but she instinctively knew to remain calm and wait. It seemed like hours before Lauren noticed ripples of water piercing the surface of the pond. She focused on that until her attention was suddenly pulled into another direction, as the gold and red leaves on the nearby trees violently swayed, before falling to the ground. The breeze picked up her hair and tossed the dark strands around her face. She closed her eyes and took a deep breath, inhaling all the familiar fragrances that accompanied a crisp fall day.

When Lauren opened her eyes, she saw him standing outside the gazebo. He was watching her with a smile on his face. She was happy to see him, but frustrated by the veil that seemed to be a constant companion at their meetings. She wanted to speak first, but was interrupted by the sounds of a tune floating lightly in the air. Lauren listened for a moment, and then opened her mouth to speak again. She stopped when she saw him put a finger to his lips. She remained quiet and just listened to the music. Lauren didn't know the tune, but it was the most beautiful sound she had ever heard. She closed her eyes and listened. When she realized what she was hearing, she opened her eyes and gasped.

"Words of wonder… words of hope… words of love… words to remind us of our past… I have loved you in our present… I have loved you in our future… I will love you always… time will hold the answers… to the question in our hearts… memories of you keep my love strong…every second that we're apart…"

Lauren blocked out everything else, and listened with intent, until she had the song memorized in her soul.

"How did you know these words? How could you have known?"

He spoke calmly and with such love, she knew she would feel his energy for lifetimes.

"How could I not know? I was right. The letter came from you, didn't it?"

Lauren was sobbing from happiness, but she was having trouble focusing. "Yes, it was from me. And I have one from you?"

"Yes, my love. From me to you."

She was about to speak, but he spoke first.

"Remember these words. Remember the music. And remember the tune that's been dancing in your mind for eons."

She smiled. "You mean 'Where or When'?"

"Yes. And my love, if you're willing, I know the music will be our key. I don't know how, and I don't know when, but we must put our trust in it."

Then Alex remembered his guide's words of wisdom. "That is, if you're a willing participate. I don't want to push you until you feel you're ready. I will always be here waiting for you. And with your help, together, we will find a way to conquer this… together."

Lauren couldn't stop the tears from openly flowing.

"Yes, I am ready. I'm no longer afraid of what I will find. It is more frightening to live without you, alone, than to seek what may be on the other side."

His smile vanished. "No. Please don't say that. With me or without me, you will succeed. I don't want to influence your judgment. Your decisions should be made without any consideration of me."

Lauren didn't understand, and confusion registered in her eyes.

"You are partly mistaken. My opinions and decisions are my own. I will always do and achieve what I must with my life. But I would be so much happier with you. I know my life would not be complete without your influence and your love. Surely we can work together and tear this veil away from us. In my heart, I know I'm ready. I would be very sad to find you no longer here with me. It would be devastating. But somehow, I know I'm stronger now, and I've learned that I would cope. I was never able to work through that lesson before. But I've grown strong in this life. I've been forced to deal with independence, and be content with it. To be able to trust my own judgments and decisions. But that doesn't take my love away from you. Your love would indeed make me complete in a deep spiritual sense."

Alex felt the warm tears flowing down his face. "I understand, and I will help any way you feel is best. In the meantime, please try and remember the music. And trust that we'll put the pieces of the puzzle together."

The music consumed them, and the words were pressed into her mind.

Feeling completely content, Lauren looked around once again, and smiled. "Please tell me why this place is so familiar. I don't understand why it means so much to me."

Alex looked perplexed. "I don't know."

Lauren pointed to the carvings inside the gazebo wall. "What do you think this means?"

Alex looked, then spoke in a knowing voice, "It means 'never forget… where or when… always remember'." He gasped aloud in amazement. "Wow. How did I know that?"

Lauren smiled in astonishment. "Because you carved those letters yourself."

They both mirrored a look of complete amazement.

She looked at the initials. "How did we know?"

She stood up to walk into his arms, but he was gone. The music remained, but he was gone from her view.

Lauren sat down on the bench and sobbed. "Why does it have to be this way?" The only comfort she found was from the music and lyrics softly playing in her mind.

She opened her eyes and found that she was back in her own bed, with the sun shining brightly through her balcony door. Lauren lay still for several minutes, trying to remember.

"Where did I go? Did I see him?" She squeezed her eyes shut tight, trying to remember. "Yes! I did."

But she could only remember bits and pieces as the dream was slowly being erased from her memory. She quickly grabbed her journal from the table and wrote fast and furiously.

"Another dream. He was there. We spoke. Gazebo. Love. Acceptance. Music. I'm ready."

Lauren looked at her words in frustration, and slapped the paper in disgust. "What the hell does this mean?"

Lauren demanded herself out of bed and into the warm shower. "I need to calm myself, and just let things be."

She stood under the steady stream of water, insisting that her concentration fall on the sound of the water hitting the tiled floor.

The sound started very soft, as if music were being played, downstairs. Then slowly, the volume increased. Lauren turned off the shower and listened closely, thinking someone was in the house with her.

The music was louder now. She listened with such intensity and familiarity, she became dizzy. When Lauren realized the music was coming from her own mind, she stumbled out of the shower and sat down on the edge of the marble tub, closing her eyes. She began singing the words as if she had known them all her life. "Words of wonder... words of hope..."

The tune and lyrics continued, as Lauren wrapped a towel around herself and hurried to write them in her journal. Then she turned on her new CD, and focused on what she knew to be fact.

"Where or when... are the same words as the ring's inscription. This much I know." Lauren paused, and then realized she wasn't ready to face the frustration again. She swiftly walked onto her balcony, picked up her phone, and called Adriana.

Alex woke himself up, screaming his love for her. His eyes burned from the morning sun, and he turned away from the open window. Frustration possessed him when he heard voices and laughter coming from the beach below him.

"Damn, it happened again. I can't believe I walked away from her. How could I be talking to her one second, then just be gone out of sight, the next? I don't understand."

Alex took a deep calming breath. He lay still for a few minutes, soaking in the small fragments he could still remember from the night before. His irritation slowly turned into a smile that covered his face.

"I spoke to her. And somehow, I transferred the song to her. How did I do that?" Alex shook his head. "I don't know how I did it, and it doesn't matter. I found her again, and she has my song in her soul. I refuse to believe that she didn't understand. I know she's enlightened, and she will remember."

Alex refused to let any sort of negativity creep into his mind.

His focus was so strong, he jumped when the phone rang. It was Donovan.

"Are you awake? How was your evening?"

Alex knew what his friend was asking.

"Yeah, I'm up and hungry. I spent much of the night writing some intense lyrics. And before you ask, yes, I saw her in my dreams. It certainly is getting more interesting. I'll tell you more as soon as I finish processing. What are you doing?"

Donovan smiled over the phone. "Vickie and I spent some quality time together last night, and she was off and running early this morning. I have several meetings later today, but thought you might want some company this morning. I printed the pictures Elliot took of your new house in Connecticut. Thought you might want me to drop them by."

Alex couldn't contain his excitement. "By all means, come over as soon as you can. I'll have coffee waiting. Why don't you bring some lox and bagels from the deli down the street from you?

I'm starving."

Donovan ended the conversation. "I'll be there in about thirty minutes. Get dressed, and I'll see you soon. But first, start brewing that coffee."

Alex hung up with a chuckle, and quickly took a shower and dressed in jeans and a t-shirt. Twenty-five minutes later, Donovan knocked on the door, and then let himself in. Alex was sitting at the table, looking at the ocean he never seemed to tire of.

"Don't bother letting yourself in unless you have breakfast."

Donovan laughed as he set the bag on the table, then helped himself to a cup of coffee.

"I thought you'd probably do what you always do when you get busy. Work your ass off and forget to eat. You'll be happy to know that I brought extra for later."

Alex ate vigorously as Donovan tossed an envelope in his direction. "They're quite good."

Alex put his bagel aside and opened the flap, pouring the photos out in front of him.

"Donovan, these are great. But when did Elliot take them?" Alex casually flipped through the photos, but abruptly stopped when he came upon a close up of the gazebo.

"He captured it perfectly, didn't he? Looks like a postcard."

Alex was concentrating on the photo in front of him and didn't answer. Donovan noticed an intensity emanating from Alex's eyes, and his body was stiff and rigid. His forehead was creased, as if he were trying to remember something. Donovan waited for several moments and then could take the stillness no longer.

"Alex, what is it?"

Alex pushed the photo further out in front of him. Donovan tried to pass another photo to Alex.

"If you like that one, then this one should bring back some memories."

He pushed the picture in Alex's other hand. Alex glanced

briefly at it, then pulled it closer to his face.

"Memory?" he asked.

Donovan was glad to finally get a response.

"Yeah, from a few days ago. Remember? We saw the initials and thought it was interesting there were three sets. Normally, you'd see two. But three? We thought it would make an interesting blow up. What do you think?"

Alex was quiet again. His mind was whirling as he put the two pictures side by side. Donovan's impatience took over again.

"What in the hell is wrong with you? What are you seeing that I'm not?"

Alex shook himself and apologized to his friend. "Sorry, Donovan. I didn't mean to ignore you."

He picked up the two photos and inspected them again. When Alex spoke, his voice was much lower than normal.

"I saw her in my dream last night. I can't remember much about the circumstances, but seeing these two pictures are causing lights, bells, and whistles to go off in my head. There just seems to be something about these two pictures." His voice trailed off in silence.

Alex tried to let go of it. He knew he was thinking too much.

"I'm obsessing. And we all know that nothing ever comes to me when I obsess."

Donovan looked over at Alex talking to himself.

"Are you trying to reassure me or yourself? I already know how it works. Don't worry. When you move on to something else, it'll come to you."

Donovan tried shoving another picture in front of him, but Alex put them all aside mumbling that he would look at the rest later. Donovan knew better than to push him. Alex took a sip of his coffee, still trying to shake off the trance. He decided changing the subject was the only way to change his mood.

"We're having our first practice tonight. We have a gig next Saturday at Jupiter's. I can count on you and Vickie, as well as everyone else you've ever met in this lifetime to be there. Right?"

Donovan laughed, seeing the old Alex returning.

"Of course we'll all be there. Is that what you were working on last night?"

Alex picked up his plate and walked into the kitchen. "Yeah, I have a new arrangement I want to try out. I just hope it works."

Donovan's curiosity got the best of him. "What do you hope works? The gigs are always a lot of fun. You're certainly not worried about that, are you?"

Alex pushed his dark hair away from his face, and sat down.

"No. Well, not really. Hell, Donovan, you know me. I'm more of a closet entertainer. I've never felt very comfortable in front of a lot of people, but I do enjoy getting together with the guys and jamming. It's a nice release."

Donovan wasn't going to let go of the previous comment. "What do you hope works out?"

Alex stood up again and walked to the patio door. "I had an idea yesterday that I hope works. I wrote a song, using the words from the letter that I wrote up in Connecticut, with the letter that I found." Alex kept his back to Donovan. "I know this sounds insane, but I thought if I could transfer the song to her, then maybe we could find each other. Surely, between that song, along with 'Where or When', something is bound to click." He didn't care that he sounded like a desperate man. "Surly?"

Donovan was glad Alex had turned away from him. Otherwise he didn't think he could ask the next question.

"Alex, how do you know if it can work? Doesn't it seem like a long shot?"

Alex didn't speak, but instead picked up the small book of Edgar Cayce's readings that he had found the day before. He quietly opened it to a page, pointed at the words, then handed it to Donovan. The room was quiet for a few moments while Donovan read it and understood its meaning. After he finished, he closed the book and handed it back to Alex.

"Wow. How did you come across that?"

Alex shrugged his shoulders. "I didn't know I had the book, and suddenly, there it was. It dropped out of my hands twice, both times falling on the same page. It all made sense to me when I read it. I meditated before going to bed, and my guide came through. She told me music would be a way to connect. It's strange, but all at once, it just seemed to make sense. I can't really explain how it happened. It just all came together. Last night when I saw her in my dream, the music and lyrics were playing all around us. It was so powerful, I'm sure she remembered it. I have no earthly idea what will happen now. But I was encouraged when she knew the song 'Where or When'. That confirmed to me the need to get the music to her. Unfortunately, I can only do things one step at a time, and only as they happen. If I look too far ahead, I could get very depressed. Not to mention scattered and frustrated. No, I have to take your advice. I need to stay out of my own way, and just let things happen as they happen. So far, so good."

Donovan watched his words carefully, and spoke in a slow drawl. "You certainly said a mouth full. But it makes sense. At least she's still coming to you in your dreams. I know you were concerned when all hell broke loose with the ring, and the lights, and all. From my point of view, it looks as though you're walking in the right direction. But more importantly, if it feels right, then you've got to go for it. And don't look back. It's a bit unconventional, but if music is the way to get to her, then that's what you need to do." Donovan thought about his last comment and chuckled.

"Getting music to her isn't unconventional. How you met her in the first place. Now that's unconventional."

The phone rang as Donovan was completing his sentence. It was Elliot calling. Alex made himself another cup of coffee while thanking his friend for taking such enlightened photographs, and then bringing him up to date about the previous night. Elliot was surprised by the current events.

"Alex, we can't leave you alone for a moment, can we? I hope you can come up with your answers about the gazebo picture. It's there, so don't worry about it. It'll come to you."

"Yeah, that's what Donovan said. It seems to be true. Every time I stop and listen, things happen. I can't wait for you both to hear this song. I just hope it works."

Elliot spoke up, "I've got a full day ahead of me, but if you're going to be around after practice, call me and we'll have a late dinner."

The other line rang, and Alex asked Elliot to hold a moment. It was the jewelry store.

"Hi, Mr. Chandler, it's Jeff from Malibu Jewelers."

Alex could feel himself tense up. "What's wrong?"

Jeff laughed. "Everything is fine, Mr. Chandler. I was calling to tell you that your ring is ready to be picked up."

Alex was taken off guard. "You said it would take a few days. Did she clean up OK?"

Jeff put Alex's mind at ease. "She cleaned up beautifully. It wasn't as difficult a process as we thought. It's ready whenever you want to pick it up. We'll be here until 6:00."

Alex was excited. "I'll be over in a few minutes. Thank you."

He clicked back to Elliot's line. "The ring is ready. I'm going to run and get it now. I'll let you know. Thanks again."

Alex picked up his keys as he approached Donovan.

"Sorry. You can stay here if you like, but I've got an errand to run. The ring's ready. I don't want to waste another minute."

Donovan grabbed his keys from the bar. "No, I can't stay. I have to be someplace in a few minutes. I'll catch up with you tonight."

Adriana picked up on the second ring, sounding exhausted. Lauren paused for a moment before speaking.

"Adriana, are you still in bed?"

Adriana yawned before answering. "I was working on research

late last night, and didn't get much sleep. I think I may be on to something, but I'll tell you about it later. Tell me what happened last night."

Lauren sounded frustrated. "Hell if I know what happened. I did everything you told me to do. You've got to hear this song, 'Where or When'. The lyrics are as beautiful as the music."

Adriana finished her thoughts. "I know. Last night I bought the song. Lauren, it's fascinating. That's part of my research, but I don't have anything conclusive yet. Just give me time. I know that song holds a huge clue for us both, but I haven't been able to figure out what it is. But enough about that. Did you have a dream?"

Lauren let out a heavy sigh. "I don't remember much about the dream. But I do remember him being there. It was intense, and a lot was said, but I can't recall much this morning. I wrote down everything I could remember. You tell me if it's anything significant."

Adriana waited while Lauren shuffled through her notes.

Lauren recited what she had partly written. "I met him at the gazebo in Connecticut. I don't know the story behind these last two words, but I wrote, 'acceptance' and 'I'm ready'."

Adriana listened intently. "You're accepting and ready for what?"

Lauren was confused. "I have no idea. I know a lot took place, and a lot was said, but I just can't remember now."

"Anything else?"

Lauren was apprehensive. "Yeah. This is the part that throws me. There was a song in my mind this morning. But the lyrics are the same words as the notes left behind at the Connecticut house. I have a strong suspicion I had all the answers last night. That's what's so damn frustrating about this. I feel I had it, and then I lost it. I'm trying to work on verifiable evidence here, and since I'm still questioning, I can't hold it to truth."

Adriana was excited. "Can you sing it to me, Lauren?"

"Yeah. It's the most beautiful thing I've ever heard. I could never have made it up myself. Here it goes."

Lauren felt a little foolish, but took a deep breath and sang the song to her friend. When she had finished, she added, "As you can see, singing isn't my forte either."

Adriana was quiet for a second, and then giggled. "You did fine. You're right, the song is beautiful. You have no idea where it came from? And you can't remember anything else about the dream?"

Lauren was frustrated again. "No. I wish I could. I know I'm supposed to remember something, but I'm at a loss. I don't get it. Why am I given this if I'm not supposed to do something with it?"

Adriana wanted to be of some comfort to her friend, but didn't know how to start. "I agree it's doubtful that song came from your imagination. I believe it's one step closer to the clues you've already been given. Maybe you should look on the bright side. Now, you have two songs to think about. They're obviously connected in some way. I wish you could remember more."

Lauren gave a nervous laugh. "Me too. It would certainly simplify my life. Adriana, you really don't think I'm making all this up?"

Adriana was quick with her response. "Absolutely not, Lauren. I don't know where this is all going, but I have some ideas I'm working on. In the meantime, don't you give up on your hopes. Continue to meditate, and write down what you remember. I can't tell you everything will come together. I pray it does, but I just don't know where it's going. In the meantime, you're learning more about yourself than you could possibly have hoped for in a lifetime. Hang in there. Between the two of us geniuses, we'll come up with something tangible. I wouldn't give you false encouragement if I thought it was leading nowhere. And at first, I was a little worried about that. But, Lauren, not now. You're too grounded to be making all this up in your mind. And believe me, I've seen some very strange things happen since I opened my bookstore. And from my experience, I would have to say that most things are possible. I think you first have to dream it before it can become a reality."

Lauren sighed over the phone. "Adriana, what would I ever do without you? You always know what to say when I need the most encouragement. I get so frustrated and confused. I'm trying to hold on to reality. But at the moment, I'm having to make it a reality based on things I can't touch, see, or hear. There's no doubt that too many things are happening in the tangible world for me to argue that it's just coincidence. You and I both know there is no such thing."

Adriana responded in sincerity, "You have come a long way. Keep up the good work. I'll meet you tonight for dinner around the corner from your house at 8:00. We'll talk then."

"I'll see you tonight."

Lauren quickly descended the stairs, heading for her office. She had to record the new song on tape before she forgot the tune. She pulled out her recorder and awkwardly sung the song as she remembered it into the machine. Then she recorded her new CD, and slipped it into her purse.

She talked to herself as she was dressing for the day, vowing to listen to the music going to work and back. She wanted to saturate her being with the tunes.

"There's a lot I'm not remembering, but by God, I'm going to remember this."

All Lauren could think about while driving to work was the gazebo in her dream. She remembered it as though it were in front of her. She could see him, and she somehow knew they were conversing on topics of great importance. She remembered his smile and all the love erupting from his heart and soul. The more she listened to the music, the clearer the previous night was becoming. Lauren turned up the volume until the sound echoed off the windows of her car. Her thinking became instinctive.

I wish you would find me, and take me with you.

She noticed herself looking in every car window she

approached on the street.

Would I know him if I saw him? Would he know me?

She scolded herself for concentrating on the people around her. "Stop it. We'll find each other. I'm not going to approach every attractive man I see and ask if he's the one."

Lauren chuckled at herself. "That would certainly get me into a lot of trouble. And I think I've got enough of that already. I'll meet him when the time is right. I must believe this. There's not one person in this world who has ever gotten anywhere by thinking negative. I know it'll happen when the time is right. Period."

She didn't say it aloud, but knew she would be distraught if it never took place. She knew her anticipation was mounting, and she noticed it was taking more concentration to keep her mind calm.

"I feel like a child at Christmas. Will I get what I've always wanted, will it be coal, or will I have to wait until next Christmas?"

She turned the volume up louder to drown out her thoughts until she reached her store, but his smile returned to her inner mind.

"I so desperately want to remember."

She sat in her car while the song completed its cycle, and she closed her eyes. Lauren suddenly saw herself pointing to the crudely drawn carvings inside the gazebo. She saw herself asking him a question. He answered, followed by a look of confusion on his face. She saw herself laughing, then casually telling him something, as if to remind him of a fact that he should have already known.

She heard a car honking somewhere in the parking lot, and her eyes flew open. She grabbed a pen and paper and wrote the memory down. Lauren glanced at her watch, realizing she had been sitting in her car for twenty minutes, and was now late for work.

"What was that all about? What was so important about the initials? What did I tell him?"

She knew it was going to be a very long day.

Alex drove to the jewelry store with his foot heavy on the accelerator. It couldn't be too soon before he had the ring back in his possession. He didn't care if he could read the inscription or not. He just needed it back.

He parked the car and raced inside. Jeff was standing behind the counter, and pulled the box from the drawer when he saw Alex approaching.

"I've got it right here for you. It looks brand new."

He was about to open the box when Alex put his hand over the lid. The gentleman looked at him strangely, so Alex spoke fast.

"That's not necessary. I'm sure it's fine. I want to see it when I get home."

Jeff's face was becoming more confused, so Alex lied to complete his story. "I have someone there who should see it first."

The look remained on Jeff's face, but he relinquished the container with a smile. Alex thanked him and casually walked out of the store. He heard the man's comment behind him. "I hope she likes it."

Alex took a deep breath when he was finally alone in the confines of his car. "You're a terrible liar, Alex."

He didn't want strangers around him when he opened the box. He wanted to see it and touch it and feel it in his comfortable surroundings, with no outside energy.

He drove fast going home, his curiosity getting the better of him.

Once inside his house, he opened the back doors to allow the ocean sounds to enter. He needed fresh air to revive his senses.

Alex sat on the couch and closed his eyes. He took a long deep breath before slowly opening the box. He smiled on hearing the creak of the lid as it opened. He took another deep breath and opened his eyes. Alex carefully took the ring from its holder, noticing how bright it now shone. "It looks brand new."

He held it up to the sunlight filtering in, and turned the band slowly. He found it easy to read now. As soon as he finished, Alex quickly lost control and dropped the ring between the cushions on the couch. He gasped for air, and fell to his knees, pulling the cushions off the sofa, still gulping for his breath. His hair had fallen into his eyes and he had trouble seeing. He finally saw the band shining alone in the light, and he carefully picked it up with both hands.

Alex sat hard on the floor and doubled over, still trying to catch his breath. He heard his own voice from someplace far away trying to offer himself some comfort.

"Alex, calm down." Along with alternating words of anxiety. "Jesus, oh my sweet Jesus. This is it! This is it!"

He put the ring to his lips, and then caressed it against his cheek.

Alex repeated the words, "This is it, this is it!" for several minutes, until he had finally calmed down, and was in control of himself.

He looked closely at the band of gold and continued to turn it around in his fingers, reading its message of love. 'Where / when… remember… my love.'

His thoughts went to every dream he had had pertaining to her. He thought about the painting in his office that lit up like the sky with verification that something was amiss. He thought about the sudden chills he would get out of nowhere, and the knowledge that she was somehow responsible. He thought about the music he couldn't stop playing on the piano, and in his head. Both songs instantly came to mind, one chord at a time. His thoughts went to the table and frame he had purchased, along with the long awakened memories in the house he had purchased in Connecticut.

He looked down at the ring and smiled. "You're my verification. I knew where to find you." Alex clasped the ring tightly in his palm. "I know she's looking for me too. This must belong to her, and I will return it to her finger."

He opened his palm and whispered softly. "I don't care what it takes; I will return this to your finger, my love."

He put the ring on his little finger, and strolled to the piano. A new composition was emerging in his mind, and he had to get it on paper before tonight.

"I hope the band can learn three songs before next Saturday." With each note he added to the song, the more his memory returned. When Alex had completed his composition, he played it, singing along. A portion of the lyrics contained the inscription of the ring. When he reached the chorus, he sang from his heart, "now and forever... where or when... always remember..."

He stopped and looked at the keys in front of him, and repeated the phrase slowly. "Now and forever...where or when...always remember." Alex stopped, closed his eyes, and watched inside his mind's eyes. He was standing at the gazebo. It changed scenes, and he saw Donovan handing him a photograph. It was of the gazebo. He was handed another photo.

From somewhere far away, he heard himself repeating the words over and over. "My dear God. This is the translation of the initials. How did I know that?"

He was losing control again, and tried desperately to regain composure. He saw himself standing outside the gazebo. She was standing inside and pointing to the initials. He spoke confidently and was then overcome by confusion. He watched as she laughed and told him something that baffled him. He opened his eyes and dabbed at the tears.

"It's all happening so quickly now. For so long, everything moved slow, at times almost stagnant. Now, much of the information is returning. But why can't I come up with the solution to locate her?"

He didn't want to think about the solution. He forced himself to be satisfied with what he had, now.

Alex recorded his new undertaking, and put all the music in his briefcase. Calmly, he walked out the door for his rehearsal.

Chapter 16

Lauren had kept herself busy, and was glad when the day was finally over. Kevin approached her during a break between customers.

"Lauren, you've been distant in the past few days. What's going on? Anything more to do with your dreams?"

Lauren looked at him with suspicion, but figuring she had already told him most everything, she decided to open up to him.

She told him about the dream and the music. She told him about the verification at the music store the previous morning. She quietly sang him the song produced the night before in her dreams. Then she waited to be chastised by her friend. How much could she count on him believing? He hadn't lived through it on a daily basis for months like she had.

Kevin sipped his coffee and looked into Lauren's eyes. When he finally spoke, it was in a softened voice.

"Lauren, I know it took you months to finally admit everything that's been happening to you. I know you expect me to tell you that you need your head examined. But I know you, and I know you wouldn't make this up. I may not understand the emotions you're going through, but I do understand that it's affecting you in a very big way. Your life is changing paths and I'll be with you no matter where it takes you. I could tell you to forget all this, and focus on the real world. But I see you're desperately trying to hang on to reality, the best way you can. I believe you, and I believe there's something to all this. I don't know what. And I won't advise what steps you should take next. But I will be here for you, and I will encourage you to do everything you can to bring this dream into your reality. How can I argue the point when there are just too damn many coincidences?"

Lauren squeezed Kevin's face with her cupped hand. "There are no coincidences, sweetie. None whatsoever. Once I learn to read the clues, I'll be just where I'm supposed to be."

She changed the subject as she refilled Kevin's coffee cup. "So, tell me about your dinner last night. Where did you go?"

While Kevin had stories to tell about his evening, it gave Lauren the opportunity to think about what Kevin had said. Outwardly, she looked as though she was concentrating on his voice, but inwardly, she was in her own world. Both were brought back to the moment when a steady stream of customers walked through the front door. By 7:00, the pair felt as if they had worked a week.

"What are your plans tonight?"

Lauren remembered, "I'm supposed to have dinner with Adriana, but I think I'm just too tired."

The phone rang as Lauren completed her last syllable. Kevin picked it up and said his hellos, then handed the receiver to Lauren.

It was Adriana.

"Hi, Lauren, sorry to do this on short notice, but something's come up here and I'm afraid we'll have to make dinner tomorrow night." She was about to continuing apologizing, but Lauren interrupted.

"Don't worry about it. I was about to phone you as well. We had a busy day and I'm beat. What happened at the store to cause you problems?"

Adriana paused for a moment and thought. "Uh, well, I just have some research to do, and I think I have almost everything I need."

Lauren was curious. "What's going on? What kind of research?

Don't you have enough to do?"

Adriana laughed outright to break her tension. "Yeah, between you and this place, I'm being kept busy. It's just the same old type of research stuff."

Lauren knew better, and ignored the uneasy tones in her friend's voice.

"OK, I think I understand. You're doing research that's driving you crazy, and you'll tell me about it in your own sweet time. Right?"

Adriana laughed. "Gee, Lauren, you're getting this psychic thing down better than I thought. Go home, and I'll talk to you later. If you need me, I'll be at the office, and then home later. Let me know if there are any new developments."

Lauren knew what she was talking about, and answered knowingly.

"If anything happens, I'll call you immediately. See you tomorrow."

Kevin handed Lauren her purse and briefcase. "Let's get out of here."

A little later, Lauren walked into her house, slipping off her shoes and placing her purse and briefcase on the table on her way into the office. She saw the red light from the message machine light blinking, and thought twice about listening to it.

"I suppose I'd better listen and get it over with. It could be one of the girls."

Though she knew had it been an emergency, they would have called her cell phone. Lauren took a deep breath and pushed the button. She sat on the edge of her desk, waiting for the machine to speak. The first message came through louder than she had anticipated.

"Hi, Lauren. It's me. Sorry I haven't phoned lately, but I've been out of the country. I spoke to our attorney. He said he'd talked to you. He's drawing up the divorce papers, getting them ready for our review. I'll be in L.A. next Saturday, but just for the day. I was hoping we could get together at his office to look them over, and sign. If this is a problem, call my office and I'll get back with you."

Lauren closed her eyes and slowly shook her head back and forth. She knew it was just a matter of time. She worried about her girls. She heard Gary's voice drop several octaves, and continued in almost a sad tone.

"Lauren, I hope you're doing well. I still worry about you. I suppose I always will. This wasn't a surprise to either of us, you said so yourself. I just want to do what's best for everyone concerned. In a few weeks, I would like for the two of us to fly down and see the girls. I think we should tell them together. Although I don't think it's going to come as much of a surprise. I see them every time I'm in town, and by their conversations, I think they're resigned to the idea. On my last visit, they asked me why we've waited so long to make ourselves happy. We've brought up two wonderful daughters. Thank God, we did that right."

Lauren was still shaking her head, tears now streaming down her face. She was sorry they no longer loved each other. But, she didn't think they ever had. Not in the way it should have been. But her daughters were well adjusted, loving, and compassionate. They wanted her happiness as much as she wanted the same for them.

Gary was completing his message. "If I don't hear from you, I'll assume that Saturday is fine. I would appreciate it if we could make it around noon. I have a late flight out. Take care. Bye."

Lauren heard the click of the phone, but continued sitting on the edge of her desk.

How do I feel about this?

She waited for remorse, and the feeling of failure and guilt, but none came. She had to admit the only emotion she felt was relief.

She picked up the phone and called her daughters. She needed to hear their sweet voices. Alexa and Alexandra were both at home, studying. She told them that she and their father would be coming to visit them. She explained they needed to discuss a few family matters. The girls were on extensions, listening together. Alexa asked whether she had been busy at work.

"Yes, it's been a madhouse. Business has never been better." Lauren gave them more details about the construction of the new store, then teased them about going to work for her when they got out of school. The three of them laughed together and talked for over an hour. The twins both had new boyfriends, cousins from Orange County. And she was concerned this could be more serious than the others. Alexandra mentioned the boys' mothers were identical twins. Warning signs went off again in Lauren's mind. *Too many things in common.*

Lauren asked if they were keeping up their grades. Alexa jumped in, "We're both getting A's. Don't worry, Mom. Our lives are going just fine. Nothing to complain about."

Lauren still marveled at how well adjusted her kids were. They were both wise old souls, much wiser and older than herself, she often thought. She was about to hang up when both girls spoke at once, and then laughed. Since the day they had said their first words, they always spoke at the same time.

Alexandra continued, "Mom, you and Dad are both very busy at work. There's no need to come check on us. We're doing great. We'll see you in a few months, and Dad drops by as often as he can. We know what you're coming here to say, and you don't have to worry. The trip isn't necessary."

Lauren was taken aback for a moment. "Honey, what do you mean? Why do you think we're coming for a visit?" Lauren was biting her lip.

It was Alexa's turn to put her mother's fears to rest.. "Mom, we know your marriage has been going downhill for years. And frankly, you and Dad both sound better and more relaxed than ever before. People go their separate ways every day, Mom. We're a close family, and that certainly won't change just because you and Dad are getting a divorce. Please, don't worry about us. We're doing just fine."

Lauren couldn't speak.

"Mom, are you there? Mom?"

Lauren was weeping quietly. "Yeah, honey, I'm here. I'm just surprised. I didn't think you guys noticed as much as you did."

Alexandra replied, "Are you kidding? We notice everything. But the primary thing we've noticed is your sudden boost of confidence. You seem to be more relaxed with life in general. I know Dad traveled most of the time when we were growing up, so it's not like we're used to having a father figure around the house. We want you and Dad to be happy. If you're both happy, then we'll be happier too. Mom, you're alone most of the time. We're so glad you have Adriana to keep you company. But you need to get out more and start a new life. Be happy the way you deserve to be."

Lauren was speechless again.

"Mom? Mom? Are you there?" The girls were giggling.

Lauren found her words. "Thank you. You have given me the greatest gift of all. Your acceptance of me, and your desire for my happiness. Yes, I've been alone for much too long, and I'm ready for a new life. However, it wouldn't have been complete without your approval. Thank you."

She heard Alexa speak up. "Oh, Mom. You're always making us happy. And you've taught us how to make ourselves happy. Now it's your turn. All this stuff you and Adriana have taught us over the years hasn't gone on deaf ears, you know."

She heard a knock at the girls' door, then a male voice. "I hope you're hungry, we brought pizza."

Lauren laughed. "I think that's my cue to hang up."

The girls said their goodbyes with their mutual reminders not to be concerned with visiting them. "We'll see you in a few months. Just keep in touch with what's happening. Now that you're going to be a free woman, you're going to start having the time of your life."

Lauren smiled, relieved at the conversation and the easiness of their relationship. "Goodbye, girls, I love you with all my heart and soul."

The girls answered, "Right back at you, Mom. Heart, soul, and beyond. And hugs to Adriana too."

As Lauren was hanging up, she could hear one of her daughters speaking to her sister. "Let's eat." Then she heard a click, signifying she was alone with her thoughts again.

"They're going to be just fine. I think everything is working out the way it was intended." She closed her eyes and looked up to the ceiling. "Thank you, God, for my wonderful kids. They teach me as much as I hope I have taught them."

Alex arrived at the studio to find all the band members waiting on him. Ron was standing in the lobby with his hands in his pocket.

"Hi, Alex. Did you bring the new material?"

"Yeah, and it's great. But we only have a week to learn it."

Ron led the way into the elevator. "We're ready whenever you are. The club's already working on filling the house. It seems we've become well known around these parts. And since we don't play full-time, we still have an enthusiastic audience. They don't listen to us enough to realize we usually sound like a bunch of amateurs. And if we know what's good for us, we'll keep it that way. If the word ever leaked out, we'd have to relocate."

Alex laughed out loud, casually pushing Ron into the studio where the band was tuning their instruments. With all the handshakes and greetings out of the way, the men immediately got down to business. They spent the first three hours working on new material, and a song he knew must be included. "Street of Dreams." Alex refused to let them continue on to other songs until he felt sure the compositions had been memorized.

Ron was surprised by Alex' energy. "Alex, you have someone special coming to the club? You're working us like slaves."

Alex gave Ron an apologetic look. "Sorry, guys, I didn't mean to burn you out on the first night. I haven't written anything this good in a very long time. I hear it in my head, and I just want to get it right."

Ron wasn't going to give up. "You still haven't told us if a special guest is coming to the club. It's obvious you're trying to impress someone. Who is she?"

Alex was silent for a moment, deep in thought. Ron felt the tension building around Alex. "Let's break for ten minutes and we'll play some of our old stuff. Alex, does that work for you?"

Alex slapped Ron on the back appreciatively. "That works for me just fine."

Alex entered the sound booth and poured a cup of coffee. He had to admit to himself he was desperate for this new music to sound the way he heard it in his head. "Why am I being such a perfectionist?

We're just doing this for the fun of it. Lighten up on yourself and the others. It'll sound great.

But Alex couldn't get her out of his head. The reason he wanted the songs to be perfect was because when he sang them, he was singing to her. As if she was sitting in front of him.

He looked up as one of the members approached. "These songs are great. And your voice has never sounded better."

Alex smiled, his dimples pronounced on his face. "Thanks. I'm glad you noticed."

Alex sat back on the couch and watched the other band members in the studio practicing the music. They were all friends of his, both casually and professionally. The band was good because they were all on the same wavelength. Very little direction had to be given. They practiced until after 11:00, before deciding to return the next night.

"Frustrated writers and businessmen letting off a little steam," Ron commented loudly as the men walked to their cars, causing the parking lot to fill with laughter. "I think I can go on record here and say it's past all of our bedtimes. We're missing the news and weather, not to mention the sports. I remember now why we don't do this for a living. We're too damn old."

Alex chided Ron good-naturedly. "Speak for yourself. Go home to Cindy. You need the rest more than we do."

Alex drove down P.C.H. with the songs blaring in his ears. His thoughts of her were very close tonight.

Will I see her? I have so much to say, but I want to be sure she understood the music. He stopped and questioned himself. *Why is it important to me that she know the songs? What difference does it make? How in the hell can I find her that way? Why can't I ever remember to ask her who she is? That should be more important than the songs.*

He called his friends and apologized for the late evening. And before long, he found himself in front of his piano again. Alex stared at the ring for several minutes before taking it off. He turned it slowly around and looked at the inscription. "Why can't I remember?" He could feel her presence all around him. He pulled his black hair away from his face, and stared at the circle of gold. As words drifted through his mind, he quickly put them on paper. It hadn't taken long before he had composed a new song. Instinctively, he made a copy for the other band members, and then went to bed. He wanted to fuse the new composition into her memory tonight. "God, please let her show up."

He undressed and put himself in a light meditative state before drifting off to sleep.

Alex saw himself at his piano. The patio doors were opened, and the ocean breeze was caressing his face. He was surprised to look outside and find it was still dark. He looked around the room verifying where he was. "How did I get in my living room? Damn it, I'll never find her here." He desperately tried to stand up from the piano, but found he couldn't move. He felt himself fighting the tension building up in his body. "I've got to get out to the beach. She'll be near the rocks. I just know it. Damn it, would someone listen to me? She won't find me here."

He tried to stand up again, but the pressure was too intense.

He slammed his fist into the keys, causing the side of his hand to burn. Alex caught his breath when he noticed the ring on his finger. It was shining bright, twinkling against the shiny wood of the instrument. "Calm down, Alex, calm down." In his mind's eye, he saw himself take a deep cleansing breath, releasing all the knots from his tense, aching muscles. "Calm down. Just let things happen as they must. If I don't find her tonight, then I'll find her another night. But for God's sake, just stay calm."

Alex saw himself playing the new tune he had written a short time before. He could hear himself thinking above the melody. "Play the song." He sang the song with the same passion as the love he felt for her.

He slowly opened his eyes and blinked hard when he saw her standing at the door. His first thoughts were how far away the door seemed to him. Alex abruptly stopped playing and watched her, but she didn't move. She was looking at him as if she wanted to burn his face into her soul. He found himself doing the same to her.

Alex loved how her dark hair fell softly on her shoulders. He could see the outlines of her body, with the light fabric clinging to her breasts and hips. He noticed the way she held her body. "She looks like a beautiful ballerina." Her face seemed almost translucent, and far away. "Why can't I see her face clearly?"

Alex barely heard her speak in a faraway whisper. "Please play the song again. I want to memorize it before I have to leave."

Alex couldn't speak, but nodded his head. He took another deep breath and sung in perfect pitch. He sang for what seemed like hours.

When he finally stopped and opened his eyes, she was gone. He was awake and lying on his back in bed. The sun was shining, and he could hear the seagulls outside, singing for their breakfast. Alex slowly turned over and looked at the clock. "How could it already be 7:30?" He closed his eyes and turned to face the ocean breeze blowing from the open door, then smiled when he saw her standing downstairs near the patio door, watching him play.

He jerked his eyes open, remembering what had transpired. "My God, she was here. She was in my house. She heard the song. God, please let her remember it."

He played the scene over and over in his head, until he was brought back to reality by the telephone ringing. He picked it up and heard Elliot's voice.

"Hi, Alex, how did practice go?"

Alex was momentarily confused. "You're calling me at 7:30 to ask me how practice went?"

Elliot laughed out loud. "Are you talking in your sleep? You'd better check your clock again. I think it's broken. It's 9:30."

Alex couldn't hide his surprise as he jumped out of bed and looked at his watch.

"I couldn't have fallen back to sleep. I've been lying here thinking about the dream I had last night." Alex looked at the clock again. "Sorry, Elliot. Let's start over. Practice went just fine. I wrote a new song last night when I got home. How about lunch today?" He didn't wait for an answer and continued. "Forget lunch. How about brunch? I'm starving."

When Elliot agreed, Alex hung up the phone and walked as far as his bathroom, when he was overcome by a strange sensation. To make it more real, he looked into the mirror, and stared deeply into his own blue eyes.

"Was she really here?"

He couldn't stop himself from running downstairs to check. He found the door leading to his immense patio closed and locked. His piano bench was pushed in, just the way he had left it the night before. Alex shook his head and trudged back upstairs to get dressed. "I guess it was just wishful thinking."

Lauren was in good spirits after talking to her daughters. She was always amazed how much they could comprehend without her having to say a word. All these years she had tried to keep up a consistently happy front, yet they knew how unhappy her life had been. She guessed they probably knew of her unhappiness before she did. She strolled into the kitchen to make dinner, but opted for a salad instead. As she chopped the vegetables, her thoughts ran to Gary. She knew she would have to see him. "At least it'll only be for a short time. I'll meet him at the attorney's office at noon, then leave as soon as the papers are signed. He'll be relieved to hear how well the girls are taking it."

She sensed many changes were taking place within her household, and wasn't sure how she felt about all of them. "I don't have any choice but to go with it. Change is inevitable, and whether we like it or not, everyone goes through some changes."

She caught a glimpse of her reflection in the window and stopped to give herself a pep talk. "Lauren, as difficult as it's always been for you, you'll just have to get used to changes in your life. Let's face it, as long as you're alive, nothing will ever stay the same. Things will go smoother when you just get used to it, and go with the flow."

She returned to her office, and absentmindedly placed the salad on her desk. "But why are there so many changes taking place at once? That seems like an awfully harsh lesson to learn."

Lauren sat in front of her computer and stared absentmindedly at the screen. "I may as well forget it. I can't get any work done right now."

She glanced at her salad, but instead, she found her attention absorbed in the music box. "It's so beautiful." Lauren ran her fingertips over the surface, tracing the pattern down the side of the box, then making invisible circles on the legs. Lauren whispered quietly in the box's direction. "What is it about your form?" She stood up and walked around to the corner of her desk, then lifted one side of the box, feeling the underbelly again. "Why are you so heavy? It just makes no sense." She placed the legs back on the desk, and then opened the lid. The music drifted through the room while she sang softly. When Lauren realized she was obsessing over an inanimate object again, she turned her attention back to her computer screen.

"This is ridiculous. I've got work to do." She pulled her hair behind her ears, and clicked on the program to begin her work. When numbers appeared before her, she looked at them closely, trying to concentrate on anything other than what she was feeling. But all the while, she was unconsciously humming the tune still playing beside her.

Lauren was completely caught off guard when she blinked and found herself standing alone on a huge patio. She could hear the ocean waves crashing in on the shore behind her. It was pitch black, but she could see a light filtering through large double doors directly in front of her. Lauren walked in their direction, but stopped when she saw him sitting at a piano.

"He hasn't seen me yet." She didn't want to take her eyes off him, but couldn't help looking around the room. It was as though she could see through the walls. Her eyes widened as she tried to memorize everything within view.

"Let's see. To the left is an office or den of some kind."

She peeked through walls, hoping to be able to understand where she was. Her eyes were drawn to a large painting on the wall. She blinked hard once, then twice, before exclaiming out loud for no one other than herself to hear. "Oh my God, it's pulsing. I've never seen so many fluorescent colors before. Why can't I make out what it is?"

Lauren squinted and let the experience be what it was. "Wow! It seems to be alive with its own emotion. This is unbelievable."

The colors from the canvas were glowing and shooting out brilliant streams of light. Without warning, the brightness suddenly dimmed, and it once again turned into an ordinary picture on a wall. She opened her eyes wider and looked closely at the couple holding hands on a beach, then gasped in disbelief.

"It's the painting. Oh God, it's the painting in my dream. How did he get it?" She felt her frustration growing, and knew she had to stabilize herself. "Where am I? How did he come to have the painting? Those people on the beach. I know who they are."

Lauren couldn't finish her sentence. Her attention immediately focused on his aura the moment he looked up and saw her standing outside the opened double stain glass doors.

He's the most handsome man I've ever seen. She could only imagine the heat his body possessed, and then realized how far away he was. She watched his large hands as he slowly pulled his dark hair from his face. Lauren noticed his shirt was pressed hard against his chest, and blatantly took pleasure in staring at his muscular body. The same body she wanted so badly, she ached for it. She could hear her own thoughts. *It's been so long, and I've miss so much about this man.* Lauren forgot about the painting as she watched him staring back at her. He seemed to give her a sense of balance, and make everything so much better. *I could thrive and grow in this presence before me. He gives me everything I've ever needed.*

Then she heard her voice from somewhere far away say, "Please play the song again. I want to memorize it before I have to leave."

She was surprised by her request, but watched as he turned to face his piano. Lauren closed her eyes and listened first to a melody, followed by the most beautiful voice she had ever heard. She could feel his pain, his anguish, and his love encompass her. She didn't know why the songs were such an important facet of their meetings, but she knew she had to listen and remember them. She was astounded by the lyrics.

"How did he know about the initials on the gazebo? How could he have known about the inscription in the ring?" She instinctively touched the chain, making sure the ring was still in her possession. "How did he know what it all meant?"

She vaguely remembered the previous dream. She saw herself translating the letters scribbled on the gazebo wall to him. She remembered being amused when he couldn't remember carving them. It had only been a few days earlier. Now, he was singing the most incredible song to her. "I never want him to stop."

Lauren opened her eyes and saw the design on the screen saver glaring back in her face. Her salad was sitting on her desk, and the lid on the music box was still open. She sat still for several minutes, trying to compose herself, before finally picking up her plate, and making her way to the kitchen. Lauren was still in a daze as she glanced at the grandfather clock. "That's impossible." She checked her watch. "That's impossible. I just dozed off for a second." She looked down at her watch again. "How can it be 2:00 in the morning?"

Lauren returned to her office, shaking her head toward the still unused computer. "Another night, I suppose." Angry with herself for falling asleep when she should have been working, Lauren turned off the lights and hastily retreated to her bedroom. She quickly took off her clothes and crawled into bed. "I'm too tired to think about anything tonight. I just want to sleep." But confusion still intruded. "Where was I all that time?"

She closed her eyes, said her nightly prayers, and quickly fell into a deep sleep. The dream started immediately and lasted all night. The same event played itself over and over again until the alarm clock signaled the dreams to be over.

Lauren wasn't thinking as she quickly jumped out of bed and retrieved her recorder. She instinctively knew there was a third song she had to get on tape before she forgot it. She sang it twice into the machine.

"When you remember the songs, we'll be together again.

Never forget, no matter where or when…

Always remember, we'll be together again."

Lauren placed the recorder in her purse and retreated to her balcony. She closed her eyes, and sang the song several more times in quick succession before looking out over the trees. She noticed a colorful hue to them, and smiled. "I love this time of year." The mornings were getting cooler, and she wrapped her arms around herself, more for comfort than to warm her body. She sat down in the nearest chair and looked up at the sky, watching a single white cloud glide by before finally evaporating. She was still in a morning daze, and wasn't ready to come out of it quite yet.

Lauren closed her eyes again, trying to retrace her steps in the dream. She saw herself standing outside of a door.

"He was sitting in front of a beautiful grand piano."

She tried to see herself as she was in her vision from the night before.

"There was something there. I just know it. What was I looking at before I focused on him?" She took another very deep breath, refusing to open her eyes until the image appeared.

"I see a wall. Yes. I looked beyond the wall. Yes, that's right. Now I see a picture on a wall."

She sat frozen in place while she watched before her, in her mind's eye, glowing colors bouncing off a painting. She saw herself squint from the bright light surrounding it. Then she watched as the iridescent intensity vanished.

She heard herself whisper to her mind, "Please let me see the picture."

In a flash, she watched as slides quickly entered and departed inside her mind. She saw herself in one slide looking at a painting on a wall, making sure it was hung properly. Then she saw herself briefly on a beach near some tall rocks. "He was there."

The slide changed again. She was speaking to her fatherly guide. She watched him hug her. She could only see his mouth moving. The slide changed again. She saw herself crying and placing a ring in a box. The slide changed, and she was burying something. She didn't have time to comprehend before there was another slide to watch. She was standing in the master bedroom at the Connecticut house. She felt a strong emotion briefly stir, but lost it when the slide changed to her standing in the gazebo smiling at the man in her dreams. The slides were moving much faster with each change. She saw herself reading the note left behind on the mantle, she saw a man reading her written note, she saw herself finding the ring in the music box, and she saw the woman in the mirror, the eyes haunting her with such pain. She saw herself lifting the music box in curiosity. The slides were fast and furious blinks of time. She quickly saw herself holding a book or journal of some kind. The next immediate slide was of her touching the music box again. She suddenly found herself back at the same double doors in her dream from the night before, and staring at a painting in disbelief.

Her eyes jerked opened, and she almost screamed out her revelation.

"It's the same picture. Was that me in all the slides? I don't remember participating in all of the scenes I just watched. But it had to be me. I know I once hung that painting. And somehow, I know I once owned the music box. And I can't explain it, but now I realize I was once the woman I saw in the mirror. I was…"

She listened to what she was saying, then felt as if she were a child about to be reprimanded for speaking of sacrilegious issues.

"Lauren, I think you are indeed losing your mind. Stop this nonsense now. Stay in reality, and work with what you have in your possession. What you can touch."

She could hear the scolding that she was giving herself, but that wasn't stopping the ache her soul was experiencing from a past remembrance she couldn't shake.

Lauren looked out beyond the trees in front of her, and begged for her guide to come to her.

"I don't want to do this anymore. It hurts too much. Everything seems to be caving in on me. Please tell me if I'm seeing what is real, or if my imagination is taking hold, and possessing me?"

She sunk deeper into her chair and waited. She felt his gentle presence, and knew her paternal guide was with her, trying to comfort her if she would only let him in. She took another deep breath and waited again. He was standing in front of her mind's eye. She could hear his words soaking in.

"You are feeling discomfort from the knowledge you are

receiving. You are locating who you are now. The totality of you. But sometimes looking into your past to see how far we've come can be painful. Continue on your path, my child. You will find what was lost to you if you keep the faith, be open, and be very, very strong."

She opened her eyes and sobbed until her tension had eased. Lauren took her shower and dressed for the day, feeling only a little better. She felt as if she were on circuit overload, with input continuing to pour in. And she worried how much more she could take before she lost it all.

She walked downstairs, still feeling depressed, but somehow finding the strength from deep within to trudge on. All she had to do was think of him out there going through the same circuit overload.

"I can't allow my energy level to fall now. I couldn't stand to think I could fail just because I'm afraid of pain. Somehow, I will deal with it."

Lauren instinctively knew that not only must she deal with it if she wanted to find what she had lost, but she must somehow learn and grow from it. All the pep talks in the world wouldn't erase her worry about not maintaining the necessary stamina.

"I feel torn in a million pieces. If what I saw was correct, and all those people were me, then I can certainly understand why it's not always a good idea to learn every detail about your past lives. It's painful as hell. And once you know of them, you have no choice but to integrate and learn from them. Otherwise, I truly believe a person could go mad."

Lauren sipped her coffee and listened to her Chris Spheeris CD. It somehow brought comfort and hope to a harsh reality. She needed to get grounded, and work on this issue.

"I'm just not sure if I can deal with it right now."

She was brought back to her kitchen by the ringing telephone. It was Adriana coming to her rescue.

"Hello."

Adriana sounded breathless. "Hi Lauren, are you busy?"

Lauren brought her mind fully back, and sat up straight.

"No, not anymore. I had a harrowing experience a few minutes ago, not to mention the dream I had last night. This experience has got to be the most detailed yet. I have another song to remember. This makes three. Some things are happening that I don't think I have any control over. Come to think of it, I don't think I ever did. But in any case, I think things are progressing in a positive manner. I repeat, I think. I have lots of questions I hope you can shed some light on."

Adriana was calling for another reason, but stopped when she heard her friend's news. "It's too early in the morning to leave me hanging. Tell me everything."

Lauren tried to find the words to continue, "To make a long story short, I was at his house last night. Don't ask me how I know this. Somehow, I just know it was his house. He played his piano, and sang the most beautiful song. It was made up with words from the inscription. He wanted me to remember it."

Adriana tightened her grip on the phone. "You're kidding! My God, Lauren, that's incredible. Did you see anything else? Do you know where he lives? How did he know about the inscription?"

Lauren was quiet for a moment, before answering slowly. "No, I don't know where he lives. I'm only assuming it was his house. He seemed rather comfortable in it. As far as this man knowing what the inscription reads is beyond me. I just don't know. We seem to know a lot more in our dreams than we do in reality. But the oddest thing of all happened before he saw me. He was playing the piano, and I was looking past him for a moment. I could actually see through walls, into other rooms. Adriana, you're not going to believe what I saw hanging on a wall in his house?"

Adriana couldn't stand the suspense any longer. "So tell me, girl, tell me."

"I saw the picture from my dream. The one of the couple on the beach. The one I saw myself hanging on a wall. It was fantastic.

One moment there were shooting colors emitting from it, and the next moment, the picture was in plain view. I somehow know it's real, and that it exists. Then he saw me. We looked at each other, he played the new song, and suddenly it was over."

Adriana noticed she had stopped breathing. "Over?"

"Yeah, I was there one moment and gone the next. Story of my life!"

"Did you get it on the recorder?"

"Yes I did, and have already memorized it. It's so beautiful. I have no idea what all this has to do with us meeting, but I'm not going to make light of anything that happens. But that's not all."

Adriana was pacing the floors now. "Yes?"

Lauren smiled as she recalled her story of seeing the images flashing and floating in front of her in quick succession. She told Adriana everything she could remember, and finished by admitting her fantasy about being the other woman.

"Does that make any sense to you, Adriana?"

Her friend paused for a moment, and concurred, "Yeah, it does. It sounds as if you're integrating small portions from a previous life into this one. Since you're remembering so much, and in such detail so quickly, I can only assume the past life wasn't too long ago. Have you asked for guidance?"

Lauren smiled again. "I'm way ahead of you. Many of the pictures were rather painful to view. I almost backed out a few times. I felt I wasn't ready. And frankly, I didn't want to feel the pain anymore."

Adriana broke in, "That's a common response. I hope you stayed with it, and fought to remain as detached as possible."

"Yeah, I did. But I had to ask for help. Basically, I was told I could go no further unless I experienced the pain, then detached from it. It was lessons I needed to learn, but it was up to me if I wanted to continue. And before you ask, yes, I'm going to continue. After everything that's happened, do I really have a choice?"

"And just remember, Lauren, you do have help from the other side."

Lauren sighed. "I was told to be strong, keep the faith, and stay open. Then the weirdest thing happened. It was almost as if I had received a pep talk from the heavens. I could feel myself become stronger, and I knew I wanted to go forward and become this new person. And no matter what happens, I knew that I would survive. That is if it doesn't kill me first."

Adriana was quiet for a moment. When she finally spoke, she whispered, as if to a child, "Lauren, I am so proud of you. You're going through so many changes in your life right now. And unfortunately, you don't have the advantage of getting used to one, before going on to the next. You're being hit by it all at once. The kids are away at school, growing up and becoming independent. You're getting a divorce, and beginning a new life. Your business is expanding, and you're busier than ever. And you're in pursuit of the man of your dreams. None of them are easy issues to conquer. But as usual, you have a grace unlike anyone I've ever met. I truly admire you."

Tears welled up in Lauren's eyes, and the only words she could mouth were a simple, "Thank you. I needed to hear that."

Adriana continued, "Now, I have news for you that may help you along, but it may also confuse you even more."

Lauren wasn't sure she wanted to hear more confusion, but her curiosity got the better of her. "If it's going to upset me, I don't know if I'm ready."

Adriana wasn't sure how to answer. "Uh, well, I don't think it's going to upset you, but it could definitely be a blast from the past."

Lauren shook her head, even more confused. "Maybe you should just tell me what's going on."

Adriana took a deep breath and began, "Remember when I was telling you about a book that seemed somewhat familiar about two people meeting in their dreams?"

Lauren spoke up quickly. "Yeah, you said the story sounded

familiar, but you couldn't remember much about it."

Adriana continued slowly, "The song 'Where or When' reminded me of the title. I read the book about twenty-five years ago, and found it inspiring. I doubt one has anything to do with the other, but it certainly perked all my senses into trying to remember."

Lauren was tapping her nails nervously on the table. "Go on."

"Once I came up with a partial name, I began my research. I have looked in every catalog you can imagine, including my own in an altered state. Slowly, it all started coming together. Needless to say, I found the name of the book. That's the good news. The bad news is that it's out of print, and has been for many years. I have no way of getting another copy."

Lauren's inquisitiveness could no longer be contained. "Adriana, what the hell is the name of the book?"

Adriana was quick to answer. "It won't be of any help to you, but the name is 'We'll Be Together Again'."

Lauren gasped, and felt she would pass out. She grabbed at her neck and massaged vigorously. The room was spinning again, and she felt weak. She was grateful to be sitting down.

Adriana could take the silence no longer. "Lauren, say something. I'm sorry I couldn't find out more. Does it mean anything to you? Lauren, are you there? Lauren?"

Lauren was in total disbelief once again, and her mind was racing. "Can it be coincidental? Of course not. Can it mean nothing at all? Maybe. Is this another clue?"

"Lauren? You're babbling. What are you talking about?"

In a distance, she heard her friend's concerned voice rising above her thoughts. She had to answer her.

Lauren forced out enough air to speak. "Adriana, you couldn't have shocked me more had you told me a spaceship was landing in my yard. I know I keep saying this, but you're not going to believe this one."

It was Adriana's turn to tap the table with her nails. "What?

Tell me before I go crazy. Did the title mean anything to you?"

"Did it ever! Let me read you a portion of the song I was told to memorize last night.

"Now and forever, no matter where or when, we shall always be together, when we remember again… When you remember the songs, we'll be together again. Never forget, no matter where or when. Always remember, we'll be together again."

Adriana couldn't control her emotions. "Lauren, how can this be? I know you're questioning coincidence, but I can't believe it. The clues just keep coming with verification you're doing what you were meant to do. But how does something written so long ago pertain to what is happening right now?"

Lauren thought for a moment, but came up with nothing more than scrambled emotions. "I don't know. I just don't know. Can you tell me when the book was written? Can you tell me who wrote it?"

Adriana was looking over her notes from the previous night's work. "It was written in 1937. I have no idea of the authors' names. There were two of them and they wrote this book under an alias, so I couldn't tell you how to go about finding out their real names. The publishing company is no longer in business either. I've checked every way possible to find out more."

Lauren was still baffled. "Two people wrote the book? Right?" She continued without an answer, "And didn't the real estate agent say the couple who built the house were both writers?"

Adriana tried to stop her, but had no argument to do so.

Lauren continued, "I know I saw the music box in the master bedroom of the house. I'm almost sure I saw the picture on the wall in the library. Am I rambling and making no sense at all? Have I gone mad? Or is it all part of the same thing?"

Adriana was deep in thought. "I don't know. This is too much, even for me. I thought I had seen most everything until now. I just don't know."

Lauren took up where her friend had left off. "Adriana, I

would like for you to have a good look at the note I took from the house. The one I can only hope is from him. See if you can get any impressions from it. There's not much more I can do until I'm given something else to work with. It seems to all be going so fast now, I'm afraid I may have trouble keeping up."

Adriana reassured her friend. "Don't worry, we'll keep up together. I'll be happy to take a look at the note. Just don't get your hopes up. No prejudgment, okay? I'll call you later, and try and come by tonight. While we're on the phone, is there anything else to report?"

Lauren thought for a moment. "Yeah, Gary phoned last night. He left a message saying he'd be in town on Saturday. I'm supposed to meet him at the attorney's office to sign the divorce papers."

Adriana wanted to be there to hug her friend. "Lauren, I'm so sorry."

"No, don't be. It's odd, but last night I was a lot more upset about it. It seems to be okay today. I don't look forward to having to see Gary under these circumstances, but at least it will finally be over. I spoke to the girls, and they're dealing with this better than we are. They actually encouraged me to seek a social life, and have fun. Oh and by the way, they sent their love to you."

Adriana smiled. "Well, Lauren, they always adjusted better to change than us. Old souls, I suppose."

Lauren giggled. "That's exactly what I think, too. But they gave you and me the credit for teaching them the ropes."

Lauren looked at her watch and knew she was going to be late again this morning. "I've got to go. I'll talk to you later today." She grabbed the phone tighter before hanging up. "Adriana? Are you still there? I just want to say thank you. I love you more than you could ever imagine."

Adriana smiled into the phone. "Yeah, I know. See you later."

Chapter 17

Waiting for Elliot was a difficult task for Alex. He was anxious to go over the new songs with his friend. He walked from one room to another, pacing the floors. Alex stopped when he found himself standing in front of the picture in his office. He gazed at two people walking on the beach, obviously very much in love. He stepped closer to the picture, and looked deep into their eyes. He refused to blink, instead opting to blur his vision.

"Her eyes look so familiar. I've never seen love look like that in anyone's eyes but hers."

Alex stopped his thoughts and focused on the male image in front of him. He envied that look. So calm and so sure of what was in front of them.

"I can only hope the kind of love I see in their eyes is real, and not the artist's imagination."

He pulled himself away, and returned to his living room, stopping again to look in the same area that Lauren had stood the night before, wrapped in a veil of fog.

"I have to believe she understood my message. I need to believe she wanted to be here, and she wants this story to finally come to a close, too."

His thoughts were interrupted by the sound of his front door opening, and Elliot's voice booming across the room. "What's up, Alex? You still hungry, or did you start without me?"

Alex turned to smile at his friend. "No, I haven't started without you. I'm starving, but before we go, I want you to hear the song I wrote last night."

Not waiting for a reply, Alex walked over to his piano and began playing. When he finished, Elliot seemed to be in a trance.

"Elliot, what's wrong? Don't tell me you didn't like it."

Elliot was visibly shaken, but didn't know why. "Alex, the words are like magic. I think you've figured out the initials on the gazebo. I didn't realize it until now."

Alex smiled, always amazed by Elliot's perceptions. "Very good, Elliot. It didn't take you as long as it took me. I suppose you also know what the ring's inscription reads."

"No, but I can almost guess. Why don't you tell me?"

Alex sat his friend down and told him all about the ring and the verification he felt was correct. The ring had once belonged to her.

"How are you going to get the songs to her?"

Alex smiled with confidence. "I think I already have. She was here in my dream last night." Alex pointed toward the stained glass doors. "She was standing over there. She asked to hear the song. She somehow already knew she was supposed to memorize it. I don't think either one of us knows why. It all seems so strange to me, now. But I have no choice but to trust the process. I would be a fool to ignore it at this point. If it feels right, I do it. I want to say it seems so easy to follow the instructions put in front of me, but at the same time, it's the most difficult task I've ever pursued. The worst of it is not being the one in control."

Elliot laughed at the remark. "Yeah, you've always had a problem relinquishing control. This must be very difficult for you."

"Gee, that's exactly what my guide has been saying. Word must get around."

The boys continued their banter while Alex locked the door behind him. During brunch, they discussed the photos Elliot had taken. Alex was visibly impressed.

"Elliot, have you thought about publishing a book of the photographs? They're certainly good enough. How did you achieve such perfection?"

Elliot thought before answering. "I'm not sure. It was as if I wasn't the one participating in actually taking them. All I did was stand there, point, and shoot."

Alex thanked him again, then changed the subject to talk about the rehearsal the night before, and how nervous he was about performing in public.

Elliot came up with an explanation that even Alex couldn't argue with. "You're nervous because these songs are your innermost desires. They're a real part of you, and very private and personal. But you'll do fine. All your friends will be cheering you on, and you'll relax once you start singing. You always do. How many people will actually know the songs are from personal experience anyways? I think two?"

Alex grinned knowingly and agreed, "How many of our group is coming?"

"I'm not sure. I'll be there, and of course, Donovan and Vickie. I would assume Vickie would invite everyone she's ever met. And don't forget Cindy. That woman knows more people than the population of most countries. Don't worry; you'll have a packed house. I'm looking forward to it in an odd kind of way."

Alex was intrigued. "What do you mean? Do you think something strange is going to happen? Don't tell me you're going to try levitating again?"

Elliot laughed at the supposed sight. "No, I can't explain it. But it's going to be fun, no matter what happens. I just think something will somehow be different. I realize I'm making no sense, and I don't mean to sound so mysterious. It may just have to do with your new songs. I'm anxious to see the reactions around the room."

A look of uncertainty crossed Alex's face. "Is there something you're not telling me? Please, no more surprises. I couldn't take it."

Elliot looked innocent enough. "No. Absolutely not. My meditations have been a little different lately, and I can't put my finger on why that is. But each time, I see myself in a room full of people. I can't see the faces, but I know it's comfortable. Where else will I be going in the next week that has a room full of people? The only person who gets out less than me is you."

They both had to laugh at their predicament, but it took Alex on a conversation he had long wanted to have with Elliot.

"You know, my friend, you really don't get out enough. You say you aren't the marrying kind, but it's been ten years. And, your son is grown and out on his own now. Maybe it's time you tried it again."

Elliot was shaking his head vigorously. "I'm not the marrying kind. I'm not even the relationship kind. Yeah, Nick is twenty-one now, and he's already out of school making his way, and doing very well. His mother is happy, so I don't feel guilty about her. Hell, how could I feel guilty? The divorce was her idea. And it's been years and years." Elliot forced a smile. "But I've got to admit, she was the smart one. She knew what was best for both of us. I count my blessings that all is well with my family, but I have no intentions of starting over. I'm happy just the way it is."

Alex looked deep into Elliot's eyes and saw a partial truth.

"You may have convinced yourself that you want no part of a relationship, but I can't say I believe it. You're such a caring person that I have trouble believing you don't ever want to share that part of yourself with someone again."

Elliot sipped his coffee before responding, "Well, if I have convinced myself of this, then I did a damn good job. I'm content having my son and my friends in my life. What else do I need?"

Alex laughed out loud. "A woman, Elliot, a woman."

Elliot dropped Alex off at his house, driving off with promises of dinner some time in the week. "I'm going to be busy practicing, so if you don't hear from me by Friday, give me a call."

Alex spent the remainder of the day practicing his new songs, in between taking several business calls. Before he knew it, he was dressing for his rehearsal with the guys.

He had recorded his compositions, and played them in the car, listening each time as if it were his first. He would usually want to stop and make changes. Sometimes as many as a hundred, but not now. He thought they were perfect the way they were. Each time he heard the lyrics to 'Where or When', and 'Street of Dreams', he would get an eerie rush of recognition, and shiver from its effects.

Alex entered the recording studio, and saw the guys already tuning their instruments.

"Well, are you ready for the big night?"

Ron grinned broadly, obviously in a good mood. "Yeah, I think we're ready. And I don't think we have to worry about a crowd. Cindy is spending the evening calling everyone and their neighbors to join us. If I know my wife, there will be standing room only."

Alex laughed. "We can always leave it to Cindy to locate the wayward misfits with morbid curiosities for our circus act."

The rest of the band clapped their acknowledgments.

It was well after midnight by the time they had completed their list of songs to be performed. Ron walked Alex out to his car, and leaned against his own.

"Alex, I don't think we've ever sounded better. Hell, I don't think you've ever sounded better. What's caused this energy you've built up around yourself?"

Alex knew Ron was a close friend, but he wasn't ready to share his dreams yet.

"There are a lot of changes taking place with me right now, and they're all positive. I feel really good about life."

Ron had a look of curiosity cross his face, and then composed himself. "There are only two things I can think of that would cause a man to feel so life affirming, and full of energy. One is business, and the other is love. Is there a new person in your life?"

Alex grinned broadly. "Ron, as soon as a new person enters my life, someone I can touch and connect with, you will be one of the first to know. In the meantime, I'm just happy for the changes."

Ron was obviously not satisfied with the answer, but let it drop. It was late and he was tired.

"Cindy's going to kill me if I don't get home."

With that, both men got into their cars and drove home.

Alex had every intention of working when he closed his front door, but after taking his shoes off at the door, he found no strength to continue. He admitted he was mentally exhausted. He opted for a quick shower, before strolling out to his patio.

"In a few more days, these songs will be out in the public. They will no longer be only my songs."

Alex was startled when he turned to go inside but was stopped by his guide standing in front of him. He laughed at himself for being so jumpy, then closed his eyes and let her touch his forehead.

She spoke first. "Any questions tonight, Alex?"

Alex thought for a moment and smiled. "No, I think I'm too tired to think. I have a sense that everything is going the way it should. I have encouraged her to control her surroundings and her fears, and I think she has chosen to accept my songs."

The old woman smiled and hugged him close. Alex was happy for the warmth of her arms. He felt such protection from her energy. He could talk to her all night, but she would have none of that.

"Go to sleep, my child. You need your rest. The highest of energy is swirling all around you, and much is still to be accomplished."

After that comment, Alex suddenly had many questions, but she was gone. Not mentally or spiritually, but physically. He knew that was his cue to rest. He walked into his bedroom, speaking now to just himself. "Well, it's my own fault. She gave me the opportunity to ask, and I didn't take her up on it."

He snickered to himself and crawled into bed.

Alex found himself in an unfamiliar bedroom. He heard music playing somewhere in the background, and noticed the door wide open, with the outside darkness flooding in.

"Where am I?"

He noticed the music was his compositions, but not his voice. His senses heightened while he waited. "My God, it's her voice. She's singing my songs. Where am I?"

He looked over to a bed, and noticed a figure breathing softly under pastille sheets. Alex pushed himself closer, until he had no choice but to stop. Not by fog or haze, but by the sheer force of energy surrounding him. Alex looked around to see what was causing him to be immobile, but saw nothing. He squinted his eyes, barely able to see through them.

"My God, it's her. I'm in her bedroom. She's recorded my songs, and playing them while she sleeps. She did remember."

He took a deep breath and cautioned himself not to lose his concentration. "But what am I doing here?"

His guide appeared at the door, partly blocking the darkness with her light. "Alex, you wanted proof that she accepted and understood, and here you have it."

Alex was taken aback. "But how did I get here?"

His guide smiled lovingly at him. "You have worked so hard to achieve a union. You need to know that she has also. But you still have more work to do to erase the karma, and bring radiance into this life. And I caution you not to get ahead of yourself. I have been so proud of your achievements. This is my gift to you. I wanted you to see for yourself that she has heard your voice and read your soul."

Alex wanted to hug his maternal escort. "Does this mean we will be together?"

She crossed the room and softly touched his face. With words so loving he wanted to cry, she whispered, "Dear Alex, if I had the power to make a match, I would. I can only assist you and encourage you. This woman has her guides assisting her as well. So don't think you are alone. You certainly are not. But this endeavor is something you both agreed on eons ago. We can pray and hope that you are both enlightened enough and strong enough to make the right choices. Not the easy choices, but the correct ones. I never said this would come without pain. Before you were brought into this life, you agreed the pain would be worth it. It's up to you both to determine whether or not it is indeed worth the wait, the lessons, and the pain.

"With or without the other, you are both learning many lessons. They won't be ignored, but I cannot help you complete the circle. On the bright side, it's wonderful that you both have come this far without too much help. You both have come this far on your own. Yes, we have hinted a little, but some people refuse to stand still long enough to recognize the hints. You did. So as my gift to you, I knew you would want to see her in her own space. She is lovely, isn't she?"

Alex took a moment to comprehend everything his guide had said, and tried desperately not to read anything into what she didn't say. He knew that he must be on the right path; otherwise this visit would never have happened. He knew nothing that had happened so far would have been accomplished if they had been on the wrong path.

All he could mutter was, "Yes, it's worth the fight, and the pain, and all the lessons we are learning. Her soul is pure, and she's the most beautiful woman, inside and out, that I've ever seen."

But she was gone. He tried to focus on the love of his life lying still, her hair flowing over her shoulders and scattering onto the bed. She was sleeping so peacefully. He would have given everything he owned to crawl into bed with her. To hold her, and to make love to her. Alex stopped and thought a moment.

"My God, I don't think I've ever actually made love before. I thought I had up until this moment. But now, I know I've never come close."

He wanted her, body, mind, and spirit. He wondered if it was sacrilegious to actually get an erection in an altered state or a dream. "No, this feels very natural. I admit freely that I would like nothing more than to feel her skin, and make love to her. I want to feel a part of her. I want to feel everything about her. I know it would be like coming home after a very long absence."

He heard her shy voice softly in the background, singing the songs he had composed. His heart felt as if it would fly out of his body. He promised himself he would never question the process again.

"I still worry that I won't have her, but I won't question anything that happens. If I could never feel her touch, I would be satisfied seeing her in my dreams."

And he knew he meant it. Seeing her like this, he knew he would take her under any circumstances, any way he could. He knew if not in this life, then another. But either way, it was only a matter of time. And with that new realization, he was back in his bed, sleeping the remainder of the night. He would later wake up feeling refreshed and confident. Ready for everything new in his life to begin.

Lauren had meetings most of the day, and was exhausted by the time she met Adriana for dinner. They talked mostly about business during the meal, waiting until they returned to Lauren's house before the serious discussions began.

They both threw their shoes off at the door in unison, and walked straight into Lauren's office. In the darkened room, both women noticed the red light continuously blinking on Lauren's recorder. She switched on the light, and looked over at Adriana.

"What do you think? Should I check it now or later?"

Adriana was quick with an answer. "Wait. We don't want to break the momentum here. We'll check it after we take a look at the note."

Lauren pulled the paper out of the safe before going to work, and was already opening the top drawer of her desk. "Don't tear it."

Adriana pushed her away teasingly. "Yeah, Lauren, I think I'll wad it up and throw it in the garbage. Gee, give me a little credit."

Lauren laughed, cringing at the same time. "So sorry. I didn't mean it the way it came out." She dimmed the lights on her way out the door. "Let me know when you've finished. No pressure, but I hope you can come up with something."

Adriana didn't speak, instead shooing her out the door with a wave of a hand. Once alone, Adriana took a very long deep cleansing breath, surrounded herself with white light, and instantly went into an altered state. She wanted to be deeper than usual tonight, so she continued counting herself down. She then asked for assistance from her guides.

Once she was at a comfortable level, Adriana began gently caressing the napkin. She wanted to detach herself, then perceive as much of the masculine energy as she could. She focused on her next deep breath, and continued stroking the content in her hand.

Suddenly, there was a man with dark hair in front of her. She noticed immediately how handsome he was. And how his energy was real and very strong. He had a positive white light surrounding him. She knew that was always a good sign, and so she let her guard down a little. Adriana was surprised by the energy she felt put into the napkin. She could sense an abundance of love. There was also an ease to this man that brought comfort wherever he was. She could feel eager anticipation and hope flow across her. "A strange combination. This man listens to his heart."

Adriana counted herself up then slowly opened her eyes, and knew his essence was gone. She grabbed Lauren's journal and wrote down everything she could remember.

"If this person is actually the man in her dreams, then Lauren can trust that he has a good soul, and is waiting for her."

Her eyes suddenly closed again, and she saw herself. She was momentarily confused, and then realized this had nothing to do with why she was there. Adriana caught a glimpse of herself in a crowd. Then she saw herself in a different crowd. People she thought she knew, but it was too quick to get a full impression of the event. She was relieved to see a smile on her face.

"At least I can assume it's a happy place."

Her eyes flew open, and she was wide awake.

"What was that all about?" She knew well enough to listen to her impressions and psychic glimpses into the future.

"Hmmm, we'll just have to see, but I'm sure it will leave its imprint in time."

Adriana summoned her friend, and knew she couldn't have been far from the door because a mere second had passed before Lauren bounced into the room, with impatience written all over her face. "Well?"

Adriana motioned to sit across from her. "Let me begin by saying that we're not absolutely sure this is the same man you're looking for." Lauren's face fell. Adriana was quick to complete her sentence.

"But. But if it is, then you can rest assured that he is wonderful."

Lauren's face perked up with a wide smile, her dimples dramatically revealing themselves.

Adriana continued, "Let me continue. This man has a lot of love in his heart, and is very self-assured. I get the feeling he's waiting for something as big as you are. This note was definitely left for a reason. He seems very trustworthy, and has a powerful energy about him." As an afterthought, she added, "Oh yeah, and he has dark hair."

Lauren laughed like a child. "I could have told you that. He sounds wonderful. At least he's not someone I should be afraid of. Right? Not that I ever felt that type of energy from our dreams."

Adriana shook her head, causing her long red hair to fall over her face. "No, judging by his energy on this note, he seems like a well adjusted person, and definitely looking for the love of his life."

Lauren stood up, pointing to herself. "And that would be me!"

They both had a good laugh to break the tension, and then Lauren asked whether she felt anything else.

Adriana shook her head. "Well, I did get one other thing, but not at the same time. I saw me in a crowd. Actually, two crowds.

Actually, two different crowds."

Lauren didn't understand the comment. "Is that bad?"

"I was smiling, so I don't think so." Then she added jokingly, "Gee, do you suppose I may actually be around more than two people at a time, for a change? I don't think I'd know how to act."

Lauren understood and hugged her friend.

"That red blinking light is driving me crazy." Adriana pushed the play button on the answering machine.

Lauren laughed. "You get used to it after a while."

There were two messages. The first one was from Cindy.

"Hi, Lauren, wanted to touch base, and let you know that we're going to a club called Jupiter's on Saturday night to listen to Ron and the band play. Believe it or not, they actually have a gig. So they won't feel too nervous, we're trying to get as many people there as possible. Although I have no idea why they should be nervous, they sound great. I know I sound partial, but they really are very good. We would love for you to make it. It's Saturday night at Jupiter's, around 8:00. We have a large table reserved. Hope to see you there. Before you think about refusing the invitation, just remember you need to get out more. I'll be expecting you. Bye."

Lauren smiled, "Well, I suppose I have plans Saturday night."

She pressed for the second message. It was Cindy again.

"Hi again. Sorry to call right back. I tried Adriana's house, but she wasn't home either. I assume you guys are together getting into trouble. I left a message on her machine, too. Adriana, if you're listening at Lauren's, I know you don't have any plans either, so we're expecting you. I'm putting you both down with an affirmative RSVP. Love you both. Bye."

Adriana laughed. "I suppose I have plans on Saturday night, too. Gee, Lauren, it's been so long. What do people actually do on Saturday nights?"

They were both tired after their long day, so Lauren walked her friend out to the car.

"Have I told you lately how wonderful and patient you are with me?"

Adriana hugged Lauren. "Yeah, all the time, but it's nice to hear it again. What are you wearing Saturday night?"

Lauren looked up toward the sky. "Um, I don't have the slightest idea. We only have a few days to figure it out."

Adriana got into her car and waved bye.

Lauren locked her doors and turned out the downstairs lights. She would abandon her thoughts of a shower tonight. "I'm too tired."

She put her pajamas on, brushed her teeth, and slid into bed. She was finally comfortable when she realized it was too quiet for her to sleep. She stepped out of bed and turned her newly-recorded tape on, and pressed repeat. She wanted to fall asleep and wake up to his words.

Lauren slept peacefully all night, but awoke with a start before her alarm rang. She lay without moving for a several moments, trying to focus on what had stirred her. She could still hear her music playing softly in the background. The sound of her own voice trying to mutter out the beautiful lyrics.

"There's something different in here."

Lauren felt all of her senses on edge and fully alert. "What happened?"

She knew her space had been altered in some way. She took a deep breath, and immediately perceived a slight impression of a male energy. "Has someone been in here?"

She inhaled deeply again, and shivered as the hair on the back of her neck raised in anticipation. "Yes, I smell a slightly familiar scent of a man."

She didn't feel frightened, and she took that sensation into account.

"I didn't dream last night. I didn't see him." She inhaled once again. "I know that scent."

Lauren closed her eyes and went into a light altered state.

She saw herself lying in her bed. Standing next to her was her male guide.

"Was someone here last night?"

He looked down at her and gently responded, "Yes, but you were well protected. He watched you sleep. His guide was with him, as I was with you. He wanted to see you. The scent you say is so familiar was from long ago. It was the same energy, as well. This is why you weren't frightened."

Lauren was confused. "Why didn't I wake up? Didn't anyone think that I might want to see him too?"

He smiled at her and lovingly responded. "Yes, we would have been aware of that. But that wasn't what took place. Lauren, please trust."

Lauren felt as if she were a child being reprimanded, but she didn't feel insulted by it.

"Thank you. Yes, I'm glad he was permitted to come here. I have a part of his energy with me now. It must have been his protection I felt over me when I woke up. I can inhale and feel his energy in this room and in my heart. Thank you."

Her master guide touched her shoulder, and was gone with a smile.

Lauren turned over and opened her eyes. She took a deep breath and felt calmer than she had been in a very long time. "Thank you."

Alex woke up with enormous vigor, feeling better than he had in a long time. His energy was boundless as he leapt out of bed, and ran on the beach for two hours. He loved running early in the morning when the seagulls were in flight, searching for food. The air was crisp and the sky was a deep blue. He ran long and hard, allowing his mind to open up to his environment. He didn't think, he didn't worry. Today, he was just a man, happily running on the beach.

When his energy was depleted, Alex trotted back home, and immediately jumped in the shower. The moment he closed his eyes, events from the night before took precedence. His breathing stopped, and he could do nothing but stand quietly in place, allowing his thoughts to flow back to her. The hot water was washing over his shoulders, but still he didn't move.

As the sights and sounds of her bedroom slowly emerged in front of him, he heard himself speak, but couldn't believe what he was saying. "I saw my guide. I remember the conversation with her."

Then suddenly it was there in front of him. The full realization took place in a split-second, and he was grateful for the bench that he took advantage of to break his fall.

"My God, I saw her sleeping, and she was beautiful. I wanted to touch, and be a part of her more than I've ever wanted anything in my life."

Alex stopped thinking, and tilted his head to the side as if he were listening to an unseen entity. When he spoke again, his voice was louder and full of excitement as it echoed through the shower walls. "She was listening to my songs?" A smile crossed his face with excitement. "She was listening to my songs! My God, we did it."

He remembered his guide saying this beautiful lady was the only one who could have permitted this to take place. That it couldn't have happened without her permission.

"For all the effort I've put forth into this realization."

He looked up and smiled to his guide, thanking her again. Now he knew why he was full of energy, and had an amazing outlook on life. "Everything is progressing."

Alex slipped into black jeans and t-shirt, and descended the stairs two at a time, grabbing his car keys at the front door. He had several short business and personal meetings, mostly touching base with those he had been too busy to contact. He wanted to be around people today, and didn't want to waste a moment. Then he called and planned a quick lunch with Donovan and Vickie.

After ordering, Vickie mentioned how excited she was about the following Saturday night.

"Donovan tells me you're planning on singing a few new songs. We're all looking forward to it." Then teasing him, she continued, "New work from the great Alex is always exciting."

Alex glanced quickly to Donovan as if to question him about how much more Vickie might know. Donovan smiled and quietly shook his head no.

Vickie continued, "Are you bringing anyone?" Alex took a sip of his water before answering. "No, I won't be bringing a date. I want to concentrate on nothing but the show."

Vickie wasn't going to be put off. "Alex, you work too hard. I happen to have a new friend who I think you would like very much. Someone Cindy recently introduced me to. I hear she's getting a divorce. You may want to meet her before she's snatched up. She's pretty spectacular."

Alex laughed out loud. "Vickie, you never cease to amaze me. You're always trying to marry me off, even when I have no intentions of doing such a thing. And in the process, you're trying to marry off this poor girl who isn't even out of one marriage yet." Vickie opened her mouth to respond, but Alex wouldn't be put off. "I'll make you a deal. When I'm ready to meet someone new, you'll be the first to know."

Vickie knew when she was being rebuffed and smiled. "OK, Alex. When you see her, don't say I didn't warn you. By that time, she won't be available. But if Cindy doesn't get to you first, I'll wait until you give the word."

Donovan winked in Alex's direction and spoke up, "Yeah, I don't know which of you is worse about trying to find this guy a wife."

Vickie pushed herself closer to Alex, ignoring her fiancé. "Just don't say I didn't warn you."

Vickie changed the subject by asking how he was enjoying his oak table and frame that he had purchased from her gallery.

"Actually, I'm enjoying everything I've bought from your place." He winked at Donovan and continued, "They have given me great pleasure indeed."

By 4:00, he was on his way to practice at the studio with the band. He felt a twinge in the pit of his stomach when he realized the gig was only two days away. He hoped he was ready.

Ron had discovered a few flaws in one of their arrangements, and they were forced to spend the next few hours perfecting it. The music never stopped, and the band worked until almost midnight.

Ron locked the doors, and walked out into the fresh air with the others.

"You'd think we were playing for the President. How did we become such perfectionists in our old ages?"

Alex laughed. "Ron, we've always been perfectionists. It's just that we aren't as young as we used to be. Maybe every now and then, we should relinquish control and just admit that things are fine the way they are."

Ron and the other band members stopped in their tracks, pretending to grab at their hearts. Ron couldn't control himself as he laughed out loud.

"Guys, is this the Alex we know? Give up control? Settle for something less than perfect? I think your recent illness did something to you. This is not the Alex I know and love standing in front of me. It just can't be. Who are you, and what did you do with our Alex?"

Alex saw the humor and smiled. "OK, so I've had a few domineering moments in my own life. And occasionally, I can be a bit of a control freak. Maybe even a bit of a perfectionist. But look where it's got me?"

One of the band members spoke up. "And where would that be, Alex?"

He thought for a moment, and then replied with a chuckle in his voice, "Happy, guys. Very, very happy." Then his voice turned serious. "But, happy or not, I've been thinking maybe it's time that I try and refrain from being so controlling. There's nothing wrong with giving up a little power in my life. Right? And who knows where it might take me."

Ron slapped his friend's back. "Right you are. And it's precisely that reason why I must get home before Cindy comes looking for me."

Alex analyzed the conversation on his drive back to Malibu. He knew he was beginning to allow himself permission to relax and enjoy life a little now. He was realizing he could still be reliable and focused without always having complete and total control over every aspect of his life, twenty-four hours a day. Now he wondered why he ever wanted to.

"Sometimes, it's better to let go and allow yourself and those around you to fly." He looked up at the stars and smiled. "I suppose there have been times, whether it's been in my work or play, that I've been a bit too stuffy for my own good."

He realized he had just learned another lesson.

Alex parked his car in the garage and entered through the side door. Slipping off his shoes at the entrance, he decided to shower, and go straight to bed. But once there, he lay awake for what seemed like hours.

He turned on his television and programmed the timer, before closing his eyes again. He recognized the movie in the background as 'A Star is Born.' It was one of his favorites. Alex listened for a moment and thought about the storyline. He thought about the extreme happiness, sadness, confusion, anger, and ultimate survival that the movie took its viewers through. Extreme examples of what everyday people go through, and could learn from. He continued listening to the dialog and knew the movie was almost over. Alex could never understand why the male character, once he could no longer control situations around him, would opt for such a drastic way out. He thought about the female lead. Even though she had enough strength for the both of them, it still wasn't enough to save him. She found herself not only strong enough to survive, but also newfound power from the situation. Alex opened his eyes and stared at the ceiling.

"Important lessons. Even with all the cards stacked against her, she survived and was strong. She didn't lie down and die because he did. She fought back, overcoming obstacles, and finding the strength and energy she never knew existed somewhere inside her."

Suddenly, the timer ran out and the television went dark. Alex laid still, thinking about the storyline, when suddenly the lessons learned were so very real to him. He heard himself speak in a loud whisper, "Why did she allow herself to get so weak after my death? Why didn't she fight back? Why didn't I help her?"

Then he closed his eyes and slept.

He didn't know where they were, but it didn't matter. They were together in a meadow full of lavender, surrounded by snow-capped mountains on all sides. He felt a slight chill in the air, but he wasn't uncomfortable. The fragrance from the blossoms prevailed over the other senses. He continued inhaling its sweet perfume, and watched in awe as the aroma encircled the top of his head in a spiraling ascension. Alex forced himself away from the perplexity in front of him, and found her staring at him from a distance. He spoke, but was unable to recognize his own voice and accent. As he approached her, he realized her clothes were not from this era.

She was wearing an elegant, long, sleeveless, black crepe gown with a cleavage rhinestone brooch in varying shades of burgundy. It was a sight he hoped that he would never forget. She looked like an aristocrat.

He asked where she came from. But now there was no sound drifting from his mouth. He walked closer to her, and saw she had long dark hair. But she didn't appear to look exactly like the woman he was used to seeing in his dreams. The dark hair was shoulder-length, pulled away from her face, and very thick and wavy. Her body also appeared slightly taller. She was still a distance away, but he felt this woman in front of him was actually many individuals in one. He could almost see the various transformations taking place. He knew it didn't matter who she was, he wanted her in his life.

Suddenly, she looked up at him, and he instantly recognized the same warm, loving eyes that were hers from the very beginning. He heard himself speak again, but in an unfamiliar voice.

"Why weren't you stronger? Why couldn't I have helped you remain and start again without me? Why couldn't I have helped you build your strength for the outside world, before I left you? Neither of us knew when we would have to leave the other. No one knows that. So why didn't I make sure you were prepared in case I was the first to go? Why was I so controlling and obsessively protective? I loved you and I trusted your intelligence, but apparently not enough to make your own decisions and form your own opinions, without my influence. Why did I do that to you? And why did you allow me to?"

She looked at him from a distance and smiled. Then she was gone. He woke up to chirping birds and the movie still playing in his mind.

After sitting through several meetings, then working after hours on the books, Lauren trudged wearily into her house. The immense pressure was beginning to take its toll. She questioned whether building the new boutique was such a good idea, after all. More often than not, she knew it was, but her body and mind were one step beyond exhaustion, and all she wanted to think about was her big comfortable bed upstairs.

She took a quick shower to relieve her aching muscles, then slid between the cool sheets. She stared at the ceiling for several minutes before deciding to find her remote control. Lauren quickly clicked from one channel to another, more out of relieving tension than to find something interesting to watch. Depending on the channel, the screen would shade or lighten her face, causing her to squint, which started bringing on a headache. She stopped when she saw one of her favorite movies being shown. It was almost over, but she was determined to stay awake and watch the end. Instead, the music quickly lulled her to sleep.

Lauren stared in shock at the purple meadow all around her. The sweet smell of lavender took precedence over the other senses. She intuitively knew this was no accident, and inhaled the scent, allowing its essence to flow to her crown chakra. Lauren could feel the immense pressure in her brow, and knew without a doubt that he was near. She turned and watched as he slowly approached. She could tell by his many facial expressions that he was already speaking to her. And he was adamant about whatever he was saying. She felt herself smiling in return, even though she had no idea what was coming out of his mouth. Lauren watched as he continued moving forward. He was close enough now for her to see his warm and questioning eyes. She knew that whatever he was trying to tell her was important, but for some reason, it didn't matter. All she wanted to do was fall into his arms, and be swept away into the purple fields, never to be heard from again.

He was adamant, and Lauren tried desperately to read his beautiful lips, but kept getting sidetracked by the essence of lavender all around her. She was about to hold up her hand to tell him she didn't understand, when a closer look at him left her motionless.

"What's going on here?"

Lauren was taken aback as she watched his clothing and appearance changing in front of her. His hair was still dark, and though it was longer from a distance, it was now much shorter. And his clothes had changed from jeans and a t-shirt to those worn many decades earlier. He was now wearing dark pleated pants, and a dark pinstriped tuxedo, with wide satin lapels. Lauren shut her eyes tightly, and shook her head. "This is crazy."

Even though he was still a short distance away, she knew that he was the most handsome man she had ever seen. She could almost feel his hot breath on her body, and knew he was the love of her life. But she was suddenly troubled at the strong resemblance of a man she thought she might have known intimately.

"Why does he look so different, yet so very familiar?"

Lauren took a deep breath, and the strong fragrance dominated again. It relaxed her, and she knew instinctively to stop questioning. *You know nothing will be solved tonight. Remember to let what you see and feel flow through you, Lauren. Just allow it to happen, and enjoy the process.*

While her thoughts were comforting, she couldn't understand what this wonderful man was saying to her. So all she could do was look into his dark blue eyes, and smile.

Until a look of immense pain suddenly crossed his face. And, without warning, Lauren suddenly felt ill. She didn't know why, but the pain struck her heart as if he had shoved a knife into it himself. "God, I don't think I'm ready to hear what he's trying to say."

Lauren raised her hand, protecting her face, as a stiff frigid breeze swept by her. When the winds calmed, she found herself looking down at him from atop a mountain. He was still talking and gesturing wildly, with the same unyielding pain on his face. Then it was suddenly all taken away as Lauren's own tormented voice woke her up. She didn't want to believe what she was saying, but the pain she felt confirmed it.

"Even though I know how senseless your death was, why wasn't I strong enough to follow through on our plans? Why did I allow myself to collapse into all that sorrow and rage? Why couldn't I just see the same purpose and vision in life without you, as I had seen with you? Why was I stupid enough to allow you to take responsibility for everything? When you left, I didn't know how to cope with independence. I was afraid of it, and I resented you because of it. And I didn't think I was strong enough. I wanted to die. I begged to die!"

When Lauren finally opened her eyes, she instinctively knew to stay calm. She felt wet tears staining her pillow, but still she refused to get emotional. Instead, she picked up her journal from the floor and wrote key words so she could later reconstruct the night's events. Her outer core was composed, but her mind was screaming with painful questions.

"Why would I say those things to him? What did they mean? Her next question was temporarily halted by the incessant ringing of the telephone. Lauren absentmindedly picked up the receiver. "What!"

It was Adriana. "Well, good morning to you, too. I couldn't reach you yesterday to see how you were. Should I ask how your evening went?"

Lauren glanced at the clock. "You couldn't reach me because I was in meetings all day, then finishing paperwork at the boutique until late last night. These meetings, decisions, and arguments with bankers, contractors, and architects are driving me insane."

Adriana spoke up with a giggle. "Too late."

Lauren continued, but now in a lighter tone. "OK, I can't argue with that. But I'll sure be glad when it's all over. We're trying to get this shop opened before the holidays. As it stands right now, we'll probably make it. Of course, today's another day. The only people in this mess who are still getting along are Kevin, Cindy, and me. I suppose that's a good thing considering the rest of them won't be in our lives after we open anyway."

Adriana sighed loudly. "Sounds like you had one hell of a day. Wish I could say mine was better, but it wasn't. I was stuck in meetings all day, too. The planets must be doing some strange things. And I'm sure the full moon doesn't help, either. Everyone I came into contact with yesterday was either irritating, or irritated. Normally, I can override these feelings and carry on. But yesterday everything got to me. I stayed calm on the outside, but I could have set a war in motion on the inside."

Lauren was nodding her head in appreciation. "How's your

day look today?"

Adriana lightly brushed her long hair from her eyes, and looked at her date book. "I'll enjoy the ride today. Not much going on. I'll go to work in an hour or so, supervise some shipments for a while, and then I thought I'd slip out, come by your place and buy me an outfit for the club tomorrow night."

Lauren had forgotten. "I'll just wear something from my closet. It should be a lot of fun. At least we'll get our minds off business for a while."

Adriana smiled. "That would certainly be a nice change."

Lauren was about to hang up, when she felt her journal lying heavily across her lap. "Adriana, do you have a sec? I want to run something by you. Do you mind?"

"Not at all. I would love something else to think about."

Lauren told her about the dream, as well as the strange questions she heard herself asking as she was waking up. She recalled the smell and sights of lavender all around her, with its fragrance entering her crown chakra. She told Adriana about the clothes and appearance that seemingly changed in front of her.

"What do you think? Could it all have been a real dream this time? Why did his appearance change to another era?"

Adriana was writing the information down as fast as she could, and didn't answer right away. Finally, there was a tone of excitement to her voice.

"Lauren, think back to the dream in detail. Do you feel as if you were blaming him for what happened?"

Lauren rolled over to get a better look at the trees swaying outside her window, hoping it would have a grounding effect.

"No, I don't think so. Maybe at one time, or in another time, but certainly not now. No, I think I was just asking for help in finding the answers. I was watching the end of 'A Star is Born' last night. That particular movie has always made me question life, and how people react so differently to it. I never knew why until now. Or do I know any more now than I did before? I don't think I know anything anymore."

Adriana laughed. "I don't think you were dreaming about the movie and replaced yourself in the lead role, if that's what you're thinking. But I do think the movie, and whatever happened in your dream, may loosely parallel each other. Think about the premise of the movie, and think about what you were asking him. Maybe the storyline of the movie did nothing more than bring out something from your subconscious. Either way, it's worth thinking about. If it were me, I'd take it very seriously. Perhaps you should be trying to answer those questions yourself."

"What about the lavender?"

Adriana thought a moment. "Lavender can be used for aromatherapy. You've used it yourself. I can think of one way it may pertain to this. Lavender is sometimes called the angel of healing and purification. It allows inner guidance and intuition to come forward. And it's supposed to bring clarity and calmness. We use it a lot for emotional, psychic, and physical healing. It does everything from calming a mother in labor and reducing the severity of labor pains, to all types of psychic impairments."

Lauren heard Adriana take a deep cleansing breath, then she continued, "Lavender was used for a reason, Lauren. Let it assist you in achieving the balance you need. Listen to your intuition and inner guidance. I would recommend you bring some lavender oil into your house, as well as in your shop. With all the emotional pressures you're going through, it will at least help calm you down. It's good for blood pressure, headaches, and even respiratory problems. And it sure won't hurt your dreams either."

Lauren opened her mouth to ask a question, but Adriana didn't give her the opportunity.

"Lauren, in light of your dreams, and with everything else that you're going through, it wouldn't be unusual that lavender would be a focal point, as well as why you felt it entering your crown chakra. I'm not sure you know this, but lavender activates the crown chakra. And one of the many qualities of this chakra is the ability to open up to and comprehend wisdom and understanding. It goes beyond space and time. It also aligns you with your higher self. So I have no doubt there's a reason lavender was used. Someone up there is looking out for you, and apparently thinks you need it."

Lauren knew deep down that her friend was right.

"Adriana, how did you get so much smarter than me?"

Adriana laughed. "I ask the same thing when you're helping me solve my problems."

Lauren smiled into the phone, and changed the subject. "How about lunch?"

Adriana was quick to respond. "Sounds like a good plan. I'll be dropping by your store today, anyway. I'll bring you everything I have that's lavender."

Lauren said her goodbyes, and lay still while trying to come to terms with her predicament.

"Maybe I'm trying too hard." She slowly re-read the words she had written just a few minutes earlier, shaking her head in disbelief the entire time.

"I don't understand any of this. What if the clues are right in front of me, but I'm too blind to see them?"

Lauren switched on her radio for comfort, and found herself singing to 'Street of Dreams'.

Alex woke up alert, pulling on his sweat pants and t-shirt. Every nerve in his body was electrified, and he hoped the fresh air and jog would burn off some excess energy. He was only a few minutes into his run when his thoughts were suddenly thrown back to the night before. Alex couldn't run fast enough to escape the confusion he felt.

Why couldn't she hear me? Maybe she heard, but didn't want to answer the questions. Maybe she didn't have the answers. And why was lavender all over the place? What was that all about?

His speed accelerated, and the sweat fell from his forehead, burning his eyes. Alex shook his head defiantly.

No, they were valid questions that were meant for both of us to answer. It's time we got down to the why and how of this thing. Why is this happening, and what in the hell is going on?

Alex stopped for a moment to stare at the ocean waves rushing swiftly on shore.

I fear this is going to be the most trying and terrifying piece of the puzzle. He lifted his eyes towards the clouds, and directed his questions. "Is this as far as it goes until we resolve some of these issues? Is this what it all comes down to? What happens if it becomes too painful for either of us? What happens if we just don't get it?"

But he knew the answer, and his voice dropped to a whisper. "If we can't handle it now, then it will probably be brought to us again, perhaps in another scenario, far in the future."

But either way, time was running out, and Alex was frightened again. "I don't want to wait for another scenario. I don't want to wait for another lifetime. I want her now. But what if I can't contact her? Or what if she wants nothing more to do with this? What do I do then? If I've learned nothing else, I've learned that I can't solve these issues for her. And I know she can't solve them for me."

Alex looked at the churning blue waters, and yelled as loud as he could to the roaring waves coming at him.

"What if we can't find a way to fix this? Can somebody out there tell me what we're supposed to do, then? Please! I can't lose her. Not again."

He stood very still, hoping the answer would appear from the depths of the ocean floor. None came. Just the deafening sound of the Pacific.

Alex shook the dread he felt covering his body like a dark, heavy cloak, and ran faster than he had ever run before. He prayed his thoughts wouldn't be able to catch up. Instead, his mind projected a vivid picture of his guide. His lungs were burning, and his knees were aching, but he refused to stop. Alex didn't know if he was trying to run to her for answers, or whether he was running away, for fear of what was to come. He felt his body finally give out and drop to the sand. He didn't care that his dark hair was stuck to his head, and his clothes were wet with perspiration. He felt the cool breeze against his wet skin, and knew he wasn't going anywhere for a while.

The face of his guide was steadfast in his mind, and his curiosity was peaking, but he was out of breath and his energy was depleted. It took him longer than usual, but once he had composed himself, Alex closed his eyes, sat quietly in place, and waited. It wasn't long before she appeared beside him, more vivid than ever before. She took his hand in hers, and spoke softly.

"Alex, you must calm down. Why are you asking yourself questions that you can't answer? Doesn't that seem like a waste of time? You were taught to start at the beginning. Are you forgetting that lesson so soon? Take one question at a time." Her brown eyes penetrated his, as she gripped his hand tighter. "Alex, do you understand? One at a time. If your love wishes to continue, then she'll have her own questions to answer. If you both feel the need to continue, and to move forward, you may find your paths very different. But that won't matter, because they will still mean the same, and take you to the same place. You must trust, and have more patience now than you've ever had before. Alex, trust the process, and be brave enough to face your fears." She bent down, kissed the top of his head, and whispered in his ear, "And don't forget to smell the lavender."

Alex opened his eyes and sighed in confusion when he found himself still on the beach, yet somehow in front of his own house.

"How grateful I am for small favors." He didn't want to walk another step, but he slowly shuffled to his patio, and deposited himself in a nearby chair. He could hear people enjoying themselves on the beach. But their noises were quickly drowned out by his own concerns. One by one, Alex wanted to remember the questions, and he forced himself upstairs to locate his journal.

He didn't care that his clothes were filthy. He sat on his bed and quickly wrote each question, not allowing himself to think about the answers until he had finished. When the last mark was written on the page, Alex closed his eyes and spoke just loud enough to hear his own voice.

"I've got to fight the nervousness rising in the pit of my stomach."

He realized how serious this had become, and knew his happiness was on the line. Alex shook off the doubt shrouding him again, and wiped the beads of sweat forming on his brow. When he felt ready, he took several deep breaths, and swallowed hard.

"C'mon, Alex, you can do this."

He took one more deep breath, realizing he was still worried, but at least the fear was beginning to subside.

"It's time to open myself up and be brave. This won't work until we both memorize the story, and remember how we failed the last time." Alex finally forced his eyes open, and read the questions, one by one.

"Could I have been so controlling?" Alex shook his head in denial. "No, that can't be. We were in love. I absolutely would not have controlled her. I can't believe this is what happened."

He read the questions again. "Maybe I was just being protective."

Alex was quickly pacing the length of his bedroom when the information suddenly stopped flowing. He stopped in the middle of the room.

"Wait! Damn it! Everything was going so well." Alex sat on his bed, and argued with his feelings of defeat. "No, Alex, you're not going to feel this way. Not without a fight. You'll work this out, then help her."

He opened his eyes wide, shocked by the words he had just spoken.

"I can't believe it. How in the hell could I still be doing it? Trying to solve all her problems for her? Trying to protect her from not feeling an ounce of pain? Trying to make everything better without first asking her permission?"

Alex needed fresh air, and walked to the balcony.

"There was strength and confidence inside her that needed to emerge. Not by what I could do for her, but by what she could accomplish for herself."

He stared at the ocean, wanting it to wash his thoughts away.

"God, I must have messed up terribly."

He heard his voice somewhere far in the distance, but every word seemed to loudly echo off, and bounce through the atmosphere around him.

"I left her with no resources, and no inner strength to fight back with. She wasn't prepared, and didn't know how to manage without me. Was it my ego that made me think I'd always be there to take care of her? Was it my fear, instead of my love for her that made me control our lives? Did I not want her to manage without me? Did I fear that she would no longer need me, or love me if she became strong and independent? God, what did I do to her? I thought I was doing the right thing. I never wanted to hurt her. I loved her more than life itself."

He quickly walked back into the safety of his bedroom and turned to look in the mirror. He saw his own confusion staring back at him.

"Was that me?" Alex wanted to calm the disturbing blue eyes.

"I don't even know what I'm talking about. I'm accusing myself of a crime I don't remember committing."

But the eyes knew the truth. They told him that he purposely took control of both their lives, and whether it was due to convenience or love, she stepped aside and allowed it to happen. Unfortunately, it ended with very severe consequences. It didn't matter that they were naive. It didn't matter what the reasons were. The end result still produced extreme negative circumstances that had reverberated forward to their current life.

"What's the story? And does it even matter?" But he knew it

did. He was hoping to avoid the pain of watching how wrong they were in the name of love.

"I did love her with all my heart and soul. I do now. I would protect her with my life. How could I not?"

His ranting stopped when somewhere deep inside, his higher self interrupted with painful truths he was hoping to avoid.

"Yes, you would protect her with your life. That is one of the many facets of love. That is not the issue. Purposefully not teaching her and equipping her to protect herself is not love. It's control, and selfishness. She was like a child. Inside, she was very strong, but was never able to manifest it. It stayed hidden deep inside. Yes, you loved her with all your heart. You still do. This is all very true. But it goes beyond that emotion. To show your love, you must also allow her to be who she is with you, as well as without you. You would have found that you could have loved her even more."

Alex couldn't believe what he was hearing. How could you love someone too much in one area, but not enough in another? He headed downstairs and sat in front of his piano. He wanted to play loud enough to drown out the voice he was hearing. But he found his fingers refused to move to the keys, and he felt his mind drifting again.

"Without her in your life, you have realized who you could be for yourself. But you have never loved anyone in this lifetime enough to obsessively protect them. Not until her. Without you in her life, she is finding out how strong she is. She is finding out how independent she can become. Don't take that away from her. You must realize there are some things you cannot do for her. There are some things she will want to do, and must do for herself. You try and take that away from her, and you take away a large part of who she really is.

"With patience and trust, you can heal the pain and erase the scars. You must allow her to do the same. You did nothing out of malicious behavior. You only wanted to protect her from all the pain and worries because you loved her so much. But, Alex, to love someone is to be there for them when they ask for your help. It's helping them save themselves, and to help when you can, but allowing them to live their own lives the way they see fit. Alex, trust what you hear and what you feel. It's real."

Alex closed his eyes and took a slow deep breath. Suddenly, the scent of lavender was everywhere. He instinctively knew this was what he needed, and allowed it to ascend into his crown chakra.

Once his body was completely relaxed, he realized this could be conquered. He didn't have a malicious bone in his body.

"Sometimes we do some rotten things to those we love the most. She trusted me, and allowed everything to go my way. She never questioned. That was one of the problems. She didn't question anything I said or did. She assumed my opinions were also hers. I suppose ignorance of a situation can still produce karma."

But deep inside, Alex wanted desperately to know the real story.

Chapter 18

Lauren calmly read and re-read the questions in front of her for well over an hour. She knew she would be late for work, but couldn't think of anything more important than what she was doing. She closed her eyes after each question, hoping to hear the answers. Instead, she found the more she read the questions, the more worried and confused she became.

"Am I ready for this? Do I even begin to understand what this is all about? What did I do that was so terrible? What did he do? Why do I have a feeling something happened that I could have controlled?" Lauren strolled outside staring at the hills, before taking a seat on her patio.

"Am I responsible for all the lessons and pain we're going through?" She thought for a moment, then shook her head. "No, it takes more than one person to create a two-person karma. Whatever the hell that means."

Lauren looked down at the trees below her.

"No, this is about the both of us. But I wonder what happened? And whatever it was, how can I fix it if I don't know the whole story?"

She waved her journal in the air, fighting the frustration growing inside her. "Why would I say these things? I can't comprehend one word of it." Lauren fought her tensing muscles, and her threatening headache. "C'mon, girl, calm down. You're not going to be able to help yourself if you don't." She exhaled noisily. "Now, think about the questions. No, think about each question."

She re-read the words that were spoken, and noticed one word written over and over again. "Lavender." Lauren picked up the phone and called Adriana. "Hi, it's me. Don't forget to bring me all the lavender you have."

Lauren had several customers waiting for her when she walked into the shop, and several phone calls to return. Before she realized the time, it was 1:00, and Adriana was bouncing in the door sharing her hellos with everyone.

Kevin put his arm around her. "I hear you're going to Jupiter's tomorrow night. You'll let me help you pick something out, won't you? I know just the thing that will look fabulous on you." Then he whispered in her ear, "It's on sale. And with your discount, you can walk out of here with almost a free dress."

Adriana laughed out loud. "Sweet words to my ears. Are you going tomorrow night too?"

Kevin was leading her to the back of the store, "I wouldn't miss it. As if Cindy would let us."

Lauren could hear their laughter fading as they turned the corner. She noticed Adriana had left two vials on the counter. She picked one up, and inhaled. "Ah, lavender." She was taken back to the night before. She could see herself smiling, before being whisked away to the top of a mountain. She saw herself looking down to see his mouth moving. Even now, she strained to hear what he was saying.

Lauren shook her head, and reprimanded herself as she slipped one of the vials in her purse. "I can't do this now. People trying to buy clothes and I'm off on a mountaintop somewhere."

Lauren took the other vial and sprinkled a few drops into an aromatherapy holder, attached to the light bulbs on the lamps. The smell of lavender delicately enveloped the room. She took another deep breath and felt a slight ache, followed by a dizziness stemming from the top of her head. However, she felt revived, and knew she could tolerate the remainder of the day.

Adriana walked in front of Lauren and pirouetted. "What do you think?"

Lauren stepped back and whistled. "Wow, you look fabulous."

Kevin teasingly took the credit. "Thanks, Lauren. I knew this dress was perfect for Adriana the first time I laid eyes on it. That Irish green perks up those eyes of hers, making them sparkle."

Adriana started giggling. "Stop it, Kevin, you're embarrassing me. I suppose you've talked me into it. Can I know how much it costs, now, or wait until my credit card bill comes in?"

Kevin was about to whisper the price, but she turned away. "No, don't tell me. I don't care how much it is, this dress is going home with me."

Lauren laughed. "Trust me, after you pay for that gorgeous outfit, you'll even have money left over to buy shoes to match. Now, let's eat."

Once the two women were seated in the quiet bistro across the street, Lauren had questions she couldn't explain away. She needed Adriana's advice.

"How do I mentally put myself in the middle of the story? I've given this a lot of thought, and you're right. There is much more to this than I can handle at the moment. Every time I ask myself any of the questions, I find I have ten more attached to them."

Adriana smiled. "Lauren, tonight I want you to go home early and relax."

Lauren was about to argue, but Adriana put her hand up in protest. "I want you to go home and relax. Take a bath in the lavender oils. Listen to your songs. I still believe they play a vital role in your remembering. After you've calmed yourself down, I want you to go to your special place in meditation, and ask what it is you need to learn. You may find that you've already started the groundwork. You wouldn't have got this far without having already learned a few lessons. You have got to believe this."

Adriana took her friend's hand. "You're much further on your path than you give yourself credit for. Lauren, believe this. I'm not saying it to make you feel more confident; I'm telling you this because I know it's true. Now it's your turn to know the truth too."

Lauren smiled. "I must admit, I'm not the same person I was twenty years ago. I look back at that person and she doesn't exist anymore. I fought for a long time, but found I didn't have any choice but to grow and become the person I wanted to be. I was forced to do things differently than I had been taught. Gary wasn't there for me. He had his own agenda and I was forced to either go along with them, or make my own way. I chose to be true to myself. I didn't realize it until we started talking about a divorce. I wished the marriage could have worked, but since it didn't, I'm glad I threw myself into the children, my work, and my personal beliefs. I've never understood why, but I've always had the urge to be my own person, so whoever I'm with will blend with me, rather than dominate. I know the difference now."

Adriana smiled broadly and pushed her long hair out of her eyes. "Lauren, you have come a long way since that girl in college. You were always a leader, but many leaders are uncompromising, or use brute force to get their way. You go along when it feels comfortable. But when you listen to yourself and know something doesn't feel right for you, then you either speak up, or back away. I remember nights you would stay home, rather than force yourself to go along with the crowd. I've never known you to condemn others for what they do. You concern yourself with your own conscience. You exude confidence and intelligence, and have a grace and poise that go beyond feminine beauty. You've learned many of your lessons in life the hard way, but you did learn them. You didn't break down, and you didn't run away. You faced them head on, and you dealt with them. And while all this was going on, you became stronger. I admire you for that."

Lauren had tears in her eyes. "Who do you think I learned it from? In reality, I followed your lead, and became one myself."

Lauren and Adriana walked out into the sunshine and crossed

the street. "Now, Lauren, promise me you'll disconnect the phone tonight, and find out what this is all about. I'll be home if you need me. I'm still researching the book I can't seem to get out of my head. So just call if you need anything at all."

They said their goodbyes with Lauren strolling into the busy store.

Kevin was ringing up a sale. "How was lunch?"

Lauren strolled by him, humming. "Enlightening."

Alex stopped at the local health store and picked up lavender oil before going to the studio. He wanted to be prepared, and knew only one way of doing that. He had to start with lavender.

He met the other band members in the studio parking lot and walked in together. Ron spoke up when he saw them entering.

"Well, this is it. If there are any changes, better have them ready tonight. Tomorrow, we bring the house down."

Alex smiled. "I think we're ready. No changes on my end. How about you guys?" Everyone shook their heads. "OK then, let's get our butts up there and practice one last time. Tomorrow's the big day."

Rehearsal went well, with Alex singing each song as if he were giving his all to an unknown entity. During a break, Ron picked up the song list. "Alex, we're playing twelve songs. Is that enough? Then he added amusingly, "Is twelve too many? I suppose we should continue playing until the tomatoes start flying. Is the club supplying full body shields?"

Alex laughed out loud. "I think we're safe with twelve. We'll be finished before anyone knows what hit them."

Ron looked at Alex through the glass and made a sign that brought Alex into fits of laughter. Everyone seemed to be in good spirits.

It was after 11:00 when they had finished the last song and packed up their instruments. Ron quickly went over the next evening's agenda with the men.

"We should arrive no later than 7:00. The doors open at 8:00. That should give us plenty of time to set up and do a quick sound check." He turned his attention to Alex. "Are you ready? No last-minute jitters?"

Alex retorted, "What the hell you trying to do to me, Ron? No, I'm doing just fine, thank you. How about you?"

"All's fine here. Shall we go?"

The other members could do nothing more but stand aside and laugh. One spoke up, "Every gig we go through this same thing with the two of you. Who will be the one with stage fright? And every time, we sound great. You both worry too much. As long as both of you show up tomorrow night, the rest of us will make you guys sound like professionals."

Ron and Alex were quiet for a moment, then realized the joke and laughed. During the drive home, Alex made sure his thoughts were focused on the following night. With the radio stations, the club, and their friends touting the gig, he knew there would be standing room only. But still, he was looking forward to singing in public again.

As he pulled into his driveway, Alex realized the only thing he seemed nervous about was approaching his front door. He knew it was time he found out what was vital to his happiness. He could go no further without answers. He knew there was mental work to do once he entered, and he prayed he was up to it.

Alex forced himself up the stairs, to his bathroom. He tried to ignore the annoying squeaky knob as he turned on the water in the tub. When the water reached a very warm temperature, Alex methodically poured a few drops of lavender oil into the steady stream. Not wanting to give thought to his actions, he casually opened the balcony door leading out to the ocean, and then slowly removed his clothes. Finally, he dimmed the lights, turned on the self-recording of his songs, and pressed repeat. Before lowering himself into the tub, he walked back into his bedroom and poured a few drops of the oil on a cloth next to the bed. Lavender permeated both rooms.

Alex glanced at himself in the mirror above the tub, took a deep breath and closed his eyes.

Lauren finished work later than she had anticipated and sped home. She was tired and wanted to take a bath and meditate before falling asleep. She reminded herself she had an appointment with her attorney the next day, then tried to delete the thought from her mind when she felt her stomach knot up.

"That can be thought about soon enough. But not tonight. For now, I just need to relax."

She couldn't lock her doors, run upstairs, and turn on the warm water fast enough. As soon as the tub was filled, Lauren stepped into the water, took a deep cleansing breath, and instantly relaxed. Her room smelled like a field of lavender. She was about to take another deep breath when she realized she hadn't turned her music on.

"No, no, I'm not doing this unless it's done right."

She carefully stepped out and rushed to her bedroom. Finally, she slipped one foot back into the tub then she realized she had not pressed repeat. She sprinted back, opening her balcony doors while she was in the room.

Lauren had almost regretted allowing the cool breeze to flow into the room. But once settled, she was glad she did. The coolness against her warm skin felt delightful. Lauren looked around once more before trying to relax, making sure everything was perfect.

She took a deep breath, letting it out slowly between her lips, and then automatically brought down her white light of protection, before asking for assistance. This was the last conscious realization she had.

Lauren found herself back at the beautiful house in Connecticut. She was in the master bedroom, staring at a woman's back. She suspected that she was watching herself in another time. Her back was to Lauren, but she knew the eyes were going to be the same as hers. She could see the hair was the same. But other than that, she knew this woman would not resemble her.

Lauren watched as the woman stood at the window, facing the dock. Lauren's pulse raced as she watched the bedroom door open, and she saw a very handsome man walk across the room to hug the woman from behind. They were both laughing as he turned her around, taking her into his arms. It was a joyous occasion of some sort.

Lauren felt she was intruding, but they obviously couldn't see her. She was trying to stay focused, but was getting confused by what she was witnessing. She thought that somehow this woman in front of her may indeed be her. The emotions were creeping into Lauren's soul, and she was finding it more difficult to stay detached. Before she knew how to stop it, she was sucked into the drama unfolding before her. Like watching a movie, she unwittingly became involved with the characters and plot. Their emotions became hers. It was a losing battle, even when she could still hear the reminders in her head to stay calm and detached.

Lauren temporarily felt a deep chill in her bones as she sensed someone else in the room, also watching this tale unfold. She could feel their essence, yet couldn't see anyone. She instinctively reminded herself not to worry about anyone else. She needed to trust the process, and to think before she reacted. She moved her attention to the couple again, and smiled. He was kissing her neck and whispering something in her ear.

I've never seen anyone as happy as these people, Lauren thought.

Lauren watched as the woman fanned the pages of what looked like a large journal or manuscript. Then she watched her place it on an oak table, next to a large music box. Lauren squinted for a closer look. *That's my music box!*

Before Lauren had time to react, the woman spoke in an unfamiliar, soft, sultry voice. "We've finally finished it. The publisher says it'll be a big hit. And, darling, I want to thank you. Without your help, this book would never have been completed on time. I wouldn't have known where to turn." She nuzzled closer to the handsome man. "It's nice being married to my partner, my best friend, and my manager. I could never make it without you."

Lauren wanted to stop breathing and listen closer. She wanted to hear what his response would be. His voice was deep, soothing, and loving.

"I promise you'll never have to worry about making it without me. That will never happen. I'll always be here to protect you. Do you think I'd let you do something this important alone? We're partners and I will do anything to make you happy." Then teasing her, he added, "You stick with me, baby, and you'll go far."

She laughed, then kissed him hard on the mouth. It was obvious the couple was happy, healthy, and very much in love. He adored her and she him. Lauren had forgotten who she suspected this woman was. *Why am I here? To see the people that once lived in my house?* Her breath caught in her throat. *My house?*

Lauren refused to ask questions for now. She was there to observe. But she couldn't shake the feeling that she wasn't alone in this parallel existence.

The handsome man continued, "Once this is on the shelves, perhaps we'll take another trip, and not come back this time. What do you say to that?"

She knew he was kidding, but played along. "No, I'll always have to come back to our home. Everything we've ever wanted was achieved in this house. This is our dream house."

Lauren couldn't believe what she was watching in front of her. She wanted to scream, but couldn't. She could hear her mind trying to reassure her, *Detach, detach, detach. Stay calm. Stay calm. Trust, trust, trust.*

Lauren watched as the woman picked up the music box and fumbled with a trap door until it opened. She gently placed the book inside the hull of the box. Then Lauren watched as the man placed the cover back in its original place and set the box back on the oak table. It looked as if it had never been touched.

Lauren was trying to recover from what was unfolding, when the woman suddenly turned completely around, and walked past her.

Oh my dear God, this woman is pregnant.

Lauren tried to remember the story she had heard about the couple who built the house. *They had no children. No one ever mentioned children.*

Lauren looked closely at her protruding stomach. She looked as if she was not only about to deliver, but also having more than one.

She followed the couple downstairs, turning occasionally to see if she could catch a glimpse of someone following behind her. She still couldn't shake the feeling she wasn't alone.

By the time Lauren reached the bottom step, everything had changed. There were people crowded in all the rooms. And the energy was oppressive and smothering. Some were talking in low tones, and some were eating and just being very quiet. *What's going on here?*

She crept back upstairs and entered the master suite again. But now, the room was somehow different. There was such distress hanging in the air, Lauren had trouble staying detached. Her eyes were drawn to the bed, where she saw the woman lying down. Her hair was wet and strung around her face. Still, she was beautiful.

Lauren heard herself ask the walls, "What could have happened to cause such a drastic change in here? Where's her husband?"

Lauren felt helpless, knowing there was nothing she could do but watch. She could feel time moving faster now. The woman was ill and running a fever. Lauren watched as the young woman refused the doctor's order to swallow the medication. All she kept screaming was she wanted to die. "I have to go be with him. He said he'd never leave me. He promised me everything would be all right."

The doctor was trying to make her see reason. "You must

think about your babies now. When your period of mourning is over, you will write more books and raise your children. You must stay strong to deliver your babies."

Lauren wanted to take the woman into her arms. She had tried to stay detached, but was now openly crying. She overheard her own voice whispering to the woman.

"You can do it. You are such a strong woman, with an immense amount of intelligence. You may be frightened now, but you must believe that you can pick yourself up, if not for you, then for your children and your business. You'll learn to find the strength you need from both. Please don't give up."

But the woman continued fighting to be left alone. The doctor put water next to her bed, and tried desperately to make her understand. "You're putting your unborn children in danger."

She had a wild look in her eyes, and was screaming at the walls, "I want my husband. I only want my husband. I can't do this alone. I won't do this alone. It's not fair. He didn't tell me how to do this."

She looked at the doctor with no hope in her eyes.

"Do you know what book we were to write next? Do you know how to manage the business and talk to our business associates? Do you know how to keep our books? No, you don't. No, no, no, no! I can't do this alone."

The doctor pushed her shoulders down on the bed. "What about your children? They need a mother they can depend on."

She picked up the glass of water and threw it against the fireplace. "No, I don't have the strength. Don't you understand? I just want to die. Let me die and be with my husband. My life is over. Why can't you see that?"

Lauren was trying to push her way against the heavy gravity, to the woman's bedside. She was speaking as loud as she could to whoever could hear her.

"Listen to me. I know how you feel, but please don't do this. You don't realize how much you accomplished without your husband than with him. You can do it again. You're hurting right now, but this pain won't last forever. You can make a new life for yourself. Please listen to me. Please."

Time was quickening its pace. Lauren blinked once, and the woman was still lying on her bed, pale as a ghost. But now, she was alone, and the house was suddenly too quiet. Her face was blotchy from excessive crying. And she no longer looked or acted of this world.

Lauren couldn't be sure if she was medicated, or still wishing herself dead. But her motions were that of a zombie. "I wonder if the stories were true?"

She watched in dark fascination as the woman slowly sat up, and slipped a ring off her finger, placing it gently in the music box. Lauren then followed her as she slowly descended the stairs, and out the back door to the trees behind the house. She carried something resembling a tiny box. Lauren sat under a tree and helplessly watched what was unfolding before her eyes. She so respected this woman. She could see the strength, compassion, and love this woman was capable of. Unfortunately, this lovely woman could see nothing but pain and hopelessness in herself. Lauren's heart broke as she watched the woman begin to sob. The woman was still beautiful, but now she looked older than her years. And it seemed her soul had vanished. Lauren couldn't understand why she was forced to witness such pain and complete despair, yet not be able to help. She watched as the woman approached an area surrounded by trees, and then fell to her knees. She watched her compulsively dig a hole in the dirt with her hands. Then the woman opened the box and took out several colorful pebbles. She heard her speak between broken sobs.

"Remember when we brought a rock home from each place we traveled? Remember we said that we could tell a story by closing our eyes and choosing one? The red one reminded us of one place, and a wonderful story would be told. The blue one told a whole other story."

She began sprinkling the rocks and pushing them into the

ground.

"Our stories are over this time around, my love. But we'll be together soon. And we'll start our chapters all over again, beginning again on page one."

Then she placed her wedding ring into the tiny box that had previously housed the stones. She replaced the lid and put it in the hole she had dug. The pitifully sad woman kneeled over the tiny grave and spoke barely above a whisper, "I've lost it all now. Everything is gone. I just wish I could come home to you right this second."

Lauren was screaming at her, "No, you don't! Please be strong. Please. This awful pain won't last forever. Show your husband that you can do it. Show him that you can carry on with what you both started. Please!"

As soon as she thought it, Lauren was rushed forward. She thought she was in another house, then realized she was watching this woman from the corner of a hospital room. She felt as if she were watching the saddest movie she had ever seen. The pain was overwhelming for her. Lauren clenched her fist, and gripped her heart. Her sobs were caught in her throat, and she was having trouble breathing. She wanted to die along with this woman. She didn't think she could take the pain anymore.

Lauren's guide suddenly appeared beside her, taking her hand from her heart, and replacing it with his own. The pain was lessened, and she was able to continue watching the story unfold.

The woman was obviously very weak now. Lauren gasped loudly when she looked closer, and saw blood covering the once beautiful lady. The doctors were working to try and save her. She overheard a nurse whispering to her, "Miss, you must help us. Be strong. Fight for your life."

Lauren could barely hear the hoarse voice coming from the bed. "I'm too weak and I'm too tired. I've lost my husband, and now I've lost my babies. I have no energy left. Please, just let me die."

Lauren fell to her knees and sobbed for the souls of all these people. The woman, her husband, and for their unborn babies. She heard herself speaking to her guide, "She could have saved those babies. She could have made a new life for herself. She knew how to do everything her husband did, but she was young and overwhelmed by it all. Someone could have helped her. She could have done it."

Although Lauren was sobbing uncontrollably, somewhere in the distance, she could hear what sounded like her voice.

"I could have done it, I could have done it. It wasn't his responsibility to take care of everything in my life. I should have insisted he show me how to do for myself. I should have insisted that he prove his love by believing that I could do something without him. I never questioned. His ideas were mine. It never occurred to me until it was too late. I never thought about handling my own life. I never had to do it before. First it was my parents, then it was him. I never stopped to think that I could be independent and strong. I was so much in love with my husband; he was my life. I didn't need anything or anyone else. I didn't think I would ever have to worry about being alone."

Lauren was sobbing harder, and hitting the floor. "It just never occurred to me. I was so angry when he left me. I hated him and then I found I couldn't live without him. I wasn't going to let him break his promise to me. We had plans and dreams. But I know if anything had happened to me, he could have continued making our dreams come true. Now I see that would have been the greatest tribute of all. To carry on our names, and to raise our children. But, God help me, I just didn't understand, and I couldn't seem to find the energy to allow me to do that. I understand why he left. It was his time. We both had lessons to learn. I think we have both learned that love does not mean keeping a person in a beautiful cage, protected from the outside world. It means allowing them to fly freely, but helping them when they ask for it. A person can't possibly protect someone from experiencing their own pain.

Sometimes, we have our own lessons to learn. Love is being there to help them through it, but remembering that it's still their pain. You can hurt with them, but you can't take it away."

Lauren's guide held out his arms, and she ran to them for comfort.

"Why couldn't either of us see it when we had the chance?"

Lauren pulled slightly away, and looked up at her male companion.

"Why didn't we see it when we had the opportunity?"

Her guide brushed away her tears. "It's a lesson you're learning now, in your current life. Lauren, do you remember what you would do when your children would come running to you after they'd hurt themselves playing?"

Lauren sniffled and thought a moment. "Yes, I would tend to their wounds. Then hold and comfort them. I hurt for them, and I wished I could take the pain away. But instead, I hugged them and sent them out to play again. As much as I hated it sometimes, I had to force myself to take a step back, and let them take their own chances, and make their own mistakes."

He smiled and continued, "And remember, as teenagers, when they thought they were in love? Remember when they would be in such pain over a breakup? What would you do for them?"

She answered slowly, recalling the past. "I would take them in my arms and let them cry their tears. Then I would encourage them not to give up on love, but instead to embrace it while it was in their lives. Reminding them that once it was over, they were to make sure they took something positive from the experience, then release it and move on."

Her guide kissed her forehead. "This is love, and these are the lessons to learn. Lauren, you have done well in this life. You have found the strength and the courage to love, to learn, and to let go. You have found the courage to allow yourself to be loved. To teach compassion and independence. You have shed many tears in the process, but you were strong, and you taught this to your children. Now you must have the courage to put the pains of the past to rest. You must forgive yourself, and then forgive him. The love will survive and grow stronger. But the first step is self-forgiveness. Seems the simplest act, but actually it is the most difficult. You've already been forgiven by the children."

Lauren pulled away and looked deep into her guide's dark eyes.

"Children? Oh my dear God. The children I lost are the children I have now? It's true, isn't it? God gave me another chance?"

Her guide smiled. "And your children gave you another chance. Now it's time to give yourself a chance. Let your defenses down, and love for the sake of loving. Be one, but be separate. Remember what Gibran said in his words of wisdom. Read the verse on marriage again, and take it to heart. Forgive each other now. This is a new life for you both. Work hard, find one another, and be happy."

She looked up again, but he was gone.

She was once again back in her own house, in her own warm tub, smelling the lavender and roses.

Alex woke up with an electric jolt running through his entire body. His bath water had turned cold, and he was shivering. However, he suspected it wasn't from the chill in the air. Taking a glance at himself in the mirror, he saw large tears running down his face. He slowly raised himself out of the tub and quickly dried off. Alex was in a state of shock while he walked into his bedroom, and instinctively picked up the cloth, deeply inhaling its scent. The fragrance of lavender overpowered him as he fell to his knees, sobbing for the pain he had just witnessed.

He could hear his voice deepening from the sobs, as he begged over and over, "Please forgive me. My love, please, please forgive me. Please learn how to forgive us."

He had never known pain like this. He felt as if someone had reached in and tore out his heart with their bare hands. Alex took another deep breath, and the smell of roses suddenly surrounded him, finally centering in his heart area. He closed his eyes before being forced to look back into the bathroom, where the story had taken place. "Where was I? How did I get there?"

As the sobs overtook him again, he knew he had the answers. Alex sat on the floor, pushing his knees to his chest, and rocking back and forth. The pain felt as if the tragic episode had just occurred.

"What was I afraid of? Why couldn't I have allowed her to be the free spirit she was? She was equal to me in intelligence. Why was my ego such that I made her believe my way was the best and only way? Was I afraid she would do better without me? Did I love so much that I wanted to protect her, or myself?"

Alex knew he didn't want to ask himself these questions. Each one hurt more than the last. Then he remembered the children.

"She gave birth to beautiful twin girls."

Loud, heartbreaking sobs overtook him again. Alex didn't want to go on. He didn't think he could survive what he was seeing. But he took another deep breath and centered himself the best he could.

"She was too weak. The babies were born dead. Her body couldn't adjust."

He was thinking back to the scene in her bedroom and the hospital. "They begged her to be strong. But she wanted to be with me. Her heart died the day I did. And I think I took her soul with me when I left."

Alex looked at himself in the mirror, and saw a man torn apart by anger and pain.

"How in the hell could I have caused such a thing to happen? Why couldn't she have gone on with her life? What was wrong with her? What was wrong with us?"

His voice trailed off. He closed his eyes and found his guide sitting next to him, gently stroking his hair.

"Calm down, Alex. The worst is over. Now you remember

what happened. You have acknowledged where you both went wrong. You both must work through this, and finally forgive each other."

Alex shook his head knowingly. "I was there. I could see everything that took place. I realized the man I was watching was me."

Alex turned to his guide, and looked in her eyes like a child.

"I was so in love with her. I wanted to do everything for her. She was my whole life, and I didn't know any other way of showing her. I didn't believe I was doing anything wrong. Now I realize to allow her to have her own strength and a certain kind of freedom was one of many ways I could have proven my love. It was my fault she wasn't able to cope. I never let her make a decision. She never questioned, and neither did I." Alex looked deeper into her eyes. "But as God almighty is my witness, I loved her with all my heart. I never meant for anything to happen to her. To our children."

Sobs were caught in his throat. "I wished I hadn't treated her like a rare porcelain figurine. I treated her as I did all my priceless possessions."

His guide spoke up to comfort him. "Alex, she chose it as well. But you must understand something. The lifetime that you just viewed was a little more complicated than a mere taking over of one's life. Alex, she was in that lifetime to specifically learn to be strong and independent. She could have loved you and been strong, too. She chose this as one of her major lessons in life. You chose your lesson to be one of compassion and allowance. It was two lessons that both of you forgot once you met. You wanted to take care of her, and she wanted to be taken care of. You are both at fault, but you have both come to realize, in this life, how important it is to allow someone to be who they are supposed to be. You know it is not your right to place your restrictions on them. They are who they are, and if you cannot tolerate it, then it is your right to leave.

"You know love does not mean taking away all the pain and lessons the other person is supposed to learn. Show them compassion, and help them as much as you can, yes. But don't keep them from understanding what they are supposed to experience. Emotions and experiences such as love, anger, remorse, courage, strength, fear, happiness. They all must be acknowledged and practiced. With that in mind, your love for each other should flourish. Unconditional love does not have an ego. Nor does forgiveness."

Alex was silent. He knew to listen with his heart. He sat looking at her for several moments before finally speaking.

"I didn't understand any of that while we were together. Once I crossed over, I understood everything. I tried to tell her, but she couldn't hear me. I begged her to give up her fears. I tried to tell her that I would give her strength from the other side, until she was strong enough. I screamed for her to listen to me. I could see her potential once I had crossed over. But her love and anger for me was too strong."

Alex's guide shook her head. "No, her fears were immense. Had she allowed love to enter her heart, she would have grown stronger. Instead of love, she allowed anger and fear to swallow her whole. But be reminded that she is not totally to blame. She took her strength only from you. She was never aware of possessing any herself. Yes, you tried to reach her and tell her that she could be brave, and could do so much more than either one of you had ever given her credit for. But it was too late. She could hear nothing but her heart breaking."

His guide stood up, lifting him up at the same time. "Alex, are you both ready to forgive? Truly forgive?"

Alex looked at her in disbelief. "You mean I still have another chance? We both have another chance to make this right with each other?"

She smiled down at him. "You've come a very long way, Alex. You had already learned many lessons before you had to experience this. Had you not understood, the pain would be much more severe. You're both aware of the roles you played. Now, you must forgive each other from the heart and soul."

He took a deep breath, enjoying the scent of roses mixed with lavender. "It smells like a wonderful garden in here." But she was gone.

Alex sat down on his bed, and looked toward the ocean before him. "How do I tell her that all is forgiven? How do I beg for her forgiveness? And, how in heaven's name could she ever forgive me?"

In a vibrancy that caressed the room, he heard, "By first forgiving yourself."

The last thing he heard was his own thoughts in reply. *It's easier to forgive her than it is myself.*

Alex turned off the lights, lay back on the bed, and instantly fell asleep.

Chapter 19

Lauren fell into her bed and dreamed she was in her bedroom with thousands of roses covering the room. She could see the pinks and reds spreading their warmth over her body, concentrating near her heart chakra.

When her alarm sounded with a steady unappealing ring, she turned it off, but kept her eyes closed. She was numb from the deep rest her body had craved. When she felt ready to face the day, she slowly opened her eyes, and watched the trees swaying outside in a rhythmic motion, trying to lull her back to sleep. Instead, Lauren picked up her journal and wrote page after page about the story and the lessons to be learned from the night before. She tried not to forget a moment. She ended the last sentence with four simple words: "Forgive myself, forgive him."

Lauren closed the book, but continued to lie still. Her thoughts returned to the events. She didn't question whether what she had seen was real. She knew it was. Her body, mind, and spirit all told her so. She now understood the lessons she had forced herself to learn in this life. But learning the lessons were not enough. Lauren realized she must also forgive herself, and then be forgiven by him. She felt she had already forgiven him. She, like him, did nothing in that life out of spitefulness and hate. They did what they did out of what they thought was love, and out of naïve innocence. She knew she hadn't lived up to the obligations in that life.

"I screwed up, big time. I took the easy way out. When it became too difficult, I wouldn't allow myself to survive. I think I literally willed myself to die. And hurt everyone who ever loved me in the process. If I was going to hurt, they were too. So ridiculous, and so tragic."

In the morning light, Lauren was able to view it with a detached mind. She knew the worst was behind her. "Unless he won't forgive me."

The doubt entered her being, forcing her to take notice. "Will I have to tell him the story? Will I have to go through it again?"

Lauren cringed just thinking about it. She shook off the dread and reminded herself that no matter what happened, she had survived this life intact, and would not make the same mistake again. She clutched the ring hanging around her neck.

"We won't make the same mistake twice. I hope and pray you can love me for who I am now."

Lauren thought about her twin daughters and smiled, even though the thought was now mixed with tears of guilt.

"They gave me another chance. And even came back, wanting me as their mother, and believing in me. Even when I wasn't sure about myself."

She couldn't deny the very special bond she had had with her daughters right from the moment of their conceptions. Lauren had gone out of her way to take good care of herself during the pregnancy. She took special care of them when they were born. She taught them to be strong and independent by her example. "I was given another chance."

Lauren's thoughts took her back to the small colorful stones on the ground.

"I wish I could have retrieved her ring. Like this one, it should be given life again."

She thought about the music box and sat up straight in bed.

"What was different about the box?" Lauren fought to remember, but failed. "What happened to the original copy of their novel?"

Lauren shook her head in distress. "Where could it be?"

She looked over at the clock. "Oh my, it's already 9:30."

She jumped out of bed and quickly showered and dressed. She didn't want to be late for her meeting with Gary. She refused to let the thought of him get her down.

"This is for the best. A part of me will always love Gary, but it's not a love made for marriage." Lauren fully realized she couldn't have become who she was without his help. "He doesn't even know what hand he played in my development. I could have broken down again and begged for his affections and attentions."

But Lauren knew she wasn't the type of woman who would do that. She knew in her heart the marriage was over for a reason. For many reasons. And she knew to hold a grudge would only amount to more karma. "No, thank you. I don't think Gary and I will have to do this again. We make much better friends than we ever did marriage partners. Gary is a good man and a good father. I chose well for what I needed at the time. But I am no longer that person, and neither is he."

Lauren took one quick glance in the mirror, then walked downstairs into her office. She meant to put Gary's legal papers next to her purse, but was sidetracked by the music box. She instinctively opened the top, allowing the music to flow into the room. She sang along with a smile. She had survived the worst of the memories, and knew she would survive the day as well.

"It'll be a picnic compared to last night."

Before she left, she picked up the phone and called Adriana.

"Hi, it's me. Do you have a minute?"

Adriana smiled. "Always. I was about to go to the store and check in with Mark. He had a few problems last night with the computer. I don't think we were meant to be born in this age of machines. I believe they are the ones with the control problem. Just when you think you have it under control, they freeze up, or change their course. I could live to be a hundred and I will never be able to comprehend what goes on in their little circuits. Apparently, Mark can't either."

She was about to continue, but remembered Lauren had called her for a reason. "Sorry, didn't mean to bore you with my little quandaries. What can I do for you?"

Lauren was giggling and almost forgot why she had called.

"Oh, I was calling to remind you about my appointment at noon."

Adriana slowed her speech. "I'll be happy to go with you if you like."

Lauren smiled. "No, that's not necessary, but I appreciate the offer. I was going to tell you I think it may be a good idea if we drove separately tonight. I don't know how long Gary will be around, and I don't feel I should rush him. He has an early flight out, but I don't want to take any chances. I'll just meet you there. Who knows? Maybe everything will go smoothly and I'll be there before you."

"Lauren, are you sure? You know I don't mind waiting for you. Is it such a good idea to be alone right now?"

"I promise I'm fine. You want to be seen in that gorgeous dress for as long as you can."

Her friend grinned widely. "I am looking forward to the evening. It's been a while since I've dressed up for anything worth getting dressed up for. All right, we'll meet there, but if there's a problem, you'd better contact me."

Adriana was about to hang up when she remembered. "My God, with all the stuff going on around here, I totally forgot to ask you about last night. What happened?"

Lauren lowered her voice an octave, and tried to explain what took place. After describing in detail the scenes, the questions, the answers, and the conversation with her guide, she felt as if she had just relived the event, again.

She brushed a tear from her eyes. "So, what do you think?"

Adriana was quiet for a moment. She was brushing tears away too.

"Lauren, that is the most tragic, yet the most enlightening story

I've ever heard. You really have come far in this adventure. And look where it's brought you? You're everything you weren't in that life. And your daughters have the mother they were born to have."

Lauren thought for a moment. "But what about their father? In the other life, this man was their father. In this life, Gary is. I don't get it."

Adriana smiled. "Because Gary has his own lessons to learn. The children were all part of it. Just like the man in your dreams. He also has other lessons besides the one with you. And so do you. It just keeps going. You know we don't always come back to the same people each time, or as the same person. For all you know, I was your grandfather in another life. Maybe you were my teacher, and I was your student. We just never know. The only thing we can hope is the positive associations we do have in our lives stem from frequent positive associations in past lives."

Lauren sat down in her chair. "Adriana, I think you were right about the lavender. Now, can you please explain the smell of roses? And what does it have to do with my heart? It really felt as if my heart was opening when I inhaled."

Adriana thought about her explanation before beginning.

"People will sometimes use the oil essence of rose when they want to open up their heart chakra. It goes well with lavender too. They will both activate, and open up the crown chakra. There are many different scents you could have inhaled, but I think rose would have suited you best. It signifies love. It's known to blend physical and spiritual love. It's also used to inspire the user. Rose strengthens and soothes the heart, which is what you need right now. And it helps soften complications in relationships. It should also help you appreciate the beauty around you, as well as invoking harmony and a feeling of well-being. It's especially good for relieving tension, depression, grief, sadness, resentment, and anger. The way I see it, this just described all your symptoms. But the most important element is that it opens up the heart, and allows love to enter.

"It makes sense to me that it should flow into the heart chakra. If you think about it, what is the heart chakra anyway? What does it do? It's unconditional love, compassion, forgiveness, balance, and understanding. It brings you peace and acceptance. The two together are a natural union. Add that with the lavender, and you seeing its scent entering your crown chakra, and I would say your mystery is solved. You are indeed being assisted from the other world. I would recommend you stop by my store and pick up some rose oil. It can't hurt. In fact, it will probably do you a world of good. Keep those scents around you today. You need as much healing energy as possible."

Lauren was always surprised at her friend's extreme knowledge on any subject. "OK, I hear what you're saying, and it makes a lot of sense. I couldn't have made that up on my own. It's obvious I'm being told what I need. I'm just curious how I knew."

Adriana interjected, "Because you have taught yourself to listen. That's all it takes. You had a hell of a night. Your worst nightmare couldn't have compared to what you lived through. You're exhausted both mentally and spiritually. If I were your doctor, I would tell you to heal yourself, and then seriously think about forgiving yourself. You can't go back and change the past. But you've already made great headway in changing your future. Lauren, forgive yourself. It's over, and you've learned from it. Don't keep happiness out of your life simply because you're misinterpreting your power. You have the power to overcome this. There's nobody out there who could go back in a prior lifetime, not to mention this life, and not find thousands of big karma producing mistakes. But that's why, by the grace of God, we are given one chance after another. Each one of us can be our own worst enemy if we allow it. Open your heart, not only to those you love, but to yourself, too."

Lauren nodded her head affirmatively. "Yeah, you're right. I know you're right. Don't you ever get tired of me saying that?"

Adriana laughed. "Are you kidding?"

"OK, I'm off to the store, then to the attorney's office, and then, I don't know. But I'll see you tonight, and if anything comes up, I'll contact you. Do I have it all remembered?"

Adriana giggled into the phone. "Yeah, I think I can depend on you."

Lauren blew her friend a kiss. "Always."

Alex never heard his alarm go off. It was the sound of seagulls soaring by his patio that finally forced him awake. He stretched his body, then jumped out of bed.

" It's 11:00! How in the hell did I sleep so late?"

He felt groggy and stiff from too much rest, but forced himself to the shower. Before stepping in, he looked in the mirror and tried to remember if he had dreamed, then shook his head.

"If I did, I can't remember now."

He felt almost grateful. Alex knew he had some processing to do from the evening before. His thoughts rolled back while the hot water splashed over his body. He took several deep cleansing breaths, attempting to dissolve all the fears associated with it. He tried talking himself into taking his new knowledge forward, and to leave the fear behind. He knew what had happened, and he realized how very painful it was to view. But he also knew that taking responsibility for his actions was just the first step.

"The final and most difficult step is truly forgiving myself."

Alex turned off the pelting water, and heard his phone ringing in the background. He grabbed a towel and stepped out of the shower, pushing the speaker button on the wall phone.

"Hello, Alex here."

"Hi, Alex, how's it going this morning?" It was Donovan. "Elliot and I are around the corner grabbing a bite to eat. Do you need a carry out? Have you eaten yet?"

Alex laughed. "Eaten? Hell, I just got out of bed. Yeah, bring me whatever you had, and let yourselves in. I just stepped out of the shower."

Donovan replied, "No problem, we'll see in you ten minutes."

Alex rubbed his face hard, determined to keep his mind in neutral. He slipped into a pair of black jeans and pullover sweater, then tidied up his bedroom before walking downstairs barefooted. He knew he would find a new perspective in daylight.

"It could be worse." Alex opened the back doors and walked out, bypassing his large patio and pool. He walked down the stone steps, and stood on the beach. He was overlooking the large rock formation that had been the meeting place for what seemed like eons.

"Hold on, my love. I'm sure we're both trying to figure all this out. And we will. We were both at fault. I hope you realize that shouldering all the responsibility is fruitless at this point. We'll get through this together, and hopefully, you'll forgive me for all the selfish acts I poured on you. Just don't give up."

Alex knew she wasn't there, but it made him feel better seeing the large rocks. It somehow made everything more real. In the distance, he heard Elliot's voice from above calling to him. Alex looked up at his patio and waved, then took the steps two at a time. His friends were making coffee in the kitchen. "What took you so long? I'm starving."

Elliot laughed and handed him a cup. "We're on time. You're the one who wasn't prepared. You could have at least made coffee."

Alex looked down and smiled. "Sorry. My mind's not all here today. I can't believe I slept so late."

Donovan walked in, putting the food on the table. "Look at the bright side. You'll be the only one not yawning at your show tonight."

It took Alex a moment to catch the joke. "Certainly, you're not saying that everyone else at my show will be yawning?"

Elliot laughed. "Alex, we aren't saying that, are we Donovan?"

Donovan stopped pouring himself a glass of milk, and looked to the ceiling, before responding. "Well, yeah, I suppose we are."

Alex laughed hard, grateful to his friends for elevating the mood, before breaking into another subject of conversation. He told his friends about his experience the evening before. He relayed all the horrid details about their fates. When he finished, his food had become cold, and his friends sat motionless with their mouths open in shock. The room was quiet for several moments, with everyone trying to find their breaths. Elliot finally spoke, barely above a whisper.

"God, Alex, that's horrific. How could something so right become so wrong? You lost your children?"

Donovan interrupted, shaking his head in shock. "I can't imagine. But I'm a little confused. How could you have produced such karma if you didn't know you were doing anything wrong?"

A crease developed across Alex's forehead as he spoke.

"That was a tough one for me, too. I didn't understand how ignorance, or being naïve, could cause such tragedy and karma. But I was forced to really examine the situation. While I was watching the scenes unfold, I could catch a glimpse of what the man was subconsciously thinking. On the most basic level, he knew what he was doing. He took advantage of her innocence, and played on it. She was brought up conservative and always taken care of. But her basic personality should have been one of independence. She was a very intelligent person, but for some reason, she didn't believe that a woman could be successful without a man. In reality, she was more creative than him. But he had the advantage of being very worldly, and male. He knew how to approach subjects to convince her that everything he did was perfect. He had become an icon in her eyes. He did everything for her. He made everything easy for her, almost to the point of living her life.

"Over time, she stopped questioning all thoughts of her own. She didn't know better at first, and when she finally consciously acknowledged it to herself, she found it impossible to change. She liked things the way they were. The problem accelerated when she gave up her independence and most of her power. She was unsuccessful in carrying out her dharma. And she basically failed to take any responsibility for her emotions and her life. She traded in growth and freedom for total comfort, and short-term security. Instead of teaching her to stand on her own, he encouraged her to follow him. He loved her more than life itself, and wanted to protect her more than anything. But you can't always protect another person from all the pains of the world. No matter what, he was determined to keep her out of harm's way. But if an animal doesn't know how to fend for themselves, what happens to them out in the wild? They die.

"She just wasn't prepared. They both did this out of conditional love for the other. There wasn't a lack of love. Far from it. Everything they thought they were doing was out of love for each other. A passionate love. But looking at the situation from a detached perspective, it was also out of fear, greed, and ego. She knew what she was supposed to develop in that life, and willingly failed to do so. He knew he was changing her to his own ways, but his ego would have it no other way. She was a prized possession to him. It wasn't a fifty-fifty partnership. He was controlling and had an enormous ego, and she refused to be strong and live her own life, or even think her own thoughts. Neither of them grew. He feared if he taught her how to be strong, she would be better than him, and she feared if she became her own person, he would no longer love her. Fear became the root to it all."

Donovan spoke up. "Yeah, but they loved more than most have ever loved. I suppose they should have loved unconditionally a little more and feared a little less."

Alex smiled. "Yes, the love was there. There's no doubt about that. But they used that love for their own selfish purposes. He could have controlled her, or nurtured her. On a different level, but one he was aware of, he chose control. Nurture would have been the correct solution. Ego, greed, and fear can do a lot in developing unwanted karma. To make matters worse, they both developed a lot of anger, and refused to forgive."

Elliot shook his head, not understanding. But Alex continued with the explanation.

"When her husband died, the woman wasn't able to cope. He had promised her he would always take care of her. She knew that would not always be possible, but she took his words as absolute truth. When he died, she was angry with him, and blamed him, refusing to forgive him. Yes, she wanted to be with him, but it was more from being out of control and weak. She couldn't find a way to forgive him, and wanted to punish him as well as herself. Seeing what was happening to her, he did get angry. He couldn't understand why she refused to be strong and independent. He couldn't understand, and in time, he had no compassion. He suddenly wanted her to be a fighter. He wanted her to carry out their plans. He wanted her to be something she wasn't prepared to be. She didn't know how to begin. When she lost the children, his intensity to all the issues increased. He loved her from the other side, but he couldn't forgive her. Both had failed to see what they had done to propel the emotions. Each thought they alone were the innocent ones. Well, they weren't. And it caused so much unnecessary pain. As we know, refusing to forgive yourself and others will only create more negative karma than one would want."

Donovan said, "So you have said you forgive her. And in your heart, you have. Doesn't that erase the karma for you both? Can you go on and meet now?"

Alex knew the answer. He had asked his own guide that question last night. "I wish it were that simple. Yes, in my heart, and on every level, I do forgive her. I don't judge her in the least. What I do feel is compassion and love. But more importantly, for my own growth, I have to forgive myself. That's the tough one."

Elliot looked deep within Alex. "Why would that be so tough? You are a very intelligent person. You have taught yourself to know right from wrong. You know your heart better than anyone. And, Alex, you know that was then, and this is now. You have come far beyond who you were then. You're learning what unconditional love is. You've learned what acceptance is. You're secure enough in yourself to not be fearful, and certainly to not make the same mistakes twice."

Alex was appreciative of his friend's words. "Intellectually, I understand what you're saying, and I agree with you. But it may take me a few days for the knowledge to soak in. As painful as it was, seeing my mistakes help. I've given this a lot of thought since last night, and I have to admit I have seen the controlling tendencies passed on in this life as well. Perhaps not as severe as before, but they have certainly been there."

Donovan stopped him. "Yeah, you tend to be controlling sometimes, but you're harder on yourself than you have ever been on anyone else. You're one of the most sensitive people I know. I've never seen you try and control someone else's lives, or their decisions. And that includes your ex-wife or girlfriends."

Elliot interrupted, "And recently, I've noticed you softening up on yourself. People can't say you don't try to be unconditional. I've learned a lot in that category from you. Alex, of course give it some more thought, but in the end, you have got to find a way to forgive yourself."

Alex smiled in frustration. "OK, and once I do that, how do I get her to do the same for me? How can this woman forgive me?"

Donovan answered quickly, "The same way you both forgive yourselves. When one is done, the other will follow. They're like magnets; unconditional love and forgiveness attract each other."

Alex proceeded to tell them about the colors, the scents of lavender and rose. He told them about the crown chakra and the heart chakra being prominent. By the time all the stories were told and discussed, it was well past 3:00.

Donovan looked down at his watch and cringed. "Vickie is going to kill me. She had a busy day at the gallery, so I promised her I'd run some errands before tonight. If I know what's good for me, I have got to go now. Otherwise, there won't be any forgiveness in my house tonight."

They all laughed as Elliot picked up his keys. "I have a few errands to run myself."

Alex cleaned up the kitchen, then sat down on the patio to clear his mind until he had to get ready and leave for the club. He closed his eyes and smiled when he inhaled the fragrances. They were still with him.

Lauren thought about the details from the night before on the drive to her appointment. She didn't want to think about Gary or the divorce until she arrived. She wanted to sort out her thoughts and try to come to a solution. She had to find a way of forgiving herself. She understood everything that had taken place between this man and woman. She felt it was mostly her fault for allowing everything to happen. And she was trying desperately to relieve herself of the guilt associated with it. Forgiving him was the easy part.

Lauren was glad when she arrived at the attorney's office at precisely noon, and found no one in the front office. She was nervous about seeing Gary under these circumstances, and wanted it to go smoothly and as quickly as possible.

"At least there's no anger with the divorce. Maybe I've learned something in this life after all."

She wished Gary happiness, and she knew he felt the same. They loved each other, but not as a husband and wife should. Even though their marriage was over, they still felt respect and good will for each other. Lauren thought about how she would have responded had he tried to seize everything they had built together.

I would have been disappointed in him, and I would have tried to reason with him, and compromise. If that hadn't worked, if for no other reason than for our girls, I would have tried everything in my power to detach and start over. Maybe the anger would have fueled the fire and kept my survival instinct active, but in time, I know I would have forgiven him. It would have just been one more lesson learned. What is, is.

But she knew this wasn't going to be the case. She was lucky that neither of them harbored any resentment. Their children came first, and she and Gary were determined to keep them away from such negative situations. It was a waste of time. And she had learned so much from this marriage. She had survived, and she had become independent and content.

"Yes, I'm proud of myself. No one can take that away from me."

She heard the front door open and saw Gary walk in. At the same time, the attorney's office door opened. Gary walked to Lauren as she stood up to accept his hug and kiss on the cheek. They both smiled at the other, then hugged again, this time less formally.

The attorney approached and shook their hands. Motioning the way into his office, he was the last to enter. Gary and Lauren both took a seat in chairs facing the desk. They waited until everyone was seated before Gary began the meeting.

"Mr. Coe, I know we've all been talking over the phone about the issues, and frankly I want to do everything fair. I've read the papers, and I'm ready to sign."

Lauren nodded her head. "I'm in agreement with Gary. We're both satisfied with the agreement, so let's get on with it."

Mr. Coe was taken aback. "In all my years practicing law, I dread divorce cases more than any other. Occasionally, I get a couple in my office who show the respect and maturity of you two. I wish I could see more. In the 'me' society that we seem to live in, it's nice to see your first thoughts were of your children, then how the other would benefit, and finally about yourselves. That shows a great deal of respect and trust. I commend you both."

Gary smiled. "Well, trust me, it hasn't been without its pain. We've both learned a lot from this marriage. And we know that we'll always remain friends."

Lauren smiled and continued, "At first, Gary and I talked about going to our separate attorneys to draw up the papers. We were going to try and go through the usual routine. But after further discussion, we decided there were no opposite sides to take, and that's what our prospective attorneys would have tried to convince us of. We wanted one neutral party that would look after us both, but with the children being priority." She turned to Gary. "I think our idea was a good one."

Gary took her hand. "Yeah, we always did better when we tried to compromise. I didn't want our lawyers hashing out our lives as if we were a piece of meat. This way was much better."

Mr. Coe pulled the file and spread it out on his desk. "Then why don't you both take a look at the agreement one last time, and if everything is satisfactory, you can go ahead and sign. Then I'll petition on Monday. Everything should be granted in a few months."

Gary and Lauren both read over the paperwork and signed where it was indicated. Neither had any remorse. They were both now looking forward to new paths.

Gary and Lauren shook their lawyer's hand, and walked out of his office together. Both were quiet until they reached the car. Gary opened Lauren's car door and allowed her to sit down behind the steering wheel. He was about to close the door when he stopped and looked at her.

"Lauren, you are such a beautiful woman. Has anyone told you that lately?"

Lauren laughed. "No, Gary, I haven't heard that in a while. Well, unless Adriana counts."

Gary returned the laugh. "I don't know why I felt I had to tell you that, but just accept it. You are beautiful both inside and out."

Lauren smiled. "Thank you, Gary. That means a lot coming from you. When does your plane leave? Do you have time for lunch?"

Gary glanced at his watch. "I delayed my flight until later tonight. If it's all right with you, I thought I'd see about packing up my things and moving them out of the house. I've made plans to store them until I know what I'm going to do with it."

Lauren shook her head. "Gary, you know you're welcome to leave anything you want at the house. It's safe."

Gary looked down at her thoughtfully. "Yeah, I know, but I think it would be best. It's mostly just the rest of my clothes, and hobby items."

Lauren understood. "Of course. You're welcome to take anything you like. Why don't we go back to the house, and I'll make us a quick lunch while you pack?"

Gary was quick to take Lauren up on her offer. "Why don't you go ahead, and I'll meet you there in an hour?"

Lauren looked at her watch. It was 1:30. "That's fine. I have plenty of time."

Driving home seemed to take just moments. Lauren had returned to thinking about her visions from the night before. The tension seemed to be loosening its grip. She knew she would meditate tonight, and begin the process of self-forgiveness. She knew that would be a start, and possibly an ending too. Then her thoughts changed to Gary. Lauren refused to think about what she would do without him over the holidays, and the parties, and the children's activities. She spoke aloud, chastising herself.

"The same as I've always done. Don't try and glamorize our lives at this late date. This was precisely how you grew to be so independent and strong. He wasn't there most of the time. He was building his career, and you were building yours. Don't make it what it's not. What it never was."

With a clear head, she smiled and parked her car in the garage. She habitually slipped her shoes off at the door, and strolled directly into the kitchen to prepare lunch. She looked at her watch again. "I have plenty of time."

Lauren had a few minutes before Gary arrived, and called Adriana to give her an update, but no one answered her private phone. She opted to leave a quick message, telling her she was mentally fine, and was preparing lunch for her and Gary. Lauren thought Adriana would find humor in that statement. She finished by saying she would contact her later. She heard the doorbell, and knew it was Gary.

Lauren answered the door and suggested he start packing while she finished preparing lunch. She knew the process was going to be difficult, and he needed the alone time to let go. She could hear him in each room as she forced herself to continue cooking. She wanted to reach out to him, and tell him that he was doing the right thing. She didn't want guilt and doubts to creep into his mind. When it became too quiet, she walked to the foot of the stairs and told him lunch was ready.

Gary was quiet as he trudged downstairs. Her heart went out to him while she watched him walk slowly into the breakfast room. His eyes were red, and he looked very tired. She didn't mention what she saw, but instead, made festive conversation during the meal. She forced him to talk about his work, and the children. She told him about the construction problems of her new boutique. By the time lunch was finished, it was well past 5:00. Lauren realized they had spent the afternoon in conversation, and Gary had much more packing to do. She didn't want to push or pressure him to finish.

It's still his house too, though no longer his home.

After an hour of pacing the living room, she finally decided she had no choice but to call Adriana and Cindy. She found Adriana in her car.

"Hi, Adriana. It's me."

Adriana heard the tone of her voice and worried. "Lauren, are you all right? Is Gary still there? How's it going?"

Lauren smiled into the phone. "Everything is fine. The appointment went off without a hitch. Gary decided to come back here and pack. We had a nice long lunch, and a longer conversation. He's back upstairs packing now. But I thought I'd better phone you. There's a good possibility I won't be able to make it to the club tonight. I don't know what time Gary will be finished, and I don't want to push him. The packing is affecting

413

him more than I thought it would. I just don't want to leave him alone right now. If he leaves early enough, you'll see me; otherwise, we can meet for brunch tomorrow, if you like."

Adriana sounded worried. "Are you sure you don't want me to come over and stay with you?" Then she realized how silly her question was. "Of course you don't need me. What's wrong with me? It's Gary, for heaven's sake. Lauren, you do what you have to do. There's no problem about tonight, except you won't see me in my gorgeous dress. If you don't make it tonight, we'll have brunch tomorrow. And if I'm lucky, I'll still be wearing the dress."

Lauren laughed out loud, but was grateful. "Are you sure? You're not angry that I backed out at such short notice?"

"Oh, Lauren, of course not. Don't worry about me. I'll know lots of people at the club. No, you just do what needs to be done there, and if you need me, just call."

Lauren was relieved. "Thanks, I really appreciate it. I'll talk to you later. Oh, and Adriana, have fun."

Lauren called and left an apologetic message with Cindy. Then finding nothing else to do, she sat quietly in the kitchen and waited.

Lauren tried to visualize the color and fragrance of lavender and roses. She tried to visualize her charkas, and the colors entering and charging them. She tried everything to relax her mind, but she was too preoccupied with Gary's energy being in the house. She would wait until he left. In the meantime, she cleaned the kitchen, then completed some much needed work on the new boutique. She hadn't realized what time it was until Gary walked into the room and sat across from her desk. He looked exhausted.

"Lauren, I hope I didn't keep you from anything tonight. I didn't realize it would take me this long, but I think I'm finished now. Everything is loaded into the car. And if I've forgotten anything, just call me."

Lauren looked up from her computer and smiled. "Don't worry about me, I had nothing pressing planned. And if I come across anything of yours, of course I'll call. You know you're welcome here any time."

Gary looked at his watch. "Gee, Lauren, I hate to go, but it's getting late, and my flight leaves in a few hours. I have just enough time to get my things organized, and get to the airport."

Gary stood up and walked to the door, with Lauren following behind him. They both stopped in the foyer and looked at each other. Neither knew what to say, so Gary took her in his arms and hugged her for several moments. He pulled her away to look at her, and saw she was on the verge of tears. Gary opened the door and turned once again to Lauren. "I love you, Lauren, and I wish you only the very best of everything. Please know that you can call on me for anything, at any time. I'll always be here for you if you need me. That goes for the kids too."

Lauren looked down at the floor as a tear dropped from her cheek.

"Of course, Gary. And you do the same. If you ever need me, you know where to find me. I love you too. Drive carefully."

And he was gone. A chapter in her life ending with the close of a door. It was over. She didn't know whether to be relieved, or cry out in pain. She climbed the stairs mentally exhausted, feeling both.

Chapter 20

Alex warmed up at home before going to the club. He wanted his voice to be in perfect pitch for the show. By 6:15, he was dressed and ready for his drive to the club. His spirits were soaring after the meditation he had had on the patio earlier in the day. He opened his mind, allowing wisdom to enter. There were no revelations, but he felt the inner work he had done was tremendous. He wanted to be ready when he next saw her.

He looked at himself once more in the mirror. He scrutinized his tightly pulled back hair, and the even tighter fitting black jeans and shirt, then decided he was ready to go. His mind wandered while he was on the road, and he was pulling up to Jupiter's before he realized how far he had driven. The nervousness that Alex was anticipating found him as he walked into the club. Seeing the other band members made him realize they were really going to put on a show. They spent the next hour setting up, and doing sound checks. By 8:00, the doors opened and they could relax an hour before going on.

He and Ron walked out from behind the stage to the tables below. Alex saw Cindy first and approached, kissing her on the cheek. He glanced around, noticing there were already at least ten people he knew.

He turned to Ron and commented under his breath, "Well, it looks as though your wife has found us a crowd again this year. How many are we expecting?"

Ron laughed and sat down next to his wife. "A full house."

Elliot walked in next, kissing and hugging everyone before sitting at the end, on the other side of Cindy. "How is everyone?"

Cindy returned Elliot's hug. "I haven't seen you in ages. How's work?"

He mocked a cringe. "Work is going wonderful. Better than I could imagine. Now, no more questions about work."

Cindy handed him a drink and all was forgiven.

By 8:45, the club was full, and there were very few chairs left at their large table. Donovan and Vickie had shown up just after Elliot. Alex almost forgot their band was the major attraction for the first half of the evening.

Cindy looked around the room, and then turned to Vickie. "I suppose they wanted to get us oldsters out early, so the young ones could take over after midnight. When was the last time you got home after midnight?"

Vickie laughed at her friend. "Only when I'm working. But who has time to do anything else?"

At precisely 9:00, the band members walked on stage and got ready. Elliot looked up, staring at the front door each time someone new came in. It didn't go unnoticed by Donovan.

"What's up with you? Are you expecting a woman, or the police?"

Elliot laughed at the thought. "Neither. I just like to people-watch."

He had no other explanation, and laughed again at himself.

An announcer interrupted the background club music, and the room went dark. The announcer's voice introduced the band with such eloquence, he received an ovation. Cindy turned to Elliot and spoke loudly above the applause, "Only in L.A."

The first chord of the music began, and the place went quiet. Everyone was there to hear the band.

The spotlight suddenly hit Alex, and he panicked for a moment. Behind him, he heard Ron's soothing voice. "We're going to do our regulars first, then let's do your songs last, Alex." Alex nodded his head and began.

Adriana slipped in quietly during the first song, but didn't go unnoticed. She was beautiful. Cindy waved to her, blowing her a kiss. Adriana did the same back. Then she waved to everyone she knew, and took the one seat left at the opposite end of the table. She looked around once more, feeling comfortable with the crowd. After ordering her drink, Adriana finally had the opportunity to listen to the band. She knew Ron. And she had seen a few of the other members in her store. She didn't know the singer, but was very impressed by him. She relaxed, and allowed the songs to leave their impressions as they flowed through her mind. She was about to take a sip of her drink when an intense psychic impression ripped through her brain. She jerked her eyes open wider, and directed them at Alex. "What is it about him?"

She tried to think back to when she could have heard him perform elsewhere. She had no memory of an encounter, but she couldn't shake the feeling she had met him somewhere before. His voice was relaxing her, causing her to fight the urge to take off her shoes and put her feet up. She giggled at the thought. Then Adriana heard someone speak to her in the background. She heard herself responding, but only physically. She was having a difficult time fighting his energy in the room. *Where do I know this guy?*

She thought about Lauren, and a solution was right at the edge of her mind when it suddenly went blank. Adriana knew she wasn't going to retrieve it in the next hour, so she decided to stop analyzing, and enjoy the show instead.

Alex was into the third song when Adriana felt a warm feeling run down her spine. She took another sip of her drink and allowed herself time to look around her table once again. She looked straight ahead, and was surprised to see someone sitting in front of her. She hadn't noticed him before. He was looking straight into her eyes. She looked away, embarrassed, but curiosity got the better of her, and she glanced up again. He was still watching her. Adriana smiled slightly, and tilted her head as if to say hello. Elliot raised his glass slightly off the table as if to toast her.

Who is this gorgeous guy in front of me? And why's he looking at me?

Adriana looked away, then glanced back again. His attention was back to the stage, and the beautiful song Alex was singing. Adriana suddenly had another psychic impression, but this time she felt she had seen the man seated in front of her somewhere.

She strongly reprimanded herself. "Girl, you really need to get out more. Everyone seems familiar tonight. You don't get out enough to know all these people."

But she couldn't shake the feeling that she knew both men from somewhere. Adriana pushed her thoughts aside and allowed the music and Alex's voice to sweep her away, until six songs had been sung, and it was time for a break. She ordered another drink when she heard the house music begin playing.

Cindy walked over to her and hugged her tight. "I'm so glad you could make it. When I heard Lauren wasn't coming, I was worried you couldn't come either." Cindy looked at Adriana again. "My God, that dress is gorgeous on you. It's from Lauren's, isn't it?"

Before Adriana had a chance to respond, Cindy continued, "No one else's clothes make me look as good as Lauren's Place. She must put a spell on us, or the clothes. I don't know and I don't care, as long as I can keep affording them."

Adriana laughed. "No, Cindy, I had nothing keeping me away tonight. I was looking forward to it. And yes, the dress came from Lauren's. She'd kill me if I bought anywhere else." She was about to continue when she heard a male voice next to her.

"I'm glad nothing kept you away. Hi, I'm Elliot." She took his hand, and froze in place. She felt herself fighting for control again. Adriana tried to speak in a solid voice, but it came out as a whisper. "I'm Adriana. I know this sounds like a line our parents would have used, but have we met somewhere before?"

Elliot laughed. "My question was going to sound as trite. I feel we have, but I can't remember where. You look so familiar."

They both laughed as if they had known each other for years.

Cindy spoke up. "Adriana owns Moonglows over on Melrose. Elliot is a magazine editor for Life and Living. Maybe that's where you guys have seen each other."

Elliot thought for a moment. "I've been in Moonglows several times, but I don't think that's where we've met. I've called there for information once or twice, but I think I'd remember talking to you."

Adriana replied, "No, it wasn't me. I would have remembered that."

Cindy reassured them both. "Adriana has the psychic touch, so if anyone can remember where or when, it'll be her."

Adriana felt a warmth run through her veins. She was about to speak when Ron and Alex approached. Ron hugged Adriana and asked where Lauren was.

"She sends her apologies, but she had some personal business to take care of tonight. I hope there's a repeat performance soon. I know she wouldn't want to miss it. You guys sound just wonderful."

Alex extended his hand. "Hi, I'm Alex Chandler. I'm glad you like our little band. You're a friend of Cindy's? I'm surprised we've never met before."

Adriana took Alex's hand, her mind's eye catching a brief glimpse of the letter that Lauren had retrieved in Connecticut. She jerked back briefly, hoping Alex hadn't noticed. She couldn't explain it herself, and she tried to catch her breath and regain her balance within a second.

"Yes, we've known each other for quite some time. I've only recently met Vickie, and have been introduced to her wonderful gallery."

Vickie heard her name and looked up. She came over and hugged Adriana, and winked.

"Yes, we've had some exciting times in my gallery."

Adriana laughed and winked back. "I'll have to come back

when I have more time to shop for myself."

Vickie brought Donovan over, and introduced them. With each hand that Adriana shook, the feeling of familiarity increased. She couldn't keep her opinions to herself any longer.

"This is turning into an evening of déjà vu for me."

She looked over at Donovan, Alex, and Elliot, speaking straight to them. "It really does seem as if we've all met somewhere before."

Elliot laughed. "Watch out. She's already used that line on me."

They all smirked at the joke, and shook their heads. Alex looked at Adriana for a moment before responding.

"I don't think we've met, but I know that feeling."

She looked into Alex's eyes again for further explanation on the flash that she had momentarily forgotten. Elliot spoke to the men gathered at the table. "Adriana owns Moonglows."

Alex's eyes rounded wide. "You do? I've been in there a few times. I come out with sack loads. I recently talked to your co-worker, Mark. He was very helpful."

Donovan nudged Alex. "That's the bookstore we were trying to get information from."

Elliot smiled knowingly. "Yes, that's right, Alex. Wasn't there something you needed to find out?"

Adriana spoke up. "I'll be happy to help you. What were you looking for?"

Alex was quiet for a moment, thinking about his question.

"It doesn't matter now. I found most of the answers from the books that I bought. You have a great place." Donovan and Elliot looked hard at Alex, not understanding why he didn't want to pursue the matter further. They caught Alex shaking his head in their direction, as he continued, "It certainly is crowded in here tonight, isn't it?"

They understood his message and let it drop.

Everyone began to notice the chemistry between Elliot and

Adriana, and politely began excusing themselves. When the two of them were the only ones left standing, Elliot looked deep into Adriana's eyes, causing her to blush.

"What do you see in there?"

She was frustrated with herself for not being more poetic, but she considered herself lucky to be able to make any sound at all.

He turned away, embarrassed. "I don't know. You're just so damn familiar. It really is a night for déjà vu."

Elliot fumbled in his pocket and pulled out his business card.

"I would appreciate you taking this."

She gladly accepted, then gave him her card. He took it from her, touching her hand in the process. Both noticed the warm chills running up and down their spines. It was Elliot's turn to blush as he spoke. "If we have met somewhere before, I don't want us to lose track of each other again. Do you want to go somewhere after the show?"

Adriana smiled. "I'd love to, but I have an emergency at the store. That's why I was late. I don't know how long I can stay. I've got to get back to work. But I agree, let's not stay strangers."

Elliot responded warmly, "I don't think we ever were."

They hadn't noticed the house music was lowered and the band members had taken their place on the stage again. Elliot pulled a chair next to Adriana so he could get a better view of the band, and of her.

Alex was now sitting on a stool, with the spotlight directed on him. He spoke in low tones, more relaxed now.

"We're going to play a few more familiar songs. But before we get started, I want to say that we'll also be performing a few songs that I recently wrote. They're very near and dear to my heart. So, if you don't like them, lie to me."

The audience laughed and sounded their approval. Alex continued, "The next six songs tell a story. A few of you will know some of the songs, others won't. But either way, I hope you enjoy them. The story is about realizing there is nothing without love."

As he started the first song, 'Street of Dreams', it was obvious the audience was held captive. His voice was smooth and professional, and each note held the deep personal feelings he was trying to convey.

Adriana and Elliot had unknowingly moved closer to each other by the time the song was over. During the second song, they didn't realize their hands were touching. It was only apparent how close they were to each other when during the third song, she felt her text go off. She had to struggle to read the message. Elliot watched her face, and knew it was an emergency when she looked up at him. She looked into Elliot's eyes as if she never wanted to forget them. He returned the mournful look.

"Do you have to go?"

Adriana nodded her head. He squeezed her hand. "Can I call you?"

She nodded her head again, and mouthed, "Yes, please."

Elliot kissed her hand, barely touching his lips to her velvet skin, and then walked her to her car. As the fourth song was beginning, Adriana turned around after the building door had closed. She stood there for a brief second, then shook her head.

"No, it couldn't have been the song."

She turned back around and followed her escort.

While Elliot walked Adriana to her car, he told her that she was going to miss the songs Alex had written. He told her the songs were about his newfound life. He suddenly stopped himself from going any further with the story. He knew not to say anymore about Alex's personal world. Adriana was so easy to talk to, he had to bite his lip to keep from telling her everything. He somehow felt she would understand, but he had promised his friend that it would stay between them. She didn't have any inclination to ask what he was talking about. She couldn't get Lauren's song out of her head. She would reprimand herself in her own dreams later that night.

He opened her car door, then stopped and looked again into her sparkling green eyes. Adriana looked away for a moment to catch her breath. Elliot touched a strand of her hair, fingering it against his palm. She couldn't help but look up into his eyes again, and they both slowly pushed forward, kissing passionately. Adriana couldn't remember a time she had been so bold, but she felt as if it was a long time in coming. Their thoughts were the same.

Where do I know this wonderful person from, and why does it feel so natural?

Nothing else was said as she pulled her car out of the driveway heading towards Melrose Avenue. She felt a smile on her face, while humming 'Where or When' with zeal. Not even an office emergency could get her down tonight.

Elliot walked back into the club happier than he could ever remember being. He sat down quietly, and watched his friend with affection.

Alex closed his eyes, taking a deep breath, and sang better than he ever had. He seemed to be in an altered state, but he could hear his voice and feel the emotion. It seemed to be coming from another realm.

When Alex sang the first sentence of 'Where or When', a rush of new energy fell across the room. Everyone was spellbound, knowing he was singing from immense personal sentiment and passion. He fought the lump in his throat and continued. And without taking a breath, Alex went right into the first of his new songs.

No one moved a muscle while they watched him sing with intense emotion.

"Words of wonder… words of hope… words of love… words to remind us of our past… I have loved you in our present… I will love you in our future… I will love you always… time will hold the answers… to the questions in our hearts… memories of you keep my love strong… every second that we're apart…"

Tears were forming in eyes across the room as he went directly into the last song without stopping the music.

"Now and forever… no matter where or when… we shall always be together… when we remember again… when you remember the songs… we'll be together again… never forget… no matter where or when… always remember… we'll be together again."

He lowered his head on the last note, and brushed away a tear. The music stopped and the crowd was quiet. He didn't notice for several moments. The room held an energy that couldn't be contained. Everyone was in awe of the electricity being emitted. Elliot began clapping first, breaking the spell. Within seconds, everyone was on their feet, dabbing at tears, and screaming for an encore. Alex wasn't prepared for such an outpouring of acceptance. He turned behind him to the other band members. They were brushing away the emotion as well.

Ron bent down to Alex. "Can you do one more?"

Alex shook his head no at first. He was exhausted.

Ron looked at him again. "Just one."

Alex obliged, singing a song that was soft and soothing to the senses. Then the evening was over before he knew it. He was mentally exhausted, and slipped out of the club after his performance, driving home in silence.

He saw the message light blinking in the darkness, before he made it into his office. It was from Elliot.

"Call me when you get home. We need to talk."

Lauren wanted answers, and was anxious to meditate. It didn't take her long to get prepared. There was nothing stopping her now. Gary was no longer an issue, and she felt ready to begin again.

She sat on her balcony, seeing only darkness amid the millions of stars flickering all around her.

"All I ask for is forgiveness. Forgiveness from him, and from myself."

She was about to take her first deep breath when the phone rang. Lauren thought about ignoring it, but remembered the time of night.

"This can't be good news."

She picked up the phone, quickly preparing herself for what was in store. "Hello."

It was Adriana, and she sounded out of breath.

"Lauren, are you awake? I really need to talk to you."

It took Lauren a few moments to grasp who was calling.

"Adriana, is that you? Where are you? Is everything all right?"

Adriana was still gasping for air, but tried to remain in control. "I'm in my car on the way to the office."

Lauren interrupted her friend. "The office? I thought you were going to the club tonight. What happened?"

Adriana tried to regain control. "I did go. That's what I'm calling about. Unfortunately, I was called away with this ongoing emergency at the office. Bad timing to say the least."

Lauren was relieved that everything was ok, but couldn't help but hear the tone of Adriana's voice.

"What's wrong? What happened tonight?"

Adriana took a deep breath and began. "Lauren, this night was a dream come true. In all my years on this good Earth, I have never experienced feelings like I did tonight. Déjà vu was the reigning queen of the evening."

Lauren shook her head. "I'm not following you. What happened, and more importantly, are you all right?"

Adriana laughed. "I couldn't be better. This is so confusing for me, and I'm trying to find a place to begin."

"OK, take a deep breath and start at the beginning. You say you went to the club tonight. What happened at the club?"

Adriana took another breath. "I went to the club. I was a little late, and took a seat at the end of the table. The band was already playing, and they were spectacular. Everyone was there, and everyone sends their love to you. Anyway, I got a huge sensation of déjà vu when I saw the singer. I think his name is Alex. He was fantastic and kept the energy in the room at an all-time high. Maybe that's what started all this. I don't know and I don't care."

Lauren wasn't getting the information she requested. "Adriana, what the hell happened?"

"I just don't understand what happened, or how it happened. I wasn't expecting anything. Isn't that always how it happens…?"

Lauren interrupted again. "Am I going to have to sit here all night until you are ready to tell me the story?"

Adriana laughed. "Oh, sorry. As I was saying, the singer was great and a very nice man. He had such charisma, I couldn't take my eyes off him. But I felt I knew him from somewhere. Lauren, I just know he's someone you would like to meet. He's a very nice guy…"

Lauren spoke up. "As if I don't have enough problems, are you trying to fix me up with someone?"

Adriana giggled. "Lord, no. I'm just saying there's something about this guy I can't put my finger on. But that's not why I'm calling. That's just the beginning of the story. I closed my eyes for just a moment, and when I opened them, there was the most beautiful man I've ever seen in my life sitting before me. I don't know how I could've missed him. But when I looked up, there he was. And he was looking into my eyes. He never wavered. I didn't know what to do. Nothing like this has ever happened before. I thought I was losing my mind. That déjà vu sensation was even more intense with him. I know without a doubt that I know this man from somewhere. I must, because I feel as if I've known him forever."

Lauren smiled into the phone. "It sounds as if you have got your first taste of love."

Adriana continued, "Just wait. As soon as the band took a break, this guy, Elliot is his name, came over to me. We couldn't take our eyes off each other. Within ten minutes, it was as if we had been together for years. The comfort level was incredible. He also had the feeling he'd met me somewhere. And before you ask, no, it wasn't a line because I used it first. He said he had been in my store several times, but if I had been there, believe me, I would have noticed him. I must have been upstairs. It figures I'd be at the wrong place, at the wrong time. Then right in the middle of things, my text went off, and I had to leave for the office. He walked me out to my car. It was so natural. We literally had no choice but to kiss. You know how slowly I go, but not tonight. I wanted him like I've never wanted anyone in my life. Without knowing this man, I know that he is the one I've been looking for my entire life. I only hope he feels the same."

Lauren was quiet for a moment, taking in all the information she was receiving. When she finally had something to say, she was soft-spoken.

"Adriana, are you sure about this? Who invited him to the club? You can't remember where you know him from?"

Adriana's voice was filled with excitement. "I am absolutely sure about this. I always wondered if I would know a soul mate when I found one. I'm glad to say I did. I want to say he did too. The look in his eyes, and the way he spoke to me, and the energy between us was incredible. I have no doubt there was a connection from the other side. Where did he come from? Hmmm. Well, he seemed to know everyone at the table intimately. And I think Cindy said that he's the singer's best friend. So, I would suppose through him. Everyone seemed to know each other. He is the editor for Life and Living magazine. I'm sure Cindy could tell us much more about him. Unfortunately, I couldn't find out too much between the music, and the damn text. I hate to call you this late, but I had to. Lauren, I think my life is changing, too. I don't feel as if there will be games played in this relationship. He seems to be a straight shooter, and our connection went far beyond those kinds of games and immaturity. I do believe it was mutual."

Lauren was thrilled for her friend. "I wish you didn't have to go to work. We'd stay up all night and talk about this. I'm glad everyone in the group knows him. Isn't it odd that there's another part of the group out there that we have never met? I can't wait to meet him."

Adriana was in a blissful state. "I know, but I suppose we have members of our group the others don't know either. I want you to meet him. Listen to me! I'm making plans like we're a couple."

She lowered her tone. "But, Lauren, I think we are. It wasn't my imagination what was going on between us. He's supposed to call in the morning. And I have no doubt that he will call, and no doubt that you will like him."

Lauren didn't know why she asked the next question. "What did you say his friend's name was?"

Adriana was quick in her response, "Alex. Alex, uh. Well, damn, I can't think of his last name now. I'm surprised I know my own name at the moment. Lauren, I'd put my money on this guy making it big if he wanted to. He's that good. Ron and the entire band were that good. If they decide to play again anytime soon, you have to come. I won't take no for an answer."

Lauren laughed. "I would love to. I thought I might know him. But I don't think I know an Alex. However, it does make me wonder why it's familiar to me too."

Adriana thought for a moment. "I don't know. He's close friends with Cindy and Ron. Also, Vickie's fiancé, Donovan. They're all really nice people."

Adriana suddenly remembered why Lauren couldn't keep their appointment. "Lauren, how did it go with you tonight? Is everything all right?"

Lauren smiled warmly into the phone. "Adriana, you amaze me. Even with all this excitement glowing around you, you still manage to remember me. Everything is fine. All the paperwork is signed, sealed, and delivered. Now, it's just a matter of waiting for the divorce to become final. Gary and I both feel fine with it. It wasn't a mistake, and fortunately, we became good friends. He packed up everything and moved out tonight. He didn't leave until late. But overall, I'm all right, and relieved it's over. I was about to meditate to find out why I did so many stupid things in the last life, then ask for forgiveness. I hope once all has been forgiven, this person and I may be able to connect the way you and your friend

Elliot have. I just have to believe in miracles."

Adriana was surprised. "Lauren, after all the verification you have received so far, don't tell me you still don't believe in miracles."

"Yes, I do believe. I just hope they can grant me my one big miracle. Conjuring up a man from my dreams is a pretty tall order."

Adriana wouldn't let her friend doubt. "It will happen, and this time, it will be right. There won't be any negative karma hanging over your heads. You've worked hard for it, and you deserve it."

Adriana pulled up to the store and turned off her engine. "Lauren, I'm here, so I'd better hang up. Hopefully, I won't be here all night. We'll get together."

Lauren was about to hang up when Adriana stopped her. "Wait, Lauren. Thank you for being there for me. I knew it would be all right to call you this late."

Lauren softened her grip on the phone. "I love you."

Adriana smiled. "I love you too."

Alex listened to the message from Elliot again. "Call me when you get home. We need to talk."

Alex listened to Elliot's tone of voice, trying to get an idea about what was so important, but couldn't. He had never heard his friend's voice sound so cautiously serious. Worried that something wasn't right, Alex immediately picked up the phone and punched in his friend's number. Elliot answered immediately. Alex didn't wait for a greeting.

"Elliot, what's wrong? That tone of voice is usually reserved for something I've done, or when you're trying to talk me out of something I want to do. Is everything all right?"

Elliot was uncomfortably quiet, then spoke slowly. "Alex, I don't know what happened tonight. I don't know where to turn. You've got to talk me through this."

Alex was getting alarmed. "Elliot, what the hell is wrong? What happened? I'll do anything you ask, but you have to tell me what's going on."

Elliot cleared his throat before he spoke again. "Alex, first of all, I want to tell you that you were terrific tonight. In fact, you have never sounded better. Your new songs held so much energy, the room was about to burst. I am so proud of you, and of your work. And perhaps it's because of the effect you had on the room tonight that made everything happen the way it did. I don't know. That's what I'm trying to figure out. Maybe it would have happened anywhere. On the sidewalk, in a grocery store. I just don't know. This is all so foreign to me, and so completely unexpected. I just don't know what to feel except grateful, thankful, blissful."

Alex stopped his friend in mid-sentence. "Elliot, I don't know what you're talking about. I'm glad you liked the performance tonight. I really am, but you aren't telling me what I want to know. Where did all of these 'fuls' come from? Grateful? Thankful? Blissful? What was so unexpected? What's going on?"

Elliot laughed at his friend's reaction. "Gee, Alex, now you know how it feels. This seems to be the kind of thing Donovan and I have had to put up with lately."

Alex was surprised. "Well, next time, slap me upside the head. Now tell me what this is all about."

Elliot started slow. "Alex, I think I have found the woman of my dreams. I said I would never go through it again, and frankly, this time yesterday I was very happy and content with my life the way it was. Now, I'm questioning everything."

Alex was stunned. "Elliot, have you been drinking? Sit down and tell me the story about this new Elliot."

Alex was trying to make light of this new development, but he was actually taking it very seriously.

Elliot continued, "Remember the woman you were introduced to tonight? The one I was talking to with Cindy? Her name is Adriana. She's the one who owns Moonglows. Alex, from the moment I laid eyes on her, I knew she was sent from heaven. I can't explain it. I've never felt like this before about any woman, and never thought I would. I feel as if she has been with me for lifetimes. The comfort level was inconceivable. Needless to say, I think we were both a bit more forward than either have the experience of being, but it was as if we wanted to make up for lost time. And there was no better time like the present."

Alex spoke up. "So she feels the same as you?"

Elliot didn't have to think about his answer. "Yes, I think so. The energy between us seemed mutual. Without knowing this woman intimately, I feel as though she is indeed everything I have always prayed for. I know her. I don't know how I know her, but I do. Have I been around you too long?"

Alex laughed. "God, I hope not. I wouldn't wish what I'm going through on anyone. If this is true love, then you are indeed one of the lucky ones. There doesn't seem to be an impossible obstacle course for you to go through before receiving your gold medal. I wish I could have been that lucky. But if I couldn't be, then I'm glad it came easily for you. Have you ever met her before?"

Elliot thought for a moment. "There was an intense feeling of déjà vu the moment I saw her. One moment she wasn't there, and the next moment she was. It was very strange. I kept trying to place where we could have met. I've been in her store, but I never saw her. I would have remembered. I wouldn't have got out of there without some sort of an encounter. We were just getting cozy when she had an emergency at the store and had to leave the club. Unfortunately, she missed your new songs. She said if you play again, she wouldn't miss it."

Alex could feel there was something Elliot wasn't mentioning, and so he asked his friend. "What else is going on with you?"

Elliot hesitated for a moment. "Actually, it's more about you. We began this whole thing with you and your dreams by going to Moonglows for information. Now that we know the owner, wouldn't it be easier to just directly ask her for help? You know she has the knowledge. I would never go behind your back with such personal information, but just say the word and I'll get you all the help you need."

Alex didn't have to think about it. "No, thank you. A few months ago, I would have been happy to share this information with her. We did in fact try, but it's not meant to be now. This relationship with whoever I'm seeing has gone beyond mere dreams. And it's much too personal for me to go around telling strangers. They would try and commit me to an asylum. No, I'd appreciate keeping this to ourselves for a while longer."

Elliot tried to be more convincing. "Alex, I'm sure she's heard every story known to man. Hell, you can't help but hear a few just walking into the place. But she's a very grounded person, and I know she would be willing to do what she can."

Alex took a deep breath. "I know you mean well, but this must be done my way. The less people who know about this, the better. For now."

Elliot understood. "All right, if it means that much to you, I won't say anything. But I sure hope this is over soon, and you find the woman in your dreams. Surely, the factor of forgiveness is the last major wall between the two of you. Have you figured out how you're going to work it?"

Alex thought for a moment. "I suppose the same way I've done all along. Just meditate, then allow it to happen. I have found that whatever happens is going to happen anyway, and the best thing I can do is just hang on, and go with the flow. But one way or the other, I hope it's almost over, too. I'm tired."

Elliot was about to speak, but Alex continued, "Elliot, I'm very happy for you. Adriana seems like a very nice, beautiful lady. And I know she'll fit in with our craziness just fine. How does she come to know everyone?"

Elliot had to think. "Well, it seems Cindy has been hiding her from us. They met through a mutual friend who owns a boutique in Santa Monica. Cindy apparently did the interior design for her. They were introduced through that assignment. They've been friends ever since. I overheard them talking about the other woman. I think she's the one Vickie wanted to set you up with. I overheard Vickie telling Cindy that she had asked, but you flatly refused. Now that Vickie has put the bug in Cindy's ear, you may be bombarded by the both of them."

Alex laughed. "Well, they can bombard all they want. I'm not interested. I have other hurdles to cross first." Alex paused, then surprised himself by the next question. "Elliot, did they say what the woman's name was?"

Elliot was confused. "What woman? You mean the woman they're trying to convince you to meet? I think her name is Laura, or Lori, or Lauren. Yeah, that's it. They were talking about her shop, with all the fabulous clothes. Every sentence was fabulous this, and fabulous that. They said she was opening another shop in Beverly Hills. Apparently, Cindy is decorating that store too. And Vickie is selling her some artwork." He continued with a smirk, "I don't know why I was left alone with those women. Karma, I guess."

Alex laughed and asked Elliot to keep him informed about the progression of the relationship. "I appreciate you not trying to fix me up with this woman too. But I'm sure you understand my heart is elsewhere, and that's where it's going to stay."

Elliot nodded his head. "I understand. I'll call you tomorrow."

Lauren opted for sleep after Adriana's call. She tried to meditate, but her mind was racing.

"I wish I could have gone tonight. I would have enjoyed watching those two fall in love. It sounds amazing."

Lauren was genuinely happy for her friend. She knew Adriana worked far too much, the same as her. But Adriana had never had a long-term committed relationship. Her store was her first love, and she was totally committed to it. Lauren was going to enjoy watching her friend blossom.

She laid in bed for a few more minutes before pressing the play button on her CD player, then turning off the lights. She was exhausted. It took only one deep breath to fall into a deep sleep.

Lauren opened her eyes and found she had been transported to an open area surrounded by a grove of trees. She turned around in her place, looking up at the tall branches overhead. "Where am I?"

She knew before she finished the sentence. She was in the backyard in Connecticut. Her thoughts went back to the night before, and watching the woman burying a box. Sadness washed over her again. "I wish I could have helped her." Lauren sat on the ground and touched the dirt with her fingertips. "How can he ever forgive me for what I did?"

She heard his voice from somewhere behind the trees.

"Forgive you? I was there. I saw what took place, and I am very much to blame, too. What we did, we did out of ignorance. I understand now that it still caused negative karma. So please don't just blame yourself. I was involved too. We both were. Can you ever forgive me for causing you so much grief and pain?"

Lauren quickly stood up and looked around. She could hear his voice, and she could sense his presence, but he was nowhere to be found.

"Where are you? Why do you ask if I forgive you? I was the one who killed our babies. I was the one who was weak and selfish. It is me who must be forgiven. I don't know how you can find it in your heart to do so."

Alex appeared from behind the trees, but kept his distance. He could see her tears and hear her painful question.

"How can you forgive me, and how can I begin to forgive myself?"

Alex came closer until she could finally look into his eyes, from a distance.

"You forgive yourself the way you are trying to forgive me. We both must understand that what's past is past. We can't bring it back, but we can learn from it, and go on to our future."

She looked up at the sky, then down at the ground, ashamed to look at him again.

"You tell me that you were also responsible. Yes, I suppose you have to take on some of the responsibility. But with my heart and soul, I forgive you. I feel everything you did was done not only out of ignorance, but out of love for me. Yes, it was conditional love, but wasn't mine for you, too? Of course I forgive you. That was never the issue for me. You are the easy one to forgive. I have no idea how you can forgive me, or how I can forgive myself. I never even tried to fight back. When you died, it was as if my soul had wings and flew to be by your side. I was left with an empty shell, with no positive emotions left in me. I wanted to die, and I didn't care if I took my children, our children, with me."

Alex moved a few paces closer. "Whatever we did is past. Have you learned anything from it?"

Lauren smiled. "Oh yes, I'm not the same person I was then. I have grown stronger, and I am a survivor."

Alex returned her smile. "Then how can you not forgive yourself? I forgive you truly and freely. There was never any doubt in my mind that what happened was also my fault. But it doesn't matter whose fault it was. We have both learned, and we have worked hard to overcome the negative habits. It's been a major issue in my life this time around. Not so much pressing control on others, but on myself. You've helped me look at that issue since we've met. You did that for me, my love. How could I not forgive you? It was never a question, and never any doubt."

Lauren smiled and tried desperately to move into his arms. She could see no veil, nothing to keep them apart. But she instinctively knew she wouldn't get any closer to him than what she was at that moment. They both seemed content with it tonight. They were there to connect in other ways.

Alex continued, "We have forgiven each other unconditionally. I suppose that was the easy part. How do we now go about forgiving ourselves?"

Lauren thought it was an impossible task, but suddenly had an idea, and smiled. She remembered what her guide had once said to her, "Open your mind, and your heart will follow."

Lauren put her hand to her heart, then closed her eyes. She visualized lavender and rose covering every area of her heart and crown chakras. She shut her eyes tighter, and took a deep breath. She could smell the fragrances flow through her being. Lauren felt as if she were covered by the aromatic sweetness. She could feel her crown chakra slowly begin to open. She watched, and felt giddy as the colors and fragrances began swirling around on top of her head. Internally, she looked down and saw her heart chakra filling up with shades of reds, pinks, and purples. She could feel the love for herself, and for her other half expanding and growing deeper and wider. Then she visualized herself transferring the swirls of glowing colors and vibrant scents to Alex. All of her chakras were now fully open and charged.

Lauren began experiencing an aliveness she could only have previously dreamed about. The sensations gave her the opportunity to feel all the love the world and beyond had to offer. In that one moment, she was actually able to comprehend and see visible love. Her entire being felt as one with the universe. She was the universe. As time stood still, there was a sensation of unconditional in its entirety. There was no need for forgiveness, or sorrow over one's past mistakes. There was only complete and total bliss. Sorrow and blame didn't exist.

Lauren slowly opened her eyes, but had trouble seeing Alex through the shades of swirling colors, and intense energy vortex surrounding them both. She saw his aura, then looked down at her own. They extended far beyond the trees, and touched each other somewhere up beyond the stars. She could feel his warmth and love holding her. She darted her eyes in his direction, and watched as he slowly opened his eyes. She could feel what he was feeling. They smiled at each other, knowing the feeling they were sharing would never be forgotten. Forgiving themselves and each other were in the past. It was no longer an issue, and it no longer existed. They both felt free for the first times in their lives.

Chapter 21

Alex awoke with the energy of a teenager. The ocean breeze was blowing the sheet lightly over his body, arousing him almost to the point of climax. He suspected it was the release of energy from his dreams. But he lay still, allowing the previous events to come into focus. He knew he would never forget what had taken place. His life had been transformed, and she was responsible for it. After several minutes, he forced himself into the shower, still thinking about how wonderful she was to come up with the idea of using colors and fragrances to help open the chakras, and allow the love to enter.

"The answer was right in front of us. Fortunately, she thought of it. I was too consumed with trying to talk her out of feeling guilty to think of a way to forgive ourselves. Using the colors and scents was brilliant."

He still remembered how her aura felt, and the energy it held. His excitement grew until he was forced to release the power and pressure from the previous night's events.

Alex quickly dried his lean, bronzed body, and walked out to his balcony. He was starving, but food was going to have to wait. Alex wanted to meditate before this rush left him. He could feel the heat from the sun bouncing off his damp skin as he made himself comfortable. He only took a few deep breaths, before finding himself at a party. Alex looked around very confused.

"What the hell is this? I expected profound insights, but instead I end up at a party?"

Alex felt himself take another deep breath to relax even further. This was another first for him, and he knew if he wanted to learn anything from it, he should allow the episode to simply unfold. But he was finding the task difficult.

"Well, if this is the way it's going to be, you may as well enjoy it."

Alex turned around to see if he recognized anyone. His eyes widened in surprise when he discovered he was standing in his own house. "How can that be? I have never had this kind of party." He shook his head in bewilderment, but continued viewing the scene. "I would never think to decorate the place like this. This is like something out of a fairytale!"

But, he looked around and recognized all of his friends. They were seated around several large round tables on the patio. He heard familiar music playing in the background. Alex's amazement increased tenfold at what he saw next.

"This can't be. I would never invite people over for a huge party, and then make them sit and endure my songs. In these strange surroundings, no less."

But he saw himself walking up to a stage and sitting down on a stool. Alex gazed all around, verifying that it was indeed his house. "There must be a hundred people in attendance."

He forced his eyes to look at each table. People were laughing and talking, waiting for the entertainment to begin. His eyes continued roving over the heads. There were no strangers among the participants.

"I can't figure this out." Alex looked up to the stars. "What is there for me to see here? Why would I do this? I know I shouldn't question, but I really don't get it."

He saw his guide appear over the heads of everyone, then point in the direction of his living room. Alex looked through the glass doors, and gasped for a breath.

"My dear God, it's her. Next to my piano. It's her!" He took another breath to calm his nerves. "Is it really her, or is she just a mirage?

He turned for an answer, but his guide had disappeared.

Without warning, his eyes shot open and he was back on his balcony drying off by the heat of the sun.

Alex couldn't move a muscle in his body, but his mind was racing.

"Wow, what just happened?"

He closed his eyes again, trying to find some insight, but found none.

His strength was suddenly zapped from his body, and it took him several moments to walk into his bedroom.

"I've got to take a nap for a few minutes."

He was too tired to question why he was going back to a bed that he had just awoken from. Alex yawned again and closed his eyes. He found himself returning to the party. But this time he didn't judge what was happening in front of him. He forced himself to look around and enjoy what was taking place. Keeping a watchful eye out for her.

Lauren woke up with a start. "Wow!" She felt a tug at her neck and saw she was holding the ring tightly in her hand.

"That was the most incredible experience I've ever had." She looked at the clock, and couldn't believe the time.

"It seems I just fell asleep."

Lauren jumped out of bed, grabbed her journal, and walked out to her balcony. She looked over the treetops and took a deep breath, letting it out slowly. Without wanting to think about why she was doing something so out of character, she allowed her gown to slip off her body and land on the deck floor.

"I feel as free as a bird in flight."

She paused a moment to look up at the sky, then down to the trees swaying in the gentle warm breeze.

"For the first time, I see everything clearly. All I had to do was trust the process, and open my heart. Everything else fell magically into place."

She heard the phone ringing softly in the background and knew it was Adriana. She answered with a giggle.

"What took you so long to call? I've been awake for ten whole minutes."

Adriana was shaken from her stupor. "Huh? Lauren, is that you?"

Lauren laughed. "Of course. Are you still in bed?"

"Yeah, I just woke up and thought I'd better call. What a night I had. I didn't get to sleep until the wee hours. I had the weirdest dreams. How about you?"

Lauren smiled. "Like you wouldn't believe. I can't wait to tell you about them. This is a new first. Why don't you come over here and we'll eat around the corner at Shanty's. We'll compare dreams."

Adriana groaned as she slowly raised herself out of bed. "All right, but give me some time. I'll be there in a few hours. I want to try and process this dream I had." Lauren then heard her friend's high-pitched laughter, "What is it with us? I don't have time to be processing dreams."

Lauren answered in a motherly tone of voice, "You'll just have to make the time. I've found they're very important. Come over when you can. I'm going to take my time too."

Lauren hung up, deciding a shower would relax her. After stepping into the warm liquid, she immersed her thoughts in last night's dream, then heard herself sigh with relief. Now she felt ready to start her day.

Lauren sat at the kitchen table, taking her time recalling, then writing the night's journey into her book. She had just completed the last word when the front door opened, and she heard Adriana's voice calling her name.

"How did you get here so fast?"

Adriana floated into the room, her aura glowing.

"So this is what it's like to feel passion, excitement, and love."

Lauren hugged her friend. "Yeah, welcome to the world of insanity. You'll never be the same again."

Adriana laughed. "This is a feeling I could get used to. And talk about the dreams? Wow!"

The girls walked upstairs to talk while Lauren dressed. "So tell me about this dream you had." Cocking her head to one side, Lauren continued in mocked confusion, "Gee, that seems strange coming out of my mouth. Normally, you're the one who asks."

Adriana's eyes sparkled. "I dreamed of Elliot. But it wasn't Elliot. I don't know where we were, but we weren't in this country. There were high mountains all around us. The village I saw was quaint and friendly. We both had the same look in our eyes, but we weren't us. Does that make sense?"

Lauren was putting her dark hair back in a ponytail, and stopped to look at her Adriana.

"You're asking me if it makes sense? Me? Jeez, right now, I feel as if I'm in the twilight zone, and our roles have been reversed. Of course it makes sense, silly. I'll bet that before going to sleep last night, you asked your guides if you had met him before. Am I right?"

Adriana looked down. "Well, yeah I did. I could have figured it out myself, but I was tired. I opted for the shortcut." Her green eyes widened. "Lauren, there is no doubt in my mind that we have been together before. Many times before, although I only saw one occasion. There was such intensity when he touched my hand, I knew immediately. We have been together before."

Lauren was interested, and sat down next to her friend on the bed. "What did you see when you two touched?"

Adriana was thinking quietly for a moment. "It's all a fog now. And that's not like me not to remember every second. But last night was just that kind of evening. When we touched, the quick impression I received was one of coming home to my soul mate. I caught a glimpse of him, but the atmosphere wasn't conducive for picking up intense impressions. My fault, of course. I had so many emotions raging in me that I had trouble staying focused. I feel I've seen him at some point in this lifetime. Maybe in a car, or on the street. I don't know, but I'll figure it out. Not that it matters now. We have finally met and connected. As I said, it was a night for strange happenings. I remember when I shook Alex's hand,; I received a quick psychic impression and a picture. I don't remember what it was now, but it shook me off balance for a moment. I don't think anyone noticed, but it surprised me."

Lauren listened before speaking. "It must have been a lot of mixed up energy, because I've never known you to forget a psychic impression. Perhaps Elliot's friend was a part of your past life, or maybe you've seen him in your store, and you were trying to remember."

Adriana shook her head, "I don't know. As you said, it's not like me." Adriana giggled. "I'm sure it was the hormones working overtime. When I saw Elliot, I could feel them coming alive. But my goodness, when he touched my hand and whispered in my ear, I thought I would fall out of my chair. I tried to look as if I had it together, but inside, I was in such turmoil. Confusion reigned."

Lauren laughed, falling back on the bed. "Yeah, that's either love or lust. Sometimes they can be confused. At first, they both have the same wonderful, mind-blowing symptoms. But in this case, I'd say you might have a live one on your hook. When can I meet him?"

Adriana looked at her cellular phone. "As soon as he calls, I hope."

Lauren touched her friend's hand. "Are you sure he'll call?"

Adriana put her other hand on top of Lauren's. "There's no doubt in my mind. It felt right from the very beginning. Yes, he'll call. He may not know why he's calling, but he'll call."

Adriana's phone made a shrilling sound, making them both jump and giggle at themselves at the same time. She grabbed it with both hands. "Hello."

She could hear him on the other end of the receiver.

"Adriana?"

She smiled in Lauren's direction. "Yes, it's me. Elliot?"

"Yeah. How are you?"

Before she had the opportunity to answer, Elliot continued before he lost his nerve.

"I was up all night thinking about those eyes of yours. And I know this is going to sound positively crazy, but I don't want to play games, and I don't want to waste any time. Adriana, if you remember anything about last night, and if you felt the way I did, would you honor me with your presence tonight?"

Adriana had never had anyone state a feeling to her in such a way. She was quiet for a moment while she tried to pull herself together. Smiling into the phone, she answered in a hoarse voice.

"You do have a way of catching me off guard. How could I turn down an invitation like that? Just try and keep me away."

She couldn't believe how straightforward they were being with each other. Glancing over to her friend, she saw a bewildered look on Lauren's face, and then a deep smile grow from it.

Elliot laughed. "Then how about I pick you up at 7:00 and we'll make an evening of it? Whatever you want to do."

Adriana didn't have to think. It was all perfectly natural between them.

"What I would like to do is call a gourmet restaurant and have them deliver several courses to my house, along with a bottle of dry wine, and a nice bottle of champagne. Of course, we can't forget a light dessert. Perhaps strawberries and chocolate?"

Adriana couldn't believe what she was saying, but she trusted her instincts, and this felt so right. She tried not to laugh when she glanced over at Lauren. Her eyes were wide with surprise, and she had a huge grin on her face. She was shaking her head up and down, with her hand in a thumbs-up position.

Elliot was quiet for a moment. "Well, now you have caught me off guard. That sounded like a wonderful idea ten minutes before I phoned you, but I wasn't going to mention it. I'm glad we think so much alike. Forget the delivery service. I'll bring it all myself. We'll have the time to get to know each other. Last night wasn't long enough."

Adriana gave him directions to her house, and told him she looked forward to seeing him again. Elliot was about to hang up, but he called out her name one more time.

"Adriana?"

"Yes?"

"I love saying your name. It goes well with the lady. I look forward to tonight. Take care." And he hung up.

Adriana held the receiver in her hand for a moment. Lauren gently took it from her and pushed the off button.

"Well, that was quite an earful. Sorry about not leaving you alone to finish the conversation, but you wouldn't have got me out of this room, under any circumstances. You two certainly have a connection all right, and it's refreshing not to have to play those awful games."

Adriana laughed. "I suppose at our age, we can't let any time slip by. If you think it's the right one, why waste time playing games? Where does it get you? They don't know who you really are, and you don't know who they are. I must say it helped that his conversation started out as a no-nonsense proposition."

Lauren raised her eyebrows. "Proposition?"

Adriana giggled. "Well, not quite. But the day's still young."

They both laughed as they pushed each other out the door. When the women had placed their lunch order, Adriana asked Lauren about her dream. "So tell me all about it. What was the dream about?"

Lauren sipped her drink before answering. "It was different. We met in the clearing near the trees at the Connecticut house. The meeting place wasn't as remarkable as what happened at the meeting. I think we made a large step forward in terms of our finally getting this negative karma crap out of our lives. We spent the first few minutes forgiving each other, but we had a heck of a time forgiving ourselves. We just didn't know how. That's always the hard part. Anyway, I remembered what my guide said about opening my mind and heart. Then I saw you telling me about the chakras, and what the colors and the fragrances meant. It suddenly made perfect sense to put it all together. I visualized lavender and roses. Their colors and their scents. Then I opened my mind, which was my crown chakra, so to speak. And that process began the opening of my heart chakra. The rest was easy.

"All of a sudden, I didn't control the situation any longer. There was a whirlwind of activity with all this stuff around us. And like buttons, the chakras just opened up and filled us with the most wonderful sensations. I've never had an experience like that before in my life, and doubt I ever will again. We were both at one with the universe. I've read about such a thing, but I never thought I'd experience it for myself. Our auras connected, and sent us shooting up to the sky. It was great.

"I woke up feeling like a great pressure had been lifted from my shoulders. I know in my heart and soul that everything is forgiven. That worry is over. Now I look forward in seeing what's next. Surely, we've done everything we can do, and gone through everything we can go through, and we have survived. Now I'm ready to meet this man. I can only hope he doesn't live on the other side of the world somewhere."

Lauren realized what she was saying and her tone lowered an octave. "No, I didn't mean that. As long as he really exists, I don't care where he is. We'll find each other, and somehow, work it out. As long as he exists."

Adriana took Lauren's hand. "First of all, how lucky can one person get? It sounds as if you had a Kundalini experience. And second, he does exist, and it's just a matter of time before you're reunited. Trust me. Remember, I'm psychic."

Lauren teased her friend. "Yeah, I can see how great you are at it. What happened last night? Gee, you don't know, because you can't remember?"

Adriana dropped Lauren off at her house after lunch.

"You don't mind if I don't come in. I'd like to go try and make myself presentable before tonight."

Lauren nodded. "Of course I don't mind. But you always look great. I wouldn't worry about it. I don't think it matters to him."

Adriana frowned. "Yeah, well, how would feel if the first time the man of your dreams sees you, you're dressed up looking like a princess? What do you think he'd expect the next time? If I don't get started now, I'll look more like a frog if he starts comparing the two."

Lauren laughed. "Adriana, you're being silly again. My psychic impression tells me that it doesn't matter what you look like. He will see only your beauty."

Adriana kissed her friend on the cheek. "Thanks. I'll call you tomorrow."

Lauren waved as her friend drove away. *It's about time she found happiness.*

Alex woke up with his mind spinning. "Damn, the day's almost gone. Where have I been?"

His meditation and dream flashed through his head. He grabbed a pen and paper from the nightstand and wrote furiously, all the time talking to himself.

"I can't believe I'm doing this. I'll never live this down if it doesn't work. But I've got to trust my gut."

The phone interrupted his thoughts. He picked it up with an absent-minded 'hello'. Elliot was on the other end.

"Hi, what's going on? You sound hassled."

Alex paused for a moment to take a deep breath.

"Elliot, I've got a favor to ask of you. Can you help me plan a party?"

Elliot was taken aback, and then chuckled out loud. "I'm fine, Alex. Thanks for asking."

Guilt crept into his voice. "Sorry. How are you? Now, can you help me plan a party?"

Elliot snickered, and let Alex have his way.

"This is sure a day for surprises. You're throwing a party? You've never thrown any more than a few informal dinner parties in all the years I've known you. What kind of party? And more importantly, why?"

Alex's voice faltered. "Well, I'm not sure myself. But I think it's to meet the woman in my dreams."

He was interrupted by the same questions that his own mind was asking.

"What? The woman in your dreams? Alex, are you telling me that you believe all you have to do is throw a party, and this person is going to show up on your doorstep? Do you know something more than I do about this? Has something changed?"

Alex laughed out of embarrassment. "I know it sounds absurd. And yes, a few things have changed. I'll briefly fill you in. We met last night in our dreams, we forgave each other, chakras opened, colors and fragrances were flying every which way, and we now believe the worst is behind us."

Elliot was mystified. "Damn, Alex, when we have more time, you'll have to go into a little more detail. And perhaps go a little slower. It sounds insanely interesting. I'm glad all is forgiven, and you can move on, but what in the hell does a party have to do with it?"

Alex shook his head, not understanding what was so difficult to comprehend.

"When I woke up this morning, I decided to meditate. I found myself in the middle of a huge party. Apparently, the meditation didn't totally convince me, because when I came out of it, I promptly fell asleep. I found myself back at the party, but in much greater detail." Alex's voice took on a pleading sound. "Are you ready to help me?"

Elliot shook his head in confusion. "Wait. Tell me what this has to do with you meeting the woman?"

Alex clicked his tongue in annoyance. "I don't know what the hell it has to do with her. When I was observing the party in my meditation, as well as in my dream, she was there. I don't know if she was attending in person, or if it was just a reflection of her. It doesn't matter, because that's all it took to convince me to do this. Call it a leap of faith."

Alex knew he couldn't do it alone. He needed his friends. "Elliot, you said it yourself. This isn't like something I'm famous for. I'm not one to give formal parties. But everything in me is screaming to trust the process, and have a little faith. You don't think that I believe this isn't insane behavior? But just think about it. You've already seen for yourself everything that's happened in this drama with her. It's truly amazing. Why shouldn't I take another leap forward and see if I fall or fly? Wouldn't you say it's about time?"

Elliot smiled into the phone. "All right, you've convinced me. What kind of party do you want to throw? A simple cocktail party?"

Alex could feel his stomach in knots. "Absolutely not. I want a dinner party. I want it all catered. I thought about inviting about a hundred close friends and business associates. And I'd like my band to play."

Elliot was laughing out loud now. "OK, and how are you going to do this, and when? Next year?"

Alex was surprised at his friend's lack of understanding. "Elliot, listen to me. I want to have this party in one week."

Elliot dropped the phone, quickly retrieving it. "Alex, are you crazy? How in the hell do you think you can carry this off in one week? The kind of party you're wanting takes a minimum of a few months to plan, and you want it in one week?"

Alex was convinced it could be done. "All right. I'll give you a little over a week. We'll have it a week from next Saturday. Can you do it?"

Elliot couldn't believe what he was hearing. "Excuse me? Can

I do it? You want me to put it all together? What in the hell do you think I am? A magician?"

Alex wasn't going to be put off. "If we work at this, I know we can pull it off. Donovan will help too. I'll work on my list today, and we can send the invitations out tomorrow by courier. I don't think people will care what their invitations look like, as long as they receive one. Personally, I don't care if they're not on the best paper, produced by the best printers in Malibu. I'll work something up and print them on my computer tonight. I know there must be agencies that handle all the arrangements. What do you think?"

Elliot knew he had lost the battle. "I think you're out of your mind, but all right. I'll locate a party service and let them fight with you instead. Any ideas where you want to hold this party?"

Alex prepared himself for another argument, but spoke his words in a nonchalant tone. "Here at my house, of course. I want the first floor decorated, and used for casual entertaining, with dinner, dancing, and the band extended out onto the patio. The stage should be set up near the pool. The tables will face the beach."

Elliot shook his head violently in protest. "You want it at your house? Alex, you are nuts! I know you have the room, but why would you do that?"

Alex smiled into the phone. "Because that's what I saw in my dream. Yes, it must be at my house."

Elliot continued shaking his head in disbelief. "And do we have a theme for this party? What are we going to tell people you're celebrating? No one will believe you're throwing this kind of a party on such short notice because it sounded like the fun thing to do. Everyone knows you better than that."

Alex saw himself as others did, and laughed. "Jesus, am I that bad? We'll tell them that it's my coming out party. We'll tell them we're celebrating love, romance, dreams, fairytales, and soul mates. Could anything else be any crazier?"

Elliot thought quietly for a few tense seconds, trying to come to terms with the entire conversation. Alex didn't rush him. He knew his demands sounded insane. But he also knew Elliot would listen to his gut instincts. Finally, Elliot responded with an added zeal to his voice.

"I'm not going to argue with you. If this is what you really want, then by God, we'll get it done. You know how I love the pressure and pace of beating a deadline. You knew that would hook me, didn't you?"

Alex just grinned into the phone.

Elliot continued, more serious than before. "Please don't be disappointed if she isn't there."

Alex was fearless. "I won't be. But don't be surprised if she is."

Elliot finally understood, and nodded to himself. "I'll do my best. Now let's get this rolling. Make out the invitation list while I call Donovan and give him the strange news. Between the three of us, we'll find a service to take over the party responsibilities. Surely we can't screw that up. What do you want to serve?"

Alex ignored the question. His thoughts were now taking him in a different direction.

"Are you going to be seeing the lady that owns Moonglows anytime soon? Adriana?"

Elliot was trying to stay open to his friend's eccentricity. "Have we entered the twilight zone? Yes, I'm seeing her tonight, and I hope every night for the rest of my life. Why? Do you want her to locate a shrieking voodoo ceremonial dancer for the entertainment?"

Alex laughed at the comment, and teased his friend, "Actually, I hadn't thought of it, but you've come up with an excellent idea."

Elliot interrupted emphatically, his voice growing in volume. "No, no, no. Let me date her for a little while before she finds out what kind of lunatics we really are?"

Alex was having trouble catching his breath from the laughter. "Okay, I suppose I'll just have to compromise on this issue. Actually, I was going to ask if Adriana might like to assist in selecting the menu. The three of us guys would just make a mess of it."

Elliot was pacing the floor back and forth, dumbfounded.

"Alex, I just met the woman. What about Vickie or Cindy?"

Alex pulled his hair back from his face in frustration. He knew he was asking for a lot.

"I know I could call on either of them and they'd be happy to help. I don't know why I would trust someone I've only met once to do something so important. I can't even tell you why I would utter such a request. I don't know where it came from. But so far, wouldn't you call everything that's happened in the last few months crazy? What's one more request?"

Elliot paused again before speaking. "I'll tell you what. If she and I hit it off the way I hope we will, then I'll ask her to help us. But if I don't feel comfortable about it, we go to Vickie and Cindy. Deal?"

Alex looked at his calendar. "Fine, but when will you know? Don't forget, the party is less than two weeks away?"

Elliot stopped his friend. "Alex, you're trying to do it again. Stop demanding everything your way! You've asked for my help. Now, give up some of the territory, and let me help. It'll all be organized beautifully. With a team effort, we can't lose. Hell, with you as captain, you won't let us lose. If you want a party, then we'll give you a party, but you're going to have to let us do our jobs too."

Alex laughed in agreement. "You certainly put me back in my place with that tactful reminder. I hope you know how grateful I am for your help. I'll get the list together today, and we'll get it to a planner first thing in the morning. Elliot, you've got to believe I've seen this party, and it's going to be wonderful."

Elliot closed his eyes. "Alex, as long as you're satisfied with the finished product, then the rest doesn't matter. I have to give you credit for staying true to yourself. Let's pray she shows up." There was a chuckle in his voice as he continued, "I've got to call

Donovan now. After hearing about this new game plan, he may bring out the white coats for us both. Maybe you shouldn't answer your door."

Alex laughed, and ended the conversation. He had work to do.

His excitement was building as he ran downstairs to his office. Alex pulled out his phone directory and began planning his list, humming his music in the background. His breathing stopped for a moment while he thought about his dream. Then his eyes fell upon the painting in front of him as he noticed a faint glow encompassing the couple walking on the beach. Alex smiled, then winked knowingly at the picture.

Lauren spent the remainder of the day catching up on neglected chores. She would often find her mind escaping to the previous night. And each time, she would stop what she was doing and smile, always touching the gold ring hanging from around her neck.

She was ready for a much-needed break when Cindy called, inviting her to dinner with her and Ron. Lauren looked forward to Cindy's perky personality and current gossip. She couldn't wait to hear about what happened at the club. Lauren loved being around Cindy. She didn't think her petite friend had ever been in a bad mood. Her brown eyes were continuously sparkling with excitement, and warmth flashed across her smile. Her disposition was contagious. Cindy and Ron were a good match. He was thoughtful, generous, and adored his wife. Cindy appreciated every moment she could spend with her husband. And except for the major withdrawal Cindy had felt when her only son moved to San Diego the year before, life seemed good for them both.

Lauren was feeling the frustration from the office backlog, when she noticed the time. "I'm going to be late." She quickly turned off her computer and ran upstairs to find something to wear, opting for a pair of maroon slacks, and a silky black and maroon shirt. She slipped into her black low-heeled pumps at the door, and was in her car in record time.

Lauren rushed into the restaurant as the couple was being led to their table. She caught up and hugged them as they made their way to a table. Cindy was her bubbly self, and had plenty to talk about. Lauren was mentally exhausted and glad to have the job of conversation shift to her friend.

Cindy took a large gulp from her glass and set it down.

"Lauren, I can't wait to tell you all about last night."

Lauren laughed at her enthusiasm. "I had lunch with Adriana today. She had plenty to say about the evening, as well."

Cindy took Lauren's arm, holding it closely. "Lauren, you would not believe the electricity between her and Elliot. One minute they were strangers, and in a blink of an eye, they were a twosome. I don't know why I never thought of putting those two together. Elliot has always been so convincing with his talk of never wanting to get into a serious relationship again, it threw me off. And Adriana was always working, making that her whole source of entertainment."

Ron interjected with humor. "Yeah, I'm surprised you haven't hog-tied them together before now. God knows, you missed that one. They make a great couple."

Lauren mentioned that Elliot had called Adriana while they were together earlier in the day. "It was like they had been together forever. And it was good to see her so happy. Do you think they have a chance in this crazy world?"

Cindy answered first, "They never took their eyes off one another. Yes, if I had to bet, I'd say it has a great chance of lasting. It's nice when two of our friends get together."

Lauren smiled, looking down at the table. Cindy mistook the act as something she had said.

"Lauren, are you all right? I didn't mean to upset you. I know you're going through a divorce. How could I be so cruel? I'm really sorry."

Lauren looked at Ron in surprise. Ron smiled warmly at her,

obviously also feeling guilty about where the conversation had gone. Lauren grinned at the couple.

"No, Cindy, you misunderstood. I couldn't be happier for Adriana. I think it's wonderful that she's found someone. God knows she deserves it. And as far as my divorce goes? Please don't concern yourself with that. I'm very content in my decision. Gary and I are friends, and I wish him well. The emotions associated with our marriage have been over for a very long time. We're just making it legal. He's gone on with his life, and I'm doing the same. I thought you knew that."

She tenderly squeezed her friend's hand. "Cindy, you're a wonderful person for worrying about my feelings, but please don't. I'm truly fine. And what's more important, my girls are fine too. We are very blessed, indeed."

Cindy looked in her eyes and smiled. "Yeah, I think you are. Now, let's just hope Adriana doesn't decide that she needs to work more, or Elliot decides he can't get into a serious relationship, after all."

Ron patted his wife's hand, and quickly changed the subject.

"Can we talk about how terrific the band was last night? Lauren, you really missed a hell of an evening."

Lauren laughed. "I hope there's a repeat performance. I heard you guys were great. Adriana says she's never heard any group play better. In fact, she said you guys were so good, you should turn professional."

Ron blushed. "We were quite good, but the crowd was incredible. We were sorry to see it end."

Cindy's brows rose, as she spoke up anxiously. "Hey, I got a call from Donovan late this afternoon. Alex, the singer of the band, is having a big party a week from Saturday. We're all a little perplexed why he's having this party on such short notice, but he said it was imperative the band play." Cindy laughed at her next thought. "I think he really got into the role of musician."

Ron interrupted with an afterthought. "If you knew Alex,

you'd understand why it's so weird that he's even considering such a thing."

Cindy nodded her head in agreement, and continued. "Anyway, it should be a lot of fun. Why don't you join us?"

Lauren shook her head. "No, I don't think that would be a good idea. I wouldn't know anyone there, and I would be uncomfortable going to his function without a formal invitation."

Ron interrupted her. "Lauren, you'll know several people. You'll know Vickie, and I'm sure Elliot will bring Adriana. And you'll know us too. I'm certain there will be a few more. Probably half the women attending are your customers. We would love to have you."

Cindy turned to her friend and whispered loudly, "Lauren, this party is going to be an event. Alex never has parties. When I asked Donovan why this was so important, he said it has to do with…" Cindy turned to her husband. "How did he put it? We don't know if it's a joke or not. It's just so unlike the Alex we know."

Ron thought for a moment, then put his hands up in a dramatic gesture.

"He said the party was to celebrate romance, love, dreams, fairytales, and soul mates." He laughed and finished his sentence. "That's a hell of a lot to celebrate. This is definitely not the Alex we know."

Cindy cut in excitedly, "Maybe he's been seeing someone on the sly, and he's fallen in love. Maybe he wants to introduce her." Cindy elbowed her husband. "No, that's impossible. I'd know about it."

Ron smiled down at his wife. "That's true. If something's going on anywhere, you're the first to know."

Lauren thought about the proposition for a moment, then shook her head with a grin. "What the hell. It sounds like it may be a lot of fun. Are you sure this Alex guy wouldn't mind? He sounds like a bit of an ogre."

Cindy laughed at her remark. "Are you kidding? Alex is one of the kindest people you'll ever meet. He's just not the party-throwing type. Especially this kind of party. So it should be interesting to see how it all turns out. Either way, you'll have the time of your life. And this may be the only time for another year that you'll be able to hear the band play. They truly were terrific. Alex sang a few new songs he had written. I don't know where he got his inspiration, but it brought the place down. I don't think there was a dry eye in the house. Ron, I hope you can convince him to sing them again."

Ron laughed out loud. "Keeping him from singing them would be more of an effort. Alex is a warm, sensitive guy. Perhaps he's not kidding about the theme of his party. We could all use a little more love."

Cindy pushed her husband teasingly. "Are you complaining?"

Ron kissed his wife's forehead. "Never. You wouldn't let me."

With dinner over, Ron led the women out the front door of the restaurant. Cindy hugged Lauren.

"I'll call you with all the info. I'm glad you changed your mind. You'll have a good time. I promise."

Lauren drove home in the quietness of her car, with her thoughts leading again to the previous night's dreams.

"I hope I see him again tonight. All the negativity is gone. We have a clear slate, and have unconditionally reconnected. Let this finally be the time to find each other."

Chapter 22

Alex completed his invitation list, and made a rough sketch on how he wanted the patio area and house transformed. He could see it clearly in his mind, and knew he wanted everything exactly as he saw it.

When exhaustion hit, he finally put the paper down. His plan would be put into action tomorrow. Invitations would be mailed out, along with follow up phone calls to everyone. He was relieved Ron had taken care of getting the band together. He knew everyone was talking about the theme of his party. Alex smiled to himself, knowing his friends were a little surprised, and not quite sure whether he was kidding or not. He had to admit it wasn't his usual serious way of doing things.

"Yes, this party is going to be what true love and romance is all about."

Looking back at the list of names, Alex laughed out loud.

"It's about time some of my friends were shaken out of their status quo. What better person to do it than myself? I'll be their example. It's all right to step out of the box and do things differently."

Alex looked up at the ceiling, deep in thought, then penciled an item to his list.

"Hundreds of candles. This has to be perfect for her. Surely the sights, the sounds, and the fragrances will open her heart, and help her to remember. It's up to her to trust what she feels." He refused to let his fear of being alone at the party enter his thoughts.

"She will be here."

Alex was ready for a good night's sleep. He needed to swim in her energy tonight. He wanted to tell her about the party. He wanted to tell her of his dreams about being with her forever. Alex lay back on his pillows, closed his eyes and prayed, giving thanks for all he had. He drifted off to sleep before completing his affirmations.

He was in a room where his party was taking place. Everyone was formally dressed in gowns and tuxedos. Alex looked into their faces and saw each one participating in his celebration. Some were dancing to the music playing in the background. Some were sipping champagne flowing freely from a fountain. He sensed that everyone was expecting him to perform. But he couldn't without her. Alex watched himself rushing from one room to the next, searching for her in a frenzied state. But each room was silent and empty. He could feel panic rising, growing ever larger with each slam of the door.

"Where are you? Please answer me. For God's sake, don't desert me now."

He watched himself walking around in circles, his brow wrinkled and drawn in distress. He watched as the Alex in his dreams looked deeply into each face he encountered. His alarm grew even more intense when he noticed the people weren't returning his stares. It was as if he didn't exist within their realm of reality.

"Why can't they see me?"

Alex watched while someone who looked like him ran to the front door, pulling it open with a great deal of force. He was more confused when he saw her standing in front of him, but looking past him into the room full of people. Alex opened his arms wide, excited to be in her presence.

"It's you. You're finally here."

She didn't reciprocate his excitement, continuing instead to look right through him.

"Can't you see me?"

She didn't answer. Alex forgot his confusion as he let himself be hypnotized by her beauty. He watched as she seemingly floated into the large foyer area. Her long flowing royal blue gown was strapless, and the snugness of the bodice pushed her velvet bosoms to overflowing. Her dark hair was pulled up, with long tentacles cascading down to her shoulders. Alex was captivated as she slowly turned her long neck in his direction, revealing her pleasure as she took in the sights and sounds of the event. Her blue eyes were glistening from all the excitement. She was wearing sapphire and diamond earrings, and a sapphire and diamond choker.

Alex knew his feelings paralleled with the man desperately fighting for her attention. He was having a difficult time keeping his panic down to a controlled level, and letting the energies flow through him without letting them affect him too much. When he noticed a dainty gold chain hanging below the choker and traveling down into the cleavage of her breasts, he felt himself shiver from anticipation. Alex could feel her energy, but knew he had none to give back. His soul was tortured, and burned to be with her. The emotions were highly charged, and he couldn't understand how she could not see him.

"How can this be?"

Alex's eyes followed her as she strolled slowly to the piano. Her sensual walk was as inviting as her penetrating eyes. She gently turned and focused directly on him. He would never forget the sweet softness of her words.

"Aren't you going to play for me?"

The room became quiet. He looked around and saw they were finally alone. A raw energy was emitting and bouncing between them, causing Alex to feel disoriented and confused.

"Can you see me now?"

Lauren laughed at his dazed look. "Of course. But where are all the people?"

Alex looked around slowly. "Perhaps when we're together, no

one else exists?"

Lauren smiled passionately, her eyes never leaving his. "I like that idea."

Alex woke up exhausted, aroused, and searching desperately around his bedroom. He had brought the confusion from his dream-state back with him. His balcony door was open, and the light of day was pouring over his naked body. He slowly closed his eyes again, more frustrated than ever.

"What the hell was that all about? She couldn't see me, and when she finally did, she left me again? Could someone please tell me what the hell that was all about?"

Alex looked up to the ceiling, with tears now burning his eyes. "I know I'm not lucky enough to figure out all my dreams, but this one has me baffled. The pain of her looking through me was unbearable. Damn!"

Alex closed his eyes, wanting to return to her. His thoughts turned immediately to the party, and his enthusiasm grew.

"I still have time to find her."

He jumped out of bed and dialed Elliot's number.

Elliot picked up dinner, wine, and dessert from a small French bistro on the way to Adriana's house. He couldn't recall ever being this excited about a date before. He chuckled to himself while trying to remember when his last serious date had been. He had dated frequently for many years, but it became more of a problem as he had less time for himself. He had met no one who meant enough to him to take him away from his work, his hobbies, or his friends.

"Until now." He shook his head, dumbfounded. "In my wildest dreams, I would have never thought something like this could happen to me. With the possible exception of her being an axe murderer, I think I could fall in love with her tonight. That is, if I haven't already. I have no choice but to let whatever happens, happen." He looked at himself in the rearview mirror and grinned broadly. "But damn, this is an incredible feeling."

Before he could discuss his emotions any further with himself, Elliot was standing at her front door. Adriana opened before he could ring the bell, and immediately took a few bags from his arms.

"Let me help you with that."

They walked into her kitchen, put the groceries on the counter, and without warning, Elliot scooped her into his arms, hugging her tightly. He closed his eyes and held her quietly for several moments, inhaling her freshness. She didn't speak, instead enjoying his familiar warmth. When he finally released her, she heard one word escape his breath.

"Incredible."

Adriana smiled, turning him in the direction of her living room. "Why don't you go light a fire, pick out some music, and get comfortable while I get organized in here." She looked into his dark eyes and winked. "It won't take me long."

He touched her face lightly with his fingers, outlining a circle around her lips. "It's been too long already."

Elliot picked up a glass of wine on his way into the living room. He immediately noticed a familiar scent permeating the room.

"Is that lavender?" She followed behind, and lit the candles. "Yes, do you like it?"

Elliot looked at her closely, noticing her eyes were much greener than he remembered. Bewildered by the turn of events, he could only whisper, "I think it's lovely."

Adriana smiled shyly, and turned towards the kitchen.

With the fire lit, and the music playing, Elliot made himself comfortable on the couch. His eyes fell to several photos sitting on the coffee table. He picked up one of Adriana with two women. He recognized Cindy as the second woman. Adriana sat down beside him, smiling at the memory.

"Of course, you know Cindy. The other woman is my best friend, Lauren Wells. This picture was taken at an open house for a new designer at Lauren's clothing boutique.

Elliot returned it to the table.

"She certainly does look familiar.

Adriana laughed. "Hey, that's my line."

He had noticed an unusual trinket hanging around Lauren's neck. He waited a moment, and then retrieved the photo again, taking a closer look.

"When was this taken?"

Adriana smiled at his interest. "Last week."

He turned the snapshot toward the candlelight.

"What's this?" He pointed to Lauren's neck.

Adriana put the picture close to her face. She knew immediately what it was, but casually handed it back to him.

"Looks like a necklace to me."

He responded quickly, "Yes it is, but it looks familiar."

Adriana wanted to change the subject. She didn't want to lie to him, but she knew better than to talk about the ring hanging around Lauren's neck. She had to find a way of changing the focus from her friend.

She turned directly to Elliot, and spoke softly. "At the club last night, it was mentioned that you and Alex had both visited my store. If I remember correctly, you were specifically looking for something. Can I be of help now?"

The question caught Elliot off guard. He wanted desperately to tell her about Alex and his dreams. He knew she would understand, but he had given his word. He shook his head, thinking to himself, *How am I going to get out of this one?*

He put the picture back on the table, and took a sip of his wine. He didn't want to deceive her.

"It was nothing really. Just one of Alex's dreams he was having trouble interpreting. We all have them from time to time. He decided to find the answer himself."

Adriana noticed Elliot's fidgety body language, and sensed she was getting only half the truth, but didn't push him. At least the conversation was off Lauren.

She stood up, and put her hand out to him. "Dinner is served."

Lauren thought she had slept peacefully between intervals of her nighttime visions. But it was daytime now, and she was sipping on coffee at her desk, feeling as though she hadn't slept at all. Circling the cup's ridge with her index finger, she tried to recall exactly what had transpired. She remembered seeing herself standing in front of a door as it was opened for her. She was relatively sure it had been a formal occasion, in a beautifully decorated house. But oddly enough, she couldn't understand why no one had looked familiar.

Lauren closed her eyes again, attempting to bring back the previous night's events. In a flash, she was standing near a piano.

Her eyes shot wide open.

"Oh my God, he was there." She tried to focus on what had ensued, and then shook her head in confusion. "Not much happened. Why didn't I speak to him? And why do I keep seeing myself near a piano?" The fog hadn't yet lifted from Lauren's mind, and she was having a difficult time making the connection.

"Why can't I remember?"

She was reaching for the phone to call Adriana when it rang.

"Good morning, my friend. How was your evening?"

Lauren laughed. "Good morning, Adriana. Obviously not as interesting as yours. Why don't we start with how your evening went? Were the emotions as powerful once you two were finally alone?"

Adriana joined her friend in laughter. "Oh yes, and more. We had a lovely dinner, then we talked. Lauren, I don't think I've had as much conversation with any man in my life as I did last night with Elliot. It's unbelievable how much we have in common. There was an immediate comfort level. It was as if we've always known each other. We talked and laughed, and generally got to know each other until late in the evening."

Lauren was interested. "It sounds like an evening made in heaven. So, I can assume you will be seeing him again?"

Adriana smiled. "Tonight for dinner at his place. I know we could go out to restaurants, but we just want to be together where it's nice and quiet. I feel as if we're catching up on lost time. I believe with all my heart that we feel the same way about each other."

Lauren put her ear closer to the receiver. "And how is that?"

Adriana continued without breathing, "He is simply the love of my life. He's the one I've been waiting for. He's someone I've known many times, and have loved many times. But it's strange to think that I didn't know him this time last week. It's amazing how fast a life can change." She laughed, and continued, "I wouldn't tell too many people this, but I think you understand. God knows, you've got your own dramas going on, and as strange as mine is I think you still have me beat. I know your dream will work out, just like I believe mine will. If I didn't know it before, I do now. Dreams can come true."

Lauren wiped a tear from her eye. "Adriana, have you two discussed anything serious yet? I know it's quick, but it sounds as if it's progressing at a very rapid pace. We've both seen stranger things happen." Lauren giggled. "I'm a living example of that."

Adriana thought a moment. "We know it's for real. You know I'm a rather grounded person, and if anyone had ever told me I would be reacting like this, I would have said they were crazy. I believe in weighing all the options and taking my time. But I don't think I have the benefit of doing it this time. Everything seems to be going at such an accelerated speed. It feels destined to be, and I have no wish to control it. I just want to ride on this wave of emotion forever."

Lauren was surprised by her friend's revelation. "Wow! This certainly sounds like a new Adriana. I think love has hit hard. I can't wait to meet him. Cindy says he's wonderful, and that seeing the two of you together was a perfect match. In fact she's kicking herself for not thinking of a match between you, before."

Adriana laughed. "Yeah, well, that's how we feel about it too. I was going to ask you about joining us at a party a week from Saturday."

Lauren finished her sentence. "I already know about it. This guy named Alex is giving it, and no one knows if the theme is a joke or not. Right? Too late, I'm already invited by Cindy and Ron. They wouldn't take no for an answer. It's actually starting to sound interesting. And personally, I'm ready for a party. I'm just glad I'm not the one giving it."

Adriana giggled. "Well, you're going with Elliot and me. He's hiring a limo, so we don't have to worry about transportation. We'll go to the ball in style. This guy lives in a big house on the beach in Malibu. It seems only fitting that we go in style. Just like a couple of Cinderellas." Adriana paused for a moment before continuing, "And as far as you not giving the party, well, I have a favor to ask."

Lauren shook her head. "No, Adriana, I can't compete with a mansion on the beach. The party stays where it's at."

Adriana laughed. "No, Lauren. It's not that. For some strange reason, Alex wants me to organize the dinner with the caterers." Adriana snickered at a passing thought. "Frankly, I believe their dialog really went like this: 'We don't want to do it, we'll ask Adriana.' There will be about a hundred people attending. I have no idea why they want me to pick out the menu, but how could I refuse? Elliot said he couldn't figure it out either. He said Alex was planning it over the phone with him, and suddenly blurted out that he would like for me to do this if it wasn't an inconvenience. Elliot swears he had nothing to do with it. I tend to think it was an easy way out for them. Whatever the reason, I could tell Elliot had trouble asking me, so I couldn't say no. I don't really mind, except I don't have a lot of time. I know you don't either, but would you consider doing this with me?"

Lauren was confused. "Why? So if it's screwed up, you can

blame me too?"

Adriana laughed. "Kind of like that. I have to meet with the catering service at noon today. Please say you'll come and help me pick out the courses. Look at the bright side, at least we'll order something we both like."

Lauren found the humor in the situation, and couldn't turn her friend down. "Oh, why not. I can pretend it's my party we're planning. I'll play Cinderella for the evening, and I'll be going in my carriage to the Prince's ball. And if I get too bored, at least I can eat well."

Adriana agreed. "Yeah, we can hide in the kitchen with the caterers if the party gets too out of hand. They'll know us intimately by the time this shindig is over. I don't think there's a price limit. I was told to do anything I wanted, and make it unforgettable."

Lauren was excited. "This is better than throwing our own party. We get to live out our fantasies through this guy. I hope he knows what he's got himself into. I think poor Alex will get his money's worth."

"That's the spirit, Lauren. Between the two of us, we can make this thing work, and perhaps make some friends in the process."

"Or get thrown out of L.A."

Adriana laughed. "Well, I guess that's a possibility too. I'll meet you at noon at Sarah's Catering. Do you know where it is?"

Lauren thought for a moment. "Isn't it the one down the street from my store? The one so exclusive I can't even afford to look in their window? Yes, I know where it is. I'll see you there at noon, and be prepared to have all your fantasies and dreams come true."

Adriana smiled with a whisper. "They already have."

Elliot was still half asleep when he answered his phone on the second ring. Alex began talking before Elliot could even react.

"Elliot, are you there? We have to get started on this party. Did you ask Adriana for help with the food?"

Elliot shook his covers off the bed. "Alex, I was sleeping."

Alex laughed. "Oh I see, like you've never woke me up at all hours of the day and night? That's what friends are for. Now, wake up and answer the question."

Elliot answered in a hoarse tone. "Yes, I asked Adriana. She said she would be happy to help out. She mentioned bringing in her own reinforcements, if needed. And before you ask, yes, we had a wonderful time last night. I think this relationship is going to last. I can't believe I'm already calling it a relationship, but that's what it is. It seems we've known each other forever and now want to make up for lost time. I didn't get home until 4:00 this morning. So you will forgive me if my mind isn't fully awake yet. I suppose love does that to you. I've never enjoyed anything like this before; therefore, I plan on appreciating every moment."

Alex was delighted. "I am truly happy for you. She seems like a very nice lady. When will I get to meet her for a longer time? The last time was for just a few minutes."

Elliot was feeling a little guilty for how easily his happiness had come to him. "Alex, I know you've worked so hard to find her. She will come to you. All this isn't for nothing. I can't promise it will be at the party, but I do believe you will have her in your life. I don't think this is a cruel joke thrown out to you by the universe. Who knows why people meet. And why it's love at first sight for some, while for others, there's turmoil to work through first. I know your love exists. There are just too many things I have personally witnessed that make my belief in your dreams so strong. Just bide your time and be true to yourself. Keep listening to that gut of yours. I never thought it would happen to me, but here I am, in love."

Alex smiled. "And that's precisely why I'm having this party. I believe in my instincts. I refuse to believe I'm wrong."

Elliot was worried about Alex's expectations. "Well, if she's not actually at your party, perhaps you'll meet her through your party in some way. You never know."

Alex knew his friend was worried for him. He knew Elliot believed the dream would come true. Just not on Saturday night.

"Don't worry about me, Elliot. I'll be fine. I know exactly what I'm doing. And if I don't, then I'll pretend I do. That's the first step to any accomplishment. If I pretend I know what I'm doing long enough, my mind starts believing it, and impossibilities are achieved. So don't worry about me."

Elliot closed his eyes, not bothering to mention there were two people involved in the meeting, not just one.

"Worry about you? Never. Now, let's get started on this list."

Alex picked up his notes. "I talked to a friend of mine yesterday. He agreed to print the invitations, and have them ready for pick up at noon today. His shop is near the caterers. Are we using Sarah's? Cindy says they're the best in town. She said no one would consider having a big party without consulting them first. Anyway, I'll go pick the invitations up, and bring them to your office. Donovan can meet us there at 1:00. Perhaps we can get them ready for delivery by 4:00. I know I'm asking for a lot from you guys, but trust me, it'll be worth it."

Elliot laughed. "Alex, when are you going to start writing another book or manuscript? I need a vacation." He pulled his list from the nightstand. "Yes, Adriana also confirmed that Sarah's is the only service to use. For a larger fee, they'll work with us on the timing. I told Adriana to enjoy herself. Think romance and choose something unforgettable. We'll get with Sarah regarding the theme, decorations, and design late this afternoon."

Alex was exhilarated. "It looks as if you have your side organized. I shouldn't have doubted you. I remember how you are about deadlines. But will Adriana have the time?"

"Yeah, she said she would enjoy it. If she gets into a bind, a girlfriend of hers will help out. She thought her friend would get a kick out of all this. Adriana was inviting her to the party as well. Her name is Lauren Wells."

Alex felt a momentary dizziness, but quickly recovered. "I

know the name. I think from Cindy. Anyway, that would be great. The more the merrier. If I have time, I'll swing by Sarah's before coming to your office and see how things are progressing. Everyone I've spoken to seems to be looking forward to the party." Alex took the phone in both hands. "Elliot, I hope you know how much I appreciate your help. Adriana's too. I know this is a call over and above the duties of friendship. I tell you my dream, and you help make it come true. How can I repay you for the trust you've shown me?"

Elliot spoke quietly. "You just did. I'll see you later."

Lauren met her friend at noon, noticing immediately how different Adriana looked. She walked in looking like a new woman.

"My God, you look like you've been reborn. So, this is what true love does for a person? Can you bottle it for the rest of us? You are positively glowing."

Adriana hugged her friend back. "Yes, it's a glow all right. Funny thing is I never knew what I was missing before. My work was my love life. But now that I know, I have a feeling Mark will be running the store more often than not." Adriana rubbed her hands together. "Now, let's take a look at those menus."

Sarah almost read their minds once Adriana described the event. She had the girls taste several samples, before making their selections. All the food and beverage arrangements were organized within an hour. Adriana turned to her friend and feigned shock.

"This is all going like clockwork. I can't believe everything would be this simple to select? And they decorate the house too? Wow! It's fun to plan these things without worrying about the cost. I could certainly get used to this kind of life."

Lauren laughed, slapping her friend with a menu card. "Yeah, it was easier than I thought. And after trying all that food, I'm stuffed. But now I've got to run. I have a ton of work to do at the store. We were busy when I left. Would you mind if I let you finish up the paperwork?"

Adriana stood up. "No, not at all. I couldn't have done this without you. But be warned, I may have to call on you again. I hope you don't mind."

"Not at all. I'll accept this kind of call any day of the week."

Adriana stopped Lauren at the door with a question. "Any ideas what you're wearing to the party?"

Lauren thought for a moment. "It all depends on what my fairy Godmother whips up for me. Glass slippers for sure."

Lauren opened the door and let herself out. She immediately reopened the door, peeking her head inside.

"How about lunch and a shopping trip tomorrow? I can spare a few hours. What's the attire?"

Adriana looked surprised. "You mean you aren't wearing something from Lauren's Place? You can't do that. I'll see about the attire. I have no idea, but I suspect it's going to be rather dressy. And yes, lunch sounds great. Thanks, Lauren, I love you."

Lauren waved to her friend through the glass and she was gone.

Adriana had just turned to the counter to complete the forms when Alex walked in carrying a large box.

Adriana had to refrain from laughing. "Hi, Alex. You may not remember me. I'm Adriana. We just sampled the courses, and put the finishing touches on your party plans. If I do say so myself, it will be spectacular."

"Of course I remember you." Alex put the box on a table and hugged his new friend. The moment he did, Adriana received another insight. She was caught off guard again, and turned rigid. Alex noticed and asked her if she was all right. Adriana was embarrassed, and decided the truth would be better than trying to come up with a story. "This may sound strange, but the other night when I touched your hand, and just now when we hugged, I got a single flash in my mind's eye. The picture was so quick, I can't make out what you're doing."

Alex was both surprised and interested. "Really? You see me?

Do you often get these flashes when you shake someone's hand?"

Adriana smiled, no longer uncomfortable. "It happens occasionally. No, actually, it rarely happens. But normally I can see the picture clearly, and more slowly. Sometimes, it's a picture of what they happen to have on their mind, or something they've recently done that's left an impression. Sometimes, it's something in the future. But I can't make out what I'm seeing with you."

Alex's eyes were wide with wonder. "That's very interesting. I've been leading a rather unusual life for the last few months. Perhaps that's what you picked up on. If it comes in clearer, please let me know. I'd be interested in what impressions you come up with."

Alex immediately felt a sisterly bond with Elliot's new girlfriend. He couldn't explain it, but it entered his mind to actually tell her about his dreams. He opened his mouth, but found he couldn't talk about this part of his private life yet.

"Adriana, tell me about the menu. I can't believe you've already made the decisions in just over an hour? I think it was a good idea to have you handle this. I can't begin to tell you how much I appreciate it. Under normal circumstances, I wouldn't have been so bold. I don't know why it was so important that you take care of this. Perhaps it was my way of getting to know you better."

She saw the warmth in his eyes and relaxed. "Actually, a friend of mine helped me out. She just left. And of course, Sarah had everything well organized. The woman is amazing. Anyone could have worked with her." Adriana handed him a notebook, and continued, "Look over the list, and let me know if you want any changes. After all, it is your party."

Alex looked over the list and smiled. "Perfect. They can actually do all this in a week? This is exceptional. I never knew planning a party was so easy."

Adriana laughed. "Believe me, it's not usually this easy. Especially on such short notice. Apparently, this party has divine intervention."

Alex grinned, drawing in his dimples further than usual. He wanted to tell her why the party plans were going so well, but backed off. Instead he turned to her and said, "Love has an energy all of its own, doesn't it?"

She blushed, but looked into his eyes. "Oh yes, it does. It's wonderful."

Alex drove to Elliot's office with his music playing loudly. It was a cool day, and the breeze felt good blowing in his hair. He followed Donovan into the garage, parking beside him.

Alex pulled the box of invitations out of his trunk, handing them off to his friend. Donovan carried them into Elliot's large office, setting them down on the conference table.

"Here are the invitations. Alex is right behind me." Elliot walked over and quickly opened the lid, pulling an invitation out to inspect. His eyebrows rose as he turned the card over. "I can't believe this was done literally overnight. This is beautiful."

Donovan pulled out another from the box and smiled. "I suppose when Alex sets his mind to do something, it's going to get done come hell or high water. We should know that by now."

Alex walked in carrying his notebook. "Did I hear my name?"

Elliot spoke up, teasing his friend. "We were commenting on the quality of your invitations. It's amazing what can be done when you know the right people, and aren't afraid to use a little brute force."

Alex smothered a grin. "Hey, I had to invite the guy to my party to get this done overnight. Not to mention paying dearly for it."

The men seated themselves at the large table and began preparing the invitations for delivery.

Donovan whispered under his breath for effect, "Sounds to me like this guy is the one who used a little brute force on you."

Alex laughed out loud. "Yeah, he did."

Elliot was anxious to talk about his new life-changing events.

"I noticed I'm already thinking of her before making a decision. I think of her all the time. I don't know where she came from, but I hope she stays."

Elliot was silent for a moment, and then quietly chuckled to himself. "If anyone had told me a week ago I would feel this way, I would have said they were crazy. I didn't want a serious relationship. Not ever again. I thought I liked my life the way it was. No complications."

Donovan interrupted with his own advice. "Don't question it. You know some things happen the way they're supposed to. I've learned to just enjoy it. It can create a sort of freedom. If anyone had told me I would fall in love with someone like Vickie, I would have called them insane, too. You just never know where love will find you, or where it will take you. How can someone put boundaries and rules on such a thing? It's never the way you anticipate it's going to be anyway. Personally, Elliot, I'm glad to see you finally falling for someone. The only person you were fooling with that talk about never wanting another relationship was yourself. Adriana seems very nice, and Vickie certainly does like her."

Donovan turned his attention to Alex. "Have you spent any time with her?"

Alex looked up from his work. "Yeah, I saw her at the caterers today. She and a girlfriend had everything done by the time I got there. They've planned a spectacular meal. I've brought a planning book for both of you to look at. The catering company takes care of every detail, so I suppose all we have to do is have these delivered, and show up for the party."

Donovan was curious. "What made you decide on formal attire?"

Elliot interjected with his own opinion. "I think it was chosen because of the romance theme."

Alex looked at his friends and smiled knowingly. "As soon as you read over the plans, you'll see just how perfectly it fits. And doesn't everyone like to dress up occasionally? Makes a person feel special. Isn't that what the evening is supposed to be all about?"

Donovan shook his head. "Personally, I find it difficult to believe we're sitting here discussing party plans, and addressing invitations. What has become of us?"

Elliot and Alex shot him a humorous glance, and spoke in unison, "Love."

The invitations were ready to be delivered by 4:00, just in time for the courier to pick them up at 4:30.

Donovan looked at the finished product, stacked high on the other side of the table. "I can't believe we're done. That went amazingly fast."

Elliot counted the number of envelopes, making sure no one had been forgotten.

"I have work to get caught up on, and a hot date tonight, but I'll be here until the courier service gets here."

Alex laughed. "Has it occurred to either one of you that I am fully capable of making sure the service picks these up and delivers them to the proper people? You've been so good to humor me like this. Once again."

The two men looked at each other and winked. They promptly walked out of the office, leaving Alex to box up the envelopes, and wait for the service to arrive.

Alex yelled through the closed door, "Thanks, guys."

Alex drove home excited about how easy the party details were coming along. Everything had been planned, right down to the valet service. When he stopped at a traffic light, Alex looked up at the stars.

"All I have to do now is relax and pray she shows up. I wonder if she'll realize this is all in her honor? The first day of the rest of our lives together."

Lauren worked until late in the evening, and was exhausted when she got home. She noticed the message light blinking the moment she walked into her office. Before answering, she sat in her chair and slowly opened the lid of her music box, waiting for the melody to filter through the room. She closed her eyes and hummed along for several minutes, while her aching muscles relaxed. When she opened her eyes, she noticed the box again.

Lauren squinted, trying to make out every detail of the beautiful object. Each time she looked at it, her thoughts went back to its size.

"The shape is so strange. What is it about this thing?"

She walked around the desk, and was about to pick it up for closer examination when she was startled by the unusually loud ringing of her phone. She closed the lid and answered the phone at the same time.

It was Adriana. "Hi, what's going on?"

Lauren fell into her chair. "Not much. Just got home. I was looking at the music box for the millionth time. I'm trying to figure out why it looks the way it does."

Adriana continued the conversation, "Not to mention the weight. We'll figure it out. It can't be that difficult. But taking it apart might cause permanent damage."

Lauren looked at her watch. "Adriana, why are you calling? Don't you have a date?"

"Yeah, but Elliot had a late meeting. Apparently, he didn't get much done this afternoon because he and his friends were addressing invitations. That's actually a funny thought. Three wealthy businessmen planning parties and addressing invitations. Good to see they don't think they're too good for such things. Anyway, he's coming over here later. He's in this area of town already. I was calling to let you know the party's attire will be ultra formal. You may get to wear that Cinderella dress after all! But, I think I'd skip the glass slippers. Nothing would be worse than picking glass out of your feet."

Lauren giggled at the thought. "You're right. That wouldn't be my idea of a good time, either. OK, I'll forget the slippers. Now I have to decide what to wear. I think I want something new. How often do I have the opportunity to buy a gown?"

Adriana thought for a moment. "Do you have anything in your shop that might work?"

Lauren shook her head. "I don't think so, but we're expecting the new holiday line any day now. Perhaps we should both wait a few days and see what develops."

"Wonderful idea. Kevin showed me a preview of that line in a book. I saw a few that would suit me very nicely. This is becoming the party of the year. For us anyway. And it's about time too. The year is almost gone."

Lauren cringed at the thought. "Don't remind me. Oh, did you finalize all the arrangements at Sarah's?"

"Yeah, it's all taken care of. You couldn't have been gone more than thirty seconds when Alex showed up. I don't think he was spying. He was very excited, and couldn't wait to see what was planned. He loved everything we picked. And you'll be happy to know I didn't take all the credit. I gave you a little as well."

Lauren laughed. "It was easy, wasn't it? It sort of arranged itself. I've thrown a lot of parties, and it was always hard work."

Adriana agreed. "It's strange how everything is working out quite nicely for a party being arranged on such short notice. I haven't arranged parties planned months in advance that have flowed this smoothly. So far, so good."

Adriana clicked her tongue, then spoke again. "The weirdest thing happened when Alex hugged me today. I received the same quick mental flash as I did when we met for the first time. I don't know why I can't beam in on what I see. I don't know if it's past, present, or future. But there's something about him trying to come through. I can't go around hugging him every few minutes just so I can solve the mystery. I told him about it, but all he said was that his life had recently been a little crazy. Maybe that's what I'm feeling. It's just odd for me not to see what's coming through once I get a flash. Oh well. In time, I suppose."

Lauren yawned. "Maybe it's because you're in love. Your brain's all clogged up. Go enjoy the evening. I'm going to take a nice long bath and go to bed. I'll see you for lunch tomorrow."

"Okay, sweet dreams."

Lauren yawned loudly and trudged into her bathroom to fill the tub with water, making sure to add a few drops of the lavender and rose oils. Within a few minutes, she had slipped into the warm cocoon and was totally relaxed.

Lauren leaned her head back, closed her tired eyes, and took a deep breath. She was surprised to see herself at a party, draped in a beautiful gown with her hair pulled up. She blinked hard, but still found herself in the same location.

"Where am I?" she asked, not really expecting an answer.

She saw people mingling, but instinctively knew that no one could see her. She heard music playing on a patio and turned to move in that direction, but without warning she found herself effortlessly transported there. The night air was slightly cool, but very refreshing. Lauren recognized the music as a romantic instrumental. She saw several couples on the dance floor, all dressed in formal attire. She stopped to watch them for a few moments, trying to calm herself.

"Everyone looks so handsome in their tuxedos and long flowing gowns; I feel as if I've been thrown in the middle of a classic 40's movie."

Lauren felt herself floating slowly to the edge of the patio. She forced herself to look down, and saw the ocean waves crashing against the shoreline. Glancing to her left, she saw a familiar rock formation, but turned away, not paying much attention to it. She was humming a new tune playing in the background, realizing the song was 'Street of Dreams', when her eyes suddenly widened. Lauren could feel her head jerking back to the left.

"Oh my God, where am I? We used to meet at that rock. This must be the same beach."

Lauren became disoriented, and couldn't put the puzzle

together. Her hair was now on her shoulders and blowing around her face. And the gown she had been wearing was suddenly gone, leaving her nude, and feeling alone and vulnerable. She fought to keep the confusion from spreading through her veins.

"How can I be having two dreams at once? Is this a multi-dimensional illusion? Please tell me what I'm experiencing. Why do I feel so sad?"

Lauren used her reserved energy to force her eyes open. She lay in her tub shivering from the freezing water, trying to calm her disturbed thoughts.

"What happened?" She tried to remember, but few details were brought to the surface.

"I know I saw the same rocks on a beach. How can that be? Wasn't I at a party?" Her stomach was churning. "Where was he? I need to know he's all right."

Tears were burning her eyes as Lauren toweled herself off and crawled into bed. She fell asleep repeating the same sentence over and over.

"Where are you?"

Alex was tired when he walked through his front door, but was too wound up to sleep. He dimmed the lights in his office, sat down, and stared ahead at the couple walking hand in hand on the beach. The painting had brought much comfort to him, and was another verification that it all existed. He was anxious for the date of his party to finally arrive. Everyone seemed to be experiencing new beginnings. And he was prepared for the same. Alex was deep in thought, but was jolted into reality by the incessant ringing of his phone.

"Who could be calling so late?"

He quickly lifted the receiver.

It was Cindy. "Hi, Alex. Sorry about the time. I didn't think you'd be sleeping. Ron and I were talking about your party, and were curious if you were bringing a date. Because if you don't have one yet, I've got the perfect girl for you."

Alex shook his head in frustration. "Cindy, you never give up, do you? I appreciate your efforts in trying to tie me down, but it just so happens that I have someone coming to the party already."

Cindy's curiosity had peaked. "Oh really? Who is she? Anyone I know?"

Alex shut his eyes, trying to come up with a sane answer. "No, I don't think you know her."

Cindy wasn't satisfied. "What's her name? Where did you meet her?"

Alex could hear Ron in the background telling her to stop pressuring his friend. Alex took a deep breath, his mind forming a blank.

"Cindy, I think I'll leave everything up in the air until the day of the party. You'll get all your answers then. Trust me, I won't be alone for my own party."

Cindy sighed. "Alex, you know I love you. I just want you to enjoy the evening. If this mystery girl doesn't work out, let me know. I have a wonderful person for you to meet."

Alex smiled into the phone. "Thank you. And now I'm going to hang up and go to bed. Sleep well, Cindy." He hung up before his friend could question him any further.

Alex walked up the stairs thinking about what he would tell people if she didn't show up. He was beginning to doubt his confidence for the first time. He lay in bed for several minutes tossing and turning before finally clicking on the TV in frustration. He knew he had to get his mind off the negativity creeping loudly in his head.

"Stop it, Alex. You've been doing just fine trusting your instincts until now. Don't let anyone try and convince you otherwise. Stop questioning how she'll arrive, and just be confident that she will."

Alex turned over on his side, facing the dark skies outside. He was too tired to fight the opposition.

"How will I know her? How will she know me? Will she be a guest? The bartender for Pete's sake? Maybe she'll work for the valet service? How the hell will I know? And what if she's with someone?"

Alex fell asleep with his own self-doubt knocking down his confidence, one layer at a time.

He awoke to a brisk wind whipping about him. He was at a party, and knew instinctively that she was there. He didn't fight the pain and fear that grew into a panic when he realized he would never recognize her. There were thousands of people glaring down on him, all pointing and laughing at his foolishness.

The scene quickly switched while he watched himself running along the darkened beach. The sky was black, making the sand below him invisible. He could hear the people still snickering in the background. He fell to his knees, feeling forgotten and betrayed by his own dreams. He sensed the warmth of his guide next to him and instinctively turned to her. She smiled lovingly, and extended her wrinkled hand to him in comfort. He gratefully accepted it, holding it close for a several moments. Alex looked away, speaking hesitantly, his voice weak.

"What if she doesn't come? What if she comes and I don't recognize her?" His worst fears and insecurities had followed him into his dreams. "And what if she doesn't come alone? Do I stand by and let her walk away again? And if by chance I do recognize her, how do I convince her of our love for each other, without her thinking I'm crazy?"

Alex shook his head. "This is insane. I don't see how it can work. I thought I did, but I'm just not sure anymore. So many things could go wrong. The primary problem being that she doesn't show up."

Alex ran his hands through his thick hair in a frantic motion.

"I will then have run out of ideas. And everyone, including myself, will think I've gone mad. No one will ever trust me or my instincts again." He looked to his ancient companion for an answer. "For all I know, she doesn't even exist on this plane. Maybe she's in another dimension. Hell, I don't know. I think I am mad. I should give up now before the pain gets any worse."

His visitor let him exhaust himself before answering. After he was quiet for several moments, she whispered, "Alex, your insecurities are speaking now. Why are you listening? Only you can turn a deaf ear. Your fear and insecurities feed on your attention. Turn your back, my child, and come with me. You have fought your demons and won. Don't let them convince you to a rematch. Turn away and be strong."

She had his attention now. "You know she exists. Are you now questioning the many lessons you've learned? Are you now questioning everything you've seen with your own eyes, and felt with your own soul? You would come this far only to give up now? Remember to open your soul and the rest will take care of itself. What is to be will be. That's destiny. But only when you are truly prepared to open yourself without hesitation will she be with you. You're the one to determine whether it's this life or another. In this consciousness or another. This is free will. All you have to do is be willing to love without reservations or question. You must be prepared to jump into the void, not worrying about outside obstacles or reactions. Do not squander your energies on fears and insecurities from your own mind, or from the mind of others. You know this already. I can advise you, but you must complete the tasks. Please, Alex, don't turn against yourself, and what you instinctively know. Trust your process."

Alex looked behind him and saw the social affair was still engaged. He could hear the music increasing in volume. His breathing was shallow as he carefully listened. He was perplexed, and looked again to his maternal guide for an answer.

"How can that be? That's my voice singing the song I wrote. I don't understand."

She lightly touched Alex's temple with the soft pads of her fingers. He closed his eyes, waiting for an answer. Instead, he found himself back in his bed, daylight streaming much too brightly into the room.

Without opening his eyes, Alex's hand felt for, and retrieved his journal from the nightstand. He wanted to quickly write his experiences before they disintegrated from his memory. When he slowly opened his lids to the sunlight, his eyes immediately widened in disbelief, and his jaw line hardened. Printed in large, bold letters on the newly opened page of the journal were three simple words: "Trust the music."

Alex looked closer, verifying his handwriting. He quickly flipped to the next page, but it also gave the same advice. His voice repeated the words loudly for several minutes before his heart finally realized its true message. "Trust the music, trust the music."

With renewed vitality and confidence, he grabbed the phone, punching in Ron's number.

"Can we get the guys together? I want a few practices before the party."

Ron responded immediately, "No problem, let's plan on 7:00 tonight. I'm sure the guys will be happy to cooperate. I'll see you then."

Alex hung up the phone, never taking his eyes off the page. "Trust the music. Of course!"

The next few days flew by in a whirlwind of activity. Alex worked with the planners and caterers during the day, spending most of his time convincing them of exactly how he wanted the layout and flow of the party to be arranged. He outlined on paper where he wanted each table placed, where each item would be set, each candle was to be lit, and where the stage and speakers would be built. He drew one sketch after another, making certain everything was arranged exactly as he had seen it.

The wall hangings, drapes and furniture were moved out, and set decorations were moved in. Electricians added dimmed lighting in some areas, and enhanced the lighting in others. Gardeners added plants and decorations inside and out. And the pool was filled with rose petals. The sound of water was everywhere, with fountains placed in strategic areas throughout. Alex knew it was important that his guests, and especially her, felt as though they had entered a dream. The fantasy and illusion had to be complete. He wasn't going to leave anything to chance. Elliot and Donovan were the only people allowed on the premises. They spent most of their time making sure the plans were precisely carried out. Whenever Alex got lost in the perfection of the upcoming event, his friends were there to calm him, and smooth over the tension it invariably created.

But on the day of the event, even they would not be allowed to participate with the final touches. He wanted everyone to be surprised. Alex was having a wonderful time putting his plans into action. He was exhausted by the end of the day, when he would practice with the band until late in the evening. Alex knew the only way to keep the insecure questions away from his conscious thoughts was to stay busy, and then fall asleep, worn out.

Every night he would visualize, and then dream of his party. He would hear his music, but he no longer dreamed of her. Every morning, Alex would wake up, staring outside, reciting positive affirmations. His patience was being tested, but he wouldn't give up. He continuously reminded himself that it was imperative he believe in his dreams, and that it didn't matter if she was no longer with him at night. His intuition was still strong, and he felt he was on the path to bring her back to him. He refused to question what would happen if she didn't show up on Saturday night. He couldn't afford to allow the fear to penetrate his mind. He knew if it did, he could be destroyed, and possibly lose her for a very long time. He missed her terribly, but refused to think about it until after the party. Whenever he felt his fear begin to rise and consume him, he would talk calmly to himself.

"Just be patient and wait. Everything will work out just fine." In his loneliest moments, he would hold the ring, stare at his painting, read his journal, and listen to his music. This gave him the proof that she did exist, and was still all around him. He depended on it to give him the strength to continue forward, one day at a time.

Lauren was busy with the opening of the new boutique, and the various meetings that never seemed to end. As each day progressed, she and Adriana were getting more excited about the party. She often commented that she didn't know why she was looking forward to it so much. Adriana thought it was because Lauren had finally agreed to come out of her shell and socialize, even if it was just for one night. Lauren couldn't be more ecstatic that Adriana had found the man of her dreams. She seemed happier than Lauren could ever remember her being. They both felt like enthusiastic teenagers again, referring to the party as the Cinderella event of the season. Everyone was gossiping about what was going to take place. Each day, the stories grew larger and larger.

The new holiday clothing line had come into Lauren's new shop, and Kevin had picked two dresses, one for each of the women.

By Friday evening, everything was ready for the party. The next day would be spent making the transformations complete. Lauren fell into bed late each night exhausted, first thinking about the work on her new boutique. But her thoughts would quickly switch to the upcoming party. She would hum the music softly to herself, and meditate about the house that overwhelmed her dreams. She knew the two houses wouldn't be the same, but Lauren told herself that it didn't matter. She forced herself to believe she was only enjoying the fantasy.

Lauren was having the same dream each night. She saw herself walking through the front door, immediately feeling the intense energy of the room. The music would be soft and romantic, and the champagne would be flowing from fountains. Everyone would be wearing smiles, and seemed genuinely happy. She couldn't remember exact details, but she could vaguely recall the house being decorated with a romance theme in mind. The one significant memory she would retain upon awakening was the moment she stepped outside to the patio area. The music she had now grown accustomed to hearing in her head would suddenly begin playing. The harmonizing tones would echo over the ocean below her, and return back in loud support of her feelings. It was as if the music were alive, and understanding her in a way that no living entity ever could. Her orgasmic thoughts would then flow directly to him.

Lauren would frantically search all around, but found she was always alone. It was she, her music, and the deep throbbing tide within. Realizing that he no longer located her in dream state, she tried to persuade herself that getting upset would accomplish nothing. She attempted to rationalized it was due to the long hours she was working. She tried convincing herself that she didn't have the energy needed to communicate in the other reality. She brought it up frequently in conversation.

Adriana knew Lauren had given herself an excuse, which was valid for the time being, but knew if her friend didn't start connecting with him again very soon, panic would begin to set in. Adriana assured her that all the events that had taken place had been for a reason. There was a reason now why she needed to put her trust in everything she believed in more than ever before. It was up to Lauren to convince herself that her dreams would come true. She knew she had worked hard on achieving everything she believed in. But she now found it was the waiting that might kill her spirit. Lauren, for now at least, had the music still playing in her ears every night. She had the lyrics to remember and hold on to. She knew the dream wasn't over. Not yet.

Chapter 23

Saturday morning was a whirlwind of activity in Alex's house, but somehow, he remained calm and relaxed. Donovan and Elliot put a conference call in to him for any last minutes changes and updates. Everyone had lost count of how many ideas had been added or deleted since the plans got underway. Donovan could hear a different tone in Alex's voice, and shook his head.

"Alex, are you all right today? I haven't seen you this cool and calm in several weeks. Are you sure you have no more changes to make? This certainly isn't like you."

Elliot laughed, adding his own comment, "Yeah, Alex, the day just wouldn't seem complete if you weren't yelling for changes. What's up?"

Alex sipped his coffee then spoke slowly. "I'm getting myself geared up for the best evening of my life. Perhaps it's the calm before the storm. I know everything we can do has already been done. The house is ready for the guests to walk through its doors and be transported to another time and place. We have to admit that our jobs are done. Now, it's time to enjoy the result of all the hard work." Alex laughed. "Damn, it does seem odd that I'm so calm. But it's much appreciated."

Alex changed the subject and asked his friends about transportation. "I never thought to ask, are you guys coming in limos?"

Elliot answered first, "Yeah, I believe they've all been booked for tonight. Everyone I've talked to is arriving in limos. It is formal after all."

Donovan snickered knowingly. "Sure, and the women wouldn't have it any other way. They're all really getting into the theme of this shindig."

Elliot appreciated the humorous remark. "I think if Adriana had her way, we'd be arriving in a glass carriage."

Donovan laughed appreciatively. "It sounds as if she's been talking to Vickie. They're all calling this the Cinderella event. And after seeing how the place has been transformed, I'd have to agree with them. Alex, the way you worked to come up with such a concept is amazing. It certainly makes the rest of us mere mortal men look insensitive and dull. Do you know how difficult it's been keeping the details secret? Vickie and Cindy are barely talking to me."

Elliot interrupted, "Yeah, Donovan, I know what you mean. Adriana's been trying to trick me into telling her the details too. I think all the women have started making up their own stories to satisfy their curiosities. You realize, of course, that none of them believe it's going to be creative and imaginative in the least. But my guess is that they'll play along with us to keep our egos intact. I think they'll be very surprised by what men can do when they put their minds to it. But personally, Alex, I am impressed with the concept. What was finally the deciding factor on this theme?"

Alex smiled. "What is more romantic than the king of his own domain finding the love of his life at a ball? They didn't know each other moments before, then they looked into each other's eyes and the transformations were complete. She was lost from him once, and he worked hard at finding her again. And once found, he would never let her slip from him again. He knew there would only be one woman in his life. The only woman that could make him complete. That's how I see it."

Elliot grinned in appreciation. "There have certainly been some big changes in you since your dreams started. Personally, I didn't think you had it in you. But aren't you forgetting something?

I believe the party planners had a hand in it too."

Alex laughed. "Yeah, I came up with the concept, and they built brilliantly on it. Without them, I couldn't have made it a reality. This place has become what I feel in my dreams. I just hope she knows it's in her honor."

Apprehension suddenly smothered the air, and his friends were both quiet. Neither wanted to mention the possible negative aspects of the party on Alex's big day. Finally, Elliot fumbled for words of encouragement.

"How could she not? It truly shaped up to resemble a fairy tale. Now, let's hope the slipper fits the foot."

Lauren and Adriana took Saturday off to be pampered before their big night. They met for lunch, then drove to the salon to have their bodies spoiled with massages, manicures, pedicures, and facials. They arranged for their hair stylist and a make up artist to come to Lauren's house in the late afternoon, after the girls had dressed. Elliot had arranged to pick them up at Lauren's at 7:00, and neither wanted to be running late.

Lauren was having her dress zipped, talking feverously, "I feel like I'm getting married again." She shook her head. "No, I don't think I went to all this trouble when I got married. Are you sure this isn't a dream?"

Adriana turned her around to look in the mirror. "No, this isn't a dream. No dream could be so expensive and time consuming. Do you know what this day is costing us?" Adriana put her hands up, but continued talking, "No, I have to say it doesn't matter. There's something about this event tonight that I can't explain. My intuition is telling me to be ready for a multitude of surprises. Can you feel it too?"

Lauren's eyes sparkled. "Yes I can. It's all I've dreamed about. Whatever takes place, it should be exciting. I'm glad to finally be meeting Elliot. It will be good to see Cindy and Vickie again too."

Adriana added, "Not to mention everyone else who will be

attending. I hear some heavy names will be joining us. Of course, I can't tell you who because Elliot wouldn't tell me a damn thing. These guys are really keeping their word to Alex about staying quiet."

The doorbell interrupted their train of thought. Adriana ran downstairs and returned with the makeup artist and hair stylist. The men gasped when they saw how beautiful the women already were. The hair stylist put down the box he was holding to hug his clients.

"My goodness, I don't think either one of you need my help." He turned to the artist. "What do you think?"

The artist laughed, agreeing with his friend. "I think we made the trip here for nothing. These girls are gorgeous."

Adriana and Lauren giggled like teenagers, enjoying the mock flattery. They both sat down in separate chairs, and the work began.

No mirrors were allowed until the job was complete. Occasionally, the two women would take a glimpse of each other and profusely compliment the other. When the unveiling finally took place, the boys removed the sheets from the mirror, and stood back.

Adriana was speechless, while Lauren burst out in laughter.

"My God, we're beautiful. We've got to get pictures of this because I don't think this kind of magic can last all night."

Adriana turned to the men and spoke in exasperated tones. "Please don't tell us we're going to turn into old hags at the stroke of midnight."

The men looked at each other and shrugged. "What are you talking about, sweetie? That beauty will last you all night long."

Adriana was having a difficult time choking down a hearty laugh, and it was left for Lauren to calmly explain her friend's comment. "Guys, everyone's calling this party tonight the Cinderella event. Adriana thought of you as our fairy Godmothers."

Adriana was now stomping her foot, howling aloud in

amusement at the words Lauren had chosen to convey her explanations. Lauren blushed when she realized she was trapped by her own words, but had no choice but to continue.

"Uh, remember? Cinderella was forced to leave the ball at midnight?"

After a purposely uncomfortable few moments, the men understood the joke and joined in the laughter.

"Don't worry, as long as you have beauty on the inside, I think it's going to be permanent on the outside. Just have fun tonight, and make sure all your dreams come true."

The girls hugged the men, with Adriana adding, "You don't know just how true that statement is."

At precisely 7:00, Lauren's doorbell rang. Adriana took a deep breath to compose herself, then opened the door. She was quiet for a moment, then Lauren heard her throaty shrill. "My God, Elliot, you are so handsome."

Elliot was having a difficult time catching his breath at the sight of her, so instead he gently took her into his arms. When he finally pulled away, he could do nothing for a moment but gaze at the beauty he had fallen in love with.

Adriana's eyes were a bright emerald green, matching the colored rhinestones sparkling from her tight-fitting black crepe dress. The shoulders were cut very low, allowing the appearance of cleavage to rise up over the fabric. Each curve of her long lean body was accentuated by the rippled material. Her pale red hair was pulled up loosely with a green rhinestone clip, with a few long semi-spiraled strands falling down the front to her breasts.

"Adriana, I have never seen anyone so beautiful in my entire life. I couldn't have imagined such beauty before you. My God, you are spectacular."

Adriana curtsied in mocked form. "Thank you, kind sir. I only aim to please my master."

Elliot laughed and gathered her in his arms again, being careful of her appearance. "I don't want to mess up your look, yet."

She laughed knowingly. "Yet?"

Lauren waited a few minutes while the couple greeted one another before entering the room. Adriana saw her first, meeting her at the bottom step. Taking her arm, she led Lauren into the living room where Elliot sat.

"Elliot, I'd like for you to meet my best friend, Lauren Wells."

Elliot turned in their direction, and immediately stood up to shake her hand. He was temporarily caught off guard by Lauren's simple, elegant beauty. Her dark hair and royal blue gown was the accent that highlighted her almond-shaped blue eyes and deep dimples.

Her easy smile helped him to quickly compose himself. He spoke softer than usual. "It is very nice to meet you, Lauren. I have heard only wonderful things about you from Adriana, as well as Cindy and Vickie. You have quite a following. And I must mention how lovely you look."

Lauren took his hand, pulling him closer for a light hug. "Thank you. I've heard only good things about you too. You look very handsome tonight yourself."

She had immediately noticed his long dark lashes and broad shoulders. There seemed to be an immediate comfort level flowing through the room, so Lauren turned teasingly to her friend.

"Adriana, I'm impressed. Are there any others where he came from?"

Elliot smiled, flushing with embarrassment. "I will be the envy of the ball with two of the most beautiful women in the world on my arms. Both of you are gorgeous."

He turned to Lauren and chided, "But I'm sure you both always look this lovely."

Lauren and Adriana laughed. "Yeah, Elliot, we clean house in our pearls, heels, and tiaras. Doesn't everyone?"

Adriana looked at the clock, and took Lauren's arm. "Well Cinderella, it's time for the big ball. Are you ready?"

Lauren took a deep breath. "As ready as I'll ever be. God knows, it will be good to get out among the living again."

Elliot opened the door for the ladies. "Our carriage awaits. Let the fantasy begin."

Elliot had champagne chilling in the limo, handing each of the ladies a full glass once they were seated and comfortable.

Lauren gracefully accepted. "Adriana, I'm liking this man more and more. I see you read minds too. This was just what I wanted. Or more appropriately, it's just what I needed."

Adriana laughed. "Yes, now you see why I have him around. He's wonderful."

Elliot blushed again and proposed a toast, "Beginning tonight, may our lives be changed forever, and may all our dreams come true."

After the first glass was consumed, the trio relaxed, talking and laughing through their second glass, and the ride to Malibu.

Lauren looked at the couple and smiled. "I appreciate both of you including me tonight. Normally, I wouldn't have intruded, but something pushed me to accept. I know you don't mind, and that makes me appreciate it all the more. Thank you."

Adriana spoke up. "We wouldn't have had it any other way. I feel the same as you. There's something about tonight that caused you to say yes. I didn't want to have to force you to come, but I would have if it was necessary."

Elliot added to their thoughts, "Yes, Lauren, this is going to be a special night for all of us. And why not? We're all dressed up, there's a wonderful energy in the air, and let's not forget all the good food we're going to consume. Thanks to the both of you."

Adriana shook her head. "You mean thanks to Sarah. She knew what we wanted before we arrived. I can't wait to see how everything's been organized. You've been so secretive about this party."

Elliot's brown eyes had a mischievous look about them. "With good reason. Alex wanted everyone to be transported to another time, and feel they were a part of this fairy tale. Or, is it a celebration? I'm not sure anymore. But if you knew everything, then the element of surprise would be gone."

Lauren looked over to Elliot. "I'm looking forward to meeting this man. He sounds like one of a kind."

Elliot laughed in a hearty manner. "Well, I don't know quite how to take that, but he is one of three of a kind. Alex, Donovan and I go way back. We're all different in our own wonderful way, but exactly the same. Once you get to know us, you can't help but love us. As far as Alex is concerned, I can't really say just where all this has come from. But I've seen his intensity soften somewhat from the conception stage a while ago, throughout the planning of this party."

Adriana finished her drink, and handed it to Elliot with a secret smile. "Well, I don't know about Alex, but what he's saying is the truth. You just can't help but love them all."

Lauren couldn't shake the curiosity. "When did all this begin? You make it sound as though the first thought of the party, and the actual follow through was over a period of time. I thought it was only a matter of a few weeks."

Elliot lightly tapped the stem of his glass. "It's a long story, and one I hope to tell you very soon. But yes, it was all slow in forming. There were a lot of changes Alex had to go through before he could pull this event off properly."

Adriana felt a psychic nudge from her gut. "Sounds to me as if you have more than a lot to tell us about this story. What kind of changes?"

Elliot laughed, shaking his finger. "No, no, Adriana. You are not going to trick me into telling you all my friend's secrets. In time, you will know more than you would believe."

Adriana smiled knowingly. "Oh, I won't have to trick you. And I'd be willing to bet the story will be just about what I would have imagined."

The game was momentarily delayed when Lauren moved her

hand up to her neck, attempting to adjust the chain hidden underneath the fabric of her dress.

"Adriana, can you help me with this chain? The ring is caught in the material."

Elliot looked casually over to the girls as they manipulated the gold jewelry. Lauren had momentarily pulled the ring out from underneath her dress, untwisting the chain. While she was concealing the ring again, Elliot caught a glimpse of the gold circle. His eyes widened, trying to get a better look. The light had flickered on the metal well enough to see that it was a gold band. He thought he saw some type of markings on the surface. He blinked hard, and finished his drink. Elliot began quickly sifting through his thoughts. He had to work at keeping his tone nonchalant.

"Lauren, what kind of ring are you wearing?"

Lauren missed the intensity of his question. "Oh, it's a wedding ring. Because of sentimental values, I never take it off."

He shook his head, not believing anything could be this easy. "Really? Is it a family heirloom?"

Adriana answered the question, sounding equally nonchalant. She helped Lauren re-hook her dress.

"It's several decades old, but she hasn't had it long. It belonged to someone who meant a great deal to her."

Elliot wasn't getting the answer to his question.

"Has it been in your family all that time?"

Lauren shook her head, still oblivious to his suspicions.

"No, it wasn't a family heirloom. Actually, I picked it up from Vickie's gallery. From the moment I saw it, I knew it was a special piece, meant just for me."

He poured himself another glass, offering one to each of the women. His mind was a whirlwind of thoughts.

Damn! How can I get a good look at it? I know it's a long shot. A very long shot, but how could the ring mean so much to her, and have such sentimental value if she bought it from Vickie? She probably didn't know the original owner, yet it belonged to someone who was special to her? That doesn't make any sense.

The questions continued circling his mind. One always bringing him to another. Elliot didn't have time to find an excuse for another look. The limo soon rounded the corner to Alex's driveway. Shaking his head quietly to himself, he opened the door for the girls.

"It was a long shot anyway."

Once Elliot helped Adriana and Lauren out of the limo, he offered each an arm, and escorted them slowly down the red carpet to the entrance. The perimeter of the front yard had been transformed into palace walls. There was a large fountain with statues between the walls and the entrance door, in the courtyard area. On either side of the doorway were palace guards, formally dressed in royal attire. Without warning, the double doors opened, and a butler escorted them to the entrance of the main room, formally announcing each of their names.

Lauren whispered in her friend's ear, "I can't believe this. It's like being a character in a story book."

Adriana took Lauren's hand. "I know. This is unbelievable. Is it the champagne affecting us, or is it the place?"

Elliot poked his head between the two girls. "It's both."

After depositing their jackets and purses, Elliot slowly escorted his dates into the main room. He was anxious to see the look on their faces as they entered. They walked under a large angelic painted domed canopy, and gasped in delight when they entered the most beautiful room either had ever seen. There were already at least half the people in attendance, and the room was swirling with energy. Beautiful music was playing somewhere in the background. The furniture had been removed, and the room had been transformed into a majestic palace garden, with ornate park benches. English street lamps were spreading a shimmering soft light in every direction. There was greenery around each bench, with hidden miniature white and blue twinkling lights. There seemed to be a glittery effect on everything in the room. They could see where the special effects led through the downstairs of the house and out onto the patio. Occasionally, they would hear the sounds of distant church bells. The three looked up at the same time and saw twinkling stars and moving clouds expanding the ceiling into something unbelievable.

Lauren leaned over and whispered to Elliot, "I feel I'm no longer in California."

Adriana was almost speechless. "I don't think we are. Walking through those doors transported us to another place, and another time. This is amazing."

One far area of the room had been transformed to resemble a palace wall. There were fountains scattered throughout the rooms, all varying in sounds and intensity. Each blended with the others, causing a gentle resonance to the ears. There was an open, elegantly comfortable feeling about the area.

The girls hadn't realized they had gone no further than the double doors, when Cindy and Vickie made their way over. After hugs were exchanged, the girls talked in excited girlish tones. Cindy couldn't control her enthusiasm.

"Have you seen the rest of the house, and the patio?"

Vickie finished the sentence, "It's not to be believed. I wish I had thought to bring a camera. Tomorrow I'll think that I had dreamed it."

The women were full of compliments for each other. Cindy and Vickie had both bought their gowns from Lauren's Place, and they looked beautiful.

Cindy looked around, whispering loudly, "At least we won't see someone else wearing our dresses tonight."

Cindy was wearing a high neck dark red satin gown and Vickie had a gold sequined off-the-shoulder gown.

Ron and Donovan found their way to the gathering, and waited their turn. After a brief moment, Vickie introduced

Donovan to Lauren. Donovan was taken aback by her poise and beauty. "It's very nice to meet you, Lauren. What do you think of the place?"

Lauren had trouble catching her breath. "I'm still reacting to it. In my wildest imagination, I couldn't have put all of this together. It's like something out of my dreams."

Cindy responded, "Just wait until you see the rest of it. Every room is decorated in an unbelievable fashion. And the patio is like entering another era. I expect to be greeted by the King and Queen any moment."

Ron interrupted as he tightened his blond ponytail. "Speaking of, has anyone seen Alex?"

Lauren looked around, her eyes shining brighter than usual. "Yes, I'd like to meet and congratulate him."

Cindy and Vickie each took one of Lauren and Adriana's arms. "Well, in the meantime, let's go get us a drink and have a look around, shall we?"

The double doors opened and more people entered. Donovan counted each one, listening to their names.

"There seems to be more people here than I remembered licking envelopes for."

Elliot shrugged. "Who knows? Alex says he has it under control. Let's just enjoy ourselves. I have a feeling a lot of surprises are going to be coming tonight. I just hope they're all good."

Ron excused himself to greet a well-known client. Elliot looked around, making sure he and Donovan were alone, and then he pushed him gently to the kitchen. Donovan was visibly surprised, but kept moving. "What is it, Elliot?"

He put his hand up as if to ask his friend to lower his voice. "There's something I want your opinion on before I take it any further."

Donovan began smoothing his jacket out with his hand. "What is it? It's not like you to sound in a panic."

Elliot pushed Donovan a little closer in the corner of the large room. The kitchen workers were running around in a chaotic turmoil, making more noise than Elliot was comfortable with. Fighting the frustration, he took a deep breath and raised his voice.

"Donovan, what did you think of Lauren?"

Donovan needed no time to answer. "She's gorgeous. Is this the woman Cindy wanted Alex to meet? He doesn't know what he's missing." He shook his head. "But it won't matter. He's hung up on a vision from his dreams. And I sure as hell hope somehow, someway, she turns up here tonight. Otherwise, I have no idea how we're going to deal with him. That's been my primary concern since all this party planning got started."

Elliot felt a worried crease form across his forehead. "I know, me too. I don't think he could handle it. I admire him for believing so deeply in his own visions and intuition. And after everything that's happened, I suppose we'd be doing the same thing. But right this moment, it's something to worry about. What if this one time he's wrong? What if the way we read it was incorrect, too?"

Donovan's face still held a look of confusion. "Is that what you wanted to talk to me about?"

Elliot moved a little closer to his friend and whispered, "No, not completely. I want your opinion on something else."

Donovan was ready to get back to the party. "Go ahead, but hurry."

Elliot nodded. "While we were driving over here from Lauren's house, we had time to become somewhat familiar, and I really like her. I didn't feel as if I were meeting a stranger at all. In fact, I'm very comfortable with her and Adriana both. Much more comfortable than I should be."

Donovan continued smoothing his jacket, unaffected by his friend's opinion. "So what's wrong with that? What are you getting at, and would you please be quick about it?"

Elliot's voice lowered another octave. "On the drive over, I saw a necklace around Lauren's neck. I admit it was a little dark."

He paused as if he shouldn't continue. Donovan had a firm

look in his eyes.

"For God's sake, Elliot, are you going to finish this story or not?"

Elliot pushed out an exasperated sound, but continued. "Donovan, she's wearing a man's ring on the end of that chain. I tried to question her about it, but none of the answers made much sense. Now, you tell me if I'm putting too much energy into this. She says its decades old. She says she bought it from Vickie's gallery, but the ring's original owner meant a great deal to her. She told me it has sentimental value, and she wears it all the time. What in the hell do you make out of that?"

Donovan stopped his fidgeting and was now standing at full attention. He thought for several moments before responding.

"I think we need to get Vickie in here. Could you see anything unusual about it?"

Elliot shrugged his shoulders. "Very little. I saw it was a man's wedding ring, and it had some sort of pattern engraved on its surface. It all happened so fast, I didn't have time to investigate. I didn't have time to think. I've tried to come up with a reason to take a look at it again without raising any suspicion. What do you think? Am I becoming paranoid? Surely, it couldn't be this easy?"

Donovan pulled back the blond locks that fell around his eyes, then peeked through the kitchen door, searching for Vickie.

"I don't think we should say anything to Alex until we know more. I'd like to be around when they meet. My mind is trying to tell me there's no way this could be her. I didn't really expect her to waltz in here announcing she's the one he's been searching for. But my gut is telling me something else."

Donovan shook his head in disbelief. "This whole night has perplexed the hell out of me. I don't know what to believe any more. What's real and what's an illusion?"

Elliot sighed in agreement. "If Alex wanted to throw everyone off, he has certainly achieved it. In any case, Lauren has no idea who Alex is. And if she is the woman he's been looking for, it may not be as simple as we first thought. And it may have nothing whatsoever to do with her. We should know soon enough. We need to locate Vickie as soon as possible. Maybe she'll remember when Lauren bought it."

Donovan shivered slightly. "Yeah, I keep remembering how Alex reacted when he was in her gallery. We thought it was due to his illness at the time, but now I just don't know. Maybe I've had too much champagne. Or maybe this whole romantic theme is getting to me. Whatever it is, I want to stay within close range of both Lauren and Alex tonight. Surely they'll have to meet at some point."

Elliot agreed. "We'll stick close by. If we see no fireworks toward the end of the evening, I think one of the girls should suddenly have the urge to see this ring she's hiding. I'm not saying it's her, but if it is, we can't let her waltz out of here as easy as she waltzed in. Somehow, we'll have to let them know the truth."

Donovan shrugged. "We'll wait and see what happens. The night is still young. Let's see if we can find Vickie alone, and locate where the hell Alex is hiding."

The men walked casually out into the large living room. It was now full, with people spilling up the grand staircase. It was a beautiful sight, with the men dressed in black, highlighted by the different colored gowns worn by the women. The whole room seemed to be cast in a spell.

Elliot moved into the crowd. "Why don't some of these people flow out onto the patio? Why are they all congregated in this one area for Christ's sake?"

Donovan just shook in head, aggravated. "Where the hell is Alex? He should be herding these people along like cattle. I suppose it's going to be our job."

The women were stopped by various friends, clients, and customers as they entered the huge room. Lauren and Adriana were both curious to see the remainder of the house, and gradually began breaking away from the acquaintances.

Adriana firmly took Lauren's hand and shifted her past the crowd, signaling to the others that they would return shortly.

"I'm going to see this house if it kills me. Are you game?"

Lauren grinned excitedly. "Are you kidding? It's open to the public. We're considered public, aren't we?"

The twosome slid against the walls, smiling and nodding to those they passed, until finally reaching the opposite side of the room. Their feet stopped at the foot of two steps, rising to the next level of the living room. The girls climbed both steps to get a better view of the crowd. There seemed to be elegantly dressed people standing on every square inch of the floor. Lauren looked out in front of her, and saw the magic casting its spell over the house. She closed her eyes, and could feel the energy pulsing through her veins.

"This is incredible. If I didn't know any better, I'd swear we're standing in the park of a magic castle."

The many props were playing with the room, making it a perfect illusion. A formally dressed waiter carefully handed the two women a drink. They gratefully accepted, clinking their glasses together. Adriana was amazed as she named all the famous people in the room. Lauren felt she wasn't herself anymore. Her mind drifted to her dreams of the party.

"This is almost like I envisioned it. How could I have known?"

Adriana sipped from her glass and smiled. "I've been telling you for years you're psychic."

Several people moved to the patio, allowing Lauren the room to step back. She stopped when she ran into a solid object. Looking behind her, she gulped for air. Adriana noticed, and grabbed for her glass.

"Lauren, what's wrong? Here, sit down."

Lauren sat down on the piano bench beneath her. She finally composed herself and spoke in a weak whisper, "Adriana, you're going to think I'm drunk, but I swear I'm not. Not yet anyway."

Adriana handed the drink back to her friend.

"What's going on? I've seen that same look on your face before. In fact, every time your dreams are involved, this look appears. What the hell happened?"

Lauren looked where she was sitting. "I don't know. I just got an intense déjà vu sensation. This piano looks just like his. I've stood near it many times." She lightly touched the hard wood with her fingertips. "The doors are always opened, but they also appear to be the same as what I see in my dream."

Adriana was beginning to take her seriously.

"Lauren, take a deep breath and center yourself. Slowly take a good look around the room. Does it resemble what you've seen before?"

Lauren swept the entire room with her eyes. After a few minutes, she turned to Adriana. "I can't tell. It looks familiar, but it didn't look like this."

Her friend gave a frustrated smile. "No, chances are it didn't. I suppose it would be difficult to make out what it looked like a few days ago."

Lauren stood up. "Let's keep looking around. This house looks like one I've always dreamed about. But, I don't know if it's been a part of my real dreams, or a schoolgirl's fantasy."

Adriana took her friend's hand. "I know what you mean. I think every woman has dreamed of living in a house like this."

The women stepped through the wide opened double doors leading to the patio, and were transported to another place, taking the sights and sounds of heaven with them. They both stopped abruptly in disbelief and held their breath. There were several dozen tables surrounding the pool. A stage had been erected on the far side of the pool, facing the ocean. When they could finally catch their breath, they found the sweet scent intoxicating. The women looked over to see red rose petals and candles floating in the pool. Huge torches had been erected around the perimeter of the patio, adding dramatic lighting and shadows to the backdrop.

Several steps below, they could hear the sound of the roaring ocean. Trees had been placed in various places, with the white and pale blue twinkling lights wrapped around them. Lauren took a deep breath and found another faint fragrance floating in the air.

"Adriana, what do you smell?"

Adriana could be heard taking a breath through her nose.

"Roses." She inhaled again. "Wait. Roses and lavender?"

A pleading note registered in Lauren's voice. "Tell me this is just a coincidence."

Adriana looked around, trying to locate Elliot. There were too many people to make that possible.

"Lauren, it's a long shot. I think the evening is getting to us both. Let's just keep a very open mind, and let things happen the way they're supposed to. Okay?"

Lauren smiled to her friend. "Yes, I agree. I refuse to make any more out of this than exactly what it is. Nothing more, nothing less. Just make sure you keep reminding me of that."

Adriana laughed out loud, and took Lauren by the arm, leading her back into the house. Everyone was in such good spirits, it was contagious. Lauren couldn't remember a time she had felt more at ease, and so happy to be somewhere.

"I don't know about you, but I never want this evening to end."

Elliot stopped the women as they were entering the room.

"You girls are difficult to find. I can't believe how crowded this place is. Have you seen our host yet?"

Adriana shook her head. "No, come to think of it, we haven't. I can't believe you haven't seen him either."

Elliot looked down at his watch. "The party has been in full swing for over an hour. Let me go upstairs and see what's keeping him."

Elliot shook a few hands on his way to the staircase, then was seen by Donovan ascending at a quick pace. Donovan excused himself from a client, and followed his friend close behind.

Reaching the top landing, Elliot spoke in hushed tones.

"You haven't seen him either?"

Donovan shook his head.

Elliot tapped lightly on the bedroom door. "Alex, are you in there? People are starting to question your whereabouts. Especially your two friends standing outside your door. How about letting us in?"

Alex opened the door a few inches, then walked away, leaving the boys to admit themselves.

Donovan approached first. "Alex, what the hell is going on? You have a house full of people downstairs, and I see you're fully dressed. So what are you doing up here alone?"

Elliot put his hand on Alex's shoulder. "Are you all right? What can we do?"

Alex sat down on the bed and shook his head.

"I've been sitting here thinking about coming downstairs. God knows I'm ready to relax and have some fun. I'm tired of drinking champagne up here by myself."

Elliot sat down next to his friend. "Then why are you in here, instead of out there?"

Alex stared down at his feet. "I'm scared to death. I'm scared of finding her. I'm scared of not finding her." He looked up anxiously to his friends. "Have you seen anyone who you think could be her?"

The two friends glanced briefly at each other, and then turned their attention back to Alex.

Donovan was confused. "Wouldn't finding her be a good thing? I thought that's what tonight was all about."

Alex looked at his friends, his blue eyes showing fear. "What if she's here and I don't recognize her? What if she doesn't recognize me? What if we walk right by each other without so much as a nod? Will she know this was all for her?"

Elliot took his friend's arm, raising him off the bed.

"Alex, she won't know unless you go down there and enjoy

yourself. If she's here, we'll know before the evening is over. If not, then we'll find her elsewhere. But either way, you have to make an appearance."

Donovan tried to make light of the situation. "Too bad we don't have a glass slipper. Try it on every woman who walks through the door."

Elliot paused briefly, and then spoke as if he were in deep thought. "Alex, are you wearing her wedding band?"

Alex raised his hand in the direction of the light. "Of course. I never take it off."

Elliot continued, but now with a stronger voice, "Fine. Just make sure you keep your hands out of your pockets. That may be one way of sniffing her out of the crowd. And one word of warning. You have one hell of a crowd down there."

Donovan snapped his fingers. "Alex, didn't you say that you suspected music might also be a key to finding her?"

Alex smiled broadly, the dimple in his chin broadening. "Yeah, I did say that, didn't I? Okay, let's go."

Elliot opened the door, leading Alex out.

Lauren and Adriana were forced to return to the crowd with Cindy. They were conversing with everyone they recognized, and had slowly made their way to the back part of the house, when Cindy caught up to them. She was anxious to introduce them to people she and Ron knew. She pushed the girls past the corridor, and barked out her usual cheerful advice.

"Come on, girls. It's time to meet new people and network. You never know who your next client or friend may be."

Adriana laughed. "Lauren, don't you feel as if you're back in college? Doesn't she remind you of our house mother?"

Cindy ignored the tease, taking Lauren by the hand and introducing her to several eligible bachelors.

She drifted briefly among each of them, finding none that interested her enough to continue long conversations. Glancing over one gentleman's shoulder, she caught Adriana's tall figure trying to get her attention, then pointing to the part of the house they hadn't yet visited. Lauren nodded slightly in an affirmative fashion, as she conversed with the men.

Alex leaned tensely against the rail, peering down from the top of the staircase.

"My God, there's no place to walk, much less find someone down there."

Elliot gently nudged him. "Well, there's no time like the present to find your place in the middle of that crowd. Perhaps you can play group leader, and get some of them out on the patio."

Several people noticed Alex walk slowly down the stairs and greeted him warmly. He was enveloped by a mass of partiers before he was able to reach the middle of the room.

After the required pleasantries were out of the way, Elliot took Alex by his arm as Donovan stepped forward stating he was needed for a moment.

Alex excused himself and gratefully followed his friends into the kitchen.

"Now I know why I've never done anything like this before. Thanks for rescuing me."

Alex overlooked the gathering from his hiding place in the bar. "Doesn't everyone look wonderful? If I didn't know any better, I'd swear we were characters in a fairytale. The house really turned out beautiful, didn't it?"

Both men nodded their heads in agreement. Alex was beginning to relax and wanted to enjoy the evening.

"I think I'm ready to start mingling."

He saw several of his friends laughing in the far corner, near the staircase, and proceeded over to them. The crush of people made it impossible to casually march through, so Alex slipped out of the patio doors on one side of the large room, crossed around the pool, and reentered through the wide double doors on the other side near the piano. As he was about to descend the two steps, he froze in place. The hair on the back of his neck stiffened, and his stomach instantly tied in knots. From his position, he could see the back of a tall slim woman with long dark hair standing several yards ahead of him. Even from behind, she was the most beautiful vision he had ever seen. Alex's throat constricted as he stared at her royal blue gown fitting tightly around her hips. His mind was screaming so loudly, he was surprised no one else had noticed.

"Her hair and body is familiar. If it's her, what am I supposed to do? I can't just walk up and introduce myself." His heart was pounding, and his frustration was building. *"Damn, am I going to be thinking everyone here is the woman I'm waiting for?"*

Alex realized he was reacting to his fears, and he took a deep breath to calm himself.

This is absurd. It's my party. What's wrong with me? Why the hell can't I do this?

His body refused to move. Instead, he felt chills begin deep in his spine, rising slowly to the top of his head. He closed his eyes to center himself again. He knew he couldn't approach her until he had got a hold of himself. She looked to be miles away from him.

I can't do it. Damn it, I'm going to lose her because of my fear. And I'm not even sure it is her.

His heart was telling him it was her. But he was too unbalanced and fearful to listen.

What the hell is wrong with me?

He looked around for his friends, but was too scattered to find anyone other than her. He stopped his thoughts for a moment, and took another deep breath, looking closely at her back again.

She's more beautiful than in my dreams. I can almost feel her soft body in my arms." The fear began to strengthen again. *"What if she doesn't know me? What if it's not her?*

He turned away for fear she would turn around and catch him gawking. He wasn't ready, and his frustration was mounting.

Why are you doing this? You've always had confidence in yourself, and in the process. Why can't you follow through now? Are you afraid it's not her? It's got to be her. I couldn't fall in love with two women. That would be a curse from hell.

Lauren was halfheartedly listening to an acquaintance, while trying to slowly edge over to Adriana. She stopped in her tracks when a chill flowed quickly up her spine. She felt someone staring a hole through her, and found herself fighting to keep her muscles from becoming a mass on the floor. She wanted to run, but couldn't move for several moments. Finally, Lauren excused herself and retreated to another part of the room. She had to be alone to compose herself.

My dear God. What is happening to me? It's got to be the champagne. I'm sure that's the reason for all these sensations tonight.

Lauren leaned against the wall, closed her eyes, and reluctantly allowed the sensations to press themselves against her. *Will I break the spell if I turn around? I don't want this familiar feeling of love to stop flowing.*

Alex watched Lauren's reaction from behind a column. He could only see the beautiful curve of her back, but he stood in awe as she stiffened, then shivered. He watched while she excused herself. Then sadness fell over him when he realized they were on separate sides of the room, and both very much alone. His eyes were glued to her as she began to slowly turn her body in his direction. Alex couldn't stop himself from escaping to the patio, and up the back stairs to his bedroom.

As her eyes focused on the piano, where the energy had been flowing from, she found no one in sight.

How can that be? Lauren shook her head in defeat. *What is wrong with me tonight? I have never been in such a mood.*

She closed her eyes again, turning inward to her guide, but the

noise of the room made it impossible to concentrate. She saw
Adriana across the room, and gratefully fled in her direction to be
consoled. But Cindy grabbed Lauren's arm from behind before she
could reach her friend. She didn't have the strength to put up an
argument, and allowed the woman to lead her down the hall
towards the back of the house. She didn't care where she was
taken, as long as she could get away from the flow of energy
interrupting her train of thought. Her mind was racing with
scenarios.

*What if I'm imagining all this? This atmosphere could be the culprit. I
have got to stay centered, and in this reality until I know for sure. Damn it,
where's Adriana?*

Before Lauren had the opportunity to ask aloud, Cindy began
talking.

"Oh, Lauren, you're not going to believe who I've met. I tried
to get you away from all those handsome men, but they weren't
going to let you loose for a moment. Have you met Alex yet? He
looks dreamy tonight. But all the guys do, don't they?"

A waiter walked by, handing Lauren another glass of
champagne. She gladly accepted and quickly finished it in one gulp.
Cindy never noticed. She was consumed with hyperactivity and
continued excitedly, "I've certainly heard a lot of gossip and
rumors tonight. I'm sure you know Alex has never had a party like
this before. Everyone was anxious to come see it for themselves. I
haven't had the opportunity to ask Alex, but other guests are
reporting this as a coming out party of some sort for him. They say
the reason the theme of the party is all about love, romance, and
dreams is because the guest of honor is a dream. Or should I say
the guest is from a dream. Well, I'm not exactly sure how you
would define it. But a dream? I'm not saying that I don't believe
him. Alex has always had a good head on his shoulders. A real
grounded type. But he listens to his intuition. I think we all try, but
usually don't believe what we hear. Apparently, someone overheard
him talking to his friends about his intuition telling him to have

this party. I'm glad I'd consumed a few drinks before I heard that one. I shouldn't talk though. It seems to work for him. How do you think he's become so successful? Probably because he listens to himself."

Lauren was dumbfounded. Her head was spinning, and she didn't know whether to laugh out loud, or beg Cindy to please stop her incessant chatter. Her mind was weaving the same thought over and over. *This night is a crazy, crazy dream.*

Lauren decided the best thing to do was agree it was nothing more than just a crazy night, and then compose herself. She tried to shake off the effects from the alcohol before nonchalantly interrupting her friend.

"Where's the host? I'd like to thank him for indirectly inviting me, and tell him what a beautiful home he has. Unfortunately, not only have I not met him, but I don't even know what he looks like."

Cindy looked around, then shook her head. "I don't see him right now, but I'd like to be the one who introduces the two of you. You'll know him by his long dark hair. It's usually pulled back tight. He's very handsome. Believe me, you can't miss him."

Lauren was grateful when Cindy saw someone she wanted to meet, and quickly excused herself. She needed a moment of tranquility. But instead, all she could think of was Cindy's comments.

Guest of honor was a dream? Well, that could be L.A. gossip. I know how that works. Long dark hair? That could be anyone in California as well.

Lauren continued talking to herself, trying to drown out her wishes. *Don't go getting your hopes up.*

But the sensation of feeling that she was right where she was supposed to be had begun to filter unknowingly through her body.

I need to sit down and just be quiet for a few moments.

She knew people would be seated for dinner soon, but she couldn't contain her oddly timed curiosity. Lauren continued walking down the long hall, suddenly stopping outside a closed door. Making certain no one noticed, she tapped on the door then entered a room.

I just need a few minutes to pull myself together.

The room was dark, and she stumbled trying to locate the light switch. Not finding one, she waited for her eyes to adjust to the dark, while reminding herself why she had to be alone.

I don't know if it's me who's going crazy, or everyone around me.

She panicked when she realized she had entered a room that was obviously off limits.

Great! That's all I need. To be thrown out for trespassing.

Lauren turned to leave when she saw a faint fluorescent glow surrounding an object on the wall. She steadied herself against the door and blinked. *What the hell? C'mon, Lauren, the wall can't possibly be pulsing and glowing. You need to get some food. You've had too much to drink.*

Her hand grabbed at the doorknob as the picture came into sharper focus. She made out two people in a framed picture on the wall. Lauren squinted so hard, her eyes ached.

"I know this picture." Lauren was fighting the urge to flee.

No, stay here! I've got to remember where I've seen this picture before!

She was once again pushed into darkness when the illumination slowly dimmed. Lauren grasped the knob and quickly turned it. Light entered from the hallway, making her less fearful. She stepped out of the room backward, and slowly closed the door behind her.

She wanted to find her group and rejoin the party, but found she couldn't move. Questions were racing through her mind, but she was denying the answers.

Where have I seen it? Why can't I think straight? What is happening to me? Damn it, I've got to pull myself together. Just calm down and go with the flow.

Suddenly, everything became quiet in Lauren's head. Somewhere within, she heard the words that brought with it a mixture of comfort and confusion.

"Become a participate, and find what was lost."

She had no idea how long she had been standing outside the room before Adriana found her. She felt her friend's warm fingers take hold of her arm.

"Lauren, are you all right? Where have you been? You look like you've seen a ghost."

She felt Adriana gently nudging her into a sitting room, and heard the door close behind them. Lauren didn't notice how beautifully decorated the room was. Her head was still reviewing the advice given a few minutes earlier. Adriana calmly sat down in front of her, and held her hand.

"Lauren, tell me what happened."

Lauren closed her eyes, searching for composure.

"Adriana, I needed to sit down. Everything was happening too fast. I thought I felt him near me. I turned and there was no one there. I don't know what happened next. Suddenly, I was in a dark room, and I couldn't locate the light switch. I closed my eyes for a moment, and when I opened them, there was a huge portrait of a couple on the wall in front of me. It looked familiar, but I seem to have temporary amnesia. I can't remember why."

Lauren was speaking in a far-away voice, but Adriana allowed her to finish.

"The really odd thing was when the painting started glowing around its edges. That's when I lost all concentration. I suppose I stood there until the room went dark again, and then got the hell out."

Adriana felt a deep pain in her gut, but remained composed. She calmly patted her friend's hand. "Lauren, do you want to go back into the room? Maybe we can figure out what's going on."

Lauren appreciated her friend's soothing voice.

"No, I'm being silly. I've probably had too much to drink, and not enough fresh air or food."

"Lauren, when you closed your eyes, could you have briefly fallen asleep, and dreamed of seeing a glowing picture?"

Lauren giggled. "I really do sound pathetic, don't I? I can't say it didn't happen like that. But I can't be sure. Either way, the sight of the portrait jarred me to such an extent that I just lost it."

Adriana looked around, not sure of what to do.

"Well, I guess so. A glowing picture would do it for me too."

Adriana was ignoring the memory in her own head. The conversation sounded familiar, but she couldn't understand why, either.

"Why don't we go sit outside? They're seating everyone for dinner, and there's going to be a repeat performance from Ron's band. Are you ready?"

Lauren smiled, happier now and much more relaxed.

"Yeah, I'm more than ready. I need to get some food into me. I just wish I could get that picture out of my head."

Adriana opened the door, allowing Lauren to lead the way.

"You've probably seen something like it in a gallery. You said you didn't get a good look at it. Maybe it just reminded you of something from your past."

Lauren stopped and turned to her friend. "Something from my past?"

Adriana pushed her forward as they followed the crowd onto the patio for dinner.

Donovan had trouble locating Vickie. He was anxious to ask her about Lauren's visit to her gallery. But people were stopping him every few minutes for long conversations. Elliot found he was having the same problem. He was searching for Vickie, but he had also lost Adriana, Lauren, and Alex.

As the crowd was being seated on the patio for dinner, Elliot caught sight of Adriana and Lauren walking from the back hall. He caught up to them and grabbed Adriana's hand.

"Hi there, stranger. I thought I'd lost you."

She turned, kissing him on the cheek. "Well, I'm glad you found me."

Donovan joined them as they stepped outside. "Elliot, have

you noticed we've lost our host again?"

Lauren laughed, feeling much better in the fresh air.

"That seems to be going around tonight. I'm beginning to believe there is no host."

Elliot glanced around as he pulled the chairs out for the ladies.

"Do you girls mind if I go try and find him again? I promise I'll be right back."

Adriana shook her head. "No problem."

Cindy and Vickie joined the women. Cindy's eyes were still wide with wonder.

"Where have you girls been? I think everyone's been lost, or in their own world tonight. But hasn't it been wonderful so far? Alex even hired a palm reader to entertain."

Adriana smiled. "Yes, it's been unbelievable."

Cindy turned her attention in Lauren's direction.

"What about for you?"

Lauren looked over at her friends, and nodded in agreement. She didn't dare trust herself to speak for fear she would blurt out everything she had just been through. Adriana squeezed her hand in moral support.

Vickie looked around their table. "Hmmm. There are eight chairs at our table, and only four people present. Where the hell are the men?"

Cindy laughed, "Ron is probably setting up the band, and God only knows where Elliot and Donovan are. We may not see them for the rest of the evening."

Cindy turned her attention in Lauren's direction, her eyes glistening with curiosity.

"Oh, Lauren, I can't wait to see who's been selected among the many handsome men to sit next to you."

Lauren laughed, chiding her friend. "Oh, Cindy, I can't wait to see either. I think I've met them all."

Donovan walked by the table, and stopped to whisper in Vickie's ear. "Sorry, I'm detained at the moment. I'll be back as soon as we find Alex. The band can't go on until he shows up. And remind me to ask you about something later."

Vickie looked concerned. "Can I be of any help? I haven't seen him since earlier in the evening. Where could he have gone? I've never seen anything like it."

Donovan snapped his fingers. "I just thought of where he might be. I'll be right back."

Walking through the near empty living area, he raced up the stairs, stopping outside Alex's bedroom door. He knocked loudly when he heard someone on the other side of the door.

"Alex, open the damn door. What in the hell are you doing? For your information, dinner is being served. Some time tonight, you'll have to perform."

Elliot opened the door. "I let myself in through the back stairs."

Donovan found Alex sitting in a chair looking in the mirror. He walked over and put his hand on his friend's shoulder.

"Alex, what are you doing? You have this huge party going on downstairs. Everyone is seated for dinner. Do you know what that means? That means it's time for you to sing."

Elliot wasn't as polite. "Alex, pick your ass up and move it downstairs now. You wanted this party. You said the love of your life would be here. If she were here, you would never know it. I've never seen you act this strange before. Stop this now, and come downstairs with us."

Alex turned to his friends, and they could see the pain in his eyes. He felt obligated to tell them what had happened.

"Guys, I think I'm scared to death. I love this woman more than anything I've ever loved in my life. I would die if I knew she was here, and I didn't go after her."

Elliot knelt down on the floor beside his chair. "Okay, so what's the problem?"

Alex wrung his hands in frustration and fear.

"The problem is, I think she is here, and I don't know what in the hell to do now. I think I felt her, and then I think I saw her, and then I just froze. Every bit of self-confidence I had drained completely out of me. I was afraid I'd make a fool out of myself by not knowing what to say. Then I worried she wouldn't know me. Then I was fearful that she was with someone else. I didn't want to know. This reaction is so unlike me. I don't know what happened. Instead of facing her, I turned and ran away."

Donovan looked at Elliot, then back at his friend. "Alex, what does she look like?"

He shook his head in frustration. "I didn't get a clear view of her. She was in the middle of the room talking to several men. She had long dark hair. I just saw the back of her."

Elliot took a deep breath. "That could describe several of the women downstairs. Do you recall anything else?"

Alex shook his head in shame. "I just don't understand what happened to me. What happens if that wasn't her? What happens if it is her, and she walks out of my life?"

Donovan was quick to verify no one could dare to leave such a wonderful event.

"Even without the host downstairs, the party is going great. But, Alex, now it's time you come play the host. You won't know who this woman is until you try again. You would never forgive yourself. And if it's not her, then you'll just keep trying."

Elliot moved until he was in front of Alex, facing him head on.

"Alex, remember all the stories you told us about your dreams? Remember all the wonderful memories you have of her? You have her ring on your finger."

Elliot tugged at Alex's hand until it was in front of his friend's eyes.

"You see? This belonged to her. And what about the note you found? Didn't you write a song from it? Think about the initials carved in the gazebo. Didn't you know what they meant? What about the painting in your office? We all saw it glow. You may not believe everything you saw, but I certainly do."

Donovan was now kneeling beside Elliot. "Alex, you told us everything your guide said to you. You wrote everything down in your journal. Would you like for me to read the last line you wrote? I don't know what it means, but I'm sure you will."

Donovan picked up the journal from the table, opening it to the last written page.

"Trust the music."

Alex blinked hard when he heard the familiar phrase.

"Trust the music." He looked at his friends, and laughed out loud. "Of course, trust the process and trust the music. How could I have been so stupid? This isn't like me at all. Hiding from my fears and insecurities."

Elliot quickly responded, "No, Alex, I would have to say that you've always met them head on."

Alex slapped his friend on the back. "And I will tonight. If she's here, I will find her. Whatever insecurities either of us may have will be dealt with. Surely she'll remember the songs. And if she isn't here, then maybe she'll be brought here by me singing them."

Alex checked himself in the mirror, and then opened his bedroom door, suddenly anxious to join his party. He felt like his old self again.

He suddenly stopped on the stairs and turned to his friends.

"Guys, you've come through for me again. I hope you're keeping score, because I intend to pay you back."

Donovan pushed Alex along. "Let's take care of this first. Then we'll find a problem of our own for you to solve. All right?"

Chapter 24

The lights had been dimmed in the living area, and softened outside. The light was now coming from the many candles, the trees, and the full moon. The band was on stage playing light tunes while the party finished their meal.

Lauren looked at the other guests, noticing everyone was still in a festive mood.

"Nothing is going to dampen the spirits tonight."

Cindy laughed and agreed. "Yeah, the party is just beginning. I fully intend to take advantage of this unbelievable energy by dancing with every man in the place."

Lauren and her friends had a table near the band, but Alex didn't know where to begin looking for her. There were so many people and so little time between the door and the stage. He hoped to catch a glimpse of her on the way. He was still angry with himself for wasting so much time by retreating to his bedroom.

"The intensity was more than I could have imagined. I was worried I wouldn't know her, but damn it, I did know her. I have to believe, without a doubt, that this woman is her. Everything about it felt right. But will she know me?"

He remembered how she looked standing in the room. Her body language was suspicious of what he was sensing.

"That's why I ran. I just panicked. But this entire party is for her. I have to believe our dreams will come true. I have to trust she will understand everything that's about to take place."

Elliot nudged Donovan and pointed toward their table.

Donovan instantly understood and nodded. He knew he had to pull Alex's attention to their table before Lauren saw him. They didn't want another escape scene like before.

Donovan walked beside Alex and stopped him from moving forward.

"Alex, do you know where our table is?"

Alex looked at him strangely. "Yeah, don't you? We all picked it together."

Elliot strolled up on the other side of his friend. "Actually, with everything happening, we forgot where we left the girls. Just so we don't look too foolish, would you just casually point us to our table?"

Alex laughed, and looked over the heads of the crowd.

"You're right up front, near the sta…"

Alex froze, not uttering a sound, or breathing a single breath. The two men looked at each other and smiled. Elliot spoke up with pleasure in his voice.

"I think we have our sighting."

Alex blinked hard and without moving a muscle, spoke in a broken whisper.

"That's her. At our table. That's the woman in my dreams. How did she end up at our table? Who is she? Who is she with?"

He shook his head and continued, "My God, after all this time and there she is. The most beautiful woman in the world. Do either of you know her?"

Elliot spoke up with a chuckle in his voice. "Actually, she's my girlfriend's best friend. Her name is Lauren Wells. She's also very close friends with Cindy and Vickie."

Donovan continued while laughing, "And, Alex my friend, this is the woman that Cindy has been wanting to set you up with."

Alex looked away, brushing tears from his eyes.

"I can't believe it! So, she isn't married?"

Elliot answered, "In the process of a very amicable divorce. Twin daughters in college."

Alex shivered. "Did you say twins? My God, you did say twins, didn't you? This is all becoming clear to me. But how in the hell can I be so happy, yet so scared at the same time?"

Donovan pressed his hand into Alex's shoulder. "Well, I hate to be the one to break it to you, but this was the easy part. Now you have to show her who you are, and hope she recognizes you. And if she doesn't recall knowing what you know, then you'll just have to find a gentle way of convincing her. Can you do that?"

Alex smiled. "I'm more than willing to take on that job."

His two friends took their seats next to their mates at the table. The women were very suspicious when they noticed the ongoing smirks on their faces.

Cindy leaned over and wanted answers.

"Okay, what's going on? You two look so damn proud of yourselves. What have you been up to?"

Vickie continued the line of questioning, "Did you find Alex?"

Adriana and Lauren laughed at looks of satisfaction on the men's faces.

"Elliot, what's going on?"

Adriana couldn't stand the suspense. Elliot turned and kissed her lightly on the lips.

"Just wait and see. This is going to be a night this place will never forget."

Lauren overheard and spoke up. "Oh, I hope there are fireworks. I love fireworks."

The boys fell into a fit of laughter before Donovan finally caught his breath long enough to speak.

"I'd say there's going to be a lot of fireworks tonight."

Alex went behind the stage and watched Lauren laughing with her group at their table. He was mesmerized by her sensual beauty. He knew without a doubt it was her. She was the one he had been dreaming of for what seemed like forever, before finally meeting her in their dreams. "At least I know where she is, and I can set my plan into motion. I can't let anything go wrong. Not now. Just trust the process."

It was now his job to convince, and her job to remember.

After everyone was seated, the lights fell dark on the stage. The crowd sipped their drinks and became very quiet. Donovan and Elliot could barely contain their excitement. They both wanted to see the look on Lauren's face when she first caught sight of Alex. Elliot turned to his friend, whispering.

"I'm glad Adriana is with her. They're very good for each other. And I think both of them will need a little grounding energy when this is all over."

As the lights dimmed, Lauren suddenly shivered and grabbed Adriana's hand. Looking over at her, concerned, her friend asked if she was all right. Lauren smiled, shivered again, and nodded yes.

Alex watched her as she silently began going through the emotions again. He noticed her shiver and grab for her friend's hand. He wanted desperately to give her support.

I know what you're going through.

He knew she felt him near, and she was feeling confused.

I wish I could make this easy for both of us, my love.

Alex stepped onto the darkened stage and sat on a stool. He put his head down, and waited for the first note to penetrate the air.

It seemed like an eternity of beautiful music before she heard someone's voice rise up through the darkness. She knew the music immediately. It was called 'Walk With Me.' A song Chris Spheeris sung on the CD she constantly played. She had always felt the words were prophetic. A beautiful song that conjured up dreams of actually finding that absolute unconditional love.

Lauren closed her eyes and waited for the first words, so she could mentally sing along. The first sound of his voice felt as though she was being brought to her knees. She jerked her eyes open, but saw only a dark stage.

She could hear the lyrics being sung, "Wandering through a misty night, searching for some signs of light, I find you. Through a tunnel in the deep, past the corridors of sleep, I find you. Open-armed you're standing there, Golden light surrounds your hair, my eyes can't look away."

Lauren's heart was beating fast and her palms were wet.

I know the voice. I would know it anywhere.

She looked to Adriana for an answer, but her friend was oblivious to Lauren's confusion. Lauren wanted to scream aloud to get her attention, but was stunned motionless.

Suddenly, the spotlight was on him. He looked up with great emotion and continued singing in her direction.

"Walk with me, through the mysteries of the night, through the darkness and light, you will find me there. Hold me now, through the weak and the strong, know our hearts will belong, to the one love we share."

He watched her very closely, feeling what she was feeling. He could see her trying desperately to remember. Her emotions were stirring, as he watched the sudden changes in her eyes and facial expressions. Her body language showed her in distress. He silently sent a prayer to her.

Lauren glanced around the table, noticing Donovan and Elliot watching her. She was fighting for self-control, not wanting to embarrass herself in front of them. But they both knew she was the one from Alex's dream. The pained look in her eyes gave it away. Even if she hadn't yet remembered everything, they knew she would in time. It was obvious to them that she was trying to hold on to reality. Their hearts went out to her, but they bowed their heads and said nothing.

Alex finished the lyrics, and knew he had no choice but to go directly into the next song. He sang 'Street of Dreams' only for her. As he did so, he watched her eyes growing wide, and knew her heart was trying desperately to put the lyrics with the singer.

Lauren knew the words were speaking to her. She knew it was her story, but she hadn't quite grasped the reality of the moment.

Alex knew it was now only a matter of time. The next three

songs would finish the story. The call would then be hers to make. He was also fighting for composure because he had no idea what he would do if she didn't remember.

Go on, Alex, you've committed yourself. Trust the music.

Alex took a deep breath and nodded to the band. He would not stop until he had completed all the songs in succession. The music began, and her face instantly paled. Adriana jerked her head in Lauren's direction, wide-eyed in astonishment. Lauren closed her eyes and fought the tears that threatened to flow. She knew her table was watching her every move. Adriana was speechless, but took her friend's hand for moral support.

Lauren began seeing lights, and then pictures flashing in her mind's eye. She saw the portrait hanging on the wall, then the carvings on the gazebo. Suddenly, the picture changed and she saw the ring she was wearing around her neck, and the inscription. The flash appeared again, and she was listening to the music playing this now familiar tune from the jewelry box. She could hear her guide somewhere in the distance speaking to her.

"Find what was lost."

As Alex began singing, she squeezed Adriana's hand. She didn't understand what was happening, but knew she was losing the battle to control her emotions. She was afraid to look up at the stage. That would mean looking into his eyes. What if they weren't familiar? It would hurt too much to hear someone else singing their song. Alex's voice was awe-inspiringly beautiful.

"It seems we stood and talked like this before. We looked at each other in the same way then, but I can't remember where or when. The clothes you were wearing were the clothes you wore. The smile you were smiling you were smiling then, but I can't remember where or when."

Lauren was hot, and having a difficult time breathing. Her mind was screaming.

These songs are for me! Then her insecurities intruded. *No, it can't possibly be. What if this is all a coincidence?*

She knew she would never get over the pain if it were. She tried to force herself to look at the man singing on stage, but found she didn't have the nerve.

Let me see him.

But she couldn't will her eyes to look up.

Alex was singing with such emotion, he was on the verge of tears.

Please look at me. Please! He kept his thoughts on her, willing her to find him.

Lauren was listening to the words and his voice, soaking in each phrase.

Is he singing this for me, or for someone else?

It was obvious the song meant much more to him than just lyrics on a page. Everyone watching found themselves caught up in his emotion. No one dared move.

Lauren wanted to drown in his voice. A voice of angels singing to their master.

Finally, she could hold out no longer, and slowly raised her head. He smiled warmly. She saw his deep dimples and long dark hair, and knew immediately who he was. She had only met him in her dreams, but she knew. They locked onto each other's blue eyes, never taking their focus from one another.

Lauren couldn't define the sensations flowing through her body, and didn't think she would ever recover. It was getting more difficult to retain the composed state of mind she needed to survive this test. She looked at his face and caressed it with her loving gaze.

He is so very handsome.

It only took a few moments before the other guests followed Alex's gaze. Suddenly, everyone's attention was drawn in her direction. Each person began to feel an intense connection taking place, yet no one was willing to give the couple their privacy. Cindy and Vickie were punching Donovan, confused by what was taking place.

No one could help Lauren face the emotions that were crashing into her soul. Such emotion on virgin territory was painful for Alex to watch. He saw Adriana holding Lauren's hand, stroking it in a maternal manner. The couple never took their eyes from one another.

Many in the crowd were beginning to understand the lyrics to the songs, and the history behind them. Others were beginning to comprehend why the party was being held, and the rumors that had preceded it. Vickie turned to Donovan with questions.

"Was this the story Alex was talking about when he sang his new songs the other night? Was it Lauren he wrote them for?"

Cindy got closer to Donovan, wanting to hear the answer. He bent over and spoke quietly under his breath. "Let them play this thing out the way they need to. Don't interfere."

Still puzzled by the turn of events, Vickie whispered to Cindy, "They look as if they're seeing each other for the first time, but the emotion is so thick, you would think they'd known each other forever."

Cindy smiled, wanting quiet. "Perhaps they have. Now hush."

Lauren was oblivious to all the whispers fluttering around her. She was struggling to decide whether she was actually in reality, or just in another dream state. Alex could see her fighting the recognition of full awareness, and wanted only to hold her tenderly against his body. He wanted to tell her that he too had felt the same crazy emotions earlier in the evening. He felt terrible that she had to endure all this confusion in front of a few hundred people. But he took a deep breath, knowing he had no choice but to continue. It was time for her to see the significance of the role she played in making the two of them a full reality. Now that he had found her, he couldn't let her walk out believing this too was just a dream.

He went directly into the first of the two songs he had written for her. Alex knew this would tell the story of their lives. It was written from the notes they had exchanged to one another in

Connecticut. He closed his eyes as tears formed. Mentally, he sent her a message.

"I have waited so very long to sing this to you in person. I love you."

Lauren tilted her head to the side, as if listening to the air. She looked back at him and held her breath.

When he began the song, she immediately felt her soul on stage with him. She realized in an instant that what she was experiencing wasn't a dream. The breeze suddenly smelled of lavender and roses. Lauren took a deep breath and tried to steady herself. She squeezed Adriana's hand and noticed tears flowing down her friend's face. She turned her attention back to him. She could hear their words combined in a beautiful melody.

"Words of wonder, words of hope, words of love. Words to remind us of our past, I have loved you in our present, I will love you in our future, I will love you always. Time will hold the answers, to the questions in our hearts, memories of you keep my love strong, every second that we're apart."

There suddenly seemed to be no one else; just their two souls finally uniting. The energy between the two was intense and quickly became overpowering. Those gathered watched silently in awe. The music continued, and Alex went into the second song he had written and sent to her in their dreams. It was the last song he had planned to sing until later in the evening. He didn't know how he would get through it without breaking down. His emotions felt like a volcano about to erupt at any moment. Having to endure the process of watching her as the truth was unveiled, and then not being able to comfort her was the most painful image he had ever witnessed. But he had learned a valuable lesson in the process of finding her again. He knew she had opened her heart, and believed all by herself. She hadn't asked for his help. But it was tearing his heart out not to give her the answers, or take away the pain.

He kept asking himself the same questions over and over.

Does she remember everything? What more can I do to convince her?

He took a deep breath and centered himself. The final song

began. She looked up at him helplessly. They were both openly crying now, with tears flowing down both their faces. The words touched her, the music hugged her, and his voice caressed her. The songs were their story. She had heard them a thousand times before in her dreams. He was singing with such tenderness, she felt she would burst with emotion. He never left her eyes. He had waited so long to look into them, to die in them. There was no one else in the world at this moment. Just the two of them. Still no one breathed.

She heard his voice sing only to her. "Now and forever, no matter where or when, we shall always be together, when you remember again. When you remember the songs, we'll be together again. Never forget, no matter where or when, always remember, we'll be together again."

She watched as he slowly moved his hand to the spotlight. A single gold ring glowed brightly on his finger. She knew instinctively who it belonged to. Lauren couldn't take the memories or the acceleration of intense emotions another moment. Everything rushed back to her in a single flash, then closed in on her. Every emotion she had ever experienced came back in a flood of turmoil. Passion, love, ecstasy, elation, concern, grief, apprehension, lust, and desire; all the emotions from all her lifetimes fell on her in one single second.

She looked helplessly to Adriana, then pulled her hand away, pushed her chair back, and bolted from the table. In a matter of a few seconds, everything came to a deafening halt. The other guests were left wondering what happened, and questioning among themselves.

Alex watched in seemingly slow motion, as Lauren pulled herself up and ran out. He watched as she raced down the stairs leading to the ocean. He knew he couldn't lose her now. He stopped singing, and called to her.

"Please, Lauren, come back. I love you."

But she only ran faster. He knew he had to do whatever it took to gain her trust. Alex was in shock, and looked to Adriana for advice. She wiped the tears from her eyes, and waved her hand as if to say, "Go after her."

Alex ran off the stage, following her into the darkness. The band continued into another song.

Lauren could hear it echoing off the waves and knew it was also one of her favorites. She continued down the stairs to the dimly lit sand. She didn't want the pain or confusion anymore. She was working hard at convincing herself it was just another dream. She looked to the south and saw the large protruding rocks glistening in the water.

"Just like the many other times I've been here."

The only light came from the full moon reflecting off the water. On the patio above, everyone was quiet and waiting, silently praying the intensity of the past hour would last forever. There were few who truly understood what had transpired. Adriana worried about Lauren, and felt she should search for her.

Elliot touched her hand. "She'll be all right. Alex won't let anything happen to her."

Adriana brushed away a tear. "How long have you known it was her?"

"Just tonight. I knew there was someone in his dreams. I knew just about every detail, but I was sworn to secrecy. I suppose had I told you, we could have saved everyone all this trouble."

Adriana smiled. "No, you were right to keep your friend's secret. I did the same. I knew what was going on. But frankly, who would have believed it? We've certainly seen their proof now, haven't we? I'm just upset for Lauren. She wasn't expecting any of this tonight."

Elliot hugged her. "I know, me too. Alex had expected she would be here. Poor Lauren was just thrown into it. But things will happen the way they're supposed to happen. It's a confusing time right now, but I know you're grateful they finally found each other."

He kissed her lightly on the lips. "And I'm grateful we found each other. I hope you realize that through all their toils and troubles, we were meant to find each other too."

Adriana smiled back at him. "Yeah, I figured that one out a few minutes ago. All of it is tied together, isn't it?"

Elliot shook his head, loving her more every minute.

Lauren continued running, trying to escape from the intense energy that seemed to be following her. She was blinded by her tears, and all the confusion. She didn't know whether to run from him, or to him. She wanted to be assured this wasn't another dream, or just a cruel trick. She couldn't endure another one. Not after everything she had just witnessed. In the background, she could hear the band continuing to play the most beautiful music, trying to comfort her soul, but causing her mind to whirl faster than her heart was beating. She needed to calm herself, but was too shaken.

"Who is he? What does he want? Does he mean the words he sang? Are these emotions real?"

Lauren was asking questions she already had the answers to. Subconsciously, she knew the answers before she ever arrived at the party. Her intuition kept telling her not to rationalize, and to just be free and accept.

When Lauren felt she was finally alone, she stared at the surf to center herself. When calmness finally took hold, she slowly turned to the shiny black rock formation ahead of her. She was grateful when the cool breeze suddenly increased, whipping up the scents of lavender and roses. She could feel fresh tears streaming down her face.

"This is where we met. Does this all really exist? Please, God, don't let this be another dream. Let me be here, where I'm supposed to be."

She turned her attention to the tunes playing above her on the patio. Then without warning, Lauren felt herself shiver and knew the familiar sensation of being watched. The warmth of the unknown energy was spreading throughout her body, then centering in her heart area. She knew he would find her.

Of course he would. How could I think otherwise?

Alex ran down the stairs at a quickened pace. His heart was begging his mind to remain calm.

"I can't let her walk out of my life now. I have to reassure her."

Alex jumped off the steps, and looked both ways. He could see a dewy figure standing near the rock formation, bathed in a pool of moonlight. He momentarily panicked.

"How do I get her attention without frightening her? I think I've confused her enough already."

He watched her hair flowing softly around her face, and felt his heart quickening in response.

"Dear God, how I want her."

Alex closed his eyes and concentrated on an answer. He suddenly remembered how well they had communicated in their dreams. He began to mentally picture the words he was thinking. Then slowly, he repeated them over and over in his mind.

"Lauren, I never wanted to confuse or hurt you. To hurt you would be an injury to my own soul. I need to explain this event was planned because we both agreed to it on another level. Our finding each other wasn't an accident. But I knew of no other way except to present you with the gifts I believed you would love, understand, and feel the most comfortable with. Lauren, I gave you my home, the ocean, and our music. I knew this would be a traumatic event, and I so wanted to cushion you. I wanted to help you believe that dreams do indeed come true. Even when I wasn't so sure a few days ago myself. I knew there was really no way to sit you down and simply explain this. It was something we both had to go through, as painful as it might be."

He watched her look up, as if listening, and then shiver. She turned around slowly, facing his direction. She knew he was there, but not sure where. She could feel his energy all around her.

"Alex, where are you? I will try to believe this is real if you will help me."

He heard Lauren's pleas. Their senses were one and the same.

Mentally, she told him of her confusion, and immense attraction to him. She told him how comfortable she felt in his home, and knew she had visited it many times in their dreams.

Alex continued to comfort her, through telepathy. He wanted to put her at ease. He told her he would continue with this form of communication until she was ready for their meeting. He told her over and over how much he cared for her, how much he loved her. He told her how he felt when he first saw her at the party. She giggled out loud at his confession of being fearful and running away.

As he spoke, she glanced around, wanting to find him, but seeing no one. Slowly, she began centering herself. The music, the sounds of the ocean, and his reassuring words and images helped her more than she could convey. She couldn't help wondering if Alex knew how much she wanted him to touch her.

Lauren looked up to the sky, and asked her question aloud.

"Is this really possible?"

"We're doing it."

She turned back to the beach and saw an intense presence of bright light. She knew that love and protection followed it. Lauren saw an image, a god with dark black flowing hair walking slowly towards her. The gentle swaying of her body to the melody helped release her controlled emotions. She could actually feel the full moon and the ocean's sound urging her on.

Alex continued walking very slowly in her direction. With each step, Lauren could feel the love pouring from him, reaching into her heart. She took the necklace from under her dress and unfastened the clasp. She looked up again to see the handsome figure nearing her. Lauren took a deep breath and waited with anticipation. She was afraid the veil would intrude and fall between them preventing their reunion.

With each step Alex took, he could almost feel her breath on his face. He didn't want to make her uncomfortable, but he felt if he didn't reach her soon, he would die. He relaxed by concentrating on the energy emitting from her heart. The scent of rose and lavender was intense. Her beauty, both inside and out, amplified with each step he took in her direction. She was bathed in brilliant white light, and he couldn't take his eyes off her.

She is so beautiful.

When he was close enough to touch her, he stopped, fearing the sheer curtain would separate them. Both could barely catch a breath, drowning in each other's eyes. He located that familiar sensation of long, long ago which now seemed like only yesterday.

Lauren watched as Alex slowly put his hand up, with his palm facing her, and waited until she was ready. She was shaking, but slowly raised her hand. It seemed to take an eternity before their palms finally touched, emitting a spark that crossed the boundaries of time.

Alex gently touched her hair, feeling the softness. Gradually, he moved his hand to her cheek, lightly brushing away a tear. Her beauty took his breath away again. He tried to think of something to say.

His only thought that translated to speech was, "Welcome home."

Nothing else needed to be said.

The electricity permeating from their auras finally met, and melted into each other. They hugged for long moments.

When she could finally speak, Lauren looked at him and said, "I've missed you."

Alex smiled. "I love you."

Then he took her into his strong arms and kissed her tenderly to seal their souls. They were one with the universe again, happy to make that commitment.

The surf was building, and the music was a constant companion adding to her comfort. Her head was spinning, but no longer with confusion. Now it was filled with total and unconditional love. Neither could stop touching, kissing, or caressing each other. It had been a long time coming.

Alex took Lauren's face gently in his hands, and smiled into her eyes.

"I don't have a glass slipper, but I think this ring may fit. I believe this belongs to you."

He gently slipped the gold band on her finger.

She was crying tears of joy as she slipped the ring from the chain she had been wearing around her neck.

"I think I have something that belongs to you too. I've kept it safe for your return."

Lauren slipped the ring on his finger.

She opened her mouth and couldn't believe what she was saying, "For now I don't want you to let me go. But some day soon, I think we need to take another look at that book we created."

Alex's eyes widened. "Do you have it?"

"Oh yes, I just didn't realize it until now."

He looked deeply in her eyes, kissed her once again, and smiled.

"I can't believe that my dreams have literally come true. We've found each other, and you're home now. In my arms. And nothing will ever separate us again. We will accomplish everything we were supposed to do. Together."

LaVergne, TN USA
12 October 2010
200138LV00009B/12/P